PRINCE MAESA

Other great stories from Warhammer Age of Sigmar

PRINCE MAESA

GUY HALEY

BLACK LIBRARY

A BLACK LIBRARY PUBLICATION

First published in 2022.
This edition published in Great Britain in 2023 by
Black Library, Games Workshop Ltd., Willow Road,
Nottingham, NG7 2WS, UK.

Represented by: Games Workshop Limited – Irish branch,
Unit 3, Lower Liffey Street, Dublin 1,
D01 K199, Ireland.

10 9 8 7 6 5 4 3 2 1

Produced by Games Workshop in Nottingham.
Cover illustration by Billy Christian.

A CIP record for this book is available from the British Library.

ISBN 13: 978-1-80026-265-2

See Black Library on the internet at

blacklibrary.com

Find out more about Games Workshop
and the worlds of Warhammer at

games-workshop.com

Printed and bound by CPI Group (UK) Ltd, Croydon, CR0 4YY

The Mortal Realms have been despoiled. Ravaged by the followers of the Chaos Gods, they stand on the brink of utter destruction.

The fortress-cities of Sigmar are islands of light in a sea of darkness. Constantly besieged, their walls are assailed by maniacal hordes and monstrous beasts. The bones of good men are littered thick outside the gates. These bulwarks of Order are embattled within as well as without, for the lure of Chaos beguiles the citizens with promises of power.

Still the champions of Order fight on. At the break of dawn, the Crusader's Bell rings and a new expedition departs. Storm-forged knights march shoulder to shoulder with resolute militia, stoic duardin and slender aelves. Bedecked in the splendour of war, the Dawnbringer Crusades venture out to found civilisations anew. These grim pioneers take with them the fires of hope. Yet they go forth into a hellish wasteland.

Out in the wilds, hardy colonists restore order to a crumbling world. Haunted eyes scan the horizon for tyrannical reavers as they build upon the bones of ancient empires, eking out a meagre existence from cursed soil and ice-cold seas. By their valour, the fate of the Mortal Realms will be decided.

The ravening terrors that prey upon these settlers take a thousand forms. Cannibal barbarians and deranged murderers crawl from hidden lairs. Martial hosts clad in black steel march from skull-strewn castles. The savage hordes of Destruction batter the frontier towns until no stone stands atop another. In the dead of night come howling throngs of the undead, hungry to feast upon the living.

Against such foes, courage is the truest defence and the most effective weapon. It is something that Sigmar's chosen do not lack. But they are not always strong enough to prevail, and even in victory, each new battle saps their souls a little more.

This is the time of turmoil. This is the era of war.

This is the Age of Sigmar.

PART ONE

THE AUTUMN PRINCE

CHAPTER ONE

THE DUST GATE

Towers of stone rose from the wreck of ages when Sigmar returned, and deserted lands flourished again. Blade and spell pushed the great enemy back, so that man, aelf and duardin came once more to live in the countries of their ancestors, and the Age of Chaos faded into bloody memory.

For all the splendour Sigmar brought, the woes of antiquity remained. Underneath new cities were old foundations, and the stones of those places were steeped in death. Teeming streets and the homes of the rich and poor alike hid secrets that were not always well buried.

Far below Shanskir was a network of ruins. When the old city fell in aeons gone, the buildings were so thoroughly toppled as to be compacted solid as rock, and were built over accordingly. But threading through this lost grandeur were the narrowed traces of old roads, and these linked wider caverns walled with fine ashlar, and lower again was a spread of sewers and cellars that all cities push under the earth, and that often outlive their destruction.

To this city under a city, Maesa, aelven prince of the Wanderer Clans, had come.

He was tall and noble, sharp-boned, with no soft edges to him; beautiful, though in an inhuman way. He wore a hooded cloak of green over a short-sleeved byrnie of such fine rings it appeared like silver cloth. Upon his back was a quiver and bow in a case next to a small pack woven from spider silk, which was topped with a carefully wrapped bundle. At his side was a sheathed sword. Disquieting violet eyes looked out from a close-fitting helm. A small pair of antlers, like those of a roe stag, jutting up from the steel, accentuated the severity of his expression.

There were thirteen in his party. Eleven humans hired to escort this single aelf. Their leader was Captain Sendel, proud in the colours of his mercenary band.

The thirteenth member stayed hidden.

The men ran hunched under a ceiling of broken statuary, the feathers on their helmets wiping damp stone. Water filthy with waste seeping down from the new city washed around their feet. Toppled temple pillars leaned from the right, meeting at the left hand a jumbled mass of blocks.

The way opened into a wider space. Draughts tugged at the flames of the torches, and a cry of alarm went up from the head of the column. A choking gurgle marked a slit throat and the end of the vanguard's life. His torch fell and was doused in the water.

'Sigmar curse it!' said Captain Sendel to the prince. 'Forward!' he shouted to his men. 'Into the Cavern of the Lost Gods. Form a line. If the skaven catch us in this tunnel, we're finished.'

His men were experienced, and obeyed without hesitation, running over the body of their fallen comrade into the space ahead. The bright flash of a sword cut down at a target Maesa could not see. A sharp squeal and a splash followed, and the scent of

Chaos-tainted blood soured the air. The men pushed forward with many shouts, locking their round steel shields together, and made ready.

The ringing of metal erupted all along their line. Daggers whistled through the dark. Shields raised to deflect them, though another man fell with a glowing blade in his throat. The small group of humans held, peering forward, their sight extending only as far as the wavering edges of the torchlight. They were blind to the shadows leaping overhead. Maesa was not.

'They are coming. Forty of them,' said Maesa calmly.

More daggers rang off the shields.

'Sigendil's light!' said Sendel. 'So many so quickly. The infestation of these tunnels gets worse with every season.' Another rain of daggers clanged off the shields. 'Men, look to your backs!' he shouted. 'For every one we kill there are two in the shadows.'

'Then I will lessen their number.' Maesa slipped past the captain, stepped over the corpse of the first man to fall and the skaven slain for his murder. Drawing his bow from its case, he moved soundlessly to stand behind the rank of humans. He drew the string, and loosed. His arrow whispered through the air. A wet smack and a pained shriek marked a hit.

A moment of quiet followed. Maesa looked into the gloom.

'They have expended their knives. They attack now,' he said. 'Above and to the front.'

'I can't see a damn thing,' Sendel said.

'Then let me illuminate matters,' said Maesa. He twisted his hand before him, spoke a word of power, and a brilliant light burst into being, revealing black-clad skaven hurling themselves from broken statues, squirming from narrow cracks in the shattered masonry. They dropped from the cavern roof, cutting and slashing into the line of men. Maesa shot down another ratman. He killed a third before the second's body had vanished into the water on

11

the cavern floor, a new arrow on his string before the one preceding found its mark. The squeals and frantic chittering of rodent speech mingled with the cries of men. The shield wall bowed back, held, then collapsed under the weight of skaven into individual melees, single men fighting two or three of the hunched figures. The skaven had begun with stealth on their side, but now they were in the open, they were overmatched in strength and skill by Sendel's men, and dazzled by the aelf's mage light.

Maesa shot another as it leapt at one of the men. Sendel came to his side, duelling two skaven that came close, his blade smashing back crude black iron, and felling the wielders.

A skaven took its chance and rushed out of a crack in the cavern wall towards the prince.

'Oh no, my friend, I think not,' said Captain Sendel. Steel connected with flesh, and its head came off with a gush of blood. Its weapon slapped into the water, turning it luminous with the poisons weeping from the blade. Sendel's sword caught in the bone of the shoulder, nearly twisting from his hand as the headless skaven flopped down. Black blood tainted the stream.

Sendel tugged at his sword, loudly cursing when it remained fast. A shrill, wordless war cry sounded overhead. Sendel looked to see a skaven falling from the distant ceiling, twin daggers ready to kill the aelf.

'Prince Maesa, look out! Above!' He yanked harder, but bone and flesh held the steel.

Maesa shot upwards, missing the creature. It came down before Sendel had the blade loose, landing softly, broad, naked feet plunging into the water so precisely they caused hardly a ripple. His own sword came out from its scabbard. The prince's sword was an uncommon thing, a jagged thorn of russet edges and black points. A sense of power emanated from the weapon.

The skaven tittered at the prince's blade. A bright pink tongue licked thin lips. Yellow shovel teeth bared in a vicious grin. It was bigger than the others, its daggers longer, their edges aglow with the sickly light of warpstone. Its long tail twitched back and forth over its head, a third blade held in the prehensile end.

'You die-die, aelf-thing! These lands of the Lords of Thirteen,' it said. Its voice was a harsh mix of squeaked vowels and lisped consonants, menacing for all its ludicrousness. 'We claim-take. This ours.'

Maesa stared dispassionately from beneath his horned helm.

'You should not have come here today, child of Chaos. Let me pass, or die.'

The skaven snickered. 'No, you die, fool-thing! Bring wooden stick to fight. Haha! You dead.'

It leapt at the prince, moving with a nervous energy that was hard to follow, but Maesa was quicker still, his movements sublimely performed, countering all three of the skaven's weapons. The aelf was lithe and supple, a war dancer, the skaven jitter-quick, both too fast for a man to beat. Weeping blades met the sword with hollow, wooden notes. Sendel cut down a lesser ratkin that moved upon the prince from behind, but he could not add his sword to the aelf's duel. Blades blurred, skaven magic set against the sorcery of plant and bough.

The weapons met again. New notes played. Aelf and skaven came closer, twitching snout to perfect nose.

'Now you die!' the skaven hissed. 'This poison kill anything.'

'I have better magic,' Maesa said. He deflected the skaven's daggers, and the point of his sword darted down, scraping across the skaven's naked thigh. Its titter at the feebleness of the scratch turned to a scream, as the glowing form of its soul was dragged from its body and sucked slowly within the blade. Spectral paws raked at the prince, finding no purchase. Ghost mouth wailed as living jaws went slack. The screech went high, falling to a deathly whisper as the soul was finally, irrevocably consumed.

The remaining skaven froze. Maesa turned to face them, his strange sword aglow.

'This is the Song of Thorns,' he sang out. 'If it pricks you, then you die forever. Begone!'

The enemy squealed in dismay. An acrid stench filled the cavern.

'Flee-flee!' one shrilled, and together the survivors turned tail and fled, vanishing into the dark as suddenly as they had emerged. Broad feet plashed in shallow water, and they were gone.

'They're running!' shouted one of the men. 'Cut them down!' The soldiers began to follow.

'Hold your ground, you damn fools!' Sendel shouted. 'They'll slit your throats the moment you are away from the light. Keep your guard up. Stand!'

Maesa's spell dimmed, and shadows rushed back. The men nervously scanned the darkness. No sound was heard. Cautiously, the soldiers stood down, and saw to their wounded. Sendel's corporal organised a party to return with those too badly injured to fight, reducing the number of warriors to six.

Sendel wiped his sword on skaven rags before he returned it to his scabbard. 'Well done, my lord prince. That was a pretty display.'

'I am blessed with a little magic,' said Maesa.

'Only a little? That blade, it is surely powerfully enchanted.'

Maesa sheathed the Song of Thorns. It was clean of blood.

'It is a terrible weapon,' said Maesa softly.

'From where does it come?' asked Sendel. 'A wooden sword? I have never seen one like it.'

Maesa appeared disinterested by the captain's question – most of his attention was on the fragments of art preserved in the rubble of the cavern wall – but he answered. 'Not wood, as you think. A blade of living thorn. You heard me name it. Pray I have no cause to do so again.'

'I mean no offence,' said Sendel, uneasy at the prince's tone.

'The weapon was Alarielle's gift to me,' said Maesa. 'It thirsts for souls. To draw it again in your presence would seal your doom, I cannot stay it. It will pierce your skin and drink your spirit. It must be fed when it is unsheathed.'

'Then I shall not ask of it again,' said Sendel.

'You are wise,' said Maesa. He ran his fingers over a portion of frieze.

'Wise? Me?' Sendel snorted. 'It is strange to hear an aelf speak of a man so positively.'

Maesa looked back at him, his piercing gaze forcing Sendel to avert his eyes. 'Men can be wise, as aelves can be humble.'

'A rarity then! I am not wise. No. Greedy, and eager to live? That I am.' He surveyed his men. Those hale were looting the bodies of the skaven and complaining about the poor quality of their plunder. A couple discussed flaying the corpses and selling the skins to the local mages, but Sendel dissuaded them. 'We do not have time!' he said.

The corporal's party set off back to the surface. The others lit fresh torches.

'We are done here, get ready to move,' Sendel said to his men, then he spoke with Maesa. 'I pledged to bring you to the Dust Gate. We are nearly there.'

'Thank you, captain.'

A blacker patch on the dark ahead suggested an exit. The water ran quicker as the space narrowed. A bubbling rush came to them on a damp breeze.

'Thank me when you are there. My men go no further than the gate.' Sendel signalled. 'Men, we go. Keep an eye out for the ratkin.'

The tunnel steepened. Not far into the corridor, the foaming water gurgled down a spiral stair.

'Down,' said Sendel.

The humans cursed at the treacherous footing, for the steps could not be seen, and they had been worn to awkward angles by the rush of the stream. Maesa was not hampered, and moved serenely through the torrent, until at last they arrived at the bottom and a tunnel in fair condition opened up in front of them. The water slowed, and deepened so that it came over their knees, where it ran as sluggishly as a canal. The light from the torches broke into scintillations on ripples the men made, and all but Maesa muttered fearfully about what foul things might live in the water. Fortune favoured them, and they travelled the length of the tunnel without mishap, coming to an ornate chamber that finished abruptly in a wall of rock. In the corners the water drained, and made its way deeper underground.

'We are here,' said Sendel. 'Pay me, and go.'

'This wall is the Dust Gate?' asked Maesa.

'Aye,' said Sendel, looking up at the rock wall. 'Disguised by glamour when the old city fell. It does not seem much, but it is a secret way, long lost, that should never have been found. I rue the day greatly that I did. It will take you to the remains of one of the great towers in Shadespire.' He reached into his tunic and pulled out a pouch on a cord, which he broke with a sharp tug. From inside the pouch he drew out a chain. A square-cut diamond flashed on the end. 'Here is the key to the gate.'

He tossed it. Maesa snatched it from the air. The aelf opened his palm and gazed into the stone, then looked back to the captain.

'There is power in this diamond. Power to open. Power to penetrate illusion.'

'There is that, but it's another thing I wish I'd never set eyes on. When you've used it, you can keep it. I'm never passing through that gate again, riches of Shadespire or not. You're on your own from here on out.'

'Then to conclude our business, take your payment.' Maesa

untied a purse from his belt. He threw it to the captain, who caught it. It clinked heavily with realmstone. 'I trust it will be enough for your services.'

'A fair exchange for that diamond? Not likely.' Sendel gave a sour smile. 'That's a king's fortune right in your fist, discounting its magical properties at that.'

Maesa's inhuman face creased in what Sendel assumed was a frown. 'I have no more money, captain. The sum is what we agreed.'

Sendel opened the pouch and peered at the gems, but did not count them. 'I never said I wanted more. Your purse is more than a fair price for my life, and that's all I want. I wouldn't wish that diamond on anyone. I thought to make my fortune from the discovery of this gate. I've learned my lesson. There's only death beyond that door.' He held up the purse. 'I'll take this tally, you keep the diamond and the secret of the gate. I brought you here not for money, but to unburden myself of that cursed key. May knowledge of the gate be lost when you die, and you will die. I will lead no more glory seekers to their deaths, and I'll be poorer but safe, and this purse will buy enough wine to wash away my memories of Shadespire, for a while.'

He held up the bag to show to his men. None of them disagreed with what the captain said.

'Good fortune to you, Prince Maesa, may you find whatever you are looking for in that cursed place. I know I did not, and neither did the other lackwits I brought down here.' He nodded in farewell. 'Men! Weapons drawn, it's a long walk back to the surface, and the rat spawn will be watching.'

Maesa waited until the jingling of war harness and soldier's grumbles faded from his hearing. When he was sure he was alone, and only the gurgle of the water escaping the room broke the quiet, he softly spoke over his shoulder.

'Shattercap. You may come forth. Take your place and tell me what you see.'

Upon the top of Maesa's pack, the cloth of his hood moved. Claws scrabbled on leather. A figure clambered up to squat upon the prince's shoulder, where it steadied itself with one tiny hand upon the antlers of Maesa's helm.

Maesa turned his head, so that the breath of the creature kissed his face.

'Well then, Shattercap?' he asked.

'What then?' said the thing. He had a voice like soft breezes in autumn leaves. His skin was greenish grey, with a covering of soft twigs and leaves around his back and elbows. His face jutted forward on a neck that seemed too long for his body. His arms were likewise disproportionate, but his legs were short, and bowed, the clawed feet pointing outwards. A pot belly sheltered below a chest drawn under hunched shoulders. His skin was all over leathery but thin looking, and somewhat seamed, while the face was that of an old and angry man. Shattercap was altogether ugly, but upon the russets and greens of the prince's garb, he did not look out of place.

'Do you see the gate?' said Maesa patiently.

Shattercap shut his deep green eyes and sniffed the air.

'I perceive nothing, oh wicked prince,' he said.

'Wicked I am not, spite,' said Maesa. 'To keep a mischief such as you prisoner is a kindness to all those your antics would hurt. Now tell me what you see, I command you.'

'I said I see nothing!' hissed the spite.

'You lie, small evil.'

'Thou hast thine own magic, use that,' said Shattercap.

'I have no need to. The gates of the shadow-wrights are well disguised, but they are never invisible. An aelf Wanderer knows where there is a way, and there is one here. See, there is the lock, disguised as a fissure in the rock.' Maesa strode unerringly to the wall, and held up the diamond to something that would seem, to human eyes, to be nothing but a small, natural indentation. The diamond slipped into it with a click, and there came a crackle of power. An oval outline sketched in light appeared on the wall, and the soft hum of magic at work filled the chamber.

'See?' said Maesa. 'The stone opens. The way is clear.'

'I didn't see it,' grumbled the spite.

'You will need to work harder in the city. There are things I cannot see that you can.'

The light pushed inward unevenly from the edges, until the archway was fully clear. The water poured out of the cave over the lip with a sudden rush. Shattercap cowered.

'Do not pinch so hard,' said Maesa. 'Curb your fear, spite.'

Shattercap peered at the wall of light. What he perceived set him quaking. 'Oh no, oh no, please, master. I will not go there. I will not go to the lands of glass and shadow. Let me free, I beg thee, kind prince, good prince.' He pawed clumsily at the prince's head.

'I am kind, and so I will not set you free,' said Maesa, brushing the spite's hands off his face. 'If you managed to evade the skaven, and make your way up to the light, then you would die in the city of men above, away from the life-giving magics of Ghyran. You know my quest. Aid me in fulfilling it, and prove your virtue. Take me where I need to go. Tell me what I must know, then I shall return you to some pretty forest, far from folk you might harm. This I swear on the nine paths of my ancestors.'

'I care not if I perish here,' Shattercap whined. 'It is a better place than whither thou wouldst go. Let me loose, I beg of thee, it is not safe. See! Something is coming!' He raised a shaking finger.

The skin of light that made up the gate flexed, and from it poured an avalanche of skulls that tocked and bounced over one another into the water.

'The remains of the damned spill from the shadowlands! It is a warning. Please, turn back, and free me from thine unkind bondage!'

Maesa shook his head grimly. 'I have purpose in Shadespire.'

The last skull vanished into the water with a gentle plop.

'You cannot bring her back,' whined Shattercap.

'I can. You remain my servant until I do. The secret to cheating death lies in the shadeglass, and you will help me find it.'

'No, please, no!'

Maesa drew his sword and loosened his bow in its case. Without a further word, he stepped into the light, and vanished.

The gate blinked. Water slapped against stone, and all was silent as the tomb.

CHAPTER TWO

SHADESPIRE

Maesa looked down from broken city walls upon a desert. All was grey. The twilit sky had no hint of dawn or of dark, no rain nor sun. Chill winds blew over featureless sands.

Behind the walls, the city was a collection of broken spires, absent of life and of death. Windows glared menacing as eyes. But outside the walls was a great camp. There, hundreds of fires burned in the perpetual gloom, and the voices of many creatures reached the travellers' ears.

'So many lights outside the wall,' said Shattercap, his fascination overcoming his fear. 'The desert smells of bone, and death! But aelf, duardin, human and greenskin, all are there. Why come they here, know they not the danger?'

'They know the dangers, small evil,' said Maesa. 'They come to pillage the city for shadeglass. Sigmar's wars demand mighty weapons. Secrets are buried in this place. For these souls, power and riches are more important than life.'

'Power and riches are not what thou seekest.'

'They are not,' agreed Maesa. The camp fascinated him with its unruly spread. Alone in the lifeless desert, already it had the appearance of a young town, with temples to many gods, and a market lit by oil lamps. Noise rose from a street of inns. Somewhere a lonely trumpet called the faithful to prayer.

'Then the captain was not so clever,' said Shattercap. 'Think how much those outside would give to gain entrance to the wall's walk as we have. He would have been mighty rich!'

'He did so, many times, but could do it no longer. Many will have died. Only a few who venture into this place re-emerge. For him, the weight of treasure was not so heavy as the burden of a guilty conscience.'

Shattercap wrinkled his nose in thought. 'Does that mean he was a good man?'

'He was good, in the end. He would condemn no more others to this half-place. Not even death is a release from Shadespire. Look to the inner wards of the city, where there are no fires but only darkness reflected in the glass. It is trapped between two worlds, a fell reflection of itself.' Maesa turned to look over the derelict buildings within the fortifications, a vista more ominous than any graveyard.

'If thou wishest to go within, then I say thou art not good.' Shattercap shuddered.

'I am neither good nor bad, small evil, I am merely desperate, and that puts me beyond issues of morality.' Maesa pointed to a huge edifice that dominated the skyline. 'There, the great tower at the heart of the ruins. Within are the domains of the Katophranes. It is the chamber of Katophrane Thanaton we must seek. He holds the answer to the riddle of death.'

Soft winds whistled over sharp glass edges. The laments of the undead moaned from dark interiors and forbidding alleys. Maesa pressed on resolutely, his eyes fixed on the great tower, his feet crunching on fallen glass.

'I like this not, not one bit at all. There are shades moving in the glass. Is every street the same?' Shattercap asked.

'They are the dead who did not die, but were cursed by Nagash to eternal half-life. Once, this was a great city, peopled by a wise folk who were skilled in magic. But they grew too powerful, and challenged Nagash's mastery over death. He is a jealous god. He regards everything that dies as his. They learned to their cost that Nagash will not be cheated. He tore down their towers, and cursed their city, moving it to this place that is not in any realm, but a place between. The inhabitants are trapped here, not alive nor truly dead, and they remain everywhere in the city.'

A ghostly scream confirmed the tale, rising up from a low moan to a deafening shriek whose echoes took too long to die.

Shattercap hid his face in the prince's neck. Maesa patted him.

'Ignore them, they can do you no harm. See, there are beauties here still. Look at this square. Such a pretty place.'

The spite peeked between shaking fingers, daring to look at the glass sides of the buildings, and the dry fountain at the square's middle. There were many mirrors set into the stone, and monuments of glass on pedestals. In most of them blurred shapes moved.

'The dead!' he whimpered. 'All in the glass! So many!'

As if provoked by Shattercap's fear, moans, weeping and screams echoed again down dark streets. He clamped his hands tight over his ears and cried to himself.

'They cannot hurt you.' Maesa slowed and cast about on the ground until he found a shard of dark mirror. He knelt and picked it up. A woman's shade, luminous and confused, looked to and fro, as if she were in a familiar room but somehow could not find

23

the door. 'I will show you. See this woman, so beautiful, so tortured? She is dead, but cannot escape this unlife.'

The woman seemed to hear him, and turned to face out of the glass. Her smeared features collected and briefly became sharp.

'Please... please... please...' she said. 'I must go to the market to fetch bread. My children will be home soon. They will be hungry, so hungry, after their day with the pedagogues. Please, I need to go. I need to feed my boys. I can't get out. How will I get out?'

Maesa watched her awhile, then laid the glass down. 'A tragedy. She is caught at the moment of the city's death. They suffer, they desire to end their pain, that is all. There is nothing to fear here, there is only sadness.'

The moans and cries coming at them rose to a climax, and cut out at once. A silence fell.

'I wish they'd come back! Quiet is worse! There is something else in the glass. A skull, glowing eyes!' Shattercap hissed at something only he could see. 'It is a great evil!'

Maesa frowned. He saw only his own reflection.

'It will be Nagash himself,' said Maesa. 'He watches this place still. He is jealous of his soul tithe.'

'Why is he looking at me, and not you?' squeaked Shattercap. 'Does he know I've been bad?'

'No, you have more magic in you than I, that is all,' said Maesa. He moved away from the square. 'We should not attract his attention.'

'No, my master. Not with what thou wishest to do.'

'Hush now. Do not speak of him.' The distant clash of weapons rang down a boulevard lined with dead trees. The source was out of sight, but close enough to make both aelf and spite look warily for it. 'Armed bands of the living contest this place. We must keep to the shadows.'

* * *

They passed swiftly through the streets, avoiding both the living and dead, and before long came to the great towers of the Katophranes, the rulers of Shadespire. Maesa consulted a mould-spotted book he took from his pack before heading within one of them. He gained entrance easily. There was not a whole door or window in the city, and the buildings were open in form, hinting at warm days when they had known the light of Hysh.

Maesa headed up a huge flight of marble stairs, so perfectly made and situated that they balanced only upon the wedge ends built into the wall, and had no central pillar. They were covered in grit and shards of glass, rags, bones and other detritus, yet they gave an impression of how the city had been in its heyday. A large roof light capped the stairs. In Shadespire all colour had drained away, but it was easy to imagine how the building must have been when Hysh rose and shone down through the crystal, flooding the tower with light.

Halfway up the stairs, Maesa turned off into a vast chamber. Chandeliers tinkled in a breeze sighing through huge broken windows, which stirred curls of dust and lifted the shreds of curtains. All was grey as old bones. Sadness clung to everything.

'Such ruin. Such desolation,' said Shattercap. He eyed a desiccated tree in a pot, and whimpered.

'Beneath the bone dust there are treasures aplenty,' said Maesa, pointing at various objects as he named them. 'Here are the jewels of emperors, and the clockwork wonders of the duardin. There is magic in these pictures on the wall. These are the personal chambers of the Katophrane Thanaton, a ruler of great power. Think of how they must have been in the days before. Ever must the glorious be lost to the jealousies of evil.'

'Then let's take his treasures! Let's be rich.'

'What would you do with treasure, small evil, eat it?' Maesa asked. 'All these splendours do not interest me. There is only one treasure I desire.'

'Does death interest thee?' spluttered Shattercap. 'There is danger here. We should leave, good master. I miss the forests. Please, take me home.'

Maesa paused by a picture whose colours were all gone to greys and blacks, but which still preserved a hint of the artist's talent. 'So you might steal mortal children, and gnaw upon the bones of innocent Wayfarers?'

'I knew no better! I promise to be good.'

'Atone for your sins in service to me, and you may return to your beloved woods,' said Maesa. 'Alarielle will judge you kindly should you mend your ways. That is our bargain.'

Maesa turned then into a smaller chamber, though still large. Eight mirrors covered in sheets stood around its periphery. Maesa walked straight to the one opposite the door, and tugged the sheet free, letting it rustle down and pool on the floor.

'According to the Book of Clovis, these are the mirrors of Thanaton. His essence hides in one of them. Use your sight. Tell me which contains the soul of the Katophrane, warn me which are traps.' Maesa went around the room, yanking the sheets down and exposing the silvered glass beneath.

'Are you sure this is the right place, the right tower?' whispered Shattercap.

Maesa pulled the last cloth free and walked to the centre of the room. 'You know it is the place. Cease your diversions. Find Katophrane Thanaton. Reveal his hiding place to me.' He put down his pack, set up his bow and stood ready.

'Oh, very well,' Shattercap grumbled. He picked a mirror and squinted hard at it, making a strained noise as he did so. 'No. It is not that one. Break it, and foil its traps!'

Maesa drew his bow and sent an arrow through the glass, shattering it to sparkling dust.

'Now the next,' said Maesa.

Shattercap squinted at the second mirror. 'Not that one either.'
Another arrow broke the mirror.

Now Shattercap was rising to his role, and quickened his efforts.
'That is not it either,' he said, pointing to the third mirror.

Maesa drew, but paused. A figure stirred deep inside, far off,
yet clear to see.

'Something moves within the glass. I see a face. Are you sure I
will not destroy that which I seek?'

Shattercap shook his head. 'It is a trap, the home of a hungry
spirit. Destroy it before the shade within comes forth.'

Maesa destroyed the third mirror. The shade within shrieked
and vanished. He drew his bow again. 'Five remain. Which is it?
This one?'

'No,' said Shattercap.

Maesa loosed. The mirror exploded into shining dust, and an
eerie howl filled the room that grew louder and louder.

'We have gained his attention. Thanaton is coming,' said
Shattercap.

A booming voice rolled out. 'Stop! Stop!'

Shattercap froze. Maesa drew another arrow and pointed it to
each of the mirrors in turn.

'Come out and speak with me!' Maesa called. 'Show yourself or
I shall break them all!' There was no reply. Maesa looked around
the mirrors again. 'Where is he?'

'There he is!' Shattercap pointed to a cracked mirror. 'In the
middle glass there.'

Maesa aimed his bow. 'Thanaton! Heed me, I seek your advice.
I will destroy your mirror if you refuse.'

'Stay your arm, my prince,' said Shattercap. 'His form gathers.
Oh, there is much magic here!'

A wavering green shadow swam into view in the mirror. It
shook and rippled, appearing like many images laid over each

other: a young man, an old man, a youth, a babe, a scholar, a leader, blurred and confusing, yet Maesa saw they were one person at different times.

'An entire life encapsulated,' Maesa said. 'All his being is here.'

The images focused, falling one into another, until a single form stared out, old yet haughty and proud of face, dressed richly, a circlet around his brow. A touch of majesty clung to him still, though he was but a shade of a man, uncertain and aethereal. When he moved, his skin drifted from his bones. When he rested, his skull glowered underneath the ghost of his face.

'Who are you?' Thanaton said, his voice rich with indignation. 'Why do you come here to destroy what little remains of the Faneway? You break the last of the ancient wonders of Shadespire in your ignorance!'

'Not ignorance,' said Maesa. 'Quite deliberate.' He put away his bow and approached the mirror until he stood an arm's length from it. 'You have kept your face and form during your time in the glass. Remarkable.' Maesa's breath made misted plumes. A deep cold surrounded the mirror.

'Stay away from the shade, my lord, he is too strong for your magic! Oh, would that we had stayed in the Realm of Life, but thou wouldst not listen to poor, poor Shattercap!'

'What manner of thing is that?' said the shade. 'What do you want, aelf? Make your request so I may deny it, and be back to my accursed rest.'

'I seek the wisdom of the Katophrane Thanaton. You are he.'

The ghost drew himself up and gripped the edges of his robes. 'Why do you seek Thanaton?'

'I hear his knowledge might be bought, for the right price.'

A calculating look floated over Thanaton's phantom face. 'It might, that it might. Come closer so that I can see you. All is dark within the glass.'

Maesa took a step forward, until his face was almost touching the mirror. Shattercap leapt down from the aelf's shoulder and scampered to the centre of the room.

'Be wary!' he hissed.

Thanaton peered at Maesa. 'You are royalty. Announce yourself, aelf lord.'

'I am Prince Maesa, of the Heartfelt Glades, last of my house, outcast Wanderer,' he said. 'I come to you with a great need.'

'Tell me what you seek.'

Maesa stepped back so he could take his pack from his shoulders. He set it on the floor, and reverently unstrapped the leather-wrapped bundle. He cradled it tenderly.

'Here in this package is all I have loved, and everything I have lost.'

'Show me,' said the Katophrane.

Maesa undid the bindings on the package and laid the leather out carefully on the ground. Inside, tied into neat bundles, were brown bones, and a skull.

'A female?' said Thanaton. He indicated the broad pelvis.

'She was,' said Maesa, staring longingly at the skull.

'Human?' asked Thanaton.

'As I said. A matter of the heart.'

Thanaton smiled horribly, showing the long teeth of the dead. He chuckled lewdly.

'Is this not a transgression for your kind, to love outside your own people?'

Maesa looked up at him. 'My so-called crimes are my own. I paid for them. They are not relevant to the service I require.'

'If you will not tell me, aelf prince, I cannot help. Begone from here.'

Maesa put his hand upon the brow of the skull. When he spoke next, it was with a low voice choked with sorrow.

'It was a transgression, one that cost me my house and my family. My kind do not look well upon humanity, but I could no easier give up breathing than not love Ellamar. When I saw her at the edge of our holdings, I should have killed her as our custom demands, but my heart was captured. I loved her instantly. We ran from my people's fury, and carved a little joy from the horrors of this age. But the spans of my kind and hers are cruelly mismatched, and it was done too soon. She wasted to decrepitude while I remained young. I wish to return her from the underworlds, for one lifetime of her love is not enough. In all the many lands of the Eight Realms, there is but one place I know where death might be defied, and that is here, in the fabled city of Shadespire.'

Thanaton laughed harshly. 'You are too late by a thousand years! Nagash determined that our art was not to his liking. He destroyed our city for our offence against his dominion.'

'You still live, nevertheless. Power remains in Shadespire. Help me. The Lord of Death demanded that her soul go to the underworld of her people, and mine will go to that of the Wanderer aelves. We shall never be together again. You must help me. I know you can. Your name I uncovered in a book lost in the stacks of an obscure library. Many tomes of forbidden lore were contained there. None were more greatly warded than the book that spoke of you.'

'A book survived that recorded the existence of Shadespire?' said Thanaton. He was suspicious, and a little amazed.

'The Book of Clovis,' said Maesa. 'It speaks most highly of you, Lord Katophrane Thanaton.'

'The wards must have been strong if they held away Nagash. All mention of this place has been removed from the knowledge of the realms. The Lord of Death will destroy those who have any truck with we of Shadespire. Those who come here to pillage our treasures will learn this soon enough, for his curse lies upon all things in the city. You will bring his fury upon yourself simply by speaking of these things, by being here.'

'If it secures me my heart's desire, then I do not care whose enmity is raised against me. I shall defy death itself, if I must.'

'Very well,' said Thanaton.

'How can I bring her back?'

'Oh, a difficult task. Do you have her grave-sands? The realm-stone of Shyish?'

'No, I do not.'

'Then your cause is hopeless. That is but the first step, and you have failed.' The Katophrane began to fade. 'I have nothing to give you, and you have nothing to offer me.'

'Wait!' Maesa shouted. 'Please! I beg you!'

The Katophrane's eyes narrowed shrewdly. 'If I were to bring her here, what would I gain in return?'

'I have nothing but an offer of service,' said Maesa. 'Bring my love Ellamar back to me and I shall serve you faithfully. You are trapped inside these mirrors. You cannot act beyond the bounds of Shadespire. I am a Wanderer. I can come and go as I please, and I will go upon your errands.'

'You will do what I ask without question?'

'I will. Anything,' said Maesa. Though his voice remained flat and oddly distant, his eyes shone with need.

'And what of your strange companion?' asked Thanaton greedily, seeing two servants for the taking.

'The forest spite is bound to me until it unlearns wickedness. It too shall serve until I choose to lift its geas.'

'Then bring your love closer to me.'

'No, master!' wailed Shattercap. Maesa ignored him, and picked up Ellamar's skull in gentle hands, and held it out to the glass.

'Closer still. Put her up against the mirror, and I will see what might be done.'

Bone clicked on glass. The chill of Thanaton's presence froze Maesa's fingers, but he did not flinch. Thanaton's face came close enough to kiss Ellamar's bare teeth. He examined her from all angles.

'Some of her essence clings yet to the skull. It appears her love for you is strong. Enough that I can bring her into the glass. I can do no more than that, and I warn you, this half-life is not to every-one's liking. When Nagash came upon our land, we expected to die, and we feared it! He had worse in mind. We were not released when slaughtered, but caught between the worlds of life and death. Many are spirits trapped in the glass of the city, doomed to relive the moment of our doom. Worse are those whose mortal bodies have decayed around them, but whose souls cannot leave, and they remain imprisoned in cells fashioned from their own ribs and skulls. They walk the land, undead, raging against their fate. Many of my countrymen have gone mad. Some have turned to Nagash's worship. Would you risk that? It is all I can offer you. My powers are warped by Nagash's judgement like all other things in Shadespire.'

'Our love will keep us sane. I ask that you bring her back. I do not care how.'

'Then you too must come within the mirrors with your belov-ed's head, aelf prince.'

'Only her skull? I will not be tricked, Katophrane, and be left with a mutilated bride.'

'It is the seat of the mind and the soul,' said Thanaton. 'The skull alone will be sufficient to summon her here.'

'Do it not, my prince!' shrilled Shattercap. 'For the good thou hast taught me, do not leave me here alone!'

'You must come within the Faneway if you will have your desire,' said Thanaton. 'I can work no magic while you are outside the mirror. You must join me, in the heart of the shadow realms.'

'How may it be done?' asked Maesa.

'By pain, and sacrifice. Take up a shard of that black glass there, a dagger shape.' A ghostly finger pointed behind Maesa to a piece of mirror on the floor.

Maesa took it up.

'Hold the point towards your heart. Like so.' Thanaton gestured at his own chest with an inverted thumb. His form shivered. His ribs glowed through his robes and skin.

Maesa did as he was told. He drew in a shuddery breath as he prepared. 'Soon, my love,' he murmured.

'Now drive it into your breast, into your heart,' said Thanaton.

'Good master, no!' Shattercap cried. He bounded over the broken glass, skidding as he came.

Maesa plunged the glass home. It pierced mail, clothes and aelven flesh as easily as water. Maesa shouted wordlessly. Ellamar's soul screamed through her jawless skull.

Maesa collapsed to the ground. Shattercap jumped onto his chest. Neither skull nor glass were in the prince's hands, and his breast was whole, but he did not breathe.

'Master,' whimpered Shattercap.

'Open your eyes.'

A voice he thought never to hear again spoke soft words, and for a moment Maesa thought himself within the cottage of the golden years, deep in the forests, far from anyone, and free to drink in Ellamar's presence until he was fit to burst with love.

It was not so. It could not be so. He was cold. No birdsong reached his ears, only silence.

'Open your eyes, my love.'

Maesa's eyelids flickered. Ellamar stared down at him. She was as old as she was when she'd died, wrinkled and frail, but she was his Ellamar nonetheless.

'Ellamar? Is that you?' Maesa's face, so often inexpressive, came alive. 'Where… Where am I?'

She looked behind her. Her bones moved out of synchronisation with her flesh, like Thanaton's had, gliding eerily under her skin. She glowed a soft, spectral green.

'Do you not see the dark deeps of the mirror?' She gestured behind her at the dark. It was of a peculiar sort, soft yet heavy, like darkness trapped in the interior of a lead box. 'This is the shadeglass. It is a substance that captures souls, much like your Song of Thorns.'

'Then I am not dead?' He struggled up onto his elbows.

'Nothing dies here,' said Ellamar. 'Nothing can.'

He got up into a crouch and took her hands in his. He too was a shade, a wisp of soul stuff, nothing more. He did not care.

'Does it matter? You are here with me, and we shall be together. Oh, thanks be to all the gods of this and all worlds! Thanaton was not lying.'

'That is not so, my love,' said Ellamar sadly. 'I cannot leave the underworlds this way. My shade can remain for but a few moments.' She looked down at herself; her bones were becoming more visible. 'My phantom fades. There is little magic here that can return my life, and none at all to return my youth. I am a hag turning into a horror, and I will soon be gone.'

'You are as beautiful to me as you ever were.'

'The underworld calls to me. You have been tricked, my love. Look behind you, back through the mirror. Thanaton has your body. His soul has escaped its prison.'

Maesa leapt to his feet and turned. He looked out onto the chamber, where his body stood, wearing Thanaton's triumphant expression. He ran forward, but though there was no glass to see from his side of the mirror, he ran full into an invisible barrier.

'I apologise, little princeling,' said Thanaton from the far side of the mirror. 'You offered me a way out, I took it. Maybe one day you will find your own escape. In the meantime, I thank you for this ageless body. Such grace your people have. I shall be sure to enjoy it.'

'You shall suffer for your treachery!' Maesa pounded upon the invisible wall, his fists tracing green trails across the black.

'I think not. Cease your beating. It is no use. You cannot escape. You must bide your time until another fool comes along, and then you may do as I did, if you wish. Until that day, I bid you farewell.'

Shattercap leapt onto the Katophrane's neck and tugged at his hair. 'Thou woundest my master, evil shade. I will not let him perish! Quickly, my prince, out of the glass, out out out!'

Thanaton turned on the spite with a snarl. 'Silence!' He lunged. Shattercap dodged the blow, only to leap into Thanaton's waiting hand. Shattercap hissed and bit his thumb, causing Thanaton to shout in outrage and dash the spite upon the floor. Shattercap skidded through the broken glass, and lifted his head weakly. Thanaton advanced on him.

'My prince!' Shattercap cried. 'Thou yet bearest the dark reflection of the Song of Thorns. Use it upon the weakness in the glass! Soul thirst against soul thirst, the magic of the aelves is far greater than that of men!'

Maesa glanced down. The only part of the glass that was visible was a faint line, the flaw in the mirror's worldly side. He drew the shade of the Song of Thorns. It writhed in his hand, its true monstrousness clear to see in this form, but he mastered it and plunged it into the crack as Thanaton raised his foot to stamp down on the spite.

The glass broke outward. Maesa stood upon the threshold between two worlds.

Shattercap laughed. 'My master, he escapes...'

Thanaton placed his foot upon the spite. 'Stop! Cease your

35

advance. If you kill me, you slay your own body. You would not kill yourself! Stop, or I will crush your familiar.'

'You misunderstand the power of this blade,' said Maesa. His ghost floated over the space between the broken mirror and his stolen body. 'The Song of Thorns is a soul thief. One scratch and you are mine.'

As Maesa spoke the last few words, he slashed with his phantom blade, nicking his wrist, and dragging Thanaton's soul from its seat. It vanished screaming into the sword.

Maesa's body fell noisily onto the glass, and lay still. Shattercap clambered to his feet.

'Quickly, good prince, thou fadest!' he croaked. 'Return to your body, before the glass draws you back in.'

'How? This magic is beyond me.' He walked to his prone form, and touched it, but his hand passed through the flesh.

'Go within, as a sleeper returns from the realms of dream and awakens, yes? Quickly! While there is life still in your body.'

Maesa relaxed. He shut his eyes. He felt the hunger of the glass around him, not only the last whole mirrors in the chamber, but also the broken pieces on the ground and the glass beyond the room, all throughout the building and the city beyond. His body was a welcome place in contrast, not the hard, sharp angles of the glass that dragged at him so strongly, but a gentle home his soul knew well.

He settled deeper, then all at once was drawn fully within.

Maesa sat up and drew in a sharp breath.

'Thou livest!' Shattercap said, clapping his hands.

Maesa scrambled to his feet, kicking glass everywhere in a clumsy haste rarely seen in aelf-kind. He searched the floor frantically.

'Ellamar! Where is she?'

'But... but she is gone, my prince!'

Maesa kicked glass everywhere. 'Her skull! Where is her skull?'

'I see it, I see it!' said Shattercap. He knuckled on all fours like an ape into the room's corner. He reached the skull and pointed. 'Here she is, master prince, her lovely skull!'

Shattercap reached to pick up Ellamar's skull.

'No!' shouted Maesa, and ran at the spite. 'Do not dare to lay your hands upon her, spite!' Maesa bent and snatched the skull up, glaring at his companion.

'Why must thou be so cruel?' Shattercap cowered. 'Poor Shattercap means no harm. I want to help, I want to be good!'

'Do not touch what is mine, and then we shall have no quarrel,' said Maesa. He moved stiffly back to the leather holding the rest of Ellamar's bones, not quite used to movement yet. He became so engrossed in tying up her bones he did not notice the glow coming into another of the mirrors. Shattercap did, and ran to tug at Maesa's arm.

'See, in the glass! Your Ellamar! Her shade is yet to leave.'

Maesa went to the mirror and pressed his hands upon the glass. Ellamar stared longingly at him. She was more solid, and wore the face of her youth, when she was the most beautiful thing Maesa had ever seen.

'Ellamar! We will be together again. Ellamar! Hear me!'

'Maesa! Maesa! Thanaton did not lie,' she said. 'Find the grave-sand. Find the crystallisation of my essence. In Shyish, in Shyish, in Shyish…'

'Ellamar!'

'Maesa…' The prince's name escaped her lips as a drawn-out sigh. 'My love, my prince, my love, my prince…' She faded to nothing, and the light in the mirrors went out.

'Ellamar!'

Maesa rested his helmed head against the glass. Shattercap approached cautiously.

'Master, master?' He tugged the aelf's tunic. 'She has gone, and so must we.'

Maesa sighed, and stepped away from the mirror, but his eyes remained fixed on the depths behind his reflection. 'Very well then. To Shyish. That is... something, at least.' He swallowed back tears, then spoke brusquely. 'Fetch me the rest of her wrappings, so I may protect her remains until the day comes when they are clothed in flesh again. I will let you touch those at least.'

Shattercap ran eagerly to do his errand. Maesa watched him.

'I am sorry I scolded you.'

'Good master, kind master,' simpered the spite.

'You could have betrayed me.'

Shattercap plucked fragments of glass from Ellamar's bandages and leathern cover. He did not meet the prince's eyes. 'I could. I did not.'

'You did not,' said Maesa.

Shattercap glanced at him hopefully. 'Does that mean I learn, my prince?'

'You learn.' Maesa joined the spite in clearing the glass from the bindings, then he wrapped the bones tightly and placed them in the leather sheet, and tied it up. 'I will seek the solution elsewhere. Let us leave Shadespire to the looters,' said Maesa. He took out the mouldering Book of Clovis from his pack, regarded it a last time, then dropped it on the floor. 'There is nothing here for us.'

He reset his pack and gear, then held out his arm. Shattercap leapt onto it and ran up to his shoulder.

'Thou wilt not release me yet,' said Shattercap, 'though I was good beyond my nature?'

'Not yet, Shattercap,' said Maesa. 'Not yet.'

PART TWO

THE SANDS
OF GRIEF

CHAPTER THREE

GLYMMSFORGE

'I don't like it here, master. Please, let us go. Too much magic, hurts my bones.' Shattercap shivered, strangely feline in his fear.

'Hush, Shattercap,' said Prince Maesa. 'They are nearly done. Be patient.'

They were at that time inside the shop of Erasmus Throck and Durdek Grimmson, providers of the finest alchemical instruments in Glymmsforge in Shyish, a realm Shattercap feared greatly.

Throck and Grimmson were comical opposites. Grimmson was a stout duardin with a blue beard and a bald head. Throck was a thin scrap of a man with a shock of white hair and a clean-shaven face. The duardin rooted about behind the counter near the floor. The man was balanced upon rolling steps, searching cubbyholes by the ceiling.

Grimmson hauled out a leather-covered box and placed it on the glass countertop.

'This is it, aelfling, the soul glass you wished for,' he said gruffly.

Throck tutted from the top of the steps at his colleague. 'Come now, Durdek! Prince Maesa is high-born and worthy of respect.'

Grimmson's granite face maintained its scowl. 'He's an aelf, and I call it as I see it, Erasmus.'

Throck shook his head, and pulled the wheeled ladder along the cubbyholes.

'My manners may be lacking, your worthiness,' said Grimmson to Maesa. 'But my work is not. I've outdone myself for you. Look at this.'

With a delicacy his massive fingers seemed incapable of, Grimmson took out a small hourglass. Its bulbs were no bigger than a child's clenched fists, decorated with delicate fretwork of silver and gold.

Grimmson flicked open a lid in the top. 'Grave-sand goes in here. Seal it. Tip it over when it's near run out. Keep on with that to prolong the life within, if you're alive. Away you go. Very simple, but that's no reason for drab work.'

'We pride ourselves on the finest equipment,' said Throck. 'Durdek here makes the devices...'

'And it's him as does the enchanting,' said Grimmson.

'It is a beautiful piece,' said Maesa. He took the hourglass from Grimmson and turned it over in his hands. 'Such fine workmanship.'

Grimmson hooked his fingers into his belt, gave a loud sniff and pulled himself up proudly. 'We do what we can.'

'Aha! Here is the other item, I knew I had put it somewhere safe,' said Throck. He slid down the ladder. From a soft velvet bag he took out a complex compass. It too had a lid in the top, covering over a small compartment. 'A soul seeker. This should lead you to the realmstone deposit you seek.'

Grimmson took the glass and placed it reverently back into the box so Maesa could examine the compass. Eight nested circles of gold, each free-moving against the others, surrounded the central lidded well. On one side of the well was an indicator made in the shape of the hooked sigil of Shyish. Maesa pushed it with his finger. It spun silently through many revolutions.

'It floats on a bath of ghostsilver,' said Throck. 'Place a token from the deceased in the well – a tooth serves, we find – and it'll lead you to their grave-sands.'

'No matter how far?'

'No matter the distance,' said Grimmson. 'We make no guarantee where the sand is, only that the compass points to it. But as you can see, it is good work.'

'Should be,' said Shattercap. 'For the amount you are being paid.'

'You get what you pay for,' Grimmson growled. 'And you are paying for quality. We are Glymmsforge's foremost makers of such devices.'

'You will find none better,' said Throck.

'Indeed,' said Maesa. 'I have no issue with the cost. Ignore my servant, he has yet to learn manners.' He handed the compass back and produced a white pouch from his belt. 'Fifty black diamond chips from the Realm of Ulgu, as you required.'

Grimmson took the bag from Maesa's hand and tugged at the drawstring, ready to count the contents.

Throck patted his partner's burly arm. 'That won't be necessary. I am sure the prince is good to his word.' Throck was awed by the prince's breeding, and couldn't help but give a bow. Maesa returned the gesture with a graceful inclination of his head. Grimmson looked at them both fiercely.

'You best be careful out there,' the duardin said. 'We sell maybe eight or nine of these kits a year, but the folks that buy them don't always come to the best end. Most go out into the Sands of Grief and vanish.'

'How do you know they work, then?' said Shattercap, slinking around the back of Maesa's head from one shoulder to the other.

'Ahem.' Throck looked apologetic. 'Their ghosts come back to tell us.'

'Ghosts? Ghosts! Master!' squealed Shattercap. 'Why did we come here?'

'I trust you have supernatural means of sustenance?' said Throck amiably. 'I do not mean to pry into your business, but where you intend to go is no place for the living. There is no water, no food, no life of any kind, only the dead, and storms of wild magic. We can provide the necessary protections, amulets, enchanted victuals.' He waved his hand around the shop. 'All you would require, if you have none of your own.'

'Oh no!' Shattercap shrieked again. 'No food!'

Maesa ignored him.

'I have what I need. My kind wander in every place. This realm is no alien land to me. I shall return in person to inform you how well your goods performed.' He picked up his packages. 'My thanks, and good day, sirs.'

Shattercap shrank from the strange sights of Glymmsforge. The sky was a bruised purple, forever brooding, its night scattered with amethyst stars. Outside the walls were the countries of afterlives ruined by the long war with Chaos, and haunted by broken souls. But in the streets of the young city, all was life lit by magical lanterns.

Throck and Grimmson was located on Thaumaturgy Way, along with dozens of other purveyors of magical goods. Market stalls narrowed the street, leaving only a narrow cobbled passage down the centre. Humans, aelves, duardin and all manner of other creatures thronged the way, and not only the living, but the shades of the dead also, for Glymmsforge was situated in the afterlife of Lyria, where some vestiges of past glory clung on.

The crowd moved slowly as its members browsed goods, creating knots of people in the flow that eddied irritably around each other. Maesa could pass through a thicket of brambles without disturbing a twig, but his aelven gifts were of no use in that place, and he was forced to shove through the throng along with the rest.

'Market days, I hate market days!' hissed Shattercap. 'Oh so many people. Where is the forest quiet? Where is the mossy silence?'

'You will yearn for their fellowship where we are going, small evil,' said Maesa. He slipped through a gaggle of ebon-skinned men of Ghur haggling over an imp imprisoned in a bottle, and reached the relative quiet of the main street.

Free of the overhanging eaves of Thaumaturgy Way, more of the city was visible to them. Rings of vast walls soared to touch the sky, holding within their compass the Shimmergate, a glimmering blue slash of light high up in the dark sky. Shattercap and Maesa were in the second district, thus close to the Stormkeep, the College of Amethyst and all the other wonders of the innermost ward.

Maesa turned his back on the central spires. His destination lay outside the city.

They returned to their lodgings in the Fourth Ward, and there Maesa arranged the equipment for their journey while Shattercap fretted in the corner.

Maesa packed his saddlebags with food, water and sustenance of the less mundane kind. He stowed his unstrung bow into its case on the outside of his quiver. The compass from Throck and Grimmson he hung about his neck in its bag, and he stowed the hourglass carefully alongside his provisions. Lastly, he took from the table his most prized possession, the wrapped bones of his dead love, Ellamar, and placed them atop his pack.

He called the houseboy to take the bags, gathered up Shattercap, and followed the servant down to the stables.

The inn's stable block housed every sort of riding beast imaginable. At one end of the stalls was a mighty gryph-charger, which rattled its beak in conversation with a pair of its lesser demigryph kin. Dozens of horses, flightless birds, great cats and more all whinnied, growled, squawked and screeched. As the air was a confusion of different calls, so the smell of the stables was a mighty reek composed of many bestial stinks. There was a single great stag in the stable: Aelphis, Maesa's mount, called back to his side when they had left Shadespire. Aelphis waited for his master, aloofly enduring the clumsy efforts of the grooms to saddle him.

'Aelphis!' said Maesa softly as he reached the stall.

The giant stag bowed his head and snorted gladly at the prince's greeting. He dropped to his knees to allow Maesa to load him with baggage.

'I am sorry, my lord, but I do not think I have your saddle right,' said the head groom. 'I never tacked up a creature like him before.'

'No matter,' said Maesa. Although the groom had made a poor job of it, he was genuinely apologetic. The prince adjusted the saddle while the groom looked on, and Maesa indulged his desire to learn. When all was as it should be, Maesa leapt nimbly upon Aelphis' back. The stag let out a bellow and rose up to his full, majestic height.

'We shall return,' said Maesa, and took his helm from a groom. Its modest antlers mirrored the magnificence of Aelphis' spread. Armoured, he and the beast were perfectly matched.

Maesa rode from the inn's yard. He would dearly have liked to give Aelphis his head, and let the beast break into a run, but the streets of the Fourth Ward were as crowded as those of the Second. Beast and rider were forced to keep their patience until they reached the eastern outgate.

A permit was required to leave the city at night. Men armed with sorcerous guns barred his path. Maesa duly provided his papers to the gate captain, who scrutinised them carefully.

No one else was leaving.

'All is in order,' said the captain reluctantly.

At a shout from the captain, the gates swung wide. The road

leading away from Glymmsforge was empty. Not one being walked the level paving. A channel of purple salt cut through the road surface a hundred yards out, interrupting its journey into desert nowhere.

'You must be an influential man to secure exit from the city at night,' said the captain, handing back the papers. 'Even so, I advise you to wait for the day.'

'I am eager to be away.'

'I have a suspicion of where you are bound, prince,' said the captain. 'I've seen plenty of creatures with the same look you have in your eyes. They were not to be dissuaded, so I will not try with you. I will give you the warning that all free folk receive from me. At the line of salt there, the protection of Sigmar ends. There are perils aplenty beyond. This gate is the frontier of life. Out there is only death and undeath. Are you sure whatever reason you are going abroad is worth your soul?'

'I am sure,' said Maesa.

'Then Sigmar watch over you. There are no others that can,' said the captain.

'Your warning is noted, captain,' said Maesa. 'But I have nothing to fear.'

The men stepped aside at a nod from the captain. Maesa's trilling song set Aelphis bounding out into the empty desert, joyful to be free of the confines of the city.

CHAPTER FOUR

THE DESERTS OF SHYISH

The road entered low hills some miles from the city, where it stopped suddenly at a half-finished cutting. Construction gear lay around, awaiting the day and the work gangs it would bring. Night-time was altogether too dangerous for mortal labour. Maesa directed the stag off the unfinished road and up to the top of the first rise, where he pulled him to a stop.

Maesa turned for one last look back. Dust kicked up by the stag's hooves blew away. From the vantage of the hillside, Glymmsforge was set out like a model for him to examine.

The Shimmergate gleamed in the sky, surrounded by the gossamer traceries of the stairs leading to its threshold. The realmgate reflected in the Glass Mere, the broad lake also encompassed by Sigmar's fortifications. Monumental buildings had spires taller even than the walls, all ablaze with fires and shining mage-light. Among the finest were the great mausolea of the celestial saints, the relics of a dozen creatures whose holy power kept back evil, joined into a twelve-pointed star by trenches of the purple salt, together making a barrier to all wicked things.

Around this oasis city, the Zircona Desert stretched its gloomy expanses.

'Look back at the city, small evil,' Maesa said to Shattercap. 'It will be our last sight of life ere our task is done.'

Tiny, whistling snores answered. Shattercap was a relaxed weight in the bottom of Maesa's hood.

Quietly, so as not to disturb the slumbering spite, Maesa urged Aelphis into a run.

Zircona's desert ran for leagues. Aelphis covered its distances without tiring. He cut straight across the landscape, bounding as quickly over crags and shattered badlands as he ran over the flats. Day's watery light came and went, and Maesa did not pause. Every third night he would rest, for aelven kind are hardier than mortal men, and sleep rules their lives with a looser hand. Aelphis slept when the prince did. At those times Shattercap kept watch. Trusting terror to keep the spite vigilant, aelf and stag rested without misgiving.

Shattered cities dotted the wastes, though whether raised by the living or the dead it was impossible to say. The metaphysics of Shyish were complex. Before the Age of Chaos cast them into ruin, many lesser afterlives had occupied the desert. As time went on, the living had come into those places, and dwelled alongside those who had lived and died in other realms. To the south of Glymmsforge, towards the heartlands of Shyish, there were mighty kingdoms yet, but towards realm's edge, where Maesa headed, only ruins remained, levelled by Chaos, and haunted by the shrieking of dispossessed gheists.

None of these wandering shades dared come near. To the sight of the dead, Prince Maesa shone with baleful power. His sword, the soul-drinking Song of Thorns, would bring their end with a single cut, and Maesa had other magical arts besides.

They passed a great city whose walls were whole and aglow with corpselight. No sound issued from the place. There was no sense of vitality, only an ominous watchfulness. The city filled the valley it occupied from side to side, and Maesa was forced to travel uneasily within the shadow of the fortifications. A wail went up from the gatehouse as he approached, answered by others from the towers in the curtain wall. Aelphis pranced and snorted at the din. Shattercap gibbered in fright. Disturbed, Maesa spurred Aelphis on. The wailing harrowed their ears as they galloped by, but nothing came out from the city, no solid nor spectral arrow, and as Maesa passed, the ghostly shrieks died one by one, until a terrible silence fell.

They left the city behind quickly. Thereafter the character of the land changed for the worse.

The night after they passed the city, they camped. All were weary, for the land took a toll on their spirits. Shattercap puled miserably and tugged at Maesa's hair.

'Master, master,' he whined. 'I feel so ill, not good at all.'

Maesa squatted at Aelphis' side. The giant stag was sleeping, his huge flanks pumping like bellows, gusting breath whose warmth the bitter lands swiftly stole. Maesa took Shattercap from his shoulder and looked at him carefully. The spite's skin had gone dry and pale. Maesa too was ailing. His face had lost its alabaster sheen, becoming pasty. Dark rings shaded his violet, almond eyes.

'It is the land. The nearer the edge we go, the less forgiving to mortal flesh it is, even to those like we, small evil, who are blessed with boundless lifespans.'

Shattercap coughed. Maesa cradled him in the crook of his arm as he hunted through his bags with his free hand.

'It is time. For you especially, a creature born of the magic of life, this place is hard. I have something here for you to ensure your survival.'

He took out a round flask protected by a net of cord. Contained in the glass was a clear liquid that glowed with greenish light. As Maesa uncorked it, it shone brighter, lighting the bones and veins in his fine hands, and flared lighter still as he held the bottle to Shattercap's lips.

'Aqua Ghyranis, water from the Lifewells of Ghyran,' Maesa explained. 'Take but one drop. Any more will change you, and we have but a little.'

Shattercap dipped his pink tongue into the glass. When it touched the blessed water he let out a relieved sigh. 'It tastes of the forests. It tastes of the rivers and the leaves. It tastes of home!'

Maesa set Shattercap down and wet his own lips. His skin tingled. His face glowed with renewed life, and the dark rings faded. He dabbed a little water on his forefinger to rub on the gums of the sleeping stag, then corked the flask and put it away.

A dolorous moaning sang out of the night.

'Best keep this out of sight,' Maesa said. 'The dead here are hungry, and will seek out a source of life such as this.'

They went further towards realm's edge. At night, the dark was full of desperate howls. Cold winds blew, carrying whispers that chilled the marrow. Thunderous storms cracked the sky with displays of purple lightning, though no rain fell. Nothing lived. The days grew shorter with every league they went, the light of Hysh paler, until they passed some fateful meridian, and went into lands perpetually in shadow, out of sight of the Realm of Light. Where the light died totally, the sky changed. Purple, motionless stars shone. Zircona was a wasteland, but belonged in part to a living world. This new desert was entirely a dead place.

Maesa slipped from Aelphis' saddle.

'We have reached the Sands of Grief. Now is the time for the magic of Throck and Grimmson,' he said. He took out the golden compass, and set it on a stone. From his spidersilk pack he took the leather-wrapped remains of his lover, then he removed the skull and set it on the ground. He knelt beside it.

'Forgive me, my love,' he said. Delicately, he took up the brown skull, and pinched a tooth between forefinger and thumb. 'I apologise for this insult to your remains. I shall replace this tooth with the brightest silver.'

Grimacing at what he must do, he drew the tooth. It came free with a dry scraping. He set the tooth aside and rewrapped his precious relics. Then he opened up the lid of the compass-box and placed the tooth within.

'Let us see if it works.'

He held the compass up to his face. Slowly, the pointer swung about, left, then right, then left, before coming to a stop. Maesa moved the compass. The pointer remained fixed unwaveringly on the desert.

'Thou hast success?' said Shattercap.

'I have success,' said Maesa in relief.

Daylight receded from recollection. Shifting dunes crowded the mind as much as the landscape. Maesa put all his formidable will into remembering who he was, and why he was there. Should he have forgotten, then his sanity would have faded, and he would have wandered the desert forever.

Time without the passing of day and night loses meaning. The compass did not move from its position. Hours or lifetimes could have gone by. The desert landscape changed slowly, but it did change. Maesa came out of his fugue to find himself looking into a gorge where figures marched in two lines from one horizon to another. One line headed deeper into the desert and the realm's edge, the other contrariwise, towards the heartlands of Shyish.

The sight was enough to shake Maesa from his torpor. Shattercap stirred.

'What is it?' asked Shattercap. His voice was weak.

'The animate remains of the dead,' said Maesa. The percussive click of dry joints and the whisper of fleshless feet echoed from the gorge's sides. Starlight glinted from ancient bone.

'What are they doing?' said Shattercap.

'I have no idea,' said Maesa. 'But we must cross their march.'

'Master!' said Shattercap. 'Please, no. This is too much.'

Maesa urged Aelphis on. The great stag was weary, and stumbled upon the scree, dislodging a shower of rock that barged through the lines of skeletons. Bones scattered as two collapsed. Like ants on their way to their nest, the animates stepped around the scene of the catastrophe, and continued on their silent march.

'Oh no,' whimpered Shattercap.

'Be not afraid,' said Maesa. 'They see nothing. They are weakly animated and have been set upon a single task. They will not harm us.' He drew Aelphis up by the line, and rode alongside it. The skeletons heading outward marched with their arms at their sides, but those going inward each held one hand high in front of empty eye sockets, fingers pinched upon an invisible burden.

Shattercap snuffled at them. 'Oh, I see! I see! They carry realm-stone, such tiny motes of power, I can hardly perceive. Why, master, why?'

'I know not,' said Maesa, though the revelation filled him with unease. Nervously, he checked his compass, in case the undead carried off the prize he sought, but the compass arrow remained pointing in the same direction as before. 'I have no wish to discover why. Few beings could move so many of the dead. We should be away from here.'

They left the name unsaid, but it was to Nagash, God of Undeath, that Maesa referred. To whisper his name would call his attention onto them, and so deep in Shyish, Maesa had no power to oppose him.

'Come, Aelphis, through the line.'

The king of stags bounded through a gap. The skeletons were blind to the aelven prince. With exaggerated, mechanical care, they trooped through the endless night, bearing their cargoes onward.

They passed several skeleton columns over the coming days. Always, they marched in two directions, one coreward, the other to the edge. They followed the lie of the land like water, choosing the path of least resistance, eroding it with their feet where they passed, forming dry rivers of bone. Not once did the skeletons notice the travellers, and soon their crossing of the lines became routine. The compass turned gradually away from their current path. By then notions of edgeward and coreward had lost all meaning. They knew the direction changed simply because they found themselves coming against the skeleton columns diagonally, then, as the compass shifted again, walking alongside them to the deeper desert. For safety's sake, Maesa withdrew a little from the column the compass demanded he follow, shadowing it at a mile's distance. Time ran. The line of skeletons did not break or waver, but stamped on, on, on towards Shyish's centre, each skeleton a progression of the motion of the one behind, so the animates were like so many drawings pulled from a child's zoetrope.

Some time later, neither Maesa nor Shattercap knew how long, they witnessed a new sight. In a lonely hollow they spied a figure. On impulse Maesa turned Aelphis away from their route to investigate.

A human squatted in the dust over a prospector's pan. From his fist he let a slow trickle of sand patter, then sifted it carefully around the pan while croaking minor words of power. Sometimes he would take a peck of sand out and put it into something near his feet. More often he would tip the load aside.

'Good evening,' said Maesa. It was dangerous approaching anyone in the wastes, but even the prince, who had spent solitary decades in his wandering, felt the need for company.

'Eh, eh? Evening? Always night-time. What do you want?' said the man. He did not look up from his work.

Maesa saw no reason to lie. 'I seek the grave-sands of my lost love. I hope to use them to bring her back, and be with her again.'

'Mmm, hmm, yes. Many come here for the realmstone of Shyish, grave-sand, the crystallised essence of mortal years,' said the man, pawing at the ground. He mumbled something unintelligible, then suddenly looked around, eyes wide. His skin was pallid. The spicy smell of rot rose from him. 'You must be a great practitioner of the arts of unlife to attempt to find a particular vein. I never met an aelf with a knack for the wind of Shyish. But I, Kwalos the Astute, necromancer supreme, I will have my own life soon bottled in this glass! By reversing it, I shall live forever. I alone have the art to exploit the Sands of Grief, whereas you shall fail!' He chuckled madly. 'What do you think of that?'

'It is most impressive ambition,' said Maesa.

The smile dropped from Kwalos' face. 'Oh, you'd best be careful! He doesn't like it when souls are taken! You take the one you're looking for, even a part, and he'll come for you. He'll not let you be until your bones march in his legions and your spirit shrieks in his host.' He looked about, then whispered, 'I speak of Nagash.'

The name streamed from his lips and away over the dunes, growing louder the further it travelled. Thunder boomed in the distance. Aelphis shied.

'Not I, though,' said Kwalos. 'I have this! Within is my life! My soul is none but my own.' He held up the bottom bulb of an hour-glass. The neck was snapped, the top lost. The glass was scratched to the point of opacity. No sand would run in that vessel, unless it was to fall out.

'I see,' said Maesa neutrally.

'The man is mad!' hissed Shattercap.

'Just a few grains more, then I will be heading back,' said Kwalos. 'All the peoples of Eska will marvel at my feat,' he said. He licked his lips with a tongue dry and black as old leather. 'I don't think you can do it, not like me.' He cradled his broken glass to his chest.

'We shall see,' said Maesa.

'On your way!' said the necromancer, his face transformed by a snarl. 'You distract me from my task. Get you gone.'

Aelphis plodded slowly by the man. As they passed him, Maesa glimpsed white shining inside his open robes. Shattercap growled.

Kwalos' ribs poked through desiccated flesh. Splintered bone trapped a dark hole where his heart had beaten.

'He is dead,' whispered Shattercap.

'Yes,' said Maesa. 'Did you only notice now?'

Shattercap scrambled across Maesa's shoulders to look behind. 'Thou knewest?'

'Only once he spoke,' admitted Maesa. 'I thought him alive, at first.'

'Should we not tell him?'

'I do not think it would make any difference, and it may put us in danger. His fate is not our business. The Lord of Undeath has him in his thrall. His doom is a cruel joke.'

Maesa directed Aelphis back upon their course and rode for a while. When he was sure they were out of sight of Kwalos, Maesa pulled out Ghyran's bottled life and regarded it critically.

'The lack of this is a cause for concern. There is enough for a few more days,' he said. He looked towards the centre of Shyish, estimating the ride to more hospitable lands. 'No more than that.'

'What do we do when we run out?' whimpered Shattercap.

Maesa would not answer.

Maesa and his companions were dying. Not a swift death, but the slow drip of souls weeping from broken hearts. Grey dunes rolled away to chill eternities. Aelphis stumbled up slopes and down slip faces, his antlers drooping to his feet. Maesa swayed listlessly in the saddle. Shattercap was silent. A few drops of Ghry-an's life-giving waters remained to sustain them. They would have to return soon, or they would die.

At the same time, they grew hopeful. Increasingly in the dust they saw glittering streams of coarse sand in green, black, amethyst and other gemstone colours. These were grave-sands, each streak on the dunes the crystallised essence of a life. Maesa looked at his compass often, hoping against hope that the needle would turn and point to one of the deposits, but he was disappointed. The needle aimed towards the horizon always. None of the coloured streaks were Ellamar's mortal days.

And then, the miraculous occurred. After what felt like years, and could have been, the needle on the compass twitched. Maesa stared dumbly at the device cupped in his hands. The needle was swinging away from their line of travel.

'Shattercap!' said Maesa, his voice cracked from days of disuse.

'Master?' replied the spite, a breath of words no louder than the whisper of the windblown sand.

'We are near.' Maesa spurred Aelphis into life. Huffing wearily, the king of stags lumbered into a trot. 'To the right, Aelphis! There!' said Maesa, intent upon the dial.

Their path took them closer to the line of skeletons they had followed for leagues. At last, the source of the animates' burdens became apparent. Where realmstone gathered most thickly, the bowl of a great quarry had been carved, and in it the two lines of skeletons joined into one. They entered, looped round, bent without slowing to peck at the sand, then walked around the back of the bowl and thence out again, carrying their tiny treasures away to their master. In the dim starlight, Maesa spied many such pits, some worked out, some seething with the flash of dead bones. Horror gripped him again. If Ellamar's sands were in one of those pits...

Relief came from the compass. It spun a little to the left, then as Aelphis followed, to the right. The compass rotated slowly around and around. Maesa brought Aelphis to a halt and slid from his back. Sand shifted under his feet. Rivulets of it ran from the dunes' sides to fill his footsteps. The grey dust comprised the lesser part of it; much was realmstone. Many colours were mingled there, many lives blended.

The prince stooped low, the compass held to the sand. By lifting individual grains to the compass rose and watching its spin, he ascertained that Ellamar's life was of an indigo hue. One grain set the compass twirling sharply. A handful made it blur.

'Fitting,' he said. 'Indigo was her favourite colour.' He took out the last of the Aqua Ghyranis, and roused the spite. 'Shattercap.'

'Good prince?' said the spite woozily.

'We shall finish this. We shall need all our strength. The servants of Nagash will come as soon as we take the sand.' He took a sip, gave a drink to Shattercap, and then tipped the last of the water into Aelphis' mouth. The stag snorted and stood taller as vitality returned.

'Help me. Pick up this sand.' He drew out the hourglass from his saddlebags and placed it on the desert floor. He opened up the lid. 'Fill it up. Carefully. Not one other grain, only the indigo, only hers.'

When lowered to the sand, Shattercap mewled. 'The dead ground burns me, master!'

'Bear the pain, and you shall be four steps closer to freedom,' said the prince sternly. 'Hurry!'

Together the aelf and spite worked, carefully plucking single grains of the sand from the dust and depositing them in the hourglass. The bottom bulb was almost full, and the remaining grains becoming harder to sift from the dust, when a piercing shriek rose over the desert.

Shattercap's head whipped up. His hands opened and closed nervously. 'Master...' he whimpered. 'We are noticed.'

Another shriek sounded, then a third, each one nearer than the last. The ceaseless, gentle wind of the desert gusted fiercely.

'Fill it, spite!' commanded Maesa. He drew the Song of Thorns. The woody edge of the sword sparked with starlight. 'Get it all. I shall hold them back.'

Howling with outrage, a wraith came flying over the ridge of a nearby dune. It had no legs, but trailed streamers of magic from black robes in their place. Its face was a skull locked into a permanent roar. In its hands it bore a scythe. This, unlike the aethereal bearer, was solid enough, a shaft of worm-eaten wood and a blade of rusted metal with a terrible bite. Other wraiths came skimming over the sands from every direction, their corpselight shining from the small jewels of other creatures' lives.

The first wraith raised its weapon and bore down on the prince. Moving with the grace native to all aelves, Maesa sidestepped and with a single precise cut sliced the spirit in two. It screamed its last, the shreds of its soul sucked within the Song of Thorns. Another came, swooping around and around Aelphis and Maesa before plunging arrow-swift at the prince. Maesa ended it before it could strike. The Song of Thorns glowed with stolen spirit.

A chorus of shrieks sounded from every direction. The undead burst from the sand, they swooped down from the sky. The watchdogs of Nagash were alert for thieves taking their master's property, and responded to the alarm with speed.

'Quickly, Shattercap!'

Maesa slew another, and another. The Song of Thorns was anathema to things such as the wraiths, but there were hundreds of them gathering, a tempest of phantoms. The spite scrabbled at the ground, his earlier finesse gone as he shovelled Ellamar's life-sands into the glass.

'Be careful not to mix the grains!' the prince shouted, cleaving the head of another wraith from its shoulders.

'I am trying!' squeaked the spite.

'I cannot fight all these things,' said Maesa. Now the wraiths saw the danger the Song of Thorns posed, they turned their attacks against Aelphis and Shattercap, and it took all Maesa's skill to keep them from harm. Aelphis reared and pawed at the wraiths, but all he could do was deflect their weapons from his hide. When his hooves hit their bodies, they passed through, leaving wakes of glowing mist.

'I have it all!' said Shattercap, ducking the raking hand of a wraith. He slammed closed the lid atop the hourglass.

'You are sure? You have checked the compass?'

'Yes!' squealed Shattercap. 'It moves no more, unless to point to the glass!'

The prince danced around the stag, snatching up hourglass and compass in one hand while killing with the other. Shattercap leapt from the sand to the prince's arm. Maesa jumped onto the back of the stag, cutting away the head of a scythe in mid-air. He reversed his stroke as he landed in the saddle to render another phantom into shreds of ectoplasm that the Song of Thorns quickly devoured.

Aelphis reared. Maesa slashed from left to right. Braying loudly, the stag leapt forward.

Invigorated by the last of Ghyran's water, Aelphis ran as fast as the wind. The wraiths pursued, more streaming from the depths of the desert to join them. Maesa slew all that came against him. He cried out when a scythe blade nicked his arm, numbing it with the grave's chill. The wraiths screeched in triumph to see his discomfort, and they closed in for the kill, but Maesa yelled the war cries of his ancestors and fought on.

The great stag flew, his hooves barely touching the ground. The wraiths were outpaced. Their dark shapes were left behind. No more came from the wastes.

Aelphis ran on for hours and hours. Light grew ahead. The Sands of Grief were coming to an end. Desert of a more ordinary sort blended into its edges. At last, Maesa arrived at a place where dawn stood still upon the edge of the world, and the glow of Hysh lit upon his face. At the margins of a wadi, grasses rattled in the wind, dry, but living. Far from the lines of skeletons and their ghoulish mines, Maesa brought Aelphis to a stop. The stag snorted. Froth lathered his skin. He shuddered from antlers to tail, spraying foam across the rocks, then settled, and blared out his throaty call.

Maesa lifted up the hourglass. He checked the compass, holding it away from the glass, but always it pointed to the sands in his hand, never back into the desert.

'The first part of the task is done,' he said. 'With this, we will be able to bring her back, and when Ellamar returns, she will not age. She will be forever at my side.'

'Yes, my master,' said Shattercap. 'But the Lord of the Undead will not rest until he has brought thee to account for thy crime, and we must find a way to steal her from whatever place she languishes within.'

'Indeed. The quest is far from over. First, we must leave Shyish, and seek out those who might instruct us.'

'Back to the city?'

'I prefer a less noticeable way. The Argent Gate is not far from Glymmsforge. We will leave Shyish there.'

'But you steal from the god of the dead,' said Shattercap. 'We will be pursued!'

'Let Nagash's servants come,' said Maesa. He sheathed the Song of Thorns. It vibrated with strange warmth from its feast, passing its strength into him. 'I will be ready. You did well, Shattercap. You are learning.'

'Learning to be good?'

'Yes.'

'Thank you, wicked prince,' said the spite. He snuggled down into Maesa's hood. But though his words were fawning, his heart retained a little flinty wickedness. His tiny fist was clenched. In it he held a single grain of Ellamar's grave-sand, kept for himself.

Unaware of his companion's thievery, Maesa set his joyous face into the dawn, and rode out full of hope.

PART THREE

THE SIGN OF THE BRAZEN CLAW

CHAPTER FIVE

A NIGHT AT THE INN

Near the Amethyst Heights on the marches of Shyish's inner realms there was a pinnacle of rock. A lonely peak, not so tall as the mountains some miles distant, but in form it was remarkable, and it was well known because of that. They called it the Brazen Claw, for it resembled a great limb stretching out of the earth, as if a giant interred alive had broken the surface of its grave only to perish upon the cusp of freedom. A column much like an arm ended in a cupped club of stone much like a hand. Four spires like three fingers and a thumb reached from this hand, straining for the purple clouds yet never snagging them. There was a fifth, the smallest finger, but that was broken off near the lowermost knuckle. The break was fresh, recent enough that the edges were sharp and the minerals within paler than the weathered exterior.

So closely did the Brazen Claw resemble a hand that the origin of part of its name was obvious. The brazen element was obscure until the turning of day into night, when Hyshbeams sparkled from the uncountable crystals of the stone, turning the pinnacle into a gauntlet of bronze.

There was no sunset upon the particular night that concerns this tale, for a storm had shrieked from the heart of the realm towards Shyish's deathly hinterlands, scourging all before it with whips of rain. Igneous nails were wet by the storm as the clouds spat in mockery at the Claw's attempts to grasp them. Wind hooted derision through the fingers. Yet the Claw reached.

Though the Brazen Claw's lust for the sky was forever denied, the thirsts of men were well slaked on that lofty pinnacle. Nestling in the palm of the stone hand was an inn. The upturned palm of the Claw was its courtyard. From the wrist, a wide road of boards curled around and away down the stone arm to the plains a dizzying distance below. The inn was large, and it needed to be, for it played host to a good deal of traffic heading out from Shyish via the Argent Realmgate, though compared to the Claw, the inn was a tiny wooden adornment. It was built right around the base of the middle finger, forming a circle, the outer parts cantilevered over the clear air, so that it appeared like a ring. Stables and outbuildings clustered round the other fingers and filled up the spaces between.

A stout sky-dock sat atop the index finger. From the palm more stairs led up to the platform shuddering in the storm, hawsers thrumming as they were plucked at by the gale. The bolts threading the timbers squeaked. A lesser construction would have shaken free, but not this dock; it was made by the Kharadron duardin for their sky-ships to use. Huge bronze collars held the dock in place, their verdigris staining the rock green. Nought could shake their hold. The dock would not fall.

No travellers ascended. None could. To attempt those stairs in that weather would have been a pact with death.

A claw of stone, black in the rain, a merry inn groaning in the winds held tight around its finger, and all around the darkness of midnight and the lash of a gathering tempest, at the very edges of the lands of death.

To this place, Prince Maesa came.

There were five of them in the inn at the beginning. Horrin would remember each for the rest of his long, long life, as he would remember everything else that occurred that night. When more immediate memories faded into the haze of years, the night remained clear.

The five were his wife, the stable boy, and two travellers. The lad Barnabus was as good as his own son, and Horrin knew him well. As the evening began, he was quietly polishing riding tack near the fire. Horrin's dear Ninian worked on tomorrow's dinner in the open kitchen, and he knew her better. Horrin himself was behind the bar. The bar and its shelves of many liquors were built into the outer curve of the building, opposite the fireplace carved into the base of the stone finger. The fireplace was crudely made, but was the room's most imposing feature, and of considerable importance.

Of the travellers, Horrin knew nothing to begin with, other than their names.

The first was a venerable duardin with hair and beard of downy grey so fine it looked like mist in the lamplight. The name he signed in the visitor's book was Idenkor Stonbrak. He was a jewel merchant, he said, from a coastal hold up Melket way in Ulgu. He said little else. He was close-mouthed, even for one of his breed, and stared into the fire with his heavy boots upon a stool, while he exhausted and refilled his long-stemmed pipe over and over, until his head was shrouded in fogs of fragrant smoke.

The second guest was a nervous man of unknown lands, pale as a man of Shyish yet not a native of that realm. Pludu Quasque, he was called. His robes were dirty with hard use, but their cut and the cloth made it obvious he had once been rich, and the dagger and sword he carried were those of a wealthy man. He muttered over a bowl of soup while casting suspicious glances at the others as readily as wayward boys cast stones.

Horrin leaned upon the bar he had made with his own hands. A canopy of rare Azyrite emberwood gleamed over the counter, following its curve exactly. Expensive amulets imbued with counter-magics hung from the canopy, resting quietly despite the roaring wind battering at the inn, reassuring him that what assailed them was solely a natural phenomenon. For all that the inn's situation was precarious, Horrin knew it was safe. It was well built, and clung hard to the stone of the Claw, so he ignored its shakings and shudderings, and the insistent hail rapping on the shingles, and the squeak of doors in empty rooms. Draughts teased candle flames into spluttering outrage. Water crept in between the roof and the stone of the finger to run down the wall in stealthy streaks. The smell of rain blew under the door, but inside it was warm, and Horrin was content. The fire burned high. The protective sigils carved into the rock around the fireplace danced with orange light. All was as it should be.

Laid upon the bar next to the visitor's book was a ledger. The figures gladdened Horrin. The Inn of the Brazen Claw was doing well. His wife gave him a warm smile. Life was good.

The wind outside roared. The timbers of the inn creaked. A shutter upstairs banged loudly, startling the outland human so hard his hand twitched and upset his bowl.

Ninian rushed over, cloth in hand. 'Let me get that for you, master,' she said.

Quasque responded poorly, and flapped his hands. 'Away, away! Oh, my robe is ruined!' he said, although the ruination was long done, and the soup stain hardly worsened it.

Thunder rolled away over the Amethyst Heights. By Horrin's

reckoning the storm's full violence would be upon them soon. The inn moaned in response to the wind's shrieks. Beams shifted in their sockets. Floorboards sang.

'A hard night,' said Stonbrak slowly, and puffed some more on his pipe. 'Fell things walk storms like this, mark my words.' His eyes glittered like gems embedded in stone.

As soon as the words were said, the wind battered at the inn, rattling the walls with hailstones. The fire died down far enough to give Horrin pause: the fire never went out, it could never go out. His heart resumed its normal rhythm as the flames climbed high, then leapt again as the door flexed in its frame.

Barnabus let out a frightened noise, dropped his brasses and ran around the back of the bar counter.

'Nobody there,' said Horrin cheerfully. He took a nonchalant step along the counter towards the place he hid his pistol just in case. 'It's only the wind.'

Three powerful knocks belied his statement.

'Wind doesn't knock!' said Quasque. He got to his feet, his eyes wide. Horrin's hand rested on the polished butt of his gun.

'A traveller then,' said Horrin, though in truth he could not guess what kind of traveller would be abroad in such a storm.

The door slammed back into the wall with a crack. Quasque fumbled through his robes to find the hilt of his sword, his other straying into his shirt to fetch out an amulet. The duardin narrowed his eyes and worked his mouth around his pipe. He continued staring into the fire, but his hand moved casually to the throat of the jewelled axe hanging from his belt.

A tall figure stood in the doorway, water streaming from his cloak. Small horns upon his head were lit by a flash of lightning. Horrin swallowed.

'Gods save us!' whispered Quasque.

The figure stepped into the light of the common room, and

threw back his cloak. The wind wailed its mocking song. The duardin's throaty chuckle ground away the silence.

''Tis but an aelf, skinny and dripping wet!' He laughed plumes of smoke into the breeze stealing around the traveller. 'Probably weighs twice his usual weight with the water.'

The traveller closed the door, shutting out the storm and transforming himself from sinister interloper to one of the company. The living were within, the storm was without, and all was back to the natural order of things.

An aelf he was, bedraggled by the weather, his long hair darkly wet. The rain's borrowed tears slid past his almond-shaped eyes. He carried three bags – two small, one a larger pack – which he placed carefully upon the floor. Now he was inside, his horns were revealed as antlers mounted on a close-fitting helm. He grasped them and lifted the helm from his head and placed it on a table. The helm's blued steel ran with water that pattered onto the wooden boards. A sword of peculiar design sat at his hip. Upon his back, unstringed in its case, was a beautiful bow. Each of the inn's occupants were granted the touch of his immortal gaze, and all felt themselves judged.

When he spoke, his voice was one of such mellifluous beauty, tears pricked Horrin's eyes.

'My pardon for shocking you,' the aelf said, 'for I can see that I did. I merely seek shelter until the sky-ship comes. My name is Maesa, of the nomad clans.' He had fine bearing. As he divested himself of his sopping outerwear, his presence grew, and Horrin knew a princeling graced his inn.

Stonbrak grunted. He removed his hand from his axe, folded his arms and went back to his contemplation of the flame's unobtainable jewels.

'It is we who should apologise!' said Horrin, recovering his wits. 'We have few of your kind cross our door, and it is such a poor evening we were all amazed to hear your knock. Few would dare the stair to the inn in this weather.'

'My mount is sure-footed,' said the aelf. 'I had nothing to fear.' He paused. 'Am I not welcome?'

Horrin dismissed the aelf's concerns with a gesture. 'No, no! All are welcome at the Brazen Claw! Provided they have the means to pay and a disinclination to trouble, of course,' he said with a quick smile.

'Of course,' said the prince.

Horrin moved his hand from the butt of the gun and rested it on the countertop. 'I assume you're here for the midnight sailing?'

The aelf nodded.

'I'm afraid it's been and gone,' said Horrin regretfully. 'Master Grindleson ran before the storm, came early and left in double-quick time to save his aether-endrins. There are no more ships scheduled until tomorrow night.'

'That is unfortunate,' said the aelf. He picked up his bags and came further into the inn, stepping down the curved stairs from the entrance into the wide pit of the common room.

'Ah, it happens,' said Horrin. 'Frightful storms we have here sometimes. You don't have long to wait. The ship'll come, should the storm blow itself out, and I never did know one last longer than a day and night. You know the duardin, they keep to their word whether it's a blood debt or a timetable. They'll be here.'

The aelf's return stare flustered him.

'What might I get for you, master aelf?' Horrin said, struggling to hold onto his smile. 'It is a vile night to be abroad. I suggest something warm. I have soup, freshly made?'

The aelf shook his head. The gesture was such a simple motion, but possessed grace a human could never match. He took up his bags, leaving his helm upon the table near the door, where it watched the company with hollow eyes.

'I will take warmed wine, with cinnaberry, and honey, if you have it.'

Horrin gave a modest smile. 'We are on the major sky routes to the Argent Gate, my lord, we have victuals to suit every palate here.'

The duardin grunted and shifted in his seat. 'Aelf diets,' he said dismissively.

Maesa glanced at him before taking a seat away from the others, yet still within the warm circle of the fire. He rested his pack against the wall, took off his bow case and placed his two smaller bags nearby; one, of rolled leather, he set by his side on the bench, the other he put on the table by his left hand.

'Do you have a thimble, silver or copper long out of the ground? No iron, nothing of the recent earth, certainly no pottery?'

Horrin glanced questioningly at his wife.

'I have my grandmother's old thimble,' Ninian said. 'That is of pewter, I think. I do not use it, it is too small for my thumb.'

'That will suffice,' said the aelf.

'For what purpose, my lord?' asked Horrin.

'You shall see,' said Prince Maesa.

Horrin bowed. 'Then my wife shall fetch it.'

Ninian bustled off, her skirts rustling.

'Clean it with pure spirit,' the aelf called after her. 'Bring it upon a wooden board. Fill it with the same drink you shall serve me. Do not touch it with anything of iron!'

'Are there any other stipulations, my lord?' said Horrin.

'None. Only make sure my glass is clean,' said the aelf. He took a pouch from his side and laid it on the table. Gems rattled. 'My mount requires stabling. He is outside.'

Horrin looked over to the wide-eyed Barnabus and jerked his head. Barnabus came forward a few faltering steps.

'Your stable boy?' asked the aelf.

Horrin nodded. 'Barnabus, that's his name. My son.'

'There is no resemblance.'

'He is my son,' insisted Horrin. 'Not by blood, but son he is to me nonetheless.'

Maesa turned to Barnabus, and spoke in kindly tones. 'Do not be afraid, Barnabus. The storm is strong, but Aelphis will shelter you, and if any evil comes, you can be sure he will lay down his noble life to protect you. You need only show him where he must sleep, and remove his saddle. He will do the rest.'

'A horse?' said the boy.

'A great stag!' said the aelf, kindling a sense of wonder in them all.

The aelf's words soothed the boy. His violet eyes did not blink. Horrin half suspected magic to be at work, though he could sense none, and the charms above the bar remained still. Barnabus nodded hesitantly and trotted to the door. He pulled his oilskin from its hook and went outside. The fury of the storm snarled into the room, and he was chased out by the bang of the door.

'Master Stonbrak here and Master Quasque are like you,' said Horrin, coming to the prince's table with a lit taper. 'They came for the scheduled flight but missed it on account of its earliness.' He leaned in and touched the taper to the wick of the larger candle in the lantern in front of the aelf.

'Move that to one side, if you please, my companion dislikes fire,' said the aelf.

'Companion?' questioned Horrin.

The aelf held Horrin's eyes with his own as he reached down to the bag and undid its drawstring. Ninian arrived at the table and set the aelf's drinks down in time to see a tiny, wizened green hand reach out from the bag, grasp the lip and pull it back.

'Cold. Wet,' said a whining, petulant voice. 'Don't like riding in the bag. Shattercap is not a round of cheese, or a block of bread.'

A homunculus stalked onto the table. Its skin was the pale grey-green of young leaves, its back hunched. The arms were a little too long for its body, the legs a little too short, the neck unusually stretched, and the flat face and the head it adorned a little too small, but otherwise it looked like a tiny man shrunk down so he might be kept in a bag.

Horrin leaned back, then in. The creature hissed at him. Ninian's hand flew up to her mouth and she gasped.

'Now, now, Shattercap,' said the aelf. 'Do not frighten our hosts.'

'Is he safe?' said Horrin. He glanced from imp to aelf and back to imp.

'While he remains under my command, yes,' said the aelf. 'And so long as his geas is respected.'

'Aha, that explains the thimble,' said Horrin.

'The thimble is for his size, but the materials are important,' said Maesa.

'Thirsty, my prince,' said the creature. It looked up at the aelf with wide eyes. Every part of them was green. The irises were the dark of forest moss, the pupils the near black of water pooled in tree boles, the whites pale and luminous as insect lights. It smelled of leaf mould and the things that hide beneath.

'Go ahead, take your fill,' said the prince. He gestured to the thimble. Shattercap scuttled towards it, making Ninian take a step back. Horrin leaned in nearer again, fascinated, so his face was only a few inches from the creature. He peered at it while it sucked at the thimble's edge.

'What is it?' asked Horrin.

'I'll tell you what it is.' Stonbrak thumped across the room. His stumpy frame rolled around an uneven gait, sending his brawny arms swinging out to knock furniture aside. He halted at the table where the aelf sat. 'This is an aelven princeling, a Wanderer of the least trustworthy and most fickle sort of all his treacherous race, and that' – he jabbed the stem of his pipe at Shattercap accusingly – 'is a malevolent spirit of the forest. It has no place in the realms of civilised folk.'

The prince gave the duardin a mild look. 'I have done you no wrong. Nor has my companion.'

'You deny he is dangerous?' asked Stonbrak.

'Is he?' said Ninian.

'A sword is dangerous, but it is safe, so long as it remains in the sheath,' said the prince.

'Pah!' said Stonbrak. 'Most swords have no mind of their own. This blade here can prick you at will.'

'I beg you, Master Stonbrak, please do not insult our guest, this is not the night for disagreements,' said Horrin, though he glanced dubiously at Shattercap.

'I should insult him,' said Stonbrak. 'I should insult him for bringing that in here.'

'He will do you no harm, I swear,' said Maesa.

'These aelves cannot be trusted, Master Horrin, cannot be trusted!' Stonbrak said. His beard bristled.

'Be calm, dear folk, this is my inn, and I see no danger in him, if the prince says he's safe?' said Horrin. Maesa nodded. 'Very well then. Ninian, get our guests a drink, on the house. For everyone!' He gave each of his guests an encouraging smile. Quasque stared back blankly.

'Please, we have a long night ahead,' said Horrin.

Quasque nodded hesitantly. 'More wine,' he said.

Stonbrak jerked out a chair from under the table and sat. Shattercap flinched from the duardin, cradling the thimble protectively. Stonbrak curled his lip.

The atmosphere thickened with more than the duardin's pipe smoke.

'I tell you what,' said Horrin, clapping his hands. 'We're all strangers here. The storm outside is blowing hard. We can do nothing but wait. Why don't we pass the time by telling each other a tale or two?'

Stonbrak would not take his gimlet eyes from the prince, but gave a shrug that might have been agreement. Horrin stepped back to include all his patrons in a loose circle, arms held wide. Quasque blinked uncertainly.

'I'll start, shall I?' Horrin was an old hand at this game, having used it many a time to calm nerves at the inn on stormy nights. It was a fine way of getting his customers to drink more, too, and he enjoyed the entertainment for its own sake.

'I'll tell you the story of how I came to make this place. That's right,' he said, waving his hand around the room. 'I built the Inn of the Brazen Claw!' He held up his finger dramatically. 'But it wasn't so simple as dragging all this timber up to the top of this eyrie, and even that wasn't simple at all...'

CHAPTER SIX

THE INNKEEPER'S TALE

When I was a young man, I decided to run away from home. My father was a tomb warden from Pandanjan, and he wished for me to follow him into the world of ancient ledgers and their endless columns of numbers enumerating the dead. But though I'm Shyish born and bred, and my father's roots go back to the Time of Myth, my mother was a landsteer from Ghur. Her people trekked the lands of that realm in giant wagons pulled by beasts we know here only from their bones. I've no idea how she came to dwell and die in Pandanjan, nor why she committed herself in marriage to so dry and dusty a man as my father, yet they knew happiness in their own fashion. She lightened his life with her joy, and passed a little of her wildness into me on the way.

Alas, every life must run its course, and every love must perish, as we say. My mother died when I was but a boy, and my father, always cold, became colder, and he decided he could not live without her. My mother's afterlife was far away from the lands where we dwelled, and difficult for one not of her people to enter.

He resolved to go there anyway. He dictated that I was to remain behind to learn his trade. I disagreed. The day he left was the day I was to be apprenticed to the tomb wardens. Instead, I took my leave of my father, Pandanjan, and my entire life.

I do not know where I intended to go. I was not my father. I did not wish to count the dead, but to drink deep of the well of life. I thought perhaps to go to my mother's people, and wandered far to find a realmgate that would take me to her part of Ghur. The Argent Gate I heard might do, so I set out to find it.

At length, and after many adventures, I came here to the Claw. No one lived in these parts then. Sigmar's light had yet to drive out the darker things that haunt the grey woods of the hills and plain, and so I was alone, and afraid. I headed for the Claw for no reason other than I could see it over the trees. You can imagine my delight upon glimpsing a small stone hut built at the base. I had witnessed no breathing being for several days, and had begun to fear I had strayed too far into unliving countries.

An old woman dwelt in the hut. She was as pleased to see me as I was to see her, and came out with a great beam of a smile as soon as I was within hailing distance of her home. She had around her hut chickens and a goat, and a patch of scrubby vegetables. I was amazed she scratched out a living in the forest, for it was a dreary place. But she managed, and she had enough to spare to feed me stew, and she appeared kind. I asked her the way to the Argent Gate. Remember that then, the duardin of the sky had yet to come to this land. This is what she told me.

'Young man, young man,' she said. 'The Argent Gate is four days' walk from here, out of the forest and over the Plains of Teeth, where howling, hungering things roam.'

'Is there a safe way?' I asked.

She shrugged, and her ancient bones popped under her black weeds. 'I do not know. I have never ventured far from this place.

There is a well and life here. What little I have are riches in this country. I count my blessings and will not go far.'

She laughed then, as did I.

'Stay the night before you go,' she said. 'You will need your strength to see you through.'

I offered her a few of the drops of Aqua Ghyranis I had, but she would not accept it. 'Hospitality to strangers is its own reward, young man,' she said. A principle I have kept to my whole life since.

Nights here are long and cold. Bruised aurorae writhe over the stars, making the trees dance. I suffered a restless night haunted by dreams of the things that hunt upon the Plains of Teeth. But I did sleep, and was awoken to a breakfast of fresh eggs, which I devoured gratefully.

'Young man,' she said to me as I ate, 'I have a favour to ask. If you would please take this basket of food and these two faggots of wood up to my husband, who works upon the palm of this claw of stone, I would be grateful.'

She pointed upward, to the top of the Claw. I was surprised, because she had made no mention of her husband, and I wondered on the nature of his labours up there.

'I make the journey every day, and I would welcome a rest for one single morning. I am old, and my joints pain me.'

'Of course!' I said, happy to repay the woman's kindness. I took the basket, placed the faggots of wood on my shoulders, and ran up the winding stairs that lead to this place for the first time. Back then the stair was narrow, a spiral ladder really. The wood was grey with age, and many spokes were missing from the sockets carved into the stone of the arm. My eager bounding became slower and slower the higher I went. Exuberance became caution, caution became fear, until I reached the top, and gratefully threw myself into the palm of the Claw.

How do I describe my feelings upon seeing this place? From a distance, the Claw looks like a claw. Up close it does not, but here, in the palm, it feels as if you are cupped in the hand of a god, which may not be too far from the truth.

There was no inn here, of course, only piles of wood like the bundles I carried, and the fireplace you see there. As you see, it is very old, carved with strange symbols. All of it, lintel, grate and chimney, is hewn into the rock itself. Everything about that fireplace is out of true, as if the maker had heard what a fireplace was, but had never seen one.

The old woman's husband was as ancient and poverty-stricken as his wife. He was crouched at the hearth, working a poker of plain iron in the fire, sending out showers of orange sparks from the chimney slot some hundred feet over our heads. He was astounded by my arrival, but his wide-eyed surprise turned to a grin of delight as I approached. He was so pleased to see me I could not help but feel a touch uneasy.

'My, my!' he said. 'A visitor, a boy!' A man, thought I, for although young I no longer reckoned myself a boy.

'I have for you this basket of food, and these bundles of sticks,' I said. I dropped the faggots and held out the basket. He took it from me, peered inside, then set it down. 'What do you do here?' I asked him.

'Ah, a strange story,' he said. 'I tend this fire, for I must. It cannot go out. It is an eternal flame! It warms the hand of this giant. The rest of him is safe down below, under the earth, but his upthrust claw here is exposed, and chill. If it gets cold, he will wake.' He winked at me. 'And we wouldn't want that, would we?'

I looked at the vastness of the claw. How could such a small fire warm so much rock? I thought, but did not say. Instead I said, 'I suppose not,' and shivered. It was an eerie place then.

'Tell me, boy,' he said. 'You have done my wife a great service. Do you suppose you could do one for me also?'

'Name it, sir,' I said. 'Your wife has been very kind.'

'The fire cannot be left untended,' he said to me. 'But I have not been down to my hut for three long years. I have hunched over this fire for so long I forget what it is to stand tall. I desire to stretch my legs and maybe...' He laughed and nodded at an alcove in the finger not far from the fire, where a dirty blanket languished. 'Sleep an hour or so in my bed, maybe in the embraces of my good wife?' He winked again, in a most repulsive and lascivious manner.

By then my sense of unease had grown, yet I felt I owed a debt to these strange people, and what harm could it do, to tend his fire for a few hours? I felt sorry for him. That was my mistake.

'By all means!' I said. His eyes lit up. He proffered me his poker.

'Then take this fire iron. Make sure the flames die no further than this point here.' He indicated a mark on the rock. 'I shall return soon.'

Naturally, he did not return. Ever. I sat all night and then all day tending the fire, hoping that he would come back, but knowing that he would not. In the morning I went down the stairs, racing to outpace the fire's consumption of its fuel. The hut was empty, the couple and their possessions gone, and the animals abandoned. In disbelieving terror I ran back up. The fire was burning low. I paid it no heed. I had decided to run. I took my few things, and made to leave. Down the stairs I went, the crack of the dying fire loud in my ears.

Upon the third turn of the stair, the earth began to shake. A terrible, low moan issued from the ground. I threw myself to the side, slipped, gripping the stairs to prevent my fall. The animals at the hut were driven wild – such a cacophony they made for so few! A great crack raced across the plain, then a second, deep and black. I looked to the forest, yearning for its freedom, then above. The arm is huge, I thought. What monster must it belong to?

I realised then what I must do. I would like to say that heroism motivated me, but it was fear: fear that the monster would slay me should it emerge from under the earth. I crawled up the stairs. The arm began to sway. Another moan came from the ground. I reached the palm. The fire was smoking out.

An awful cry issued from beneath. This was my only chance. I took up a fistful of dried moss, and cast it on the fire, piling kindling upon it. In my panic, I nearly extinguished the last ember, so thrust my hands into the hot ash to shift the fuel, hoping it would catch.

Stone rumbled. I looked up. The fingers were closing! They were once straighter than they are now. Perhaps it was too soon, or perhaps the titan had been asleep too long, but as they began to close, the little finger broke, and fell away. Blind now with terror, I blew through my snot and my blubbering onto the fire. The shaking grew and grew, the fingers ground and popped. I thought I would fall or be crushed by the demigod's clenched fist.

The fire burst into life anew. The shaking stopped.

For a year I was alone, building up the fire, then racing to the ground to collect what wood I could and what food I could find. The first wanderer came, and I had it in mind to do to him what the old man had done to me. But then I thought on my misery, and realised it was only my own foolishness that had condemned me, and that I had no right to make another suffer in my stead. I shared the food I had and explained my situation. The traveller tarried a few days, bringing me food, and wood, while I steadfastly refused his offer to tend the fire. 'Hospitality to strangers is its own reward, young man,' the old lady had said. I think she meant it. The old man and his wife were not bad people, only trapped by cruel fate.

The first traveller left. When the second wanderer passed by, I gained a jewel from him out of his pity and his kindness. The third was a carpenter, and he stayed a month to help me build a warm house, which is now a store on the far side of the yard. So with the third, fourth and fifth; as each stranger was treated with kindness, I was shown kindness, until one day the duardin of the sky came with an offer. They had designs to build a platform for their packet ships here, and to use this place as a way station. I agreed, and the inn was my reward; they provided the lumber and aided me in its building. Now people come here every day. I am good to them, so fate is good to me. I am a rich man, with a fine wife, a good home, and servants in the summer months to help me tend the fire, although I can never leave, and the fire must never, ever go out.

A log popped in the grate. A tumble of cinders spilled onto the hearth.

'You could leave,' said Quasque. He blinked. He had very large eyes, somewhat yellow-looking in the whites. 'Someone else could take on your curse.'

'I could,' said Horrin. 'They could.'

'Then why are you here?' asked Quasque.

'Because I am always here!' he said with great cheer. Ninian brought him a wooden pint pot and kissed him fondly. Horrin raised his beer in salute. 'Brewer, carpenter, farrier, I have learned to be them all. Hundreds of people come here. Tales from every land I hear. Burning a few logs is no great price to pay. I am glad for my fate.'

'Kindness is its own reward,' said the duardin sarcastically. 'What a fine moral.'

'You do not believe so, master duardin?'

Stonbrak snorted by way of reply. 'I've got a story for you,' he said. 'I'll tell it now.'

He tapped out his pipe on the sole of his massive boot, and

scratched a horny fingernail around the bowl, sending flakes of char showering onto the table. Shattercap sneezed and retreated to his master's side. The prince petted him absent-mindedly, his calm violet eyes fixed on the duardin's glowering face.

'It is a tale of vile aelven treachery in return for such kindness as you describe.' The duardin pulled out a stained pouch of tobacco from his tunic and refilled his pipe. 'You are wrong, innkeeper, and you will soon hear why.'

CHAPTER SEVEN

THE MERCHANT'S TALE

The wind was full of mischief. It ran about the inn, banging shutters and shouting down chimneys. Draughts batted at the inn's fire. Cold gusts puffed under doors and raced away, hooting at the fun. The rain was less showy, but as determined to get in. Following shyly, it pattered then drummed, then thought better of its racket and went back to pattering. Through gaps in the flashing on the inn's conical roof, it insinuated itself into the fabric of the building, dripping in fat drops to a spot on the floor, and darkening the giant digit the inn was built around. Once within, the water stayed. It was persistent when the wind was flighty.

Idenkor Stonbrak ignored the trembling of the building. The unpredictable forays of cold that snuck up under his collar could not discomfit him. He was duardin, enduring as rock. It would take millennia for any storm to wear away one so solid.

He lit his pipe with a sulphurous match, pulled deeply upon the ivory mouthpiece, and appraised the group around the table with a merchant's eye. Horrin, Ninian and Barnabus he judged worthy, and did not linger on them long. When he looked to Quasque his eyes narrowed until they glinted like coal seams at the back of a mine gallery. Stonbrak took in Quasque's spoiled finery and hunted face, and saw a disquieting story behind them. But his gaze remained the longest on Maesa and Shattercap, who had crept back onto the table boards before the prince. On the verge of saying something he might regret, Stonbrak clamped his lips shut, puffed smoke like an engine and shook his head.

'My turn then,' he said eventually. 'This is my story. A sad tale of broken contracts.' He cleared his throat, and took on a storyteller's airs.

You might guess I am not of this realm, and you would be correct. I hail from Barak Gorn, a mighty port upon the shores of the Whispering Sea, in Ulgu near Melket, if you've ever heard of that. Now, Barak Gorn was built in ages past by the ancestors of my ancestors, and though once it was a fine and marvellous place, when Chaos came it lay in ruin until the Age of Sigmar began, and drove back a little of the darkness.

When the time came to return, my people were among the first to leave Azyr and reclaim Barak Gorn from obscurity. I was a beardling. It was a long time ago now, but I remember well the sorrows of what we found, and the joys of restoring former glories to the halls and the quays.

Stonbrak's eyes lost their focus behind the smoke wreathing his face. He was quiet for so long, Shattercap spoke up.

'Is that all?' the spite asked Prince Maesa in confusion. 'So short a tale. Not worth the listening.' He folded his spindly limbs about himself in such an awkward way he resembled a dead spider, until he shrugged and twitched, so that he was suddenly sitting cross-legged, sharp elbows out, hands clasped around his thimbleful of wine.

Stonbrak snorted. 'All? All! I'm only getting started, you impertinent imp!' He took his pipe from his mouth and jabbed the stem at the spite. The fine leaves on Shattercap's shoulders quivered. 'A pause for thought was all that was. Now, where was I?'

'Forgive Shattercap,' said the prince. 'He has no manners. You were speaking of your home, worthy friend.'

Stonbrak nodded gratefully. 'I was.'

'I have heard stories of Ulgu!' said Horrin. He lifted his drink. It was his third of the evening, and his cheeks were flushed. He enjoyed his ale as much as his stories. 'Though of course I cannot go there.' He waved a hand at the fire by way of explanation. 'It is a realm of mists, where nothing is as it seems.'

'That it is, master innkeeper,' said Stonbrak. 'All thirteen lands of it, a confounding place of intrigue and shadows, where it is never either truly dark or truly light.' He moved his pipe around his mouth. 'A strange place to find the likes of we duardin, you might say, but duardin are not so affected by Ulgu's inconstancy, for we are as steadfast as stone. Mist does not bother rock. Rock is impervious to illusion. Even so, my sort are considered secretive among our race, and our numbers in the Realm of Shadows are small.' He sucked his pipe. The bowl grew bright, glinting from his eyes in such a way it was easy to imagine tiny foundries hidden in his skull. 'However, there are many aelves in Ulgu, of strange kindreds. The princeling's kind are prone to plays of light and shadow, and not always for the best, as you shall see.'

He took a drink from his beer mug, wiped the suds from his beard, and recommenced both his smoking and his tale.

Barak Gorn has neighbours. A race of aelves whose halls also overlook the misty sea. These aelves dwell in the mountain, in a manner similar to some of my kind. Once the two cities were one, but when we were forced from our port, they hid themselves away in their deepest halls and remained there throughout the Age of Chaos, an act some of my people saw as a betrayal, but the more level-headed of us know to be pragmatic. In the dark years they withdrew into themselves, become stranger still through their isolation. We call them the *skuru elgi*, or the grey aelves, because of the colours they wear to blend into the mists, and the magic they weave about themselves to hide. They are tricky creatures, never get a straight answer out of them! They are apt to disappear in the middle of conversation, and they never smile. They are, not to labour the pick in the stone too much, a miserable bunch.

But business is business. My kind and theirs did much dealing before the dark times, and do so again now, for they marvel at our jewels, and their nobles ever have rare sea-gold to pay for them, though the hurts of the old times are slow to heal. Their gold brings us to the heart of this tale.

In my clan there was a worker of gems so fine his renown spread far and wide. He could capture the very essence of beauty. His works of gold carried the warmth of flesh. With cunning cutting, he trapped light inside gemstones. You can imagine how valued such stones are in shady Ulgu. His skill was unsurpassed...

Let me tell you a little of our city. The cliffs at Barak Gorn lean out to roof over the shore, combining the best of cave and harbour in one. Naturally, so great was the craftsman's wealth that his shop had a fine spot overlooking the sea. On the few days there is no mist, you can see all the way to the horizon from its window, and when the fog draws in and chill water runs down the glass, which is practically every day, there was the comfort of Barak Gorn's lid of stone pressing down above, and reaching its arms around the harbour. It is a tonic to a duardin soul, the permanence of the rock, the indomitability of the earth. Shadows and mist are nothing compared to the solidity of those things.

* * *

Stonbrak tapped out his pipe and refilled it unnecessarily, using the action to keep from looking at his audience. Maesa saw his sorrow clearly enough, caught the reddening of the duardin's eyes, and noted well Stonbrak's reluctance to name the jeweller.

'My cousin Bertgilda worked with the craftsman in his shop,' he said, striking a match upon his boot. He put the flame to the bowl and sucked until its tiny coals glowed. The foundries in his eyes flared. 'It is from her I have the detail of this tale.'

One day, one of the grey aelves came into the shop. The doorbell did not ring, nor did the craftsman hear the door close. My cousin noticed him only by the dampening of the air. Thinking that a heavy fog had come into the harbour, Bertgilda looked up from her work, and found that the mist was thin, and day as bright as it can be in our realm, but that the shop was cold. Grey vapours withdrew under the door, and in front of the counter stood an aelf of high birth, not unlike your guest here, master innkeeper. His grey cloak was beaded with moisture. I tell you, I meet these aelves and wonder, have they never heard of fire? They are perpetually damp.

A sharp elbow from Bertgilda alerted the craftsman to this customer, and he raised his eyes from the jewel he was cutting. He was methodical, not prone to rushing. He pushed back his loupes from his face, folded the paper he worked upon, and from it poured tiny curls of gold into an envelope. Frugal, he was. Very frugal. Only then did he speak with the aelf.

'How may I help you, sir aelf?' the craftsman asked. He was a stout-hearted soul, not given to shock, and had had many dealings with our aelven neighbours. They often did things like appearing out of nowhere. Shifty beggars. The aelf looked upon him with grey eyes as cold and treacherous as the winter sea.

'I am to be married to a princess of a foreign nation,' he said.

His voice was peculiar, Bertgilda told me. Gravel churning in a mountain stream. Musical, as the voices of aelves tend to be, but with a rasping edge they rarely have.

The inhabitants of the inn glanced at Prince Maesa. The prince gave them no comment on the peculiarities of aelven voices, but sipped his wine, his attention given fully to the duardin. Stonbrak continued.

'It is a great union of peoples,' the aelf said, 'bringing together kindreds that will bless all this country and bring new trade and wealth to your city as well as mine.'

'I see,' said the craftsman. He was careful, and waited for the aelf to outline his needs. Some duardin might rush in to negotiation, scenting treasure at the end of a bargain involving princesses, but the duardin of Barak Gorn are of Ulgu, and alive to the dangers of hasty contracts.

'These aelves covet watergems above other jewels,' continued the aelf.

'Do they?' said the craftsman. This did pique his interest. Watergem is a rare diamond. It is named for the movement in its heart. Look into a middling example, and you will see the dance of sunbeams piercing the waves on turquoise seas. They say if you look into a perfect stone, the deeps of faraway oceans might be glimpsed.

'I require a necklace to be made of such diamonds, to these measurements.' The aelf placed a roll of paper on the countertop. He had no interest in the marvels displayed under the glass – understandable, considering what he was carrying, as our craftsman shortly discovered. The aelf pulled a velvet pouch from his side, and upended it, scattering the contents on the countertop. Gems spun across the polished glass, and when they ceased their movement and clinked against the frame, the pounding of waves on distant shores filled the shop.

Upon the counter were eight of the most exquisite watergems the craftsman had ever seen. From each shone the light of Hysh cast upon a different sea, in a different realm. It takes a lot to surprise a longbeard like he, but the craftsman was dumbstruck. This was a king's fortune, his ransom, his estates, fortress, armies and more.

'Where did you get these?' the craftsman asked.

'My beloved gave them to me, and swore she would not be wed until they had a setting fit for their beauty,' said the aelf. 'I wish them placed into a necklace of purest moonsilver. It is my bride price for the match, so I am willing to pay well for your efforts. How much for your best work?'

Ordinarily this question would have offended, for a duardin *always* does his best work, but the craftsman was so shocked that he blurted out a price rather than the threat of grudge-making. He had not taken leave of his wits completely, and the price was high.

'Do this for me within the week, and I shall double it,' said the aelf.

'Half now,' said the craftsman, who was no fool.

'All when complete,' said the aelf.

It goes against every instinct of a duardin to take work without pay, but these gems were of such high quality that surely the aelf had the money. No one less than a king could possess such wonders. Mayhap that should have given the craftsman pause, but greed ever was the curse of our kind. Precious things are our greatest weakness.

'Very well,' he said. 'Double. In a week.'

The aelf nodded.

'Before you leave,' said the craftsman, 'what is your name, for my ledger of works?'

The aelf paused before speaking. 'You do not require my name. My entrusting to you of these gemstones is my bond. I will return, in a week.'

The aelf said no more, and departed. This time, he used the door.

The craftsman laboured long hours over that necklace. Twice he made the mounts for the gems, twice he melted down the moon-silver and began again. The cost of the materials alone was enough to beggar him, and he sought the money from the lenders of the Granite Brotherhood. A foolish move for anyone who is not abso-lutely certain of riches to pay them back, but our craftsman was sure.

Finally, he was done. Weary from days of sleepless toil, the craftsman removed the lenses from his eyes and sighed with sat-isfaction. Truly, this was his greatest work. The necklace was the finest he had ever made. Those few who saw it compared it favour-ably with the greatest works of the Age of Myth, and that was only if they could speak through their tears of joy.

The week passed. Then another. The craftsman's delight turned to fretting. The aelf showed no sign of returning for his goods. He sent messengers up to the skuru elgi mountain, but without a name he was at a loss to find the commissioner of the piece. His descriptions did not help. You aelves look much the same to us. The craftsman was perhaps too coy about what he had made. If he had revealed he had the stones to the aelves, things might very well have turned out differently, but he did not, keeping to his bond of confidentiality instead.

A reckoner of the Granite Brotherhood paid the craftsman a visit, insisting that he repay the money he had borrowed. When he saw the necklace, he softened his tone, and urged the craftsman to sell it, whereupon he would be able to repay the debt and be enriched in the process.

'It is not mine to sell,' the craftsman said.

'The aelf is in breach of contract,' said the reckoner. 'You are free to do with it as you will.' The craftsman said no. The representative insisted, several times, but the craftsman was an honourable sort, and steadfastly refused.

The Granite Brotherhood gave him a week more to find the money. 'After which time has passed,' their reckoner informed him, 'we shall seize your goods, as we are legally entitled to, and you will be ruined.' Such is the price of honour.

The craftsman hid his worries from the reckoner, but they were growing, until, four nights after the Granite Brotherhood came, he received a message, delivered by an unseen hand to the side of his bed, and written upon paper damp with the mist.

My apologies for the delay, it read in flowing Aelfish script. *Owing to unforeseen circumstances I have been unable to collect the item you fashioned for me. However, I need but to see it, and I will be able to pay you the sum in full. I have absolute trust that the piece will be exquisite. I cannot come into the city, and require delivery. Bring the necklace with you to Eskbirgen's Cove at midday, where I shall meet you. Come alone! There you shall receive your reward. Once again, my most heartfelt apologies.*

It was signed with an X. Naturally, our craftsman was outraged. This aelf had broken his bond to him. Being a duardin of the shadow realm, he had expected the course of events to run crooked, but now he was facing betrayal, ambush, or worse! He had no choice but to comply. The sum involved was great.

The cove was a league outside of Barak Gorn and well known to him. It is a beautiful spot, if you like that outdoors kind of thing rather than a good ceiling of bedrock over your head. But it had something of an ill reputation. Before he left for the cove, our craftsman took his pistols from the workshop strongbox. He loaded one for himself and gave the other to Bertgilda, and asked her to follow him, and told her to secrete herself in the cliffs over the cove so she might keep watch.

'In this way,' he said to her, 'we may foil any aelven trickery.'

The craftsman set out first, Bertgilda half an hour behind, in case the shop were being watched. The craftsman took the Long Stair out of the city cave, up through the overhang and onto the clifftops. All trade goes to and from Barak Gorn via the ocean and the realmgate in the deepest hall. There are no roads to the port. The Long Stair's exit is carefully hidden. Were you to pass it by, you would not see it – not even you, Wayfarer. A thin trail, no wider than that made by goats, winds across the cliffs. If you look down from the top, there is no sign the city is there. Well it is so, for Ulgu is a tormented realm even now.

To the north of Barak Gorn, the bulk of the aelves' mountain is grey in the mist. In the late morning, the time our craftsman departed, Hysh spreads itself through the vapours, giving indistinct light. It never gets lighter in Ulgu. Under those conditions the mountain appears like a steel cut-out laid upon brass. That the aelf had not asked for the item to be delivered to the aelven kingdom gave him no end of concern, but if he wished to be paid, he had no choice but to follow the aelf's wishes. More or less. He was carrying his gun, you will remember.

Bertgilda followed him later. The fogs thickened, and though the cliffs are free of trees or other such vegetation, and the close turf smooth and without rocky eminence, she only caught sight of her master once or twice ahead, and then only by the bobbing of his lantern, for even at noon it is wise to light your way in our realm. The fog was full of the whisperings of misbegotten things, but a duardin maid is as a brave as any male, and she made her way to the cove without mishap. Through drifts of mist she saw the craftsman was already waiting upon the beach. The sea heaved with slow waves, not one cresting, the water dull as unpolished pewter, and thick as oil. It slopped upon the shingle, but in the misty noon light the waves raised not so much as a clack of stone on stone, or the faintest hint of the rushing hiss one should expect of sea on shore. It was silent, almost deader than Shyish.

'No offence,' said Stonbrak.

'None taken, I assure you,' said Horrin, though Ninian scowled.

Stonbrak leaned forward, his massive head shadowed by candle and firelight, making chasms of his wrinkles and caves of his eyes and mouth. His voice lowered, evoking the watchful quiet of the Realm of Mist. The storm, too, lessened in ferocity, rapt as the listeners.

No one else was about. Bertgilda found a spot where she could observe, primed the pistol loaned to her by the craftsman, and hid herself. She did it well. She had a little runecraft to her, did Bertgilda. A scratch here and there, and the application of certain metallic salts, and she was hidden as well as could be. When the aelf came down to the shore from the clifftop path, he passed her right by without so much as a glance in her direction. His boots scuffed the stone not four handspans from her nose, and she was not seen. She pressed herself against the rock and soil and held her breath until the aelf was past. Only when she heard the aelf hail the craftsman – 'Master jewelsmith!' he said – did she poke up her head to watch.

The pair met upon the shore. He was arrogant, like most aelves. But this one, he had an air of desperation, and though he tried his best to stand tall and haughty over our craftsman, his gaze kept drifting sideways, as if he expected his worst fears to emerge from the sea, and pull him under. The craftsman stood with legs apart, his fingers hooked into his belt. He was the very picture of indomitability. He looked confident, Bertgilda said, he looked stubborn.

'Do you have the necklace?' said the aelf.

'Do you have my payment?' the craftsman said. He patted the butt of his gun.

'You shall have it, I promise,' said the aelf, and he appeared sufficiently apologetic that our craftsman lost a little of his anger. 'Please,' the aelf pleaded. 'Let me see the necklace.' He looked nervously over the water again. 'She will be here soon. She is my love, but we must not anger her.'

The craftsman thought nothing of this. Duardin women are notoriously fiery of temper too, and with a people as mercurial as the aelves, well… Let's just say I am glad my wife is no aelven female.

'His isn't either!' hissed Shattercap, jerking his thumb over his shoulder. 'You be nice, beard-bearer. Make bad thoughts about the poor prince. His wife is–'

'Silence, Shattercap,' said Prince Maesa, so firmly the spite cringed. 'Pray continue,' he said to Stonbrak's questioning expression. Maesa left no doubt that he would not speak further on the matter.

The necklace was presented. The light of eight seas shone into the grey aelf's face. His unfriendly demeanour was banished as he wondered at the work.

'Truly you are a master of your craft!' the aelf said. The craftsman bowed.

'I am,' said our craftsman, and he took the necklace back. The aelf's yearning gaze followed it all the way into the pouch. 'Now. My payment,' said the duardin.

The aelf shrank in on himself, for he was rightfully ashamed, and gave the craftsman a desperate look. 'You must give me the necklace and go.'

'Are you mad?' said the craftsman. 'You will pay me!'

'I will, I will,' said the aelf. 'Payment will be left here. You must leave the beach, turn your back on the sea. Do not look to the water, or it will go badly for you. My lover has the gold, and I swear by Mathlann, who she worships, I shall leave it here for you.'

'Lies!' boomed our craftsman. His voice rolled out over the lazy slap of the water. His talented hands drew his pistol and pointed it at the aelf's head.

'I am sorry!' wailed the aelf. He clasped his hands together. 'I did not wish to trick you, but this is the only way.' He blinked. 'I told you a little mistruth. I have no way to pay you myself.'

'Then I shall blow your lying aelven head off!' roared the craftsman, who by then had had more than his fill of aelven nonsense.

'Wait, wait! I mean for you to be paid! She has riches beyond compare. She is beauty incarnate. She will give you what you seek, I swear, but please, you must leave. Get away from the water, for your own sake!'

'I,' said the craftsman through lips flecked with rage's spittle, 'am an honourable being. I have endured questioning, and innuendo, and threats because of the funds I borrowed to make your necklace. I refused to listen. Our contract is binding, but you have invalidated it. I am going, and I will sell this necklace of the eight seas to recoup my loss.'

'You mustn't!' said the aelf. Ignoring the gun held at his head, he ran to the shoreline and back again. His feet whispered over the stones. The click of the hammer drawn back halted him, loud and clear in that listless, leaden bay.

'Goodbye, master aelf,' said the craftsman. He began to back away.

The aelf remained staring out to sea. 'Oh no, I have erred. I have erred most gravely!' A haunting horn note echoed from the cliffs, penetrating the mists, and travelled far out to sea. 'Too late!' the aelf said in anguish. 'She comes!'

The craftsman paused. 'Then she can pay me herself,' he said, his pistol not wavering one hair's breadth from the aelf's head.

Bertgilda watched with mounting horror. She wished to shout that the craftsman should flee, but he was her elder, and she had no right to tell him what to do. The scene took on the feeling of a dream. The sea boiled not far from the shore, and from the waves a pale-skinned aelf maid rose. Although she left the water, it did not appear to leave her. Her hair and clothes moved with the slow dances of the drowned. Fish darted through the air beside her. If she swam herself or flew towards the shore, Bertgilda could not be sure, for she seemed to do both. Her account was confused. Her recollection of events was slipping from her when I heard the tale, and the second time I spoke with her about this matter, she had forgotten most of it, all in the space of a day! Aelven witchcraft.

The aelf maid floated to the beach, her feet not once touching the floor.

'You have the necklace?' she said.

'Give it to her!' the aelf hissed. 'If you value your life, please! If she is satisfied you may depart with your soul and your sea-gold. Ah,' he said, as he saw the expression on the maiden's face. 'At least your soul.'

Still holding up the gun, the craftsman pulled out the necklace and raised it for the aelf maid to see.

She gasped with pleasure and drifted nearer, not once touching the jewellery, but caressing it with her gaze. As she peered into each watergem and saw the worlds entrapped therein, she laughed, and said in delight, 'A fine gift you have brought me, my dryshod love. A worthy price for my affection.'

A look of pure avarice gripped her. The look she gave my kinsman was far, far worse.

'You have another item for me, I see.'

The aelf looked at the craftsman. 'Please!' he said 'Run!'

Too late did our honest jeweller see the peril he was in, and even when he did, a duardin does not run. Never! He fired his gun. The report of the shot banged off every stone and out into the mist. But the violence of the noise was all the shot availed him. The bullet slowed, as if caught by water, and drifted down, scaring apart a shoal of fish swimming in that uncanny ocean surrounding the foreign princess. The maid descended upon him, hands outstretched. His gun fell to the shingle.

What act of sorcery the aelf performed, I cannot say. Bertgilda was gripped by an awful, unnatural terror, and could not watch. The last she heard was the craftsman's strangled groan, the awful scream of the male aelf, and a mighty splash. She lost her senses for a while. When she regained them the aelves were gone. The craftsman, by a miracle of the ancestors, lay upon the shingle, eyes wide, still breathing. At first she laughed through her tears, until she found her attempts to rouse him failed, and she realised his body lived utterly devoid of mind.

Upon his chest was a weed-wrapped net full of treasure dragged from cursed wrecks. The promised payment for his work.

Stonbrak pulled hard on his pipe, his exhalations filling the space around the table with a cloud of smoke. The fire was burning low, lighting the room through the pipe's exhaust much as Stonbrak had described Ulgu, a glowing mist, never bright, never truly dark.

'Bertgilda returned to the city half out of her wits,' he said. 'Days later, our clan heard a rumour. An aelf of low birth had taken the most precious treasure owned by the mountain king and used it to buy the hand of the daughter of a foreign lord. That treasure was eight watergems.

'For some time, the grey aelves argued with us about the fate of the craftsman. Eventually, the Alder Council declared the craftsman at fault on account of reckless brokering; the aelves admitted their share of the blame. His creditors called in their loan. The sea-gold covered the debt, and his family were lucky to avoid penury.

'I learned all this when I returned home. The craftsman's deathless state persisted for some days before he expired, but he never once spoke again. By the time I saw Bertgilda, she was ill of mind, though I managed to piece together the events from what she said before she forgot them all. She lived, thank Grungni, but it took her a long time to recover.

'Every day for ten years I walked from the city to hammer on the mountain gates of the grey aelves. Their guards and their functionaries spoke with me, but their high lords would not see me, until, annoyed by my persistence, they paid blood money for the craftsman's death and told me that was to be the end of it. Unwilling to risk relations with our neighbours, the Alder Council ordered that I drop the matter. I did, and though they assured me I did so honourably, it stung me.'

Stonbrak grumbled into his pint pot. 'From this tale I learned three things. Generosity is a weakness. Always take payment up front.' He jabbed his pipestem at the prince. 'And never trust an aelf!'

Maesa sipped the last of his wine and gestured for more. Horrin hurried off to oblige. 'Surely the message of your tale is that greed is a weakness?' said Maesa. 'Pride, a desire to maintain his honour and goldlust were his downfall. Can you not see?'

'And you imply these are flaws?' Stonbrak slammed his pot down. 'Not at all. Pride drives a being to do his best. Honour, to maintain it. Greed is good, so long as it does not overrule sense,' said the duardin. He clamped his pipe in his teeth with an audible click.

'Yet all three led to his demise.'

'Life,' said Stonbrak coolly, 'can be cruel.'

'Who was this craftsman to you?' said Maesa. 'I guess he was close, from your sorrow.'

'What of it?' snapped Stonbrak. 'He was my clansman, his dishonour tarnishes the reputation of all his kin. Enough to shame me twice over.'

'He was more than a cousin or an uncle, I think,' said Maesa.

Horrin returned with a jug of wine. 'I'm sure his highness here meant no offence,' he said cheerily, keen to head off disagreement between his guests. Before either could reply, a strong gust buffeted the inn, and a rattle of hail. He looked up momentarily as the structure shifted. Dust sifted down from the rafters. The building settled.

'I seek merely to understand,' said Maesa.

'Not much to understand,' grumbled Stonbrak. Horrin poured.

'Then tell us,' said Maesa. 'Who was he?'

Stonbrak removed his pipe, grasped it hard in both hands, and stared at it.

'His name was Jurven. He was my brother. I loved him dearly,' Stonbrak said shortly, embarrassment clamping his jaw so he bit off the words. Then he softened with the sentimentality his kind hide so well. 'When we were young, people assumed I would be envious of him, but it was not so,' he said. 'His works were a marvel. I lacked his perfect skill, but I never had any feeling for him other than pride in his ability. As I could not compete, I became a merchant, travelling the realms beyond Ulgu to sell his crafts, and many a pretty profit I turned. It was while I was gone that tragedy befell him.'

Shattercap reached up his cup to the innkeeper. 'More, more!' he said.

Horrin looked to Maesa. The aelf nodded.

'Just a little more,' he said.

Horrin obliged, tipping a few drops into Shattercap's thimble.

'I tell you what else I learned,' said Stonbrak. He patted his axe. 'I don't use firearms after what I heard. I trust my life to my axe.'

Runes glimmered on the shaft and head, fading only reluctantly when his hand left the metal. Barnabus crept up to Ninian, and snuggled into her. Warmth enveloped the company.

'Now,' Stonbrak barked. 'You have had your story from me. I nominate this aelven princeling next.' The wind was dropping, but the rain picked up, its nervous fingers rattling on the shutters. Thunder cracked.

'The weather is improving, perhaps,' murmured Quasque. 'The storm breaks. Perhaps the ship will come sooner?'

'I am afraid not,' said Horrin. 'The eye of the storm is closing in on us. There will be a drumbeat of thunder, a dazzlement of lightning!' He had consumed all his fourth drink and much of his fifth while listening to Stonbrak, and was thoroughly set in the storytelling mood. He was eager for more. 'The eye will drift over, and linger awhile. When it goes on its way, we'll have more wind, more rain. There is plenty of time for more tales,' he said. 'Will you, could you, tell us a story, Prince Maesa?'

'I could.'

'I would like to choose!' said Stonbrak. 'An aelf like him will have lifetimes of tales, but there is one in particular I would like to hear.'

'Is there?' said Maesa. 'And which is that?'

'I want to know about him,' said Stonbrak, pointing at Shattercap. 'Tell me how you came into the company of this little monster here.'

Shattercap hissed.

Maesa set his glass down. 'Very well,' he said. 'I shall.'

CHAPTER EIGHT

A SHORT BREAK

Shattercap grinned slyly. 'This is the best story!'

'That may be,' said Pludu Quasque. He was the quietest in the company, the storm frightened him, but the promise of Prince Maesa's tale woke a little of his curiosity and he peered at the spite. 'I have some experience with arcane creatures.'

'My name is Shattercap!' said Shattercap indignantly. 'Not creature!'

'It is a forest daemon,' said Stonbrak dismissively. 'No good can come of having it around.'

'Then why do you wish to know where he comes from?' asked Horrin.

'For protection's sake,' said the duardin sternly. 'Stories have a power of their own. Useful magic, when dealing with things like that.'

'He is not a daemon,' said Quasque. 'Is he?'

'He is not,' agreed Maesa.

'He is a spite,' said Quasque.

'He is,' said Maesa.

'I have read of spites, but never seen one, until now,' said Quasque.

'You are familiar with the breed?' said Maesa.

'Book learning only,' said Quasque bashfully.

The wind was dropping as the eye of the storm circled around the Brazen Claw. Each dying roar drew out a shudder from Quasque, but his fear was lessening as the wind dropped, and his spine uncurled slightly so that he looked a little less hunted.

'I would be...' Quasque said. Thunder clashed. He cringed. His voice rose, as if he were stifling a shriek. He swallowed, and composed himself. 'I would be grateful for any information you could provide. I am, ah...' He licked his lips. His eyes darted at his fellow travellers. 'A student of the esoteric arts.'

More thunder, then... quiet. The wind had dropped to a sigh.

Maesa drained his second drink and motioned for his glass to be refilled again. Horrin leaned over to pour from the bottle.

'While you're at it,' said Stonbrak loudly, 'you can get me another.'

'Of course, Master Stonbrak,' said Horrin, and bustled off.

'And bring the whole cask this time!' Stonbrak shouted. He grumbled at his pint pot like its emptiness was responsible for the world's ills. 'Manling measures,' he complained.

'The spites are creatures of magic and spirit,' Maesa said.

'So, a daemon,' said Stonbrak. He peered into his pot in case any beer had escaped his attention.

'Not a daemon,' said Maesa, refusing the duardin's attempts to irritate him. 'Though inclined to mischief they are not things of Chaos. They are aelemental beings. They have free will, or else how would I be able to teach Shattercap here how to be good?'

Shattercap burped and grinned from ear to ear.

Maesa stroked the tiny spite's back, rustling the leaves there. 'To change, one must have the power of self-determination. A daemon is a product of its monstrous patron, and can make no choice that would lead it away from its master's essential character. Spites are born of the woods and trees. They are the will of moss manifest. They are the dreams of branches. They are the thoughts of ferns, and the musings of grass.'

'A plant daemon then,' said Stonbrak. He refilled his pipe. Quasque produced a small brass pipe of his own from an inner pocket, held it forth, and gave the duardin a hopeful look. Stonbrak rolled his eyes. 'Very well,' he said, 'but this is duardin smokeweed. I'll warrant it'll choke a strip of crackling like you dead.' He tossed his tobacco pouch over the table. Quasque took it up gratefully, and filled his pipe bowl to the very brim, to Stonbrak's scowling annoyance.

'Like all things of free will,' continued Maesa, 'a spite may make the wrong choice. They can be enslaved, or dominated by those of greater will. They can be evil of their own accord. So although he is most assuredly not a daemon, Idenkor Stonbrak, he is dangerous, as you have asserted.'

Horrin came back with a small keg under one arm and the other hand supporting a tray crammed with drinks balanced in that magical way common to barkeeps everywhere. He set the keg down before the duardin with a thump. Stonbrak licked his lips.

'That is more like it!' Stonbrak said.

Horrin passed out drinks to the others, explaining that he thought it better to make sure everyone was well supplied, then Stonbrak said he was hungry, and Quasque requested the location of the privy. Barnabus was falling asleep in his foster mother's arms, and she nudged him towards his spot by the fire. He awoke and loudly refused to go. Their argument over his bedtime started a flurry of activity. The travellers toileted, Horrin fetched food. Barnabus won a reprieve from his bed. For a brief while the inn was all a-clatter, evoking a sense of busier nights, so that a sense of safe conviviality outdid the storm's menace.

Finally, relieved, refreshed and with plates of bread and cheese in front of them, they were ready to continue. Horrin was the last to sit. Before he did, he ostentatiously noted down the fare consumed upon a slate, peering at each traveller and counting the provisions they had consumed not quite aloud but in such a way they were sure to see, in case any of them assumed greater generosity of Horrin than he actually possessed, and attempted to duck the bill.

Throughout all this, Maesa watched, his violet eyes staring off into far places, his fingers idly massaging Shattercap, who trilled and purred under the attention.

'I think we're all ready,' said Horrin.

'Then I shall begin,' said Prince Maesa.

CHAPTER NINE

THE PRINCE'S TALE

'I am a wanderer among Wanderers,' Maesa began. 'It is many long years since I fell in love with a human woman against the custom of my kind, and so my people and I parted on bitter terms, but the sorrow I felt for the sundering could never compete with the happiness Ellamar brought me, and we lived decades in bliss. They were gone too quickly. I am an aelf – a human life is brief as a spring afternoon to us. A moment's joy, then centuries of sadness.'

Maesa's perfect face transformed into a vision of sorrow so exquisite the others dabbed their eyes. Even Stonbrak tugged his mist-grey beard and coughed uncomfortably. Maesa smiled.

'I would not have had it any other way...'

So it was I found myself alone. I left our home to fall into the embrace of forest thorns, and set out to journey. I knew not where I was going, but following whatever path I found my feet upon, I passed through many realms. Weighed down by grief, I shunned company, that of other aelves especially. I turned aside from the secret ways of my folk, but walked the realms like any mortal man, passing through the throngs of humanity where they still persisted. At other times I traversed the wastes made by the Dark Gods, or wilds protected by profound magics of elder ages. While my body walked, my soul traversed endless cold voids of grief.

After a time, I wandered far from all the throngs of people, good or evil. For years I did not speak a single word from the languages of man, aelf or duardin, immersing myself in the silent speech of far deserts and deep green places. Many times death tried to claim me, from thirst, or exposure, or broken-heartedness. I welcomed it, encouraged it, but every time it came near, something in me awoke, and pushed me towards life, forcing me to drink, or to eat when my pulse faded, or to fight when I was threatened. These years went on for so long I cannot remember them all, nor all the places that I went, nor how many times I called to death then shunned it.

Nothing lasts, not nations or stars, or even grief. Eventually my isolation came to an end, although as the day dawned I had no inkling of its significance.

I had returned to Ghyran, scarcely aware that I was once more in the realm of my birth. I recall the morning. A veil was lifting from my eyes, and I saw more than I had for some time. I walked a road much overgrown by blind oak and goldenbough. Old roots had heaved up the surface in the slow ploughing ways of trees. Once, the road had been a wide thoroughfare, and although there was little of Chaos in the land thereabouts, the populace was long gone. We Wanderers are gifted in the reading of the wilds. Patterns in the trees hinted at lost fields. Undergrowth tangled on levelled settlements, made verdant by the ash of ancient conquest.

Presently I came to a high wall surrounding the ruins of a great city. Breaches from the city's sacking put out mossy ramps of tumbled stone. Trees grew from cracks in the facings, wrecking the stone more thoroughly than any war engine ever could. The marble had greened, and the statues were broken and thrown down from the parapet. Nevertheless, the wall remained impressive, and in its artfulness I saw the works of men, duardin and aelf combined. This was a city of the Age of Myth. Looking upon it I was saddened by the thought of higher eras when peace was the norm. Remarkably, it was the first time I had considered anything other than my own pain since Ellamar died, although the significance of that too was lost on me at the time, so brief the thought was.

The road led through a gateway whose arch had collapsed, mounding the cobbles with ivy-gripped stones. Within the walls it was much as outside, a verdancy grown thick on the wreck of lives, trees' high canopies raised over shattered houses and public buildings. So much of what I saw was covered over by green that it was hard to gain an impression of who had dwelled there, but in open parts I saw fragments of statuary that had escaped the ravages of time, and they suggested a sophisticated people. Perhaps I might have explored under other circumstances, but I had the urge to leave the place. Its desolation sharpened my own sorrow, and I quickened my pace.

The city was vast, mile after mile of broken streets. I became wary. There are many strange places in the realms, and it is easy to become trapped within them. The calls of daytime creatures gave way to the impatient cries of hunters awaiting the dark. I realised I could not cross the city before nightfall and searched for somewhere to sleep. No roofs remained upon the buildings, all were fallen into deep forest soil. There was no sign that people had existed there at all; that is, until I found the track.

A simple road overlaid one of higher artistry, cartwheel ruts carved through centuries of leaf mould down to the stone beneath and, alongside, a footpath compacted to smooth hardness. I was amazed: people lived there yet. I touched the ground, feeling the residual warmth of a passer-by who I judged not ten minutes gone. I could have turned away, ordinarily I would have, but discovering signs of life in the green tomb of the city, and feeling loneliness more keenly than grief for the first time in ages, I found myself following the track.

Shortly after, I saw three people. Humans, of unremarkable appearance, two men with wary eyes and a girl nearing womanhood. I followed them. They were canny in their woodcraft, but they did not see me. They could not. A Wanderer is invisible among the trees if he chooses to be.

Soon I heard noises ahead, and spied a wooden wall. A village was built within an open space in the city. A dozen families, no more, hidden away in the sprawl of ruins, their simple homes of wood and scavenged brick built upon the broken accomplishments of their forebears. In those times before Sigmar came down from High Azyr, it was rare to see people living free, and I marvelled, for I sensed no taint of Chaos in the air. I wished for a closer look, so sprang noiselessly up a tree, running the branches, leaping from one bough to the next, until I was at the edge of the clearing, and close enough to the palisade to see inside.

The fortifications were disguised by carpets of ferns encouraged to grow in the cracks between the timbers. So strong was life's magic there that the planks of wood sprouted, adding further green to the screen of leaves. These efforts were not enough to hide their home from my eyes, but any other would pass it by without notice. The houses within were similarly camouflaged with living plants, but in spots bright yellows and blues flashed boldly, and fine wooden carvings guarded the beam ends. The village bore few signs of war or suffering. The people were well fed, free of disease and other signs of poverty. And yet they were quiet and watchful as they worked.

It was no more than a hamlet, but to me, who had dwelled in wild silences for so long, the scene seemed monstrously loud and crowded. Affected by misgiving, I retreated into the leaves. Watchful people can be unkind to strangers. I decided to sleep where I was, close by their dwellings, and be away early in the morning. I had nothing to fear. I would not be seen if I did not wish to be, so fell into my sleep easily.

I was woken from dreams of Ellamar by weeping coming from the village. The night calls of insects and the screeches of owls could not mask it. The misery of the crying stirred sympathy in me, for the sound was the sound of my own grief, and I yearned to go near it, and see sorrow outside of myself, the better to cope with my own. Foolishly, perhaps, I dropped from the tree, clambered over the wall, and went silently across the village.

Some way inside the walls was a small shrine. A woman knelt there before a pile of children's things: clothes, toys and tools made for immature hands. I could guess the reason for her anguish well enough. Soundlessly I approached. She did not see me. I watched awhile. I could have left without her noticing me at all, but to my own surprise, I spoke.

'You have lost a child,' I said. The words sounded strange. I had not heard my own voice for such a long time.

She was on her feet in an instant. To her credit, she did not scream, but stared at me, the whites of her eyes glinting in the dark.

'Do not be afraid,' I said. 'I am a friend. I mean you no harm.'

'An… An aelf…' she said, in quiet wonder. Quickly she wiped the tears from her face.

'That I am,' I replied. 'Do not cry out. I heard your weeping, and could not keep away. Your sorrow called out to mine.'

'Who are you?' she said.

'I am a traveller who has lost the one he loved,' I replied.

'Are you a warrior?' she asked.

'When the time demands, I am,' I told her. 'In this moment, I am a fellow griever.'

She looked back to the pile of belongings, little more than rags and wooden dross, but each fragment infused with pain.

'Why do you weep?' I asked.

'My sister's child is gone, along with others,' she said.

'Where?' I asked.

'The forest takes them,' she replied.

I expected she meant beastmen, or other fell beings who taint the wilderlands with their presence. It was not so.

'It is the trees,' she ventured. 'The trees take them.' She took a step closer towards me. 'You are a lord of the woods,' she said. 'Perhaps you can help us.' Her eyes sparked with fresh notions, and before I could stop her, she called out to her people.

They were quick and quiet, I freely admit, coming upon me while I was talking. I was surrounded in a moment by a circle of spears. My hand flew to the hilt of my sword. I could have killed every last one of them, but I did not wish to.

'We will take you to Gurd,' she said, 'our leader.' She was calm. The others were suspicious. I could feel their urge to slay me.

'What if it's a trick? What if he's shifted shape?' one of the men asked. 'What if he is an agent of darkness come to worsen our misery?'

'Are you a shapeshifter in the guise of an aelf?' the woman asked me.

'I am a Wanderer, as you see,' I replied. 'Nothing more.'

'If that is so, you will not be harmed,' she said.

'Then I will not harm you either,' I said.

'You could try,' said the man.

'I would succeed,' I said to him.

I allowed them to take me to their chief. The woman was good to her word. The men were nervous. Their spears shook with their fear and the desire to kill, but not one attempted to hurt me.

'An aelf,' said their leader, once he had been roused from his bed. He was aged. I smelled the death waiting for him, a few brief years away. His mouth was caved in with a lack of teeth, his cheeks were crumpled as dropped cloth, yet his eyes were sharp. 'Well,' he said. He sat heavily on a rough stool, and poured out mead from a jug into a horn cup. 'Sit,' he said. 'Will you drink with me?'

'I will,' I said. He poured a second cup for me, and pushed it across the boards. It was sweet-smelling, not refined as aelven wines are, but not without savour. I drank it gladly.

'I am Gurd,' he said.

'This woman told me,' I said. She had come into the chieftain's house with me, a hut no bigger than any of the others. The men waited outside. 'She did not introduce herself.'

The old man snorted with good humour. 'Kelloway,' he said. 'That's her name. She's sly, probably worried for enchantment, giving up her name to you.'

'I am no mage, though I have some magic. I am only a Wanderer.'

'A pity,' he said, and meant it. 'A mage would be useful.' He shrugged. 'I have not seen an aelf for decades. They are long gone from these parts, as are most men. We are the few that remain, untouched by Chaos' evil.'

'I am as surprised to find you as you are me,' I said. I spoke honestly. I sensed no wickedness to this Gurd.

He looked at me with calculation. 'You are of high birth though, I can see that.'

I did not deny it, for I am a prince. Gurd drained his cup.

'For generations this forest has sheltered us from the Dark Gods,' he said. 'We honoured the spirits that linger here. They protected us, we protected them. But of late, they grow greedy, vengeful. They take things they have no right to.'

'Your children,' I said. The old man nodded.

'Seven now, over the course of a year. We keep the windows and doors barred, and the young ones under watch at all times, but somehow they steal within our homes and take them – it's always the youngest, the suckling babes. A birth is a cause for mourning now.' He became grave. 'We cannot leave this city of our ancestors. Beyond the boundaries of the forest, the hordes of Lord Fangmaw hold sway. We do not know what to do. Perhaps if we had a better understanding of why the spirits turned against us, we could placate them, and reforge our alliance.' He looked at me imploringly. 'Your kin has ancient association with the Sylvaneth. Could I convince you to go to them, and speak with them as our ambassador?'

'You have sent an embassy before, I assume?' I asked.

'Of course,' Gurd said. He looked troubled. 'That is how we know who is responsible. We found our wise woman's bones tangled in vines thirty-three days after she departed, along with her guardians, not far from the walls. In the past it was our enemies left out this way for us to see, now we find we are the victims.' He leaned forward, and spoke urgently. 'Kelloway's niece went missing only a day ago. There might still be time for her, if you hurry.'

Kelloway tensed, awaiting my answer.

I sipped at my mead as I sip this wine now. I had no real desire to venture into the deep forest and seek out the children of Alarielle, for they can be vicious, and the ancient compact between my kind and theirs is void, broken by our actions, and they have little love for us any longer. But I thought of the sorrow of the woman Kelloway for her missing niece, and how it had touched my own. Something in me had awoken after a long slumber. A change like that does not occur by chance.

'Where is the child's mother?' I asked.

'Where do you think?' said Gurd. 'Beside herself with grief.'

That made little difference to me, for I had not tasted her pain. It was an abstract, but I realised I wanted to go. I was recovering from my loss.

'Very well,' I said. 'I shall visit the forest-born, and return the child, if I can.'

And so it was agreed. I set out at dawn.

Gurd's people directed me to the glades where, according to their tradition, the creatures of the forest dwelled. They met rarely, and none had seen a dryad for some time. I detected none of their presence, even as the woods got thicker. Giant trees stretched limbs towards the sky, their leaves casting shadows that flooded the forest floor with inky gloom few plants could tolerate. Soon I was in near-total darkness interrupted by scattered jewels of Hyshlight, rare wealth indeed in that gloomy place. The air was stifling.

I have known all manner of forest, yet none daunted me so much as that forsaken wood. A forest guarded by the Sylvaneth is a place of fecundity, but this land was dying, the trees watchful and their hearts black with spite.

Shortly after, I entered a burnt patch of the forest, where blackened earth showed through leaves turned to white ash. The trees were charred some way up their trunks, weeping amber tears of sap from their deepest burns, and their spirits cried out in silent pain. In the middle of the devastation was a tangle of charcoaled branches that could be mistaken for tree limbs, but were, sadly, the fire-slain bodies of dryads.

I skirted the burnt ground, not willing to defile it with my tread. The bodies were much reduced, and so it was hard to see how many lay there. Were all the Sylvaneth of the forest dead, supplanted by wicked powers? Yet I saw no beast-sign, or the works of evil men. Disquieted, I passed further on.

The land rose, gradually at first, then steeply. The trees

thinned, allowing a wind to refresh me. Green showed upon the forest floor again. I smelled the icy breath of a mountain ahead. Broad-leaved giants dwindled, replaced by smaller, hardier breeds with knuckled roots that clutched the rock into splintered submission; then they too failed, and straight-bodied pines who aimed themselves at the sky like arrows took their place. Turning to look back, I could see for league after league across that part of Ghyran. The forest stretched on towards the realm's centre. The way I had come, I saw the ancient kingdom hidden beneath its cloak, as surely as a child's model hidden under a blanket: the lines of roads and the blocks of cities, the stumps of towers and citadels, reservoirs choked with reeds. Away from Hysh was another story. There, the forest abruptly ended in a black plain riven with rivers of molten rock and tortured mounts spewing flame. There were hundreds of thousands of dead trees at the border of the two landscapes, scorched as spent matches. The might of Chaos drew near, and I wondered why this forest had held so long, with its frightened, remnant folk, and why it was only now beginning to succumb.

Ahead, the soaring mountain touched the sky. Great beasts wheeled around its snowy peak, and the light of glorious Hysh burned most brightly over it. Up there, I was sure, I would find my answers.

Sure enough, as the trees dwindled to isolated shrubs, and tussocky meadows took their place, I found tracks in the earth. Small tracks, less than a day old, and less evident than the signs of the burden they dragged up the slope.

'Spites?' asked Barnabus, his eyes wide.

Maesa nodded. 'A dozen of them, or so I judged. With no more trees to scamper through, they had been forced to go over the ground. Now I had their trail, I made swift time. As the meadows gave way to slopes of scree, I found a dell scooped from the mountain's side, and there, set back in permanent shadow, was a castle of living trees and huge boulders bound fast by roots.'

Barnabus' eyes widened. 'Alive?' he said. He became downcast. 'I have never seen anything like that, and I suppose I never will.'

'You are of the Realm of Shyish,' said Maesa. 'What is mundane to you would be wondrous to someone of Ghyran, to whom a living fortress is the most ordinary of castles.' He leaned in a little closer to the boy. 'Look around you with new eyes, young human. You dwell in an inn cupped in the palm of a slumbering demigod. Is that not marvellous enough?'

Ninian ruffled Barnabus' hair. The boy frowned thoughtfully.

I strung my bow; I did not know what welcome I would find in the fort. I scaled the walls and found no one within. The walls were dying, the roots were dry and losing bark, while mountain winds rattled withered leaves put forth from the tower trees. A beast cried in the sky far above, otherwise there was nought but silence. Stealthily, I headed deeper into the castle.

Beyond the walls was a grotto burrowed into the mountainside by roots as thick as a man, and gated with a screen of vines. They were also dead, and falling apart. I wondered if I would find anything alive in there at all, then I heard voices, high, whispery, like restless twigs scratching one another. I nocked an arrow to my string, and stepped through the vines into a cave filled by a lake a thousand strides across.

A giant black tree climbed from an island in the lake. The trunk was immense, its branches braced the cave roof, holding it up. Light fell through holes in the rock and shone upon the tree, and reflected from the water. Like the wall trees, the great cave tree was dying.

I finally spied my quarry. The spites struggled down a path to the lake shore, dragging a bundle behind them that was most burdensome to their feeble strength, though it was but a babe deep in enchanted sleep. For all the effort it took them, the spites moved quickly, rolling the slumbering child into a small boat made of a single curved leaf. Their leader leaned over the side and with huge, webbed hands paddled the leaf, spites, baby and all, across the water to the island. As I followed the boat along the shore, the source of all this misery became apparent to me.

A seat had grown into the wood of the tree, and in it a great Treelord was enthroned. Treelords are mighty creatures, wise, powerful and quick to wrathfulness against the enemies of Order, but this one was injured grievously.

Fire had consumed his left side. His bark skin was peeled back to the fleshy wood, which was pale with illness, and wept a foul, reeking sap. His face was likewise blackened, one eye burned out, his crown of branches and leaves scorched away. He sat crooked, leaning away from his wounds. His mouth worked with pain. The whorls in his skin, which should shine true with the pure light of jade magic, pulsed an angry redness. In desperation, he sought a terrible cure. All around his throne were heaped the remains of hundreds of creatures. I saw the bones of orruks and humans mingled with those of simple beasts of the wood. All of them were deathly white, drained of life completely, awaiting but a single touch to knock them into dust. The Treelord's feet were rooted in the depths of the bone pile. From the dead he drew new life. He wore a necklace of lambent seeds, and by this adornment especially I knew he had lost his senses, and descended into madness. A terrible fate awaited the child.

The leaf-boat reached the far shore. The spites jabbered, singing high-pitched songs as they struggled the sleeping babe from the boat towards the pile of bones. I could have walked away, and left the child of men to its fate. Many aelves would have done so. I could not. I looked at the baby and thought only of the child my darling Ellamar desired, but we could never have. I drew my bow. The creak of it roused the Treelord from his pain. He opened his remaining eye and looked at me.

'An aelf, and a Wanderer at that,' he said. His voice was the grinding of roots breaking bedrock, slow and deep and powerful. At his speaking, the cracks of the great tree's bark around his throne shone with a hundred eyes, and more spites crawled out: the court of this wounded king.

'As life made me so, I am Maesa, exile prince,' I said, using the formal words that were part of our people's common bond long, long ago. They could not be denied, even after our sundering, and the Treelord was forced to respond in kind.

'And as life made me, I am Svarkelbud, called the Black,' he said, naming his own evil. He did not wish to, and he spat the words unwillingly. 'I do not care for aelves. I have not seen your kind since you betrayed Alarielle, and left Ghyran to its fate.'

'That was long ago,' said I. 'Before I was born.'

'You cannot escape the guilt of your people. It is yours as it was your ancestors,' said the Treelord firmly. He clenched his good hand. 'You have no right to be here, nor to call upon our ancient alliance. Begone, you are not welcome.'

'I will gladly go, with the child,' I said.

The Treelord laughed. 'Now we come to it. An aelf at the beck and call of savages. How noble. That is impossible. I must heal. The forest must persist. The child's soul is ripe with life's potential. By consuming it I shall grow strong, and the slaves of the Dark Gods will feel my wrath again!' His cry turned into a pained, splintering cough. He clutched his wounds. Sap ran through his fingers. 'I will not allow you to take it,' he said, his voice hazed with pain. 'I require its essence.'

'Where are your dryads?' I asked. 'I will speak with them.

Perhaps we can come to another arrangement that will bring you back to health. You are dying. I can help.'

Once more he laughed. 'Traitors! The dryads are dead. After I was wounded by the slaves of the Blood God, they entreated me to leave this place and head to the Lifewells, where I could be remade. The journey is too far, the process too long. I would have been rooted there for many years, and my forest left at risk. They did not approve of my alternative.'

He laboured to speak through the pain of his wounds. Time was running short. The spites had the sleeping child upon the shore, and were moving it to the pile of bones at the Treelord's feet.

'By fire I was wounded, by fire they perished. By my hand!' roared the Treelord. 'They opposed me, so they died, and became acquainted with my agony.' His voice lost a little power. He hunched over himself.

'You wear their soulpods,' I said.

'They were unfaithful. They were punished,' he said, as if this justified his atrocity.

'You hunt the people who are your allies.'

'Where were they when Lord Fangmaw burned me with alchemical flames? Hiding in their hovels! For too long they have intruded upon my realm,' insisted Svarkelbud. 'They have earned their fate.'

'Their city is swallowed by your trees, I would say you intrude upon theirs,' I said. 'You go against the teachings of the Goddess of Life. Let me help you. End this madness.'

'Alarielle is gone! Driven away. What loyalty do I owe her? I am king in this domain!'

The spites chittered and screeched at me from the trunk of the underworld tree, more mischief in the gathering than in a troop of apes. Their cohorts raised the child above their heads and bore it to the mound of bones. I had my arrow aimed upon the Treelord through the conversation, but switched it now, sending it at the foremost spite bearing the child, a sinuous thing wearing the form of a glowing, four-armed snake, and struck it dead. Already I was moving forward, my hands pulling a second arrow from my quiver and letting fly. It buried itself, fletch-deep, in the chest of a waddling thing fat as a barrel. I made the shore of the lake, slaying more of the spites before my feet were wetted. Cold, subterranean waters beckoned, who knows how deep, but though I am not a mage, I have my magic. Murmuring certain words, I sprang onto the water's surface, and sprinted across without sinking, loosing arrows all the while.

The spites struggled with their load, half dropping the slumbering infant, jolting it awake, and it began to cry.

'Cease your meddling!' roared Svarkelbud. He heaved himself to his feet, sheets of hardened resin cracking from his wounds and letting flow the sap blood they staunched. Screaming with rage, he thrust his roots deeper into the ground. They burrowed through stone quick as my arrows, and erupted in a spray of water from the lake. Tips of iron-hard wood speared upward, but I was gone. Swift as the wind am I, too fast for the Sylvaneth. Svarkelbud called to his court of mischiefs. Spites crawled head first down the tree, carpeting the shore, brandishing thorns and splinters of bone. The babe was but fifty paces from me. Perchance I was already too late.

Maesa paused and looked at Shattercap. 'A spite of medium size, grey-green of skin with leaves upon his shoulders, stood upon the squalling infant's chest. In his hand he held a dagger of bone raised to puncture the child's throat, and steal its life away.'

'Me!' exclaimed Shattercap. He clapped his hands.

'You,' said Maesa.

In desperation I called out, 'Do not harm the child!' Although he most certainly had harmed others, the spite looked at me, and for the briefest instant, his face lost its ferocity, and he looked upon the child with something approaching tenderness. It was enough for me to spare his life. I drew my sword – a plain steel blade, not the one I bear now, or my task would have been considerably easier. When I reached the child, I struck with the flat, knocking this creature, this Shattercap, unconscious. I severed the life threads of a dozen more spites to clear me a little more space. I nocked my final arrow, whispered fires upon its tip, and sent it winging towards Svarkelbud. The Treelord saw the shot, but could not prevent its striking. It was the last thing he saw in this life.

The arrow plunged into his remaining eye and burst into flames. His roaring was so terrible that his spites scattered, leaving me free to snatch up the crying babe.

On a whim, I took the spite also, stuffing him into one of my pouches. Svarkelbud lashed out in every direction with his arm and roots, forcing me into such a display of acrobatics I amazed myself. His hand swept down, and I leapt upon it, and jumped again, swinging my sword to cut free the necklace of soulpods. I caught the string as it fell, and landed upon the dry, dry bones. Then I was away, down the shore, over the lake, as Svarkelbud's roots and wrath burst stone, water and bone all around us.

Soon enough I was clear. I paused to see. Svarkelbud's head was ablaze. Sylvaneth fear the flames. They fear the smell, and the heat, for in their hearts they remember the screams of trees consumed by forest blazes, and they dread the same fate for themselves. It was worse for Svarkelbud the twice-burned. In his madness and his panic, he forgot the water all around him, but blundered about, beating at his burning head with his hand and wailing treachery. He banged into the underworld tree, and fire leapt from his head into its dry, dying leaves, setting them alight. At that moment I fled.

From a safe distance I watched the castle burn. The reign of

Svarkelbud was done. For a single aelf to slay a Treelord is a deed of legend, yet nevertheless I am ashamed of it.

'The forest?' said Horrin, his drink forgotten and mouth dry.

'I do not know what happened to it,' said Maesa. 'Not long after, Azyr opened, so I hope the people remained until Sigmar's storm swept down, and the trees grow there still. I did my part to ensure it was so, for I found a grove, by a spring, and there I planted the soulpods of the dryads slain by their own king. Given time, they would have sprouted and taken up guardianship. I hope that is what occurred.'

'What happened to the baby?' asked Ninian, who was clutching her foster son tightly.

'Returned to the mother in the dead of night. I did not speak with the villagers again, but left a token so they would know it was I who had brought the child back, and that she was not some changeling. Then I left the woods, and headed into the wastes beyond, my eyes shedding the scales of grief. After so long, I had something of a purpose – the rehabilitation of my new companion.'

'Why did you not kill him?' said Stonbrak in tones of outrage. 'You said yourself these things are dangerous, and witnessed them at their worst.'

Maesa smiled sadly. 'Spites are things of magic. Those in the castle were enthralled to Svarkelbud. But Shattercap hesitated before murder, despite that. There is a seed of good in his heart, and I have been carefully nurturing it.'

Prince Maesa sat back in his chair. Shattercap grinned a horrible smile of teeth pointed and hooked for the catching of frogs, slithering things and children's fingers.

'If I cannot see good in him,' Prince Maesa said, 'what chance is there for myself? I too have done many terrible deeds.'

The company fell silent. Soft rain kissed the roof. Wind caressed the eaves. Thunder rumbled a long way away.

'We are now at the centre of the eye of the storm,' whispered Horrin.

Unexpectedly, Pludu Quasque blundered to his feet, knocking over his goblet. Stonbrak swore and flicked wine from his hand. The rest dripped to the floor, slow and thick as blood.

'I'll speak now!' said Quasque. 'Yes,' he nodded, and glanced nervously at the windows with his wild, jaundiced eyes. 'I'll tell you what happened to me, while I still have the time...'

CHAPTER TEN

THE SORCERER'S TALE

The sound of the storm being now much diminished, many small noises crept out to be heard. Wood crackled in the fire. Beams sighed. The soft drip of Quasque's spilled wine was awfully loud. Every scuff of movement from the travellers seemed amplified, and when Stonbrak scraped back his chair, everyone but Maesa grimaced. Somewhere deeper in the inn, a clock chimed sixteen. The very middle of the night.

Pludu Quasque looked at them dumbly, blinking like a sleep-walker suddenly awoken.

Stonbrak cleared his throat. 'You were going to tell us your story, lad,' he said gently. 'You're last. It's your turn.'

Quasque swallowed: a slow, heavy action that lent him a some-what toadlike aspect. 'I was. My story. Yes,' he said.

'Go on then,' Horrin encouraged.

'Yes,' Quasque said again. He wiped his hands on his stained finery, and sat back down unsurely, whereupon he took a deep breath, and began.

'My name is Pludu Quasque,' he said, though they all knew this already. 'And I am from Hysh, the Realm of Light.'

Horrin raised an eyebrow. The few humans he had met from the Realm of Light seemed to glow with an internal radiance, their eyes especially. Quasque was instead pallid as any native of Shyish, unhealthy looking, and his eyes were dark.

'Though,' Quasque said hurriedly, 'I may not look it to you.' He patted at himself, almost as if he were checking he was still there, and smiled sadly. 'Once upon a time, my clothes shone with Hysh's light. My skin was deep brown, as lustrous as burnished copper, not this chalk you see. I am filthy and poor now, but then I was rich, and from a respected family.' He paused. 'And I was young. Very young.' His gaze remained downcast. 'We make such foolish errors when we are young, as Master Horrin's tale attests, but his youthful mistake gained him all this.' Quasque's frightened eyes swivelled about to take in the room. 'This inn, a foster son, a loving wife. My error has brought me nothing but pain.'

Anger coloured his pasty cheeks. He looked up, shocked, as if he had been rebuked. The company waited for him to continue.

'I was born in Yllur Suvas, one of the Sevenfold Towns upon the edges of the Girdle Sea. Our homes perch perfect and clean upon the slopes of the Eldoir Mountains, so glorious, so pure.' He bowed his head. 'You will have never seen such a place, and probably never will. We of the Sevenfold League have the trust of the Lumineth and of the Tempest Lords. Ours are favoured settlements, granted rights and charters others do not enjoy. Therefore, we are among the most secretive of nations.'

'But why?' asked Barnabus. 'If you enjoy such beauty, why not share?'

Quasque glared at the boy. 'Because we perform magic of such delicacy a stray thought can send all awry! We are the favoured of the aelven realm-lords, taught their secrets, elevated to the heights of their knowledge.'

'I sincerely doubt that,' grunted Stonbrak.

'What would a shadow duardin of Ulgu know of the glories of the Realm of Light?' Quasque pointed a grubby finger upward. 'Nothing!' Again, that anger. 'The streets of Yllur Suvas echo to the chanting of songs that have been sung unbroken since the realms came into being, whose words were taught to my people by aelves of such refinement they are almost gods.'

As Quasque spoke, he calmed. A little regality stiffened his spine.

'I was a noble. Am a noble,' he said, directing a venomous glance at Maesa. 'My lineage is as great as a lesser aelven house, generations of great wizard lords reaching back, back, through light...'

He trailed off. The wind sighed.

'That should have been enough. It never is. The day I left for the Lyceum Radiance in Settler's Gain to learn the higher arts, my father came to speak to me. He and I had argued much as my youth passed and my manhood approached. All youths argue with their fathers. Young Barnabus here will fight with you soon enough,' Quasque said, gesturing at the boy cuddled into his foster mother's side. She kissed his head.

'Not yet,' she said softly.

'It shall come,' Quasque said. 'His last years of childhood shall be a blight on you, a shaking as great as this storm, and when it blows out, he shall be away, off on the path of manhood, leaving the shivered timbers of memory behind. That is childhood's curse.' Quasque took a swift gulp of his wine, and continued.

I and my father argued more than most. In my arrogance I would not listen to him, and he, filled with an elder's superiority, would not hearken to me. So it was we avoided each other until the day I left, and he came down from his tower of mirrors only when I stood in the cab of my chariot, my rods of control grasped tightly. I stared ahead, over the glowing manes of my Xintil stallions. The horses were his gift to me, worth the fortunes of a dozen kingdoms. I never thanked him.

'My son,' he said. 'Remember that the Wind of Hysh is the finest, most delicate of all the eight magics.'

'I know this,' I said to him, curt as only a son can be to his father.

'And that it can only be controlled with great concentration. True mastery takes many years.'

'This I know too.' I wished he would go. Why could he not just glower from his high study as I set out. This is what I had envisaged: the noble son departing his unjust father, the tears of the women shining in the constant light of our realm. I wore my finest make-up, black kohl about my eyes, my beard so beautifully oiled and my hair concealed beneath my conical golden crown. The scene was perfect except for him. He was embarrassing me.

Embarrassment is worse than a sword cut to the young. Father would not relent, bidding me beware the sin of pride. The day was getting on, I was late leaving, being sluggish out of bed. The heat of the Girdle Sea was rising as the lights of its waters came alive. I stood tense, wishing only that he would go.

'Know also that the Wind of Hysh cannot easily be manipulated by a single man alone.' My father put his hand on the rail of my chariot. 'Son, son. Look at me.'

I would rather have not, but I did, and the look of love in my father's face almost broke my youthful arrogance. How I wish it had.

'No man is a fortress,' he said. 'You are young, sure of yourself, but the way of our people is to work together. To sing the songs of dawning and of evening. We are of ancient stock, well blessed, and that comes with certain responsibilities. You must listen to your aelven tutors. Remember, we are not Lumineth. We can never be. But we can learn from them. You do not know everything that you think you know.'

'I will make my own way, my own name,' I said proudly. I was so arrogant!

'You will, but listen to me. You–'

'I have heard enough,' I said. 'Farewell, father.' I set my face forward, and spoke the words to set my stallions in motion.

The animals we have in Hysh are nothing like the beasts of lower realms. They are beautiful, more glorious than the creatures of Azyr, even. In the steady light of the Girdle Sea, my horses shone like suns, with skin of lemon light and manes of lustrous gold. Rados and Solios they were called. They leapt as swift as beams of light, pulling my chariot from its resting block. My car was of Lumineth make, finest magic. The wheels ignited, and I roared from my home, out through the gates, down the hills of shining crystal and then straight out over the waters, whose glorious waves the hoofs of my horses trod as easily as the solid ground.

I did not look back.

Quasque waved to Horrin for a goblet of wine. His manner had become imperious along with his voice. Horrin poured for him.

'The light, is it good, or is it bad for plants?' asked Shattercap. 'Tell me, Master Quasque, does the light burn the trees?'

'In Hysh, the trees shine with light,' said Quasque.

'But what of the moss, does it not dry?'

'The moss? Also suffused greatly with radiance,' said Quasque. 'For Hysh is the Realm of Light.'

Shattercap frowned. 'Does it not blind the birds?'

'No, master spite,' said Quasque. 'For their eyes shine more brightly than Hysh does in the sky here. Everything is light.'

'The ferns, the moths, the katydids, the bats, the owls, the blooming flowers,' chanted Shattercap, creeping forward, 'the soil, the water and the fish, are they not scorched then by such dry brightnesses?'

'All these are blessed with their own lights,' Quasque said tersely. 'It is Hysh!'

Shattercap picked at his teeth with one of his long nails.

'I think I would not like this place. Too much light.'

'It would not like you,' Quasque said. He drank his wine down in a single measure, slammed down the cup and gestured for more.

Horrin poured, but as he did, asked with a small laugh, 'You do have a means of payment, sir?'

Quasque's agitation returned. Maesa spoke quietly.

'I will pay for his refreshment, innkeeper. Pray continue, mage of Hysh.'

'Thank you,' said Quasque. Horrin topped his glass.

I arrived at the Lyceum Radiance, one of the most prestigious academies of magic in Setter's Gain, full of pride, only to discover my father was right. The study of light magic is hard for a mere human, and yet I thought myself the better of any man. It soon appeared that was not so. I regarded myself above the choruses of acolytes, whose songs form the foundation for our magic, focusing Hysh's insubstantial wind so that greater mages might manipulate it. When tested on the lower stages of proficiency, the basic chants were beyond me. During incantations my voice stood out for its roughness. I fumbled my words. I barely had enough control to rise from the ground to the lyceum portal. I was hardly better than earthbound. A humbler man than I would have recognised his shortcomings. He would have worked harder. He would have sought instruction after begging forgiveness. Not I. I was much too arrogant for that. I placed the blame on everything and everyone else but myself. I blamed our servants. I blamed my classmates.

I blamed the hour of the day or the weather. The one person I did not blame, and who was most obviously at fault, was myself.

The master of our college at the Lyceum Radiance was an aelf named Ireath Talvari, a great mage. He took me into his study to speak with me. He offered kindness, but my pride heard only rebukes, and he received the same treatment as my father. I applied myself to the higher incantations, neglecting the lower. I reached too high, too fast, and so I always failed.

Eventually, close to expulsion, I began to understand. I learned a little humility. I abandoned some of my pride. I redoubled my efforts.

'Another short tale?' said Shattercap. 'Like beardy's? Is that it? You were bad, but then good, then all over?' He blew a raspberry. 'Boring!'

'Mine was not short, imp!' grumbled Stonbrak. 'You mistook the beginning for the whole. You heard the matter of my brother's betrayal and death not an hour gone by!' The duardin shook his head, his mist-grey beard rustling over his clothes with loud disapproval.

'You must learn to wait to hear the whole of a tale, Shattercap,' said Maesa.

The spite shrugged. 'Thou art wise, good prince, but I think I learn quicker than quack-quack here. I am small, but if I were to be as tall as he, then he would still be the bigger fool.'

Quasque was ashamed. 'You are right. Pride trips a man. Envy ruins him totally.'

'Envy?' said Ninian.

'Yes,' said Quasque. He looked fiercely at the innkeeper's wife, as if imploring her to understand. 'There was another student at the lyceum. His name was Hamanan Kekwe and he exceeded me in every way. Were this a true parable, he would be my opposite in humility and diligence. But he was not. Kekwe was as arrogant as I, more so. But the sting of it is that he was far more talented. He had an easy way with people. The acolytes liked him. Women liked him. Our Lumineth tutors liked him.' His face hardened. 'But I, I hated him, and I envied him.'

Quasque's sudden timidity was crushed by his hatred, and more of the youth re-emerged from within the frayed man.

'Arrogance, pride, hatred. Three of the twelve forbidden urges, as we enumerate them in the Sevenfold Towns, but I had more than that! I was rash. I was thoughtless.' He shuddered, and hunkered over his goblet.

Hyshians have a reputation as aesthetes. But youth will behave as youth does wherever it blooms. We drank. We students caroused. In the lyceum's collection of magical wonders is the stonewrought form of a great aelementor. Aturathi, the weeping sage: he is the spirit of the bald knoll of Aturath around which the Lyceum Radiance sits. It is a small mound compared to the great peaks of Hysh, but its roots go deep, its stone is threaded with theldrite, and they say Aturathi's wisdom was as profound and as rich as the rock in which he dwelled.

Truth was his domain. In ages past, from his throne in the lyceum, he gave counsel to the worthy. Aturathi would answer truthfully any question put to him in good faith, and would verify oaths, making any promise binding. There was great magic in the marble of his body, but the greater part of Aturathi's essence was invested in the eyes of aetherquartz set into his mask.

Aetherquartz is the very essence of light, the realmstone of Hysh. Our magic is airy, and not given to crystallisation. It must be coaxed into coalescence. Alas, it is coveted. Some centuries ago a sneak-thief of the ratkin dared the halls of the lyceum to steal the gems. He was found out, and slain, but not before he had prised free one of Aturathi's eyes. He perished half in the rathole leading from the realm, struck down by spears of light. But when the paw of his corpse was opened, the gem had gone. They say the soul of the thief took the gem with him when he died, down into whatever afterlife the ratkin call their own.

Aturathi's power was broken by the theft of his eye, and his body of stone reduced to a statue. He remained seated upon his throne, the carving between seat and demigod indivisible, his hammer across his knees, and he spoke no more. It was said that only one oath would he verify. If anyone pledged to retrieve his eye and replace it in the empty socket, only then would he speak again. No one dared say those words near the statue, in case the legend proved true, and the speaker doomed themselves to an impossible quest.

The students' tradition was to drink at Aturathi's feet and pledge promises to one another. The intention to pass our examinations, to be faithful to our friends, to excel, to better the world and bring honour to our school. Foolish things, and I was the biggest fool of all.

I remember it so clearly. Brass lamps shone along the hall in the twilight that passes for night in Hysh. A few of my fellows played harps strung with moonbeams. The deserts of Xintil are rarely cold, and the air was balmy. Hysh is a paradise of logic and serenity, and I yearn for it still.

We took it in turns to make our boasts and promises to the silent aelementor. Kekwe's turn came.

'Oh, great Aturathi!' Kekwe called up to the statue. 'I swear most faithfully to study hard and rise through the hierarchy, to find fame and fortune as one of the most high lords of light, to honour my people, my house, and our kind benefactors, the Lumineth! Hurrah!'

The group responded 'Hurrah!' and drank, sealing the promise.

Kekwe bowed with a flourish, a little unsteadily, and another student got to his feet. We were all drunk, though none as drunk as I. Kekwe was accompanied by a beautiful girl named Messana, of the Lyceum Shining Snake. I lusted for her myself, and hated that Kekwe and she were pair-bonded.

'Only one of the most high? Why not the highest!' I roared, waving my drink like a sword, interrupting the student before he could begin his oath. 'Why not pledge to become the Grand Luminance himself?'

Kekwe's good cheer fled. I had challenged his honour in front of his friends, and insulted the highest human mage in Xintil. Of course, Kekwe could not pledge to become Grand Luminance. That was as near total disrespect as one could get, and would be viewed poorly by man and aelf alike.

'Then what will you pledge, Pludu Quasque, small lord with the mighty opinion of himself? Why do you not pledge to be the Luminance? Surely,' Kekwe said mockingly, 'with all your talent and all your wisdom, you are better equipped for the role than I?'

His barb stung me. I was drunk. I was young, and I hated Hamanan Kekwe with my very soul.

'I will do better than that!' I said. I raised my goblet to the aelementor and my wine slopped in glimmering waves to the floor. I turned my eyes up to Aturathi's stern face, where one yellow eye stared out from the bull-helm, the other an empty socket. 'Oh, mighty Aturathi, I swear solemnly upon your sacred visage, and upon my heart and the immortal light of my being, that I, Pludu Quasque, shall not rest until I have ventured from this realm, recovered your missing eye, restored it to you, and released you from your plight!'

The group gasped. Messana put up her hand to her mouth at this rash oath. Kekwe was horrified, and his concern overcame his animosity. 'Stop! Pludu, you should not!' But it was too late.

'Hurrah!' I called, sealing the oath with a gulp of wine.

Not one of my fellows responded. The music and laughter stopped. They looked at me with absolute disbelief.

'It's just a story,' I sneered. 'You're all fools to believe old tales. More stories to keep the old strong and the young weak. This is no true aelementor, it is just a statue.'

But the temperature dropped. The lamps flickered in a sudden breeze.

'THE OATH IS NOTED!' boomed a divine voice, the first time Aturathi had spoken since his eye was taken.

And so I was doomed.

The storm rumbled but quietly, far away from the inn.

'I will not dwell upon the shock that went through the lyceum,' said Quasque, 'or the reaction of my tutors. Some mages intervened on my behalf, pleading for clemency. Others called to place me in the crystal asylums that float over the city. And yet, the oath had been made. The most high argued I should be sent to fulfil it, for I would be doomed if I did not. The city was in uproar. My parents were sent for.

'Before they arrived I took my chariot and fled Settler's Gain for Tor Elid, where the scandal had yet to spread, and whose realmgates were not barred to me. The fate of oathbreakers who have sworn before Aturathi is so terrible I will not speak of it here. He had verified my pledge. I had no reason to doubt his wrath should I abandon it. I needed a way out.

'In Tor Elid's libraries I worked harder than I ever had as a student. There, I found there was no escape, and realised the scale of the task I had set myself, that I must travel to the Realm of Death itself, and seek out the place the dead ratkin go. Fool I was. One cannot simply come to Shyish and enter any afterlife one chooses.'

'We know this,' said Shattercap.

Maesa wet his lips with his wine, his almond eyes staring at Quasque as the mage continued to speak.

There are underworlds where the living are not welcome, or cannot go at all, and in all of them the God of Undeath's jealous eyes are everywhere, seeking out interlopers and thieves. The perils inherent to the realm of Shyish alone would see me fail a thousand times over. I had so much to learn, much, much more than I would have needed to gain my accreditation from the lyceum. But fear gave me the application I lacked while in school. I fled again, and my education took a different path.

From a shaman in Ghur I learned how to walk between realms in spirit form. From a wizard whose soul was half lost to Chaos I learned some secrets of the ratkin: that they call themselves skaven, that they are everywhere, and that their capital is a realm to itself. I consulted necromancers, daemonologists, thanatothurges, cartomancers, hedge wizards, high mages, academics, historians, adventurers, tomb robbers and more. From most of them I had to keep my purpose secret. All of them discovered what I intended, sooner or later. Some urged me to break my oath, others drove me away. Two tried to kill me, fearing that the nature of my quest would bring the God of Undeath's attention on them for instructing me. Little by little, my power grew, though the magic I wield now is very different to the energies of Hysh. I learned a little of all, from the purest, to the most debased. From each of the eight paths of magic I took something, and also from those outside the established colleges – the corrupt, the prohibited, the evil.

Step by step, I became a sorcerer.

'Did you ever find the eye?' asked Barnabus quietly. All at the inn were enrapt.

'Hush,' said Ninian. 'Let him tell his story.'

'The darkest tale yet,' muttered Horrin.

'Yes!' piped up Shattercap. 'Do you have it? Did you get it? I like jewels. They are so pretty!'

'I am coming to that part. More wine, please, if you will, master innkeeper.' He looked to Maesa. The aelf nodded his assent. 'I am sorry, Prince Maesa,' said Quasque. 'I abuse your generosity, but this part of the story is hard for me to tell. I...' His hand shook as he held up the goblet to be filled. 'I have never told it before.'

His glass recharged, Quasque took a long drink to steady himself.

It was years before I was ready to come to Shyish. When I arrived, years more effort awaited me. I had not learned the location of the skaven realm. I travelled from the living kingdoms to afterlives of all kinds; those that throng with souls as solid as you or I, ones that were faded places serving nations long since gone to dust, and whose last inhabitants were mindless shades weeping on the winds. Others were overrun by Chaos and twisted into perverse form, and many, many more fallen under the sway of the Great Necromancer and become part of his unliving empire.

I saw kingdoms where the living and the dead lived side by side. Places where the living hunted the dead, others where the dead hunted the living. I witnessed the heavens and hells of men, duardin, aelves, and many more races, both good and ill. But never once did I see a shade of the ratkin, or hear any notice of where they go when they perish. I had no news of the eye of Aturathi either.

The years rolled on. My early manhood passed by in dark places. I was embittered by my quest. I came close to giving up more than once, and would have done had I not found a reference to the Library of Forgotten Tomes.

It was a single passage in a book written by a madman, a dead one at that, but it gave me hope. It described a library towards the centre of Shyish where all things that have been forgotten are recorded. Not only living things die, you see, but dreams, and hopes, and knowledge; they too have lives and deaths.

This was it, the only place I might discover where the soul of the ratkin thief had gone, along with Aturathi's eye. After a year of searching, I found the library. What I saw there I will not speak of either. There were many things too terrible to describe, but wonders also. The library is a place of infinite capacity where all knowledge that has been known might be rediscovered. Perhaps it was once a place of learning, but the Great Necromancer's domain has overtaken it. The black pyramids and obelisks built around it appalled me. Shyish is a horror compared to Hysh, a place of cold instead of warmth, of gelid shadow rather than soothing light. Surrounded by buildings of lifeless realmstone, the wondrous library moulders, unattended, more silent than a grave, yet it is not uninhabited.

I was there for nine years. Eventually, in a wing dedicated to the history of a lost world, I found history after history concerning the ratkin. These are not selective works as written by men, but the tiniest details of every life that was ever lived and every thought ever had. It is maddening to read the lives of skaven. They do not think like us, and the echoes of their souls scratched madly inside my skull, but my obsession drove me on, until I happened on a book detailing a place unlike any other.

I had found the realm of the skaven after death. It is called the Realm of Ruin.

There were several books on Aturathi that hinted at the great secrets of the realms. Had I wished to follow the trail of those references, I would be the most learned man alive. But I was intent. I needed to know where the eye was. I had to have it, and free myself from my oath. Another year passed, until I found that too: the jewel was in the tower of a rat daemon whose name I dare not say aloud. I was tempted again to abandon my quest and remain, for anything that has been known is there, and more than once I came across the remains of scholars who had entered the library, and died drunk on knowledge. Little by little, day by day, the light of Hysh in me dimmed, but it never died. Had it guttered out, I would still be there, but my obsession saved me. I found a map to where I must go, and prepared to depart.

From the library I learned spells of the direst sort that would allow me to make my way to this Realm of Ruin. I prepared for the journey, forging a dagger of the kind the skaven use to cut their way through time and space. My essence was still too bright for the place I had to go, so one half of my soul I burned out with fire stolen from a daemon I lured into the library. The last stages required sacrifices I could not bear to make. I needed magic, lots of it, and it was there in the person of my horses. They knew what was coming. I could not bring myself to do it for weeks, until brave Solios gave himself nobly to the cause. I shed my last tears when I plunged this sword through his noble heart. Those things done, I was ready. With the dagger of Chaos-tainted realmstone I cut a slit in the world, mounted Rados, and plunged into the secret ways of the ratkin.

I left the realms entirely, galloping through a place between. I was not in the heavens that we see in the night skies of every realm, but some other place. The underside of the sky, that is the only way I can describe it. From my vantage I could see each of the realms floating by, gargantuan islands in oceans of magic, and other places beyond – most dread of all a glow, far away, where evil gods dwell. It was inverted: a sky of light, with stars black, but it was at the same time a swirl of sorcerous colour, an ocean of possibility. I tell you gravely all, my friends, that the skaven riddle the place between the realms. Their burrows stretch nets to snare the cosmos in every direction.

I followed a tunnel unlike the others, which are used by living ratkin. It was separate from their network, accessible in few places, and once entered vast and black, full of streaming shades, uncountable millions of them, a tide of rats running before a flood, all heading down, down, to one place.

'The Realm of Ruin!' squeaked Shattercap.

'Indeed,' said Quasque. 'The shades were skaven dead, scurrying to whatever fate awaits their kind. The numbers were staggering, an infinity of rat-souls, pouring on, on, down the great tunnel, which grew and grew, becoming the throat of a vortex marbled with green and crackles of purple lightning. The rushing swarms filled every surface.'

'Didn't they attack you?' asked Ninian.

'They were ghosts, hardly aware of me, and they recoiled from the light of Rados, so we passed untroubled,' said Quasque.

'The end came suddenly. We appeared over a grey sea covered with rubbish of every conceivable kind. The rat-souls tumbled from the tunnel into the water, where they squealed and thrashed, until forced under by the torrent of others following them. I saw only a little of the opening, which was huge and shaped like the bell of a black trumpet, for Rados bore us away quickly, his glowing skin a glare in that benighted place. We reached the shore, and he set down, his light illuminating a desolate beach crammed with mounds and mounds of refuse.

'I patted my horse's steaming neck. Alarmingly, his light was fading. Flight was a gift to him from my father, as Rados and Solios were his gifts to me, but I had pushed him too far, and without the magic of our sacred realm, there was no way to refresh his strength. I did not have much time. As we rode across the desolate land, he grew dimmer, and for the first time in my life, I saw shadows on his golden coat. He grew dull, like unpolished brass. He was dying.'

'You didn't come with your horse, master. I did not stable him for you,' said Barnabus.

'Quiet now,' said Horrin softly.

Quasque gave Barnabus a sorrowful look, and drank some more.

The Realm of Ruin is a terrible place. Piles of stinking refuse are heaped as far as the eye can see. Every rise is a mound of rubbish. Distant mountains reveal themselves to be yet more rubbish. The water was scummy, and had an oily, chemical scent. It was gloomy, but never truly dark, the clouds being lit by green bale-lights.

The worst thing about the refuse is its nature. It appears of uniformly brown, midden shades, but look closer and riches can be discerned. Once seen, they are everywhere. In that place are the broken glories of thousands of races, millions of nations; perhaps, even, the gnawed loot of entire worlds. Huge rat daemons stalk the valleys between the mounds and sometimes, with no predictability, a vision of a sprawling city appears in the sky. Its appearance lights up the Realm of Ruin starkly green, then just as quickly as it arrives, it is gone, plunging the land back into the dark.

So it was we came in time to the tower the book said held the eye of Aturathi. I rode up onto a hill, and spied the tower situated close to the shore. Half its considerable height was buried in stinking rubbish. I saw a swarming around off to the tower's west, inland, away from the sea. My eyes were drawn towards it, and I beheld the flash of magic between the yawn of twin realmgates – small as coins at that distance, but large of scale, I thought. The clash of metal and discharge of great guns sounded on the edge of hearing. War had come to the Realm of Ruin.

I dithered a little. My path would take us close to the battle. I had no choice. I urged the faltering Rados on towards the tower, my eyes always on the battle. One realmgate was of seething amethyst magic, the other a ragged tear green with skaven sorcery. From the skaven side poured a legion of armoured ratkin, urged on by the scourges of their daemons into a horde of undead I cannot properly describe. Vast armies of skeletal remains animated by the will of the Great Necromancer. Huge clouds of spirits soaring over them. Opposing the rat daemons were giant constructs of bone and flesh, and the corpses of monsters raised to a semblance of life. The forces on each side appeared to be limitless, and as I watched, the front lines of the battle stretched outward, engulfing more of the piles of rubbish. My path took me up a rise made almost entirely of potsherds of dizzying variety. From there I watched.

There were dread generals of the deathless legions riding the sky over the dead. They cast magic from their wands. Squadrons of vampire knights charged freakish beasts with rodent's heads. Skirmishing ghouls loped ahead of lines of skeletal archers who fired without tiring. Protected by phalanxes of armoured skeletal guardians, syphons fashioned from the bones of godbeasts extended fleshless jaws, racks of lead pipes sucking up the souls of the skaven as they died. I was witnessing a war not over territory, but spirits. The Lord of Death regards all dead things as his by rights, and it seems even the souls of so mean and tainted a race as the skaven lie within his claim.

On their side, the skaven responded with alchemical cannons and strange machines. Monstrous beasts waded into the armies of the undead. Warpstone-powered weapons scythed down swathes of the foe. Both sides suffered terrible casualties, but more warriors poured from the holes in space to join the fight. I would have been noticed were the two sides not so absorbed in each other's destruction. Certain I would not remain undetected for long, I rode down the slithering pot heap, towards the tower by the sea.

I reached a grey beach. The battle was out of sight. Though the clamour continued loud enough to hear, it was not sufficient to drown out the rush of the dirty surf. Bright pollutants swirled in the water, and all along the beach, foam made extravagant, quivering heaps between lines of tide-washed refuse. I urged the dying Rados up the slopes of refuse clinging to the tower, hoping that if I were quick, I would be able to leave that terrible place and save his life. It was not to be. I dismounted to search for a way in, the entrance being hopelessly buried. The sound of Rados falling had me rush back. At my return he opened his eyes a final time and whickered softly. The last of the light left him, his body heaved and his coat dulled to mundane flesh. I stroked his muzzle as he breathed his last, whispering that his trials were over.

If only that were true! I was in an uncanny realm, and so witnessed his gallant soul rise from his body. It shone with a measure of the light he had in his life, and he climbed upward, heading, I was sure, to a just rest in shining fields.

A tear slipped down Quasque's nose, and into his wine.

'Something grabbed at him and yanked him ferociously across the sky towards the battle. His soul, so serene a second before, screamed in terror, then he was gone behind the mountains of filth, certainly consumed by the spirit syphons of the undead.'

Quasque's narrative ceased. He broke down, and wept silently, his back heaving with sobs. Ninian put her hand on his. Horrin got up, and rubbed his shoulder.

'This one is on the house, good sir,' Horrin said, refilling Quasque's goblet. But Quasque would not be consoled, and the party had to wait for his weeping to subside before the tale continued. The wind began to blow again, and the rain fell harder.

Lightning flashed around the shutters, followed by a boom of thunder, very loud, that came close behind. Shattercap squealed and scampered up Prince Maesa's arm, fidgeting around the aelf's neck until Maesa plucked him up and set him back on the table. The fire bellied in the grate. Wind shrieked, then again, before settling once more to a constant moaning.

'The eye of the storm is passing over,' said Maesa. 'That is all, Shattercap. The wind returns.'

'Don't like it, oh wicked prince,' growled the spite. He sniffed. 'Smells wrong.'

At this, Quasque recovered his dignity, and said, 'Then I should be quick and finish.' He drained his cup again, and continued.

The tower was made of iron, and though it was heavily rusted, its walls were unbroken. Dark apertures high above I took to be windows, but they were beyond my reach. I thought myself defeated at the final hurdle, until, on the very far side overlooking the sea, I found a balcony. It was above my head, and I was obliged to haul myself up to gain access. In this way I arrived within the tower, covered in filth and streaked orange with rust.

I expected resistance in the tower, and primed my battle magic, but there was no sign of souls, living or dead, only the sickly smell of decay and the crash of waves on the beach.

The centre of the tower was taken up by a spiral stair. On each level was a single room. I peeked into them as I passed upward. They were all empty, save one, wherein lay sprawled the immense skeleton of a rat creature crowned with horns and dressed in tarnished armour. Beneath an outstretched claw a second skeleton was pinned, this one human and armoured in a style I did not recognise. Everything in there was rusty, covered in dust, except the sword, still bright with magic, jammed in the ribs of the creature, and the obvious cause of its death. This must have been the owner of the tower, slain by a hero long ago. I had not read the story of this encounter in the library. A terrible thought took me, that Aturathi's eye was gone, and I hurried on to the upper-most room.

In a chamber lit by thirteen tall windows was a chest of greened bronze between two thrones. In the thrones sat the mummified remains of skaven warlords aglow with magic. I dismembered these quickly with my sword, threw their limbs out of the windows and placed their heads away from their bodies. This done, I turned my attentions to the chest. It was locked, but nothing to the magic I had learned, and I opened it with a minor cantrip. Immedi-ately the heads began to chatter their jaws, and the bodies roll about. Had I not dealt with these things first, I would have had to fight them.

Inside the chest was a rotting leather pouch that fell apart the moment I lifted it. Out tumbled a single drop of exquisitely carved aetherquartz, yellow as a tiger's eye. I sobbed with relief, but could not delay. I heard the battle's roar coming closer to the tower. Neither undead nor skaven would forgive my taking the treasure.

There was too much iron around me for me to flee magically, cer-tainly the builder's purpose in using the material, so I ran down the stairs to the balcony and back out onto the grim shoreline. I believe my opening of the chest had alerted the death lords to the eye's presence, and I had the terrifying notion their armies had come to seize that very jewel. From over the horizon came the moaning of phantoms. A charge of phantom cavalry galloped soundlessly up and over the mountains of refuse. I had but moments to escape. I sliced at the weft of reality with the tainted knife. The edges of the beach sucked inward, and a hole opened onto a tunnel. I had no clue where it headed, but threw myself headlong within. The gap closed over my head. I had escaped.

* * *

Quasque took a shaking breath. The storm built in ferocity, approaching the power it had shown earlier in the evening.

'I was lucky,' said Quasque. 'I was able to cut an exit from the tunnel before I was discovered by the ratkin. Luckier still, the place I emerged was in the gentler parts of Shyish, many thousands of leagues away from the terrible places of the realm. Though alive, I was alone and impoverished. My horses were dead. My possessions were lost. The dagger disintegrated with the last cut. All I had left you see here, these clothes, my sword, a tiny amount of realmstone. My troubles were far from over.' He smiled. 'But I finally had this.'

He reached for a pouch by his side, and reverently withdrew a large yellow gem. He set it on the table with a click. Golden light shone into the inn, soft as a summer's day.

Shattercap's eyes widened. Involuntarily he reached for the gem, then self-consciously snatched his hands back. The company leaned in, except for Maesa, who remained impassive.

'Now that is a pretty stone, and no mistake,' said Stonbrak greedily, his eyes glittering.

'The eye of Aturathi. Pure realmstone of Hysh, beloved of the Lumineth,' said Quasque. 'With this, I could purchase a duchy. It is a shame I will not have the chance to fulfil my promise.' He picked up the stone and put it back into the pouch.

'What do you mean?' said Stonbrak. The wind shrieked outside. The inn trembled.

Quasque looked up defiantly. 'I regret to tell you that since retrieving the eye, I have been pursued across Shyish by the agents of the Lord of Death. I took it from a realm of the dead, and all those places, and all things within them, the God of Undeath deems his by right. Nagash!' Thunder boomed at the speaking of the name. 'I thought I had finally managed to outrun them. From the Argent Gate in Ghur one can go to Irb and the realmgate to

Hysh there, but this storm.' He smiled bitterly and waved his hand over his head. 'The sky-ship's early departure... It has delayed me just long enough. It cannot be natural. He knows everything. Nagash...' His voice dwindled to a whisper.

A shriek came from outside.

'That was not the wind,' said Maesa. He was on his feet, sword in hand, before the next scream blasted around the inn. Shattercap scampered up his arm.

The amulets above the bar jumped, and set up a constant jangling.

'By the gods!' breathed Horrin. 'What have you brought upon us?'

'I am sorry,' said Quasque, 'they are here.' His smile became crazed. 'The Hounds of Nagash have come.'

CHAPTER ELEVEN

THE HOUNDS
OF NAGASH

Manic light gleamed in Pludu Quasque's eyes, and he sat down hard.

'They are here,' he whispered again. His fingers fluttered nervously against each other. Screaming blended with the wind's music, adding wordless lyrics of misery.

Stonbrak got to his feet, drew his axe, and joined Maesa facing the entrance. The aelf hurriedly strung his bow. Something heavy slammed into the other side of the door, shaking it in the frame. Ninian screamed. Barnabus gripped her waist and whimpered.

The door leapt again. There was a deafening cry. Sharp nails scraped against the wood, scratching and scratching; there was a moment of silence, then the soft creak of timbers tested by inhuman strength. Grave-cold seeped into the room, chilling the air to mist and spreading a web of frost up the walls. Iron nails and studs gathered small thickets of ice. Over the bar, Horrin's warding charms swung out from the wood and strained towards the door.

Maesa watched in silence. The wooden edge of the Song of Thorns gleamed with the magic of Ghyran.

'Curse you, mage, for what you have done!' growled Idenkor Stonbrak. He hefted his axe. The runemarks upon the head glowed with cold fires.

'It's not my fault, I was a boy, a foolish boy!' Quasque collapsed into tears.

Shattercap scampered onto Maesa's shoulder, craned his neck and sniffed deeply. 'The dead, master. Thou knowest it is the dead at the door!'

'What manner of undead are they?' growled Stonbrak at Quasque.

'The Hounds of Nagash! Can you not hear them bark?' blubbered Quasque.

'What?' spat Stonbrak.

'A breed of Nighthaunt,' said Horrin softly. 'They are well known to we of Shyish. They chase down those that displease the Great Necromancer. It is said they were cruel hunters in life, now doomed in death to wear the skeletal heads of their hounds in place of their own. They are implacable, and will track down their quarry wherever they may be.'

'Then they are wisps, and wisps pass through solid matter,' said Stonbrak. He groped for his pint pot and drained the last of his ale. 'Let them come! I have a surprise of steel for them. My axe will see to their second deaths, as will that stick of the aelf's, I'll warrant. It has a gleam of magic almost as good as my own.'

'My sword is inimical to such ghasts,' said Maesa softly. 'But the Glaivewraiths are deadly, and hunt in packs. We must be ready.'

'Oh, I'm ready,' said Stonbrak.

The thing picking at the door planks moved away to try the

window. The shutters rattled violently. Plaster dust shook from the bouncing frame. Streaks of water ran from fresh cracks. Ice spread around the window. The glass broke. A plant on the sill withered and died. Ninian screamed again. Barnabus was crying, but he stood up, fists clenched.

'Go away!' he shouted bravely.

Horrin rested his hands on his foster son's shoulders. He smiled through his fear. 'They cannot get in,' he said quietly.

Maesa looked at the innkeeper.

'The charms over the bar,' Horrin explained. 'I have many, from all manner of wizards. They cannot get in.'

'They will not last,' said Maesa. 'This magic is strong, and yours, alas, is not.'

Horrin glanced at the bar. All the charms were shining red, and smoking with the dust burning from them.

The first shutter fell still. The thing outside moved on. There was a brief pause before the next shutter shook to a furious pounding.

Stonbrak narrowed his eyes. 'The aelf is right. Your charms will be insufficient, Master Horrin.'

'Barnabus, come with me,' said Horrin. 'Fetch the silver balls for my gun, and bring the daggers out for you and your mother. Barnabus!'

Barnabus was panting, staring at the patches of ice spreading all along the inn wall. His breath steamed from his mouth, thin threads at first, then huge billows. The temperature dropped rapidly, carrying frost deeper into the room along the beams. Shattercap shivered.

Noises were coming from the first floor.

'They're trying the shutters upstairs!' said Ninian.

'I said they can't get in,' said Horrin, but he no longer believed it.

All the shutters and the door commenced banging at once with great ferocity. Things outside shrieked and screamed.

'Your gun, innkeeper,' Maesa said. 'Now!'

Horrin nodded dumbly and hurried to the bar, dragging Barnabus with him.

The charms floated parallel to the wall, straining on their chains, now glowing brighter than a tree of candles. As Horrin took up his gun, the first charm exploded, showering the room with hot fragments that hissed on the spreading ice.

Barnabus scrambled over the counter. He rummaged about and shoved a rattling box at his foster father. Horrin half spilled the contents and swore as he fumbled powder and ball into the mouth of his gun. Shaking hands took three attempts to push the ramrod home. Barnabus scrambled over the countertop again, clutching a pair of identical sheathed daggers to his chest. He gave one to Ninian, and drew his own. As soon as it cleared the sheath, flames licked along the edges.

'Now that's more like it!' said Stonbrak. He was shifting about, eager to fight. Maesa stood completely still, the Song of Thorns pointed at the door. Shattercap hissed.

Horrin finally succeeded in priming his gun. He pulled back the hammer with a click.

'All your weapons are enchanted?' asked Maesa.

'This is Shyish, what use is a weapon of any other sort?' said Horrin.

The banging stopped. The party waited tensely. Soot sifted down the chimney. A cold wind blew out from the fireplace. The flames in the grate sank.

Horrin paled. 'The fire!' he said. 'The fire must not go out!' He banged himself on the furniture as he rushed to the hearth.

Another charm exploded, then another. The whole string of them went off like duardin firecrackers, banging in succession until only one remained. Stonbrak growled at a fleck of molten gold burning his cheek. Frost raced over the bar, up the bottles shelved behind. Glass broke as the contents froze solid.

Maesa kept a wary eye on the last charm. It floated, buzzing with failing magic, flickering like a firefly heading deep into the woods.

More soot fell down the chimney, damping the fire further.

'They're going to come in through the bloody fireplace!' Stonbrak shouted.

'The fire! The fire!' Horrin wailed. He tossed dried mosses onto the sinking flames. They sputtered, but would not take. Barnabus ran to his side with a flask.

'Try this, Master Horrin!' he said.

Horrin uncorked the flask and upended it over the fire. Thick oil glugged onto the embers. The fire roared up and Horrin cheered. His jubilation fled when a bone-chilling wail echoed down the chimney, and the fires died back again.

'Get away from the fireplace,' Maesa said.

'It cannot go out!' Horrin was in a panic, spilling matches and kindling as he tried to revive the fire.

The last charm exploded. To Maesa's aelven vision, the chain fell slowly, each link clinking in turn on the wood. Broken charms rippled along the length as it swung to a stop. As the last link stilled, the candles in the bar room extinguished all at once. Lightning flashed somewhere in the depths of the storm, sending sharp slivers of light spearing through the gaps in the woodwork. Maesa saw a shadow moving fast outside.

'The fire,' Horrin groaned. The last spark winked out.

A moan fluted down the chimney.

'Get away from the fire,' the prince repeated.

With a rush of soot and ash, a cloaked thing plunged into the room. Horrin threw himself aside. It sped over his head, wailing piteously. Green and ghastly light flooded the bar. A canine skull jutted from under the figure's filthy cowl. It had no legs, its body and robes blended into a long, glowing tail of magic. Clawed hands swept at Maesa as it flew by. It raced around the room, its passage leaving a trail of ice and soot upon the walls. The touch of its spectral form knocked pictures down and shattered glass ornaments. As it came at the group again, a glaive appeared in its hands, solidifying from shadows: a black wooden haft hardened by centuries in a tomb, a sword-long blade eaten with rust but still sharp as death's bite.

The ghast levelled its weapon and sped towards Quasque, who let out a low moan. Ghost fire glowed in the thing's empty eye sockets. It shrieked triumphantly as it stooped to kill. From far away came the baying of hounds and the shouts of wicked men intent on their quarry.

Maesa stepped in front of the ghast. The Song of Thorns sang through the air, intercepting the blade before it could claim its prey. Green sparks fountained along the point of contact. Maesa encountered a wiry strength he had not expected, and the ghast pushed him back, its fleshless muzzle snapping in his face.

Stonbrak gave a shout and threw. His axe blurred through the air, cleaving through the phantom as if it were composed of nothing but mist. The blade dragged the stalker into shreds of vapour. The runes cut into the axe's steel flared. The phantom discorporated into nothing, and Stonbrak's weapon thunked into the wall.

'That's you done,' said the duardin matter-of-factly. He clumped across the room to where his axe was embedded, and grasped the haft.

'Master duardin!' Maesa called.

Stonbrak looked back. Maesa dropped the Song of Thorns. His lithe arms moving too fast to follow, he plucked an arrow from his quiver, drew his bow and loosed. The shaft sped towards the outraged merchant, passing his nose by a finger's breadth, and buried itself in the skull of a second wraith emerging through the wall. It disappeared with a moan and shower of grave dust. Another ghast plunged through the door. Horrin snatched up his gun and fired. The bullet burst into pink fire as it punched through the phantom, sending it shrieking back to the netherworlds.

'We need to remove ourselves from here,' Maesa said. He looked at the finger. 'I do not think they can pass through the body of the god.'

Stonbrak tugged out his axe, and brushed the dust from his arm with distaste. 'Then we go upward, into the storm,' he said. 'There's too much ground to cover here, too many ways in. We should hold at the sky-dock, keep our backs to the stone, and await my cloud-dwelling cousins. We might be able to hold them off for long enough.'

'Boy, which way to the dock?' said Maesa.

'The stairs are here, good sirs!' Barnabus said. He hurried to the far corner of the room and opened up a door.

'But the fire!' Horrin said.

More shrieks passed close by the inn. Nothing attempted entry.

'Maybe they've learned caution,' said Stonbrak. He hauled Quasque to his feet. 'Up you get, master mage.'

Horrin was stacking the fire anew. 'The dead know no fear at all,' he said.

'That is not true,' said the prince. He picked up his sword, fetched his helm from the table and put it on, and stowed his packs under a bench. 'They know fear of failure, for their lord will punish them if they do not bring their quarry down.'

'I cannot go,' said Horrin. 'I must relight the fire!' None of the matches would ignite, so Horrin took up steel and flint and sent sparks fountaining into fresh kindling. It did not take, and Horrin cursed.

'It will not burn while they are assailing us,' said Maesa. 'Come.'

The ground stirred beneath their feet.

'It is beginning!' Horrin said.

Shifting timbers moaned. The inn pitched like a storm-tossed ship. Objects fell from the tables and bounced across the floor. Only Maesa rode the motion with any dignity. Stonbrak stumbled. Ninian gripped at a table. Quasque wept all the harder. Chairs toppled over with wooden clatters.

'We must leave now!' Maesa said.

Barnabus waved frantically at the dark stairwell. Tears glinted in his eyes. The boy was terrified. 'This way, this way!'

The room swayed again. A rumbling pitted itself in competition with the storm: the low-bass, tooth-jarring scrape of stone on stone. The few bottles behind the bar that were not frozen in place fell to the floor and shattered. Wood splintered. Windows burst in warping frames.

'Don't need to tell me twice, lad.' Stonbrak shoved past Maesa, dragging the shivering Quasque with him. Ninian went to her son's side.

'Please watch my family,' said Horrin. 'Help them live the night through. I have to stay here.'

Maesa nodded. 'Very well.'

Horrin smiled. 'Thank you for your story, good aelf. Maybe, tomorrow, you can tell me an–'

A howling wraith burst upward from beneath the inn. Its phantom glaive point slid through Ninian's chest with no resistance. Horrin's eyes and mouth went round in shock. When the tip emerged from beneath her sternum, it suddenly phased into solidity, parting Ninian's skin with a sudden rush of gore.

Barnabus screamed. Ninian opened her mouth to speak, but a sheet of blood poured over her jaw in place of words.

The phantom passed through Ninian's dying body, stilling her heart and covering her in frost. It raced with a shriek at Maesa in order to get to Quasque. Maesa sidestepped at the last possible moment, brought down the Song of Thorns and decapitated it. The hound skull fell towards the ground, the body began to dissipate, but then the Song of Thorns glowed ruddily, and the shreds of the doomed hunter's soul were sucked screaming into his blade.

'Grungni's beard!' Stonbrak swore.

'Ninian… My Ninian…' Horrin stood, hands trembling.

The inn shook, and lurched upward.

'Go, leave the fire. It is too late!' said Maesa. 'Get them all out, duardin, they are coming in earnest.' He spoke no louder than a whisper, yet the words flew with the force of an arrow.

'As you say, aelf,' said Stonbrak. He marched across the room to grab the shivering Horrin. More of the phantoms slipped through the walls as if they were not there, weapons transitioning from ghostly to solid forms. Maesa set himself against them, covering Stonbrak's retreat. The ghosts clacked their canine teeth together, drifting into a line six wide.

Stonbrak cast hurried glances at them, hustled Horrin to the door, shoved the humans into the stairwell and slammed the door behind him.

The wraiths attacked.

They came at Maesa in a group, glaives pointed at his heart. The Song of Thorns flashed out and took the heads from two of the weapons, causing their bearers to wail and discard the hafts, which boiled into glowing smoke. One of the disarmed wraiths raced at the prince. Maesa leapt lightly onto the table, parrying a flurry of jabs from the others, his eyes ever on his principal opponent as it reached out with its heart-stilling touch. A swift thrust from the Song of Thorns, and its soul was sucked away into the prison of his sword.

The others became wary.

'There are more terrible things in these realms than Nagash,' Maesa told them. 'This weapon I bear was the gift of the Goddess of Life. It is deadly to your kind. Come at me, and know a true end.'

They tried to surround him. Maesa followed their movements, switching his stance just enough to execute deflections and counter-attacks. The inn's movements increased, not fits and starts this time, but a smooth, purposeful motion towards the ground, steady as a piston drop. The ceiling cracked as the great finger poking up through the roof twitched. Furniture upended and skidded down the sloping floor. Maesa leapt from tumbling chair to sliding table, his feet light, as if the battle were a well-choreographed dance and not a struggle against death itself. Muffled shouts came from upstairs. The phantoms, not anchored to reality, were taken unawares, and passed screaming in fury through the walls and floor as the building moved away from them. The great stone digit the inn was built around flexed. Timbers cracked with such force that splinters exploded across the room.

'Master!' wailed Shattercap.

The inn tipped sideways, then stopped abruptly. Furniture crashed down. Aelven grace was no protection, and Maesa was flung clear across the room, landing in a tangle of broken wood and glass. Shattercap gibbered terror into his ear.

'Master! Master! Master!'

'Silence,' said Maesa. The inn had come to rest on its side. One wall was now the floor, another the ceiling. All surfaces were broken and bent. 'Ellamar,' he said.

Maesa sheathed his sword and pushed himself out of the debris. He searched frantically for the package containing his beloved's remains. Finding it, he tied it across his back, leaving his pack, and clambered for the door to the stairs, now above him and hanging open. He leapt, grabbing the edge of the turned-about doorway and hauling himself lightly upward. Once inside the stairwell, he ran along the walls, for the stairs hung broken over his head, all while the great tremors of the god's waking splintered the timbers further.

Maesa found Stonbrak in a heap of armour and beard.

'The others, where are they?' Maesa demanded.

'Ran ahead!' Stonbrak said, pushing broken plaster off himself. 'Quasque fled gibbering up there after them. He refuses to use his magic.' Stonbrak spat a huge gob of saliva and dust from his mouth. 'What by the Six Smiths was that?'

Maesa peered out of a crazed window onto a vista of grey grasses and black-barked trees.

'The arm of the demigod has come down. We are on the plain. We do not have much time before it fully wakes, I think.'

In answer to his warning, the hand shifted, and the inn tilted a little way back towards its proper position. Horrin shouted from somewhere ahead.

Stonbrak got himself up, and immediately put his heavy boot through the laths of the wall currently making the floor.

'I do not think this will end well,' said Maesa. He sprang ahead, barely troubling the fractured building, while Stonbrak swore and blundered.

The upper floor of the inn was ruined. Maesa pushed through a rent in the wall to emerge onto a slippery mess of tiles caught in the angle of a gable. Water ran from the smashed inn in floods. Rain pounded at his eyes. The fingers of the god were half curled, the giant hand resting blade down on the ground, the mighty thumb blotting out most of the sky, black stone on black clouds.

Atop a higher portion of the ruin, Quasque held Barnabus to ransom. He had the boy's flaming knife pressed up against his throat. Horrin balanced on the tiles. He'd lost his gun, and stood helpless.

'Get back from me!' Quasque shouted.

'Leave the boy, Quasque,' said Maesa. 'Let him free to his father.'

'No!' said Quasque. He searched the sky for the ghasts. 'When they come back, I'm going to give him to them. Then they'll leave me alone. I'm sorry. It's the only way. I must return the eye!'

Maesa withdrew his bow from its case and nocked an arrow to the string. 'They want you, master sorcerer. Spilling that boy's blood will make no difference.' He drew, taking sure aim on Quasque's head.

'He's just a stable boy! I am a mage of Hysh! I carry an aelementor's eye! It is obvious who should die!'

'You are just a man, for all that,' said Maesa.

Quasque laughed wildly. 'I know the spell that will see me safe!' He stiffened. From the corner of his eye, Maesa glimpsed what Quasque saw: looping down through the sky on trails of ghostly vapour came the Glaivewraiths. They flew at the terrified sorcerer.

'Drop the knife, Quasque. I will protect you.'

'No!' Quasque shrieked. 'You don't know what I've lost. I won't let them take me. I'm sorry, boy,' he wheedled. 'I've avoided this until now. It can't be me, so it has to be you.'

'I have killed many creatures, both fair and foul, during my cursed life,' the prince said. 'But I will not stand by to see this boy's soul carried off. It is your error that led to your predicament. He is innocent. If you will not let me help you, let him go and face your punishment.'

'No,' sobbed Quasque.

'Then you leave me no choice,' said Maesa.

The ground lurched as he released the string. The giant fingers of the god curled in. Maesa's shot went wild. Horrin slipped and fell tumbling through the torrents of water pouring from the god's hand onto the mud of the plain.

Maesa swayed in time with the movement. He plucked another arrow from his quiver, and drew his bow, only to see Quasque vanishing over a pile of timbers, dragging the boy with him. The inn was high up on the god's hand, giving the aelf a good view out over the plain as it bulged upward. The turf broke, soil ran in muddy torrents, massive boulders beneath lifted up like jagged teeth opening.

A stone head as large as a hill burst through the earth. The land further out rippled, and a second hand punched its way from the ground and reached for the sky. Lightning flashed, stabbing into the giant's splayed fingers. The left hand fell and hit the ground. The elbow angled upward. Palm flat, the giant pushed, heaving its shoulders free. The hand bearing the inn curled tighter, stopping before making a fist that would have crushed them all. Wood shattered as the god pushed hard on the earth. Slowly, water and mud running off its face and from its mouth, it forced itself out of the ground. Its shoulders emerged, then its chest and back.

Horrin slid towards the gargantuan hole left in the plain by the demigod hauling itself out of the earth. Maesa watched, unable to help, then shouted in relief as Aelphis leapt down the crags of the grounded fist, and hurtled towards the man. He tilted his noble head to the side as he charged at him. Horrin grabbed onto the points of his antlers, and Aelphis bore him away. The stag ran as fast as he could, bounding from crumbling sod to falling boulder, brown water surging up to his chest, his head bowed by the weight of the innkeeper.

'Take him to safety, Aelphis!' Maesa cried.

The stag tired near the lip of the growing crater as the giant lifted one leg free from the ground, placed its foot flat, bent forward, then pushed, and dragged up the other leg from its subterranean prison. Water, soil and rock tumbled into the gaping void it left behind. Aelphis dwindled in Maesa's view as the giant rose higher and higher into the sky until finally it stood tall in the storm. Lightning flashed all around, thunder roared. The giant roared back, a cry of rage that chilled Prince Maesa's soul.

Aelphis jumped from rock to rock plummeting into the hole. For all his speed, he was going nowhere, until finally the avalanche slowed, and he raced free, galloping off to the side of the rising god, and finding safety among the trees.

Stonbrak shoved his way out of the building just as the inn tilted again. The giant brought up its palm to its face to see the drama unfolding there. The motion led Stonbrak to slip, and he would have fallen to certain death, had not Maesa loosed his arrow at the duardin, pinning his clothes to the wood of the inn. The whole ruin groaned, and Maesa was forced to run and leap as his stag had, until the palm was flat and the ruin of the inn of the Brazen Claw, still clinging to the finger of the giant, was brought up before a stone face as tall as a cliff. Eyes of fire peered from sockets deep as caves at the inn and the tiny figures around it, much as a man might examine a beetle scurrying over his skin.

Stonbrak was left hanging by his cloak from a high beam, struggling and cursing against the arrow.

'It is ironwood, it will not break,' said Maesa, 'you must draw it out.'

'The god does not like us,' said Shattercap. 'I see it! It will devour us!'

'Its thoughts are slow,' said Maesa. 'We have time to save the boy yet.'

'He's there!' said Shattercap, pointing to the stairs running around the giant's finger to the platform high above. Stairs and dock were both in disarray, but being of duardin make they were not easily dislodged. Quasque was dragging the boy after him. In the sky, the ghasts circled about, floating up the side of the giant after their prey.

Still peering at its palm, the giant god took one ponderous, earth-shaking step. It moved slowly at first, but each stride carried it hundreds of yards away from its grave, and became quicker like a rockfall building speed, until it was moving over the land like the wind.

The storm boomed around them, thunder mingling with the thump of the god's feet so that it seemed the ground exchanged blows with the heavens. Rain flew at Maesa in horizontal rods. The Glaivewraiths shrieked in the turbulent air left by the god's passage. One bounced from the chest of stone, and was torn away by the wind.

'Help me down!' growled Stonbrak, still slapping fruitlessly at Maesa's arrow.

Maesa's eyes squinted against the wind and rain. Quasque continued his clumsy ascent, hampered by Barnabus' struggling. A flash of lightning lit them as Quasque threw the boy against the stone, and slapped him hard across the face with the back of his hand, stunning Barnabus into submission. Thereafter his ascent became quicker.

'Release yourself,' Maesa told Stonbrak. 'I must save the boy from his fate.'

The prince ran to the broken stairway. His feet flashed over cracked timbers and bent iron pins, bearing him unerringly upward.

Behind him, Stonbrak growled and yanked the arrow hard. He fell loudly to the palm.

'Wait!' the duardin called. 'Wait!'

Maesa lost Stonbrak's voice in the storm. He rounded the finger quickly, then again, gaining on the fleeing sorcerer. In little time he had caught up to Quasque. Barnabus was unconscious, draped over the sorcerer's shoulder.

'Stop!' shouted Maesa.

Quasque glanced back. He grinned in triumph and hurried on.

'Master!' shrieked Shattercap. 'The wraiths!'

Maesa switched targets from Quasque to a trio of ghasts bearing down on him. His arrow pierced the first, tearing it to rags of ectoplasm. The second two met their end to swift blows from the Song of Thorns. They were pulled wailing into the sword, but valuable time was lost in their slaying. Maesa recommenced his pursuit. The god held its palm mercifully still in its fascination with the unfolding drama, but the plunge of every step rocked the aelf, and its great fingers twitched and moved with the motion of its walking, making the way perilous.

The god curled its fingers. The stairs shifted. Overhead, the damaged sky-dock swung from the fingertip by threads of iron and steel.

Around and around the finger Maesa went, daring creaking, wet wood, and slick iron staples where the steps had been torn away. Quasque evaded him, pushed on by terror. By the time Maesa caught up, Quasque had reached the sky-dock, and lodged himself firmly into an angle of wood, his feet braced against further movement. He had laid the insensible boy across his thighs, the dagger again to his neck.

Quasque was muttering the words of a spell. Maesa whispered to Shattercap. The spite jumped from his back and vanished into the rain. The prince drew his bow.

'Quasque, let him go!' Maesa shouted.

Quasque opened tormented eyes. 'I can't,' he said. He spoke the words of his spell quickly. The shrieks of the stalkers were coming nearer.

Maesa loosed his arrow. It sped at Quasque's face, but flashed into nothing.

'I have a great deal of magic. Have you not learned your lesson?' sneered Quasque.

Maesa put his bow away, and drew again the Song of Thorns.

Quasque finished his spell. A nimbus played around Barnabus. A phantom outline of the unconscious boy overlaid his physical being. Quasque grinned at the prince. 'You will strike me down with your soul stealer? I would not, if I were you. Already you provoke Nagash's wrath by stealing the essence of his servants. They are but scraps of being. If you take my soul, then his attention will be fixed on you.'

'It already is,' said Maesa, 'but it is not my time yet.'

'Aye,' said Quasque. 'I know what you hide in your satchels. The grave-sands of Shyish are his as much as this jewel I carry. You are a thief like me. I wonder, how far behind my hunters are yours?'

'That, you will never know,' said Maesa.

'You've already lost,' said Quasque. 'My magic has loosened the boy's soul from his body. I must now strike the final blow, put the mark on him, and I will be free for a while. Long enough to fulfil my oath, in any case.' He raised his dagger to strike. The wraiths howled.

A tiny figure darted out from behind a leaning post. Shattercap, his teeth bared, leapt upon the sorcerer's arm and bit hard. Quasque howled. Maesa lunged, his blade piercing the shield of magic around the sorcerer, and with its tip he knocked the dagger from Quasque's hand. Quasque jumped up. Barnabus fell down, and slid towards the drop at the edge of the tilted platform, where he caught upon a broken post. Quasque shook his arm until Shattercap was flung free. The spite went crying over the edge of the dock, and was lost in the storm.

Maesa watched him go. 'You will pay for that.'

Ghost light shone through the rain. The distant baying of hounds carried on the wind.

'Save me!' Quasque pleaded.

'By your own actions, you have damned yourself,' said Maesa. He sheathed his sword. 'Prepare yourself for Nagash's judgement.'

'Please!'

Five stalkers floated down towards the dock. They passed by Maesa, bony snouts twitching up and down as they sniffed at him. Maesa held up his hands.

'It is not me you want, your quarry stands there. The mage of Hysh.'

As one, the ghostly huntsmen turned, black eye sockets locked on Pludu Quasque. Their blades pointed at him. They surged forward, each voicing a soul-piercing shriek, and transfixed the screaming Quasque with their rusty weapons.

Quasque's death was not quick, and he screamed all the way through and beyond. He aged rapidly, his skin wrinkling and sagging, his teeth falling out, his hair growing long and fine until it blew away on the wind. Weakening bones and failing tendons drew him into a hunch. He was ancient now, but still alive, still screaming, even as his flesh turned to dust and yellowed ribs emerged through disintegrating skin. As his body vanished, his soul was left, howling in agony, pierced by five blades it could not escape no matter how hard he writhed.

The last of Quasque's mortal body fell away. The wraiths rose up, carrying his screaming spirit with them.

They floated into the storm. One of the ghasts pulled its glaive out, and turned to face the prince. It uncurled its bony finger and pointed. Magic flashed in its eye sockets; the baying of hounds rose over the giant's footsteps and the thunder. Then the five wraiths and their spectral prey faded from being, and the barking dwindled to nothing.

CHAPTER TWELVE

THE GOD WALKS

Maesa wiped the rain from his eyes. He looked up into the face of the god, who stared back with unguessable intent.

Seeing the drama done, the god's face moved into a grinding frown.

The fingers twitched. The hand moved. Barnabus hung on the edge of death. Maesa leapt for him, scooping the boy up and slinging him across his back. Maesa grabbed a plank of wood and swung himself back onto the remains of the sky-dock platform. He secured a safe position, and through the driving rain saw a mountain approaching, the first of many rocky fangs lining the horizon. A cliff of stone black in the wet loomed ahead, close by the god's right hand.

The giant reached out.

'Shattercap!' Maesa shouted. 'Shattercap!' But he could see his companion nowhere.

Maesa raced away from the sky-dock as the finger extended towards the mountain. The palm bent back. The cliff drew closer.

Stone rushed by. The god scraped its fingers against the rock to wipe off the inn, dislodging a tumble of boulders. The dock caught on the mountain and, with a screaming wrench of metal and broken timber, came free. The palm got closer and closer to the stone, tilting so that it too became a cliff parallel to the mountain face.

Maesa ran along the cracks of the god's palm, then through the chasm between its fingers. From behind came a squealing and shattering as the Inn of the Brazen Claw snagged on stone and was crushed to matchwood. Maesa leapt for the mountain cliff, legs wheeling, one hand clamped about the boy's wrist. He slammed into the mountainside, sliding down, tearing the skin on his hand until, at last, his feet found purchase upon a grassy ledge. With great effort, he shifted his weight, and fell into a crouch, coming to rest a hundred feet above a slope of scree.

The giant strode on, the hand still trailing against the rocks, showering bits of shattered wood onto the land below. Like a man divesting himself of something distasteful, it wiped its fingers back and forth on the stone, then upon its leg. It bit at the staples in its fingers and spat them like bullets against the mountain. The inn removed, with quickening strides the demigod headed off towards the mountain peaks, and vanished into the rainy night.

Barnabus moaned on Maesa's back. Though slight, the aelf was strong, yet now the ache of his exertions threatened them both.

'Rest easy,' Maesa said, panting. 'Do not move suddenly.'

Barnabus opened his eyes and gasped.

'I said be easy,' said Maesa.

With some difficulty, Maesa guided the frightened boy from his back and onto the ledge. The angle of the cliff there was not too steep, and the ledge was wide enough to keep them safe, but the climb down was hard, and Maesa doubted Barnabus could make it. He looked upward, and saw a more difficult climb above where the rock grew steep again.

'Ninian... Horrin...' the boy said. He kept his eyes screwed tightly shut.

'I am sorry for your loss, boy. Ninian was a good woman. Your foster father escaped. I saw it myself. My Aelphis took him away from the ghasts and the god, he will keep him safe until we return. Sit. Put your back against the rock. We are in no danger here.' Maesa's words were true, but the boy was beginning to shiver. He could die of the cold. How long that would take, he did not know. Humans lacked the fortitude of aelf-kind.

Barnabus took one look at the drop then shut his eyes again. 'How will we get down?'

'I will find a way,' the aelf said. He checked over the bag holding Ellamar's remains. Finding it to be whole, and her bones unbroken, he started to look for a descent. The ledge went for a dozen yards in one direction, a little less than half that in the other. Everywhere he looked, the stone below the ledge's lip was smooth for many feet, without handholds.

The rain eased to drizzle. The wind dropped its voice to a gentle whisper. Away to the east, Hysh was approaching the edge of the realm. Already the sky was turning silver, and the clouds were breaking.

'The weather turns,' said Maesa. 'That is a good start. The day will warm you.'

He tried a few times to lower himself down, but his feet rasped on featureless rock. As he was about to make another attempt, a piping voice called from above.

'Master!'

'Shattercap?' Maesa said. 'You live!'

'Yes, yes, I live.' Shattercap landed with a soft thump upon the grass. There was the hiss of rope on stone, and coils of it piled on top of the spite. He groaned, and picked himself up, then shook his fist above. 'Stupid beardy!' he shrilled. 'Rope's too long!'

He untied the line at his waist, showing it to Maesa before nonchalantly tossing it over the edge.

'Shattercap stayed alive on purpose. Stupid beardy didn't save me, no, no, not at all. I make sure to stay alive all by myself to save nice master!' He poked his thumb into his chest. 'Shattercap good spite, yes?'

'Yes,' said Maesa. 'You are a good spite.'

The spite stuck out his chin in delight.

'Though I suspect the rope is not yours, but rather Master Stonbrak's,' Maesa said. 'Which means he must at least have found you, if he did not save you.'

Shattercap scowled. 'Stupid beardy,' he said again. 'Shattercap needs no rope for this little climb.'

From above came the clash of hobnails on stone, accompanied by heavy breathing and rough curses. Stonbrak rappelled efficiently if gracelessly onto the ledge. His face was badly grazed, and one eye swollen shut, yet he grinned at Maesa, exposing a missing tooth.

'I'll wager you thought me a goner, eh?' said Stonbrak. 'Not so easy to kill off old Idenkor Stonbrak! Takes more than wraiths or gods to put an end to a duardin of Ulgu.'

'Or, indeed, mountains,' said Maesa.

'Mountains! *Mountains* he says! Mountains won't kill me, aelfling. Ha! You might get duardin floating in the sky, living in manling cities or rolling about in the fireplace, but the only real duardin is a mountain duardin if you ask me, and what kind of mountain duardin goes anywhere without a good bit of rope?' Stonbrak winked.

Maesa looked him over. There did not appear to be anywhere the duardin could have stashed his rope. He bowed.

'Your kind are a marvel to me,' he said.

'And yours an irritation to me,' said Stonbrak, 'but I won't hold it against you, because that was a great deal of fun.' He peered over the edge. 'Now then, I've got about two hundred foot of good strong line here. Should be more than enough to get us down.'

Stonbrak attached the rope to the rock by means of a small iron spike hammered into a crack. He went first, followed by Barnabus, who was accompanied by Shattercap, hissing hard encouragement at him. When Maesa at last reached the bottom, Stonbrak gazed mournfully upward.

'Be a shame to leave my rope behind,' he said.

Maesa drew his bow and shot off an arrow without looking. The rope went slack, and a few seconds later came racing down the cliff, tangling up the merchant.

'My thanks, master aelf!' Stonbrak said, his voice muffled by the line. 'Ow!' he shouted, as Maesa's arrow bounced off his head. Shattercap scampered up to him and snatched it up with a glower.

'Come on!' Barnabus said. His teeth were chattering, and he was running about to keep warm. 'We've come a long way, I have to get back. I have to see if Master Hor–' He paused. 'If my father is all right,' he said firmly. He started off.

Stonbrak untangled himself from the rope and began to coil it. 'Don't run far, lad! The night might be over, but there are many perils in these parts!' he called.

The striding god had covered miles, and had taken them high into the foothills. On the grey plains hung a mist turning gold in the light of rising Hysh. Maesa looked up towards the mountains. He saw, far off towards the snow line of the highest peak, a glint of bronze catch the sun. It flashed as it proceeded upwards, then was lost.

'Brazen claw indeed,' he said.

'Your highness!' Barnabus came running back. 'Your highness, look what I found!' The boy held out an eager hand. He turned it up, and opened it.

In his palm was the lost eye of Aturathi, the sage of Hysh.

'Oooh,' said Stonbrak and Shattercap simultaneously.

'You should take it, your highness,' said Barnabus. 'Please!'

'Perhaps you should, to pay your way,' said Maesa. 'You have lost much. It will be some recompense.'

'No!' said the boy in horror. 'It bears a curse. Besides, it is worth a fortune. Horrin'll want to keep it, but we will be in danger if we do, not just from the dead,' he gabbled. 'Take it back to Hysh. Put it back where it came from. Then we'll be safe. Then...' He became downcast. 'Ninian...'

'She died protecting you, my boy,' said Stonbrak, gripping the youth's shoulder and shaking him. 'Remember her bravery, and honour her. Now, if you'll give me that pretty thing, then...'

Before Stonbrak's eager fingers could pluck the gem up, Maesa's hand closed over it.

'I will do as you say, Barnabus, and return the eye to Hysh, in memory of your foster mother. Maybe Aturathi will give me his counsel. There are matters he could help me with. For that I thank you.'

'Oh no you don't!' said Stonbrak. 'We won that bauble together!'

'Then you are more than welcome to accompany me, master duardin.'

Stonbrak stroked his beard, his eyes beady and fixed on Maesa's palm.

'Knowing the Lumineth, they will be grateful to have their treasure back, once adequately prompted. There will be a reward.' He cleared his throat. 'Then I might well come with you,' said the duardin. 'To see the world set to rights. Any treasure paid for tasks done and all that will be gratefully received. But even if there's not riches involved I'll come,' he added hurriedly, 'it's the moral thing to do.'

'Come with me or not, I do not care,' said Maesa. 'First we must make our way back to the site of the inn, and deliver this boy to his father. I must recover my steed, and my belongings. We cannot make the Argent Gate by land. The Plains of Teeth are deadly. We must hope that the sky-lords are true to their schedule and return to the site of the Claw.'

Stonbrak looked up into the lightening sky. 'It's not natural, duardin living in the clouds. We need stone under our boots and stone over our heads! Nonetheless, they are duardin, and now the storm is done they will return to their schedule.' He looked out over the misty landscape. 'Ten miles, I'd say.' He sniffed. 'We'd better get on with it.' He'd wound his rope into a fine coil, and he now secreted this beneath his beard. After he did, he peered at his chest and moaned. 'It'll take ages to fix the links on my mail coat, it's damn near practically ruined.'

'Then ask your cousins on the boat for aid,' Maesa said. 'They are also skilled smiths, are they not?' Shattercap scampered up onto his perch on Maesa's shoulder. When the spite was comfortable, the prince strode off down the hill. Barnabus followed. 'The voyage will take three days or more, and there will not be much to do.'

'What shall we do to pass the time? It's customary to swap tales on voyages, and I'll guess you have many more to tell,' said Stonbrak, trotting to keep up.

Maesa kept his eyes on their destination.

'Like at the inn? I beg your leave, master duardin. I for one have had enough of tales for now,' he said.

PART FOUR

THE
HUNGERFIEND

CHAPTER THIRTEEN

THE PLAINS OF TEETH

The airscrews of the duardin ship chopped at the sky. Beneath the keel, forest thinned and gave way to plains of grey grass that raced with silver waves. Further on, the grass became patchy, the black earth around its roots exposed. Ivory blots appeared between, growing bigger and merging together, until the grass and earth became islands in a plain of yellowed bone, and eventually petered out completely.

Heavy steel boots thudded on the riveted deck as the crew attended to the ship. At Prince Maesa's side, Captain Thringsson rested armoured hands on the rail. His sigh of pleasure at the view rattled metallically in his breathing pipe. Though the sky-cutter sailed only a few thousand feet above the ground for the benefit of its passengers, the duardin crew retained their high-altitude gear. A metal facsimile of a duardin's face served Thringsson as a visor. Morning light glinted from the bronze and steel. It was ornate, as befitted a person of his status, with eyepieces of clear crystal.

'The Plains of Teeth,' said Thringsson. His voice echoed in his helmet. 'A spectacular sight.'

'It looks like sand at this height, even to me,' said Maesa.

'Aye, but as we go further into the desert, the teeth increase in size,' said Thringsson. 'At the edges they are tiny, the teeth of crawling things, fishes, frogs and other small creatures.' The duardin looked at Shattercap, who sat wrapped in Maesa's hood against the cold. 'Teeth like yours, forest spirit.'

Shattercap slowly looked down and curled his lip before returning his attention to the bone-white wastes.

'Deeper in they become immense, the teeth of leviathans, and dragons, and godbeasts, so large you can see them easily from up here. You can practically count the wealth.' Thringsson sniffed loudly. Although these duardin of the air were strange to Maesa, they were still duardin, and had mannerisms that matched Stonbrak's. 'Some of my people come here to mine the wastes. A pretty penny in ivory, just waiting to be picked up. There's a clan up Barak-Zon that do nothing else but carve the stuff. Wealthy as the karak kings of old, so they say. Rumour is, at the desert's heart, there's mountains made of molars, and fells of fangs.' He chuckled, and his mirth echoed beneath the golden beard of his mask. 'The teeth of gods and monsters, can you imagine such a thing?'

'You have not travelled to see?' asked Maesa.

'And risk this old lady?' Thringsson patted the gunwale. The metal of his gauntlet clicked. 'Not likely. I've a good trade going here, running the packet through to Ghur. It's dangerous enough sailing the skies of Shyish without looking for trouble. There are bad things out there.'

'I have heard there are dangers in the desert,' said Maesa.

'Aye, there are,' said Thringsson. 'In the air above it too.' They looked out across a sky that was unusually bright for Shyish, almost the same blue as that of kinder realms. Thringsson sucked his teeth thoughtfully. 'It's getting worse everywhere in Shyish. Strange tidings. One thing's for sure, I and my crew won't be heading back this way for a while.'

Maesa turned his steady gaze on the captain. 'What rumours?'

'Haven't you heard?' said Thringsson. 'All sorts of talk. The dead are restless.' He grunted. 'Well, more restless than usual. They say the Great Necromancer is on the move, that he has designs on the other realms.' He lowered his voice. 'They say he plans war. I am surprised you have not heard.'

'I have errands of my own,' said the aelf.

'We'll keep a sharp lookout while we're sailing here. The Argent Gate is the swiftest road for Ghur, but it is a perilous one. We might need that bow of yours, lordly aelf, before our voyage is done.' He gave one last look to the horizon. 'I'll be seeing you,' he said, then sauntered away.

'Not if I see thee first,' said Shattercap darkly, though not quite loud enough for the duardin to hear; he was nervous of Thringsson's pistol.

Maesa patted him absent-mindedly. A side wind blew the aelf's hair into long, whipping cords. They flew directly away from the dawn, and the desert was still in the grip of earliest day. Further out, it remained dark, yet already Maesa could see what the duardin said was true. The ground became uneven, badlands made of teeth. Clouds rushed in scattered groups, their undersides stained orange by Hysh's swelling power. It was beautiful. Despite his long life, Maesa had never before flown upon a Kharadron sky-ship, and the experience fascinated him.

Flecki Grimsdottir's Pride was not particularly big; Maesa had trod the stones of floating castles, and islands in the sky as large as countries. The realms were replete with wonders of all kinds, yet the ship was remarkable, a hundred-foot-long artefact of metal held up against gravity's insistence by a combination of ingenuity and magic. Three globular aether-endrins took the place of sails. It was richly appointed to attract paying passengers, of which it carried a score in small but luxurious cabins. Cannons manned by watchful duardin sat upon the forecastle and the poop deck, and more guns bristled from the sides.

'There are enough firearms upon this vessel to put a hold tower to shame,' said Idenkor Stonbrak as he joined Maesa at the rail. His words were neither said as a compliment or in envy, but were a dour, grumbling mixture of both.

'The captain insists this is not a ship of war,' said Maesa, 'but must sail dangerous skies.'

'It's a lot of unnecessary firepower, that's what it is. Show-offs, they are,' he pronounced. 'What kind of duardin lives in the sky?'

Stonbrak popped his pipe in his mouth and cursed as he attempted to light it, as each match he struck blew out in the wind. Over his armour he wore a fur-trimmed coat, and slitted goggles over his eyes against the light. Being a duardin of Ulgu, the brightness pained him, and made him irritable. He groaned and gave up when a match head sparked, fell free and burned a hole in his beard before blowing out like all the rest.

Shattercap giggled. Stonbrak scowled.

'Aren't you cold, aelf?' he said.

'I am rarely cold,' said Maesa.

'Typical,' said Stonbrak. He looked into his pipe bowl disappointedly.

A crew member came up and stopped directly in front of the merchant. Stonbrak peered at him. For a moment they stared each other down like bull tauruses about to fight, slit goggles to crystal lens, then the Kharadron lifted up a small blowtorch, which ignited with a button push. A soft, roaring spike of blue flame burned steadily. Stonbrak put his pipe back in his mouth. The other duardin lit it for him and went away without a word.

'See, show-offs,' grumbled Stonbrak. His beard blew back over his shoulder. His mane of grey hair pushed flat against his head. 'Still,' he said grudgingly, 'this Thringsson's got a talent for commerce. He was bragging about it to me. The passengers are where the real money is.' He gestured with his pipestem at the few other passengers strolling the deck. 'Carrying mail between the free cities of Sigmar avails him of the licences necessary to enter each. But the passengers pay more. Quite clever, I have to admit. He makes so much from them, he offered to rebuild the inn of Master Horrin so passengers have still got someplace to gather, though Horrin's going to need a new name for it, and the money will only be a loan.'

'What do they hide beneath their helmets?' said Maesa, watching the crew. Condensation beaded the metal and the rigging of the *Flecki Grimsdottir's Pride*. The duardin were busy mopping water up from the deck, and knocking the hawsers holding the ship to its endrin globes, making them vibrate and sending the water leaping off in bright silver sprays.

'What? Their faces, of course,' said Stonbrak. 'They rarely remove their helms, but I hear they're duardin through and through. Apart from showing off so much,' he said in the direction of a passing crewman. 'And apart from living with thin air under their boots rather than good, honest stone!' he added, even more loudly.

'Many a wicked face has hidden behind a fair mask,' said Maesa.

'True, but can't you see these are honest folk?' said Stonbrak, suddenly leaping to the Kharadrons' defence, now they were being criticised by an aelf. He shook his head. 'You are suspicious people. They gave me the tools to fix my armour.' He knocked his knuckles against his chest. 'They found me the gold to make this!' He grinned broadly. A finely made replacement for the tooth lost at the inn glinted in the morning. 'Fine people.'

Maesa raised his eyebrow, but said nothing.

The lookout by the bowsprit straps leaned back in from his perch and called through a cupped hand 'Realmgate ho! The Argent Gate is in sight!'

In the distance, over the desert, a gash of silvery light split the sky. Its top and bottom were embraced by floating machines placed there in ancient times. Near these the edges of the gap were smooth, but towards the centre, away from the devices, the boundary between the gate and the realm of Shyish was in flux, and shimmered violently.

'Aha! We are nearly there. Duardin ingenuity. You can't beat it. You'd never find anything like this built by an aelf.'

'Thou art bald,' said Shattercap mockingly.

'I am not!' blustered Stonbrak.

'Yes thou art, I see the shining of pinky skin. The wind has blown your hair flat.' Shattercap tittered. 'That is why thou combest it so high! So vain, master merchant.'

A cry from far below distracted Maesa's attention. He looked over the gunwale of the ship.

'I ought to knock you from the damn aelf's shoulder,' growled Stonbrak, plumping up his hair. 'Bald indeed.'

'Quiet, the both of you.' Maesa's keen eyes darted across the landscape. 'I hear something.'

'What?' said Stonbrak. He thrust his head over the edge and stared at the desert. 'By Grungni's second-best hammer, that is a long drop,' he said uneasily, though pride prevented him from bringing his head back in. 'What are you looking at? I hear nothing.'

'I cannot be sure, a thin screech. There!' Maesa pointed at movement on the desert floor where a jumbled pile of giant tusks were heaped, their arches making dark caves. Stonbrak squinted through his goggles, not seeing what the prince discerned. By the time he spied the pale bodies of the things below, they were already squirming their way out of their lairs and spreading membranous wings to leap into the air. They flapped laboriously at first, moving up into the sky with effort, but once airborne, their flight steadied, and they beat swiftly towards the *Flecki Grimsdottir's Pride*.

'Is it me, or are those beasts rather large?' said Stonbrak. 'I am not one to shy away from a good fight, but we are a long way from the ground.'

'Captain!' Maesa called up to the ship's wheel, where Thringsson was speaking to the helmsman. 'Captain! I would have a word with you, of some urgency.'

Thringsson caught the tone of warning in Maesa's voice, and clanked down the steps from the stern.

'Beasts approach from the ground,' said Maesa. He pointed to the bat-like shapes rising towards them.

Thringsson cursed and turned back from the rail. 'All hands, battle stations,' he bellowed. 'All passengers below. Now!' A whistle shrieked three times. The crew stopped what they were doing and their movements stepped up a gear. They hurried about, pulling covers off swivel guns, while the broadside cannons pushed their muzzles out of their hatches. The ship's purser rounded up the collection of rich merchants and officials braving the cold, and herded them downstairs.

'Can we run for the gate?' asked Stonbrak.

'We can, but we won't outpace them. Mister Grundun, full speed ahead. All power to the aethermatic endrins!' he shouted to his helmsman. 'Best get below if I were you.'

'My companions and I will aid you,' said Maesa.

'We will?' shrieked Shattercap.

'Of course, of course,' said Stonbrak. He loosened his axe in its loops. 'What are they?'

'Terrorgheists, undead beasts,' said Thringsson. 'These here are unbound, wild, deadly, an odd breed. We've got a fight on our hands.'

He shouted out more orders, and made to go.

'How?' said Stonbrak. 'How are they odd? Apart from being undead bats with a forty-foot wingspan?'

They could hear Thringsson's grin in his voice. 'This lot eat teeth.'

'They wants my teeth!?' Shattercap clasped scrawny fingers over his mouth.

'Aye!' shouted Thringsson with a laugh, clambering back to his captain's station. 'The fresher the better.'

Shattercap whimpered. Maesa took out and strung his bow. The Terrorgheists were flapping towards the ship, approaching the same altitude now, and gaining from the stern. *Flecki Grimsdottir's Pride* hooted from steam vents and aether-whistles, pushing forward. The aft gun boomed, spitting out a long harpoon that hissed back the way they had come at the first Terrorgheist. It shrieked and folded its wings like crumpled paper, causing the gunner to let out a shout of triumph, but the beast had dodged the missile, which fell clearly away to the ground as a thin black line, missing the beast entirely. The Terrorgheist righted itself, and with a piercing shriek beat its wings again and came at the ship, its fellows close behind.

'An additional half share to the first one to bring a gheist down!' Thringsson bellowed. The promise urged his crew on remarkably.

'Just get it here to my axe,' growled Stonbrak. 'All this faffing about with harpoons!'

Maesa counted seven of the great bats. They split as they approached, seeking to surround the Kharadron vessel. Thringsson's crew was only fourteen in total, but every one was heavily armed according to his own tastes, a selection of pistols of differing designs supplemented by swords, gaffes and other blades, all humming with the power of the duardin's strange alchemical sciences. One of Thringsson's officers opened up a locker and passed out long guns to the four not working the ship's heavier weaponry. He whistled shrilly, and gestured at Stonbrak.

'Oi! *Khazbokigrin!*' he shouted. 'Want a gun?'

Maesa knew a little of duardin speech, but he didn't recognise the word. Stonbrak, however, bristled.

'Why I ought to...' he growled.

'What?' said Maesa.

'He called me "little mining stone foot". It's their idea of an insult.'

The Kharadron Overlord approached and held out the weapon. 'Pull the trigger here,' he said, in outrageously accented common speech. 'Point the–'

'I know how to fire a gun!' said Stonbrak, and snatched it from the officer.

'Not one like this, mud clumper,' said the officer. 'And you, fancy elgi, do you want one? Minimal charge, I'll cut you a fine deal. But I'll bet knowing your sort you'll want to keep to your sticks.' He said this in an altogether insolent way.

'My bow will suffice,' said Maesa.

'Aye, well, make it count,' said the officer, and returned to his duties.

Flecki Grimsdottir's Pride lurched upward as energy poured into the aether-endrins. Brilliant light glowed from the portholes set into the spheres containing the mechanisms. For a few minutes the ship had the better of its pursuers. They did not fall back, but neither did they gain upon the vessel. The Argent Gate's silvery shine grew in the sky.

'Come on!' Thringsson shouted. 'Come on, lads, bring her up. Full power!'

The boat's bell clanged. The aether-endrins hummed. Slowly, they pulled ahead.

Were it not for a quirk of fate, the *Flecki Grimsdottir's Pride* would have outpaced its pursuers, but Maesa felt the wind change, switching capriciously from abeam the boat to astern. The great bats' ragged wings bellied like sails. Sped on, they came shrieking at the ship.

The sky harpoon flung out its missile again, this time catching one of the Terrorgheists in the wing and ripping away the leathery membrane. The beast fell out of the fight in an uncontrollable spin, fluttering to the plain far below.

'Aha!' cried Thringsson. 'Nothing stops a duardin packet ship!'

'Take that! And that!' shouted Stonbrak. 'Ha ha!' he cried triumphantly, as aether-bullets from his borrowed weapon drove one of the Terrorgheists back. 'See that, princeling? I'll down it yet! I'll have it properly dead, so swear I, Idenkor Stonbrak!'

Maesa followed another of the beasts with keen aelven vision. When it was close enough, he drew his bow, tracking the passage of the creature below the boat, and loosed the arrow. For a moment it appeared that it would miss, arcing away from the beast, and Stonbrak snorted, but the Terrorgheist moved over currents in the air, pitching up at the exact moment required for the arrow to punch through its left eye into its rotten brain, ending its unnatural half-life. It fell like a wet rag through the sky.

'Thou wert saying?' said Shattercap slyly. The duardin muttered something foul-tempered under his breath and fired his own weapon at the foe.

Aethermatic weapons cracked and popped all around the skyship, driving back the creatures from its sides. One gheist chanced the endrins, but the crew were quick to defend this most important and vulnerable part of their craft. Stonbrak joined them, and this time he had cause to shout with glee, as his shot punched a big hole in the creature's side, causing it to scream and flap clumsily off.

The ship was close to its goal. The gate was a shimmering curtain the colour of moonlit rain that screened out the sky.

Stonbrak grinned. 'Yes, by Grungni and by Grimnir! See the genius of the duardin at work, aelf! We're home free!'

'I think not,' said Maesa.

The Terrorgheists were not done. As the gate filled their view from top to bottom, a beast mightier than the others landed on the prow. The ship dipped. The duardin crew opened fire on it at once, but it clambered on board, smashing aside the foregun with a head as huge as a cart. A duardin was sent flailing over the side by a flicked wing, his safety line paying rapidly out and snapping taut.

The magical gate that led from one realm to another was within a spear's cast of the boat, but Thringsson grabbed the wheel from his helmsman and spun it hard to the side, sending the ship into a lurching turn.

'Kill it!' yelled Thringsson. 'Get that thing off my ship! We'll not get through till it's gone!'

A swivel gunner brought his gun round and blasted a shot from his cannon at point-blank range. It was loaded with scatter-shot designed to hole the wings of enemies like the gheist, and it shredded the skin to tatters. The beast squealed. Its head plunged down on its long, flexible neck, and bit the gunner in half. The ship swayed as the Terrorgheist knuckled its way up the deck. Duardin fired guns at it, breaking holes in its furred hide. Thick, rotten blood poured from its wounds, and it shrieked again, so high and sharp Shattercap clapped his hands over his ears and sobbed with pain.

Flecki Grimsdottir's Pride swung away from the Argent Gate. The silver wall gave way to blue sky.

'What is he doing?' Stonbrak said. 'Go through the gate!' he shouted. 'Flee, captain, flee!'

'Not likely,' shouted Thringsson back. He was still working the wheel hard, spinning it through his hands. 'The gate is warded on the Sundsfor side, and the magic will break us in two. We'll go through without it or not at all.'

The beast clambered its way forward, weirdly agile on the deck. It knocked Thringsson's crew aside and bit off their limbs. Screams mingled with its roars and the sound of overworked engines.

Stonbrak braced himself against the angle of the deck. Maesa stood lightly.

'Are you not going to do anything?' Stonbrak asked. 'Shoot it through the eye or something – you bloody aelves are always going on about how marvellous you are with those bows of yours. Kill it!'

Maesa quietly unstrung his bow, and put it away.

'Oh, that's just marvellous,' said Stonbrak. He hefted his axe. 'I'll do it myself then. I've lived a long time anyway. *Khazuk-ha!*' He shouted a war cry older than the realms themselves, and hurled himself into battle.

Stonbrak joined the Kharadron duardin in a hopeless fight. Their aethermatic weapons chewed into the Terrorgheist's body, but the beast used its wings to shield its vulnerable parts. Though the skin was delicate, the bones of its massively elongated fingers were hard as iron, and the duardin could not land a telling blow. Stonbrak's axe shone with runic power. Kharadron blades hummed with arcane science, but the Terrorgheist pressed them back, slaying one of the crew and seriously injuring another.

Stonbrak found himself face to face with the snarling beast. His axe bit deep through fur, bringing forth a welling of necrotic fluid. The creature hit him in return with its forelimbs, hurling him backwards hard, into the rigging.

'That won't do, my little friend,' said Stonbrak, and clambered back to his feet, ready to fight on. He grinned at the creature's weakened state.

A blur in grey and green passed in front of him. Maesa danced around the beast, provoking it to strike him with its fanged maw. He leapt as it bit, and as easily as if he mounted a stair, stepped onto its neck, and drove his wooden sword down.

A blinding glare of green magic shone from the back of the creature's skull. The beast doubled, a spectre lifting from the corporeal form. As its mortal body died a second time, the bound soul flapped madly, poised between life and death, before being sucked away into the Song of Thorns with a shriek Stonbrak would never forget.

The others took fright and flew madly away, the last shots of the duardin chasing them back towards their roosts. Maesa stepped down from the back of the creature. Even now, it was desiccating and curling up into itself. Greying lips shrank from sword-long fangs. Eyes shrivelled to black pits. Ears dried and crumbled. Its tendons dried and muscles withered, pulling it into a smaller, pathetic shrivel.

'What manner of sword is that?' said Stonbrak. 'I saw it suck in the souls of the ghasts at the inn, but this...' He toed the desiccated corpse of the great bat. Its skin broke at the gentlest touch, collapsing to dust that blew off in the wind.

'Never ask me again,' said Maesa, sheathing the Song of Thorns. The blade made a wooden clack on the scabbard.

'Yes, never ask him again,' said Shattercap.

'But why?' said Stonbrak. 'What are you hiding, Maesa?'

The aelf strode past him. Shattercap hopped around on the prince's shoulder and stuck out his tongue.

The ship's bell rang three times.

'All clear!' shouted Thringsson's mate.

The lookout clattered back down to the shattered remains of his post. 'All clear!' he called

'All clear!' one of his fellows responded from the stern.

'Make that corpse secure!' Thringsson commanded. He slid down the rails of the steps leading from the poop to the main deck. 'I know plenty of sages who'd pay for the remains,' he said to Stonbrak. 'Enough to get them bidding against each other.' He laughed to himself. 'Bring us about! Back on course, lads! Lower speed for safe passage. We make for Ghur.'

Maesa helped the wounded as best he could. Four of Thringsson's crew were dead. Another three were badly hurt. The duardin knocked over the side was hauled up by his wire. The ship came about in a wide arc, and headed directly for the Argent Gate.

Shining metallic air confronted them, bright as quicksilver. The ship pierced the veil dividing Shyish from Ghur. Ripples spread across the surface as the vessel passed through, and as the veil moved over them, the sheen became a silvery haze, and the other side was discernible. For a moment Stonbrak and Maesa were in two worlds, blue skies edged with purple over a plain of teeth to the rear, a city basking in an amber noon to the fore.

Then they were through. Shyish was behind them. Ghur spread out its wild lands in every direction. A city of flat-roofed white buildings stepped down an immense, slope-topped mesa. Gargantuan walls protected it. Dusty plains stretched away to a ring of mountains some miles in the distance.

'Here we are then,' announced Thringsson as his shaking passengers emerged into the daylight. 'Gorksmak Crater, and the city of Sundsfor in the kingdom of Estraga. Welcome to Ghur.'

CHAPTER FOURTEEN

INTO GHUR

Maesa and Stonbrak disembarked at Sundsfor at Kharadron docks built into the top of the mesa's cliffs. Thringsson wished them well only after they had paid the remainder of their fares. Maesa and Stonbrak collected their luggage from the hold. Thereafter they passed through the Kharadron enclave, which was large, Stonbrak muttering all the while about the odd ways of his cousins, but in truth they seemed not all that strange once they entered the streets of the city.

Sundsfor had a large population of duardin of many nations. There were duardin in exotic robes made for hot climes. Fyreslayers walked and talked with Dispossessed. Wiry warriors in painted leather armour rubbed shoulders with those sweating in heavy suits of plate, and, most scandalous of all to Stonbrak, duardin whose beards were part shaved into outlandish patterns, the bare patches between dark with tattoos. The diversity on display did not stop with Grungni's folk, and the rest of the city's inhabitants were drawn from all kinds of creatures, from hulking ogor mercenaries to secretive aelves and rarer beings besides.

'What I don't understand is why supposedly intelligent folk pay these sky pirates so much,' said Stonbrak, as they walked down one of the city's streets. Not one of them were level, but all comprised broad steps, dozens of feet wide and nearly as many deep, that led down from the mesa's peak. 'It's criminal, I say. And did you see them? They were glad their crewmates were gone! Bigger shares all round, I heard them saying to each other! Where's their honour? They need some competition. They've got arrogant. Those aether-ships are impressive, I'll grant you, but I'd like to see them out-fly a paraffin vapour gyrocopter.' He shook his head. 'That'd give them a run for their money. Times are changing, that's for sure, and not for the better, mark my words. Time was you'd never get a duardin behave that way. Never!'

Maesa ignored him as much as was polite, dropping as few interjections as possible into the conversation, if it could be described as such. Stonbrak didn't seem to notice or to mind, but kept up a steady stream of grumbling about the state of the realms, and of duardin and of men, and how things were less impressive than they had been in the past.

Maesa's own thoughts were occupied with the tasks to come. The acquisition of Aturathi's eye offered him great hope, so much that he thought his heart would burst with it. He had secured Ellamar's grave-sand, and if he could restore Aturathi, he could ask the aelementor how to bring her back for good. He sensed the end was near, that his years of wandering were coming to a close, and soon he would hold his beloved in his arms again. Such joy had him in its grip he fought to control it. If Maesa gave in to it, it would overwhelm him, and he might wander far and forget his purpose as he lost himself in sensation. Maesa therefore put his considerable self-restraint into action. Stonbrak would never know that Maesa could have burst into laughter, kissed him and danced wildly down the street-steps of Sundsfor with him in his arms. It was all hidden. Maesa kept his facade intact: alert, cold, dignified, deadly.

Sundsfor possessed three realmgates of note. None would take them directly to Settler's Gain in Hysh. Quasque had said he planned to travel to Irb and take the gate there, but Irb was distant, and Maesa would know if there were a quicker way.

The Institute of Cartomancers operated in a building dry with the dust of old paper. Robed men went about serious business, their servants pushing wheeled carts piled high with atlases and rolled maps. Whispered conversations hissed through high halls. Giant, framed depictions of lost kingdoms hung on the walls, their ink faded and parchment fragmentary. The maps the prince sought were new, kept as scrolls within towering stacks that occupied most of the establishment.

Gloved hands trembling with age unrolled one such scroll upon a shining table. The man was extremely ancient by human standards, though nothing in years to either the duardin or the aelf. He knew his business, and when he traced the lines linking realm to realm his fingers became firm. A boy servant kept the scholar's gossamer-fine hair off the map, and he peered through his many-lensed spectacles with grave authority.

'Departing through the Hyshian Gate of Sundsfor will take you to the Realm of Light, but it is many years' travel from there to Settler's Gain in Xintil. I have plotted a route through several realms to see if there is a quicker method of arrival, but such traversals of multiple realmgates can be perilous, and it seems foolish when, like you say, there is a realmgate in Irb that will take you directly to your destination.'

'I know these ways,' said Maesa. 'I am interested in new routes that may have opened in recent years.'

'How recent?' croaked the old man.

'Within the last century, maybe longer.' Maesa's perfectly smooth face creased in a frown. A sudden disquiet had him. 'I have passed this way before. But when…?'

'You didn't tell me you'd been here before,' said Stonbrak.

'I have. I…' The memory was elusive. 'I cannot remember,' he was forced to say. 'I have been here, but how and when and with whom, I have no recollection.'

'I thought you aelves forgot nothing,' said Stonbrak.

'I…'

'Is there something amiss?' asked the sage. He remained absorbed by his map, clearly more interested in ancient marks than his clients.

Maesa shook his head. 'It is not important.'

'Well, there are no other routes than these you see here. Nothing new, nothing ancient reopened, nothing lost rediscovered.' The sage looked up very slowly, as if afraid his head would fall from the stalk of his neck. He smiled apologetically. He had grey teeth.

'Then Irb it is,' said Maesa.

'How far is this city?' asked Stonbrak.

'Three hundred leagues,' said the sage. 'It is the quickest route to where you wish to go, and assuredly the safest, though no road through the realms is entirely without danger.'

The sage continued to peruse his map, tracing the loops of the realms' orbital tracks with his finger, as if he longed to join them in the aether. His velvet glove rasped on paper, but his other hand reached out and patted the plain wooden box at the edge of his table, into which there was set a hole.

Maesa deposited a small Ghyranese emerald. The man, without looking, patted it again.

'More daylight robbery,' muttered Stonbrak, as Maesa added a second gem.

'Tell me, lord prince,' said the sage. 'Your kind is well known for their mastery of travel. I am learned in such matters, and know of your hidden networks of glades that link the realms. Why do you not travel that road?'

'I am not welcome in the greenways any longer,' said Maesa. 'Good day, sage. We thank you for your services.'

'Costly services,' harrumphed Stonbrak.

Shattercap poked his head out from under Maesa's hood and bared his hooked teeth at the sage, but he was lost in the wonders of places he would never see. Shattercap contented himself with giving the man's servant a grin that would haunt his nightmares forever.

They passed back out into the white streets and the heat of the day.

'These Hyshians better be glad to get their stone back,' said Stonbrak. 'This trip is getting expensive.' He sniffed at the air, and pulled up his belt. His stomach gurgled with lordly volume. 'I'm hungry. What do you say to a spot of lunch?'

Maesa nodded. His joy was less now, clouded with dismay. He wracked his mind to place his visit to Sundsfor, but he could not.

'That would be agreeable,' said Maesa.

During lunch Stonbrak consumed a quantity of mead and became irksomely wistful, reciting sad tales of lost duardin glories, of which he seemed to have an inexhaustible supply. As they moved through the city afterwards, he complained often about the brightness of the day. 'I am a duardin of Ulgu!' he would say to anyone that would listen.

Sundsfor was large, and the going through its streets slow. The afternoon passed and the heat dropped, and more people came out of their workshops and homes to make their way to the city's night markets. To avoid the crowds, the companions kept to the wider thoroughfares. Nearer the great walls circling the city, the mesa became steeper, with the lowermost wards built into the cliffs themselves, and the streets meandered back and forth to accommodate the increased gradient. Hysh sank from the heavens, flashing off the gold statues adorning the citadel of the Sundered Brotherhood Stormhost at the top of the mesa. Duardin rune lamps ignited with small cracks as the shadows deepened, and the city took on a carnival air. With a sigh of relief, Stonbrak removed his goggles.

By nightfall they reached one of the main gates. It remained open, and a flood of people were coming and going. Maesa and Stonbrak went out onto a viaduct built out from the gate that, in contrast to the city streets, struck out arrow-straight and dropped with gentle declivity directly towards the plain.

'Now that is proper engineering,' said Stonbrak admiringly.

At five miles long, the viaduct took some time to traverse. Traffic was kept in orderly lines, inwards and outwards, by duardin and human guards in the city livery. Gate castles every mile spanned the road, and in two places the viaduct was broken by immense metal drawbridges decorated with images of Sigmar and the duardin brother gods.

At the foot of the causeway was a lesser town, close to a shanty at the edges, and poorly planned compared to the great city on the mesa. Hawkers crowded the road, shouting out their wares and services, not all of them of a good and clean sort. Maesa and Stonbrak headed for one of the better inns, intending to set out across the plain of the Gorksmak at dawn. Stonbrak consumed even more mead and ale at the inn.

Daybreak brought a sore head for the duardin and a hearty if unsophisticated breakfast for them both. At Maesa's insistence, they secured a mount for Stonbrak. He would accept only an emora, a stumpy, flightless bird with legs as thick as his own, but if Stonbrak hoped to find a docile, slow beast, he was mistaken, for it was swift as the wind and sharp-tempered. Eventually, after

Maesa had watched the wailing duardin borne round and round in circles, he caught the emora's reins and bound its beak, then led it away from the scruffy town at the terminus of the viaduct.

'Duardin do not ride!' said Stonbrak. 'I don't see why we can't both just walk. You're walking,' he added. They went against long streams of wagons laden with meat hunted on the plains beyond the shield mountains.

'You must ride, because when Aelphis returns to me, you will not be able to keep up, and you are too stout for him to comfortably carry.' Maesa gave a sly smile.

'Something's got into you, prince,' said Stonbrak. 'Your manner's changed.'

'I am in good spirits,' said Maesa.

'He is happy, fat bearded one,' said Shattercap. 'Dost thou know happy, or art thou all a-grumbly the whole time?'

'I liked it better when you were hiding in the aelf's hood,' said Stonbrak.

'No need to hide now! Out in the countryside. Very nice too,' said Shattercap. He breathed the air deeply. 'I smell trees!'

'In all this dust?' Stonbrak coughed.

After a time, the three of them went off the highway. Sundsfor had no agriculture of its own, trading meat for grain. Aside from a few scrubby fields of vines lining the road, the plains were largely unspoilt: arid, rocky, but covered in a savannah of tall grasses that supported a wealth of life. Sundsfor stood white and mighty in the centre of the crater, the Argent Gate shining in the sky over the citadel, dominating the landscape for leagues, but it and the road to it with its crawling ant line of carts were the only signs of civilisation. In less than three hours they had entered the true wilds, where creatures bounded from the underbrush and hungry beasts watched from dry woods.

Towards the mountains circling the crater, the ground rumpled.

They crested several ridges, each higher than the last, when unexpectedly a moist, forested valley opened before them. Maesa led Stonbrak's mount down a path the duardin would have never seen. Woodland silences engulfed them, broken by snatches of birdsong.

'You knew this was here!' said Stonbrak.

'Yes,' said Maesa.

'Why did you not tell me where we were going?'

'You were surprised by the forest?'

'Yes, I was,' said Stonbrak.

'Then the emotion you felt was worth keeping our destination from you.'

'Too busy getting used to this damn cockerel you've got me perched on,' said Stonbrak. The emora made a rattling call. Stonbrak pulled a face and shifted about. 'My backside's getting sore.'

'You must grow accustomed to it.'

Shattercap snored in Maesa's hood.

The sound of rushing water came to them from further in the forest, and soon they reached a gorge. Maesa turned widdershins, working his way up the gorge. Though of impressive depth, the gorge ended suddenly at a waterfall where a river fell loudly from the mountains. Clouds of cool mist rose like smoke from the depths, and where the trees parted, the light of Hysh coloured them with rainbows.

To the side of the waterfall was a glade full of dappled light. At its centre was an ancient stone covered in ivy. There were dolmens all over the realms, and as such Stonbrak thought it unremarkable, until Maesa dropped the reins of the emora and said, 'We are here.'

As the aelf approached the stone, green light shone from carvings the duardin could have sworn were not there moments before.

Nervously, Stonbrak slid from his mount's bony back. Maesa reached the stone, the foliage rustled and parted. The aelf pressed the flat of his hand against the rock. The green light burst from the carved channels and sped into the air in looping patterns, circling the aelf before winding themselves together into an arch of vines made entirely of light. Flowers budded on the arch. Creatures like Shattercap peered out from between the stalks. The spite awoke and crouched low, hiding from his fellows, his ears flat against his head in a gesture of submission, though they were all much smaller than he.

'You look upon something no outsider gets to see, Idenkor Stonbrak. This is a greenway gate to the ley-roads, the means by which my broken kindred move from realm to realm. This waystone marks the entrance. Only one of my blood can open it. You will never see this again. Count yourself privileged.' Maesa left one hand pressed against the rock, but cupped the other to his mouth and let out a trilling call.

The spites in the gate branches clambered over the foliage. Those with wings flew round the glade in dizzying displays. Stonbrak was no great lover of green nature, but he found himself entranced.

Again, Maesa trilled. This time, a booming call replied. A tattoo of rapid hoofbeats sounded from the gate, growing unnaturally loud, until the glade shook, and Aelphis burst from within trailing the magic of Ghyran. He came kicking and prancing with joy, as lively as a young faun, gambolling round his master with evident delight at their reunion. Magic from his transit glimmered all over his fur, and he seemed greatly invigorated by the trip. He came to Maesa, bent his head, and with a tenderness that moved the gruff Stonbrak, nuzzled the prince.

Maesa removed his hand from the stone. The lights faded. The gate disappeared, its vanishing marked by the blinking of tiny, spiteful eyes.

The glade was a glade. The stone was a stone. No sign of the secret greenway was left, only Aelphis attested to its presence.

The ritual done, Maesa set about loading the beast with his

packs. From a sack he took out riding tack that seemed far too small, until he unfolded it, and by some cunning contrivance it became a saddle and bridle large enough for the beast. Stonbrak swore at his own mount as it pecked hard at the earth.

'It would be mighty handy if we could go that way,' said Stonbrak.

'We cannot,' said Maesa. 'The gate would not have accepted you. Even an aelf of another kindred would struggle to pass through.'

'But you could have gone,' said Stonbrak.

'I could. I chose not to.' Maesa rearranged Aelphis' burden. Shattercap jumped down and sniffed suspiciously at the stone, pressing his hand against it repeatedly in the hope of gaining a reaction.

'Why make it harder for yourself? I am pretty sure my company is not what kept you from going that way.'

'No,' said Maesa. He beckoned to Shattercap, who reluctantly left the rock and scurried back up the prince's cloak. Maesa leapt onto the stag's back. It took Stonbrak considerably more effort to remount his own beast.

'So tell me why, then,' he said when he was in the saddle.

'Because my crime of love is so great in their eyes that if my people caught me in the greenway, they would kill me,' said the prince. 'Now, I suggest you improve your riding quickly. We have a long way to go.'

CHAPTER FIFTEEN

OVER THE MOUNTAIN

They left the crater by means of a hidden pass. From there they descended the mountain's outer slopes into arid wasteland. In winter, hard rains carved gullies into soft stone then fled along the channels, leaving the place parched and deadly in other seasons. A day's uncomfortable riding had them across and into better terrain of open woodland. These woods got thicker, until they merged into a forest full of animal cries and beady eyes.

Maesa took an overgrown road where a surface of fitted stone poked through the leaf mould. A further range of mountains climbed up the horizon, much bigger than those circling the crater, and the track followed, passing through the ruins of a town. As the trees thinned again, the road became clearer, and the aelf and duardin encountered signs of life. At first, burnt-out campfires and the detritus left by hunters, then little farmsteads appeared in clearings, where hobbled goats munched weeds and kitchen gardens occupied terraces. A man and two children watched them pass from some distance away. Sweet blue woodsmoke fragranced the air.

'These houses are ancient, newly repaired. Civilisation returns,' said Stonbrak. He waved at the children. One waved back. The other pressed into her father, who watched stonily over the head of his long woodsman's axe.

'Thousands of years will pass,' said Maesa, 'and these lands will still not see the multitudes of people they hosted in the Age of Myth.'

'Aye, well,' said Stonbrak, looking up at the bare peaks standing guard over the farm. 'At least there are proper mountains here.'

The mountains more than fulfilled Stonbrak's idea of what mountains should be, and without the road would have been all but impassable. In places, it had collapsed and been renewed with lesser skill, but it continued, cuts carved by the ancients taking it directly through the rock where there was no easier route. They went through a village made of mountain slate, the buildings all piled on top of each other on the brink of a cliff. They saw far over the forests fuzzing the foothills. Beyond the trees, the plains were golden expanses, the vegetation on them bright suggestions, like colours on a map. The village people hid themselves away as the pair passed through. A few scrubby fields occupied what little flat land there was. Cairns marked the boundary of the settlement, pennants of ribbons fluttering and snapping from the tops.

Stonbrak peered closely at one as they passed.

'Grungni's beard! Those are skulls, not rocks,' he said. 'What kind of place is this?'

'There is magic on them, masters,' hissed Shattercap. 'Weak magic, poor magic, but magic.'

'Do you sense evil?' asked Maesa.

'Is fear for your children evil?' the spite responded. He was shivering, and had wrapped Maesa's hood about himself again. 'Is it evil to keep snapping teeth away from plump, young flesh? Is it evil to fear the grip of bony hands in the dark?'

'Wishing to avoid those things is not evil, you confounded nuisance!' said Stonbrak.

'Then, wise prince,' said Shattercap, ignoring the duardin, 'there is no evil here, only terror.'

They left the village and ascended. The road switched round above it, and the meanness of hovel and field was accentuated. Stonbrak turned in the saddle of his riding bird.

'Not a soul dares come out,' he said.

'Fear in the night,' said Maesa. He looked at the cairns. 'The dead walk.'

'I thought we'd left all that nonsense behind us in Shyish,' said Stonbrak.

'Something is changing,' said Maesa. 'Everywhere.'

The road wound on and up, nearing the sharp shoulders of the mountains. Loose rock lay dangerously on the slopes above, yet no rubble was scattered along the route, and the travellers guessed someone tended this high way, remote though it was. The route turned around a crag, then led downwards into a corrie seemingly scooped by godlike hands from the mountainside. A dark tarn lay mirrored in the basin. They then knew that the route was maintained for certain, for visible at the back of the corrie was a stone traveller's cabin in good repair, with an attached stable, and as at the village, cairns ringed it, adorned with the same flapping ribbons.

'We'll stop here for the night,' said Maesa.

'Are you sure?' said Stonbrak, peering uneasily about. The light was fading, and he had moved his goggles onto his forehead. 'Maybe we should press on.'

'We will be caught in the open, and you will be cold,' said Maesa.

'I will not!' protested Stonbrak.

'Nevertheless, Shattercap is freezing. I smell snow on the air, and the mounts are tired.'

Stonbrak nodded reluctantly. 'Aye, I'd welcome the chance to use my own feet.' He slipped out of the emora's saddle, and stood with bowed legs. 'Oooooh, that hurts.'

'Stable the beasts,' said Maesa. He came down from Aelphis. 'I shall scout a little. Shattercap will remain here with you.'

Shattercap was blue and shaking head to foot, his teeth bared and clamped hard together. Maesa picked up the spite from his back. He did not complain when Maesa dropped him into Stonbrak's arms, but attempted to burrow into the duardin's beard for warmth.

'Stop that, you little...' muttered Stonbrak, but Shattercap looked so dejected he relented, and parted his beard for him.

Maesa vanished. Stonbrak looked all around but could not see him. He strained his ears but could not hear him. Feeling suddenly exposed, the duardin went about bedding the animals down, whistling defiantly against his own sense of unease.

By the time the aelf came back, it was dark. Aelphis and the emora were in the hut's stable with blankets draped over them, and Stonbrak had a fire going in the simple stove. He hummed an old smelter's song as he prepared a meal from some of their supplies. His encouragements to Shattercap to join in fell on deaf ears, and the spite stared into the fire, shivering miserably.

Maesa announced his return with a sharp series of whistles, then opened the door into the shelter's common room.

'Stew!' said Stonbrak with a grin, gesturing to the pot bubbling on the stove. He lifted the lid and scraped the vegetables he'd been chopping into the mixture, then dusted off his hands. 'Dry stuff mainly. There's nothing to eat in here, and a long list of fees for the use of the hut.'

Maesa said nothing, but sat in a chair by the long table that filled half of the room.

'I paid the fees,' said Stonbrak pointedly.

Maesa glanced at him. He had his hands pressed together. He seemed cold for once. 'My thanks,' he said.

Stonbrak sat in front of him. 'What did you see?'

'Nothing,' said Maesa. 'Some lights in the far western clouds that could have been a storm. The pass goes up again past this vale. It is growing colder, and it will definitely snow tonight.'

'And?' said Stonbrak, filling his pipe.

'There is a presence here. He can sense it better than I.' He nodded at the spite.

Stonbrak's face set. 'Yes. A sense of being watched.'

'We will take turns in sleeping tonight,' said Maesa.

'You don't sleep much anyway,' said Stonbrak, lighting his pipe.

'Tonight I must,' said Maesa. 'This landscape is hard on my soul. There is little of the magic of Ghyran here. It drains me.'

'Then I will take first watch. This country suits my kind,' said Stonbrak. He sucked on his pipe thoughtfully. 'What do you think our watcher wants?'

Maesa shivered slightly. 'It has the touch of death. What else does Nagash want, other than for the living to be the dead?'

Stonbrak nodded and peered at the coals in his pipe bowl. 'Maybe some stew will cheer us up,' he said.

The next day, a steep path took them down into a valley full of resinous pines and thick, perfumed silences. Not long after, they heard their first bird, and the joyful bubbling of streams. The road ceased its back and forth, the incline became shallower, and broadened out so that Maesa and Stonbrak could ride together side by side once more.

The road clung to the side of a ravine where a white river grew fat on tributaries rushing from the peaks. Still they saw no living being.

Evening came quickly. The sky turned a deep blue, then black. To their relief they saw the lights of a substantial village ahead, and before long reached a wooden gatehouse built across the road. Skulls mounted on spikes lined the parapet, dangling bunches of bronze charms. Three men manned the gate, and called out a challenge in some impenetrable local language. When they got no response, they tried the language of Sigmar's realm.

'Halt! Who goes there?'

'Travellers,' said Maesa. 'An aelf and a duardin, we are. Maesa of the Wanderer Clans and Idenkor Stonbrak, merchant of Ulgu. We are passing through on our way to Hysh.'

'You're a long way off the God's Road,' said one of the other guards. His accent was thick, melodious. 'Few come this way. What's your business?'

'Like he said, we're passing through. There is no need for suspicion!' barked Stonbrak. 'We are people of honour. Let us in, we will not trouble you long, and if you have an inn, we'll eat and drink there and make you all a little richer in return.'

The men looked at one another. They didn't appear to know what to do.

'Charms don't say anything,' said the second. He pointed at the wards hanging like fruit from the stakes.

'All right,' said the first. The third remained silent, and goggled at them in disbelief. 'Open the gates.'

'It's not my turn,' said the second.

'Just do it! I'm watch master tonight.'

'Grungni grant me patience,' said Stonbrak out of the side of his mouth. 'This is a crack crew and no mistake. You'd think they'd never seen a duardin come out of the mountains.'

The single gate creaked open. The goggler peered out from behind.

'Light the torches while you're at it,' said the leader. The second guard grumbled and fetched a long burning brand that dripped pitch onto the ground. He lifted it to touch the gate torches alight.

'Welcome, welcome,' said the leader. He lit candles in the skulls with a spill to make their eyes glow. 'Inn's that way.' He pointed up the road. 'Have you had any trouble out there?'

'Only an oppressive feeling in the high pass,' said Maesa to the man, once they'd passed under the gate. It was a crude affair, a single row of palings with a rickety platform behind it.

'Then you're lucky. Dark things are afoot round here. Best be indoors.'

They rode on. The gate shut behind them.

'That wood was fresh cut, and I suspect they are new to the business of watchmen,' said Stonbrak. 'What is going on here?'

The reception they received was lukewarm at best. People watched suspiciously as Maesa and Stonbrak rode down the road. The houses were hidden in the trees, built on large rocks, with foundations of drystone and walls of split timber. The road crossed the river in the village centre on an elegant single-span bridge, and by its side there was a square, surrounded by bigger stone buildings, these mortared and fairly built. One of these was an inn, and the travellers went in.

The locals inside spoke quietly, and watched the strangers suspiciously. The innkeeper was a man of few words, but polite enough, and served them roast ribs. He even found a passable wine for Maesa to drink.

'There is something odd happening here,' said Stonbrak. He lowered his voice to match the quietness of the others in the bar.

Maesa nodded. The prince ate nothing of the food given them, but fed morsels to Shattercap hidden away under the table. Maesa watched the door so intently, Stonbrak couldn't help turning around to look himself.

As he did, it opened, and a man in fine clothes entered. He looked around the bar. As soon as his eyes lit on Maesa and Stonbrak, he hurried to them.

'Uh-oh, here we go,' said the merchant.

The man approached. 'You are the strangers?' he said.

'I don't recall living here, and I don't see many of my folk here, so I'd say your guess is a fair one, manling,' said Stonbrak.

'Good, yes, of course,' said the man nervously. 'My name is Donagelli. I am one of the village council here. I have come... Er, may I?' He indicated a spare seat.

'Please,' said Maesa.

'I just wanted a quiet meal,' said Stonbrak, pointedly tearing meat from a rib.

Donagelli sat down. 'Yes, before I start, are you, well...' He swallowed nervously and worked his hat through his hands. 'Are you warriors? Fighters I mean?'

Maesa put his goblet down. 'I have been. I can be. It is not all I am.'

'I'm a merchant,' said Stonbrak.

'Oh,' said Donagelli disappointedly.

'You will not find a duardin who is not a warrior as well as whatever else he is,' said Maesa.

'Thanks,' said Stonbrak sarcastically.

Donagelli brightened. 'And, if I may ask, since you are an aelf...' He spoke quickly to cover his nerves. 'Do you have magic?'

'A little,' said Maesa.

'More than he lets on,' said Stonbrak gruffly. He doggedly ate his food.

'My friend here has his own enchantments,' said Maesa. 'Runes upon his axe.'

'Oh that's just great,' said Stonbrak. 'Get me completely involved, why don't you?'

'I have a request,' said Donagelli. 'A task. The village council, that is to say, my fellows on the governing table, they chose me to come to you to ask that...'

'What manner of evil troubles you?' Maesa interrupted.

'You know of it?' Donagelli said.

'We felt something in the mountains,' said Stonbrak. 'A beardling with a head like a brick could tell there was something nasty up here.' He tossed his bare bone back onto the plate and looked at Donagelli for the first time. 'Piles of skulls. Enchanted trinkets. Nervous incompetents on a new wall. Why don't you just tell us what's going on? Get it off your chest, manling, so we can decline to help, get a good night's kip and move on.'

'Forgive my friend Idenkor,' said Maesa. 'We have had a hard journey.'

'Yes. Yes, of course, well...' Donagelli looked back and forth between the two, asking permission to continue.

'You may go on,' said Maesa. The innkeeper returned and filled Maesa's goblet. He hung around the table until Donagelli jabbered something at him in the local dialect, and he departed with a scowl.

'Something is hunting us,' Donagelli said. He leaned down onto the table and whispered. 'It started last year, taking our livestock from the high fields. We heard mountain nomads up there had lost people, and we prayed that it would not come near us. But it does. It comes down at night from the peaks. The charms don't scare it any more. It has become bolder. Last week it ventured into the lower pasture, even within sight of Widow Amanta's cottage. We are not safe here. There is talk of abandoning the village, but where would we go? We have been here for generations, through the time of Chaos, and before. This is our home.'

'What are we talking about?' said Stonbrak. 'Be more specific, manling. Big, little, dead, alive, wild, intelligent? There are as many dangerous things in the realms as there are stars in Azyr. What is it?'

'They say it is huge, a grotesque phantom, yet somehow of solid flesh. Long arms, no legs, a terrible mouth. It lives in the place of the dead.'

'Dead then,' said Stonbrak. 'I suppose you want us to go and hunt this thing? Well I'm not interested. Pointy-ears here and I have business in Hysh. Isn't that right?'

Maesa stared at Donagelli. His violet eyes sparkled enigmatically. 'We will help you,' Maesa said.

Stonbrak rolled his eyes. 'Perfect.'

'Now?' said Donagelli. 'I can show you the way. I–'

'Of course not now!' snapped Stonbrak.

'If it hunts at night, we will hunt it in the day,' said Maesa.

'Both of you?' said Donagelli.

'Three of us,' said Maesa. Shattercap poked his head up over the edge of the table. Donagelli gasped.

'Very well,' said Stonbrak. 'Mine's four pints please.'

'What?' Donagelli had gone pale. Shattercap stuck out his tongue at him.

'Do you want us to help you or not? We require payment,' said Stonbrak, pointing at the bar. 'Four pints of your weak manling ale would be a good start. Now. And another plate of meat.' He jutted his chin out at Maesa, making his beard quiver. 'Better get skinny here some more of that grape juice he likes too.'

CHAPTER SIXTEEN

NAGASH'S CURSE

Hysh was high, and the sky dazzling. Wind blew over rocks and through the boughs of a solitary tree no taller than a full-grown man. The hollow knocking of wind chimes made of bones played sinister music. They hung from the gnarled branches of the pine, femurs making xylophone notes, skulls a hollow clocking. They jounced and leapt in the current of air coming off the mountains. Cold came with it, gathered from the high places where no man had ever ventured.

Maesa, Donagelli and Stonbrak strode a rough path. In places it was slick, the bedrock polished bright by generations of feet. Round stones waited to roll under careless boots. Whitewashed rocks marked out the way, but it had been long since the paint had been renewed, and they were hardly any different in colour to the unpainted stones. Stonbrak's boots crunched loudly on ice and gravel. Donagelli's footsteps were lighter and further spread. Maesa made no noise at all, nor did he disturb the stones he stood on.

Stonbrak's pace was as relentless as only a duardin's can be, and he reached the tree first. He stopped in its small shadow, and looked up through his goggles at the chimes.

'That's a grim display, and no mistake,' he said. He took out his kerchief and mopped his brow, then drank from his canteen. The smell of small beer wafted from the top, and he let out an appreciative burp.

Maesa came to a soundless halt beside Stonbrak. Shattercap leaned forward on Maesa's shoulder and sniffed warily.

'I do not like these bony fruit, wicked prince. I do not like their knocking music. The tree is old, old as time. I like it less.'

Donagelli was last to the tree. He was mountain born, but panted in the rarefied air.

'The bones' chimes are not pretty, but they keep back the spirits of the mountain,' he said. 'Before the fiend came, the bones warded this path of the dead to our burial ground. They kept us safe from restless spirits. They warded the monster away for a while too. Not any longer.'

Shattercap hunched low onto Maesa's shoulder. 'And the fiend is beyond?'

'Pah! I doubt it would want to snack upon a mouthful of twigs, forest daemon,' Stonbrak chuckled. 'It might use you as a toothpick after, mind.'

Maesa laid his hand on the tree. It was only a little taller than he. The trunk was twisted round on itself so that it had become fat as a barrel, and was covered with grey, scaly bark.

'You say it haunts the heights all around this place?'

Donagelli nodded fearfully. 'Yes, the pass you came through, and the meadows around the village, above the valley, the tent villages of the high herders. We have not been past the way of bones for months, not since the first of us began to die...'

'Then you are brave to show us the way,' said Maesa.

Stonbrak harrumphed.

'We shall see what can be done. Go back to the valley, Donagelli.'

A look of profound relief broke across Donagelli's face. 'You do not wish me to come with you?'

'Your presence will not be necessary,' said Maesa.

'Thank you, your highness, thank you, master duardin!'

'Wait for our return for three days, no more,' said Maesa.

Donagelli frowned. 'What are we to do if you are not back by then?'

Stonbrak grinned broadly through his beard. 'The good prince means we will not be coming back at all, in that case, so I'd move out if I were you.'

'Very well. Three days, I understand,' said Donagelli. 'Sigmar be with you.'

'Go,' said Maesa.

Donagelli turned gratefully away and started back down the path, his footsteps crunching quickly. He stopped and he shouted over the wind.

'The burial ground is not far. You'll find the beast near there, if it is not inside the walls. That was where it was seen most often, before we abandoned the mountain to its hunger!'

He resumed his descent as quickly as was safe. He was soon out of sight.

'Coward. See him run. Shattercap is scared but Shattercap is going!'

'For once you and I are in agreement, twigling,' Stonbrak grunted dismissively. 'If he and his people had an ounce of iron to them, they'd be up here to burn the thing out themselves.'

Maesa let his hand trail down the bark. 'Do not be too unkind, master duardin. These people are right to be afraid. The being that haunts the mountain cannot be easily overcome. They are not mages or warriors.'

'Ha! Everyone is afraid,' said Stonbrak. 'Courage is hammering fear until it is sharp, and useful. Cowardice is letting fear master you. Is it your habit to help every creature who comes to you for aid? I was looking forward to a day's rest. Now I find myself up this freezing mountain with a monster to face before breakfast.'

'No one is forcing thou to go, bearded one!' Shattercap hissed. 'Not like me,' he whined. 'Poor Shattercap has no choice. Oh, wicked prince!'

Maesa turned away from the tree. The knocking chimes framed his horned helm. 'I help those who I might, Master Stonbrak. There are many injustices in these realms. I am responsible for more than a few. It is my duty to put right those I can.'

'Put it like that, I can see why every peasant with a problem should get a hearing,' said Stonbrak. 'It's not like we have anything important to do.'

'You may mock me, Idenkor Stonbrak, but know that your help is appreciated.'

Stonbrak shrugged the collar of his cloak higher. 'You realise this thing they describe, a great phantom yet of flesh, bearing no legs but with monstrous arms, and beset with an unreasoning hunger that can never be sated...' He sniffed hard. 'It is, in all likelihood, a Mourngul.'

'It is almost certainly so.'

'You know these things are mightily powerful, ravening spectres, and are difficult to lay to rest?' said Stonbrak.

'I have faced worse foes,' said Maesa.

'Go back to your jewel-shop if thou art afraid,' said the spite.

Stonbrak laughed. 'Afraid, afraid? A duardin is never *afraid*, twigling. Besides, I could do with a good scrap. I am merely worried for your master. He is, after all, only an aelf.'

'I thought thou wert interested only in the shinies,' said Shattercap.

'There's more to a duardin than treasure, little twig. I like a fight.

Still, my blade will grow blunt for lack of use if we're not quick, and my stomach's rumbling.' He pulled his runic axe from the loop on his belt. 'It'd be nice to slake my thirst and fill my belly before nightfall. Let's be about it.' Stonbrak pushed on up the hill. 'Are you coming, little twigling?' he called over his shoulder.

'Yes,' said Shattercap miserably.

'He goes where I go.' Maesa drew the Song of Thorns. It rasped out of its scabbard with a round, wooden sound. Once free, its edges glimmered with green magic, and it hummed faintly. 'From here we walk with our weapons drawn.'

'Aye!' Stonbrak shouted back. 'I'll rely on good duardin steel. You stick with your pointy branch, noble prince.' He started to whistle.

Together they headed to the burial ground.

The three of them passed into a deep gulley. Wind carrying an abrasive cargo of grit rattled on Stonbrak's armour. It hooted and moaned through natural sounding chambers, mournful as the clatter of the bone chimes.

'Good stone round here,' said Stonbrak. 'Solid grain. You could make a fine hold in mountains like these!'

He looked up and around the canyon. His armour jingled as he ran his gloved hand along the wall. The leather rasped.

'Very good stone. A shame about this ravine though. If the roof hadn't worn through, this would be a very adaptable cave. I can see it now, carved into shape, good steps, not too deep or steep, alcoves for guards. A good position, defensible. I suppose it could still be covered over...' He frowned to himself, picturing elegant windows in the lumpy rock.

'Duardin have not lived in these mountains for centuries, Master Stonbrak,' said Maesa.

'Perhaps they will again. It is time for the Dispossessed to hew new halls into the mountainsides. Or all other right-thinking people will assume we've all set ourselves on fire, or ascended into the clouds like that Thringsson.'

'Many ways, for many lands,' said Maesa. The gulley was wide enough for them to spread out a little. Maesa walked the centre of the path, while Stonbrak stayed close to the walls.

'Cultural diversity is all fine if you're an aelf, but what about tradition, and the old way of doing things? Our customs served us for generations before all these new-fangled sky-ships. And the Fyreslayers! Maniacs! Arsonists to a duardin. If I had my way, it'd be back to picks, stone and well-crafted–'

Stonbrak's diatribe was brought to a halt by a loud squelch. He screwed his eyes shut.

'Oh my ancestors, what did I step in?'

'He didn't see it!' Shattercap tittered. 'Didn't smell it. Stupid pipe dulls his nose.'

'Oh, these boots are new!' Stonbrak lifted his foot and scraped it on the stone. A blackened carcass was jammed into a small hollow in the rock.

'Then trim your hairy eyebrows, so you can see where you are going!' crowed Shattercap.

'Bah! I'm not afraid of a little blood and guts, spite,' said Stonbrak. Leather creaked and mail jingled as he got down onto his knees to examine the carcass. 'This is a fine mess,' he grunted, then sniffed at it. 'Ach, but that smell! It doesn't look long dead, but it stinks so! Was it… was it a goat? Hard to tell, it's so chewed up.'

Maesa watched him. 'The Mourngul eat, but can never be satisfied. All they consume falls from their ragged stomachs. It is a terrible fate, all the worse because it is suffered by those driven by hunger to desperate acts. Those cursed are rarely guilty of anything other than the need to survive. Nagash is a cruel god.'

'True, aelf, the realms are rarely fair places.' He poked at the animal a few times with his axe haft, then got up. 'I need to cleanse my lungs after that.'

He rummaged through his pouches and fished out his smoking gear, stuffed his pipe, then struck a match in the shelter of a cupped palm. He put it to the bowl, then puffed until he was breathing wreaths of smoke.

'By Grungni and all the Six Smiths, that's better,' he said around the mouthpiece. 'Nothing like a lungful of good duardin smoke-weed to kill off a bad smell.'

'Silly duardin, burning leaves and breathing them.' Shattercap blew a raspberry. 'Stupid!'

'I'll smoke you if you don't learn some manners,' said Stonbrak.

'Hush now, Shattercap,' said Maesa.

The wind blew harder, pelting them with sand. A haunting cry rose and fell ahead.

'We are close,' said Maesa. 'We must be ready.'

'Now that's grand news,' said Stonbrak. Smoke gathered around him quicker than the wind could carry it off. 'If the fiend is near, it means we can have breakfast soon.'

The gulley dwindled to a crack in the rock, and the path left it by steps cut into the stone at the side. At the top, the path continued, lined now by skulls on stakes, to a level area of ground. They were far above the valley. A low wall surrounded grave markers of wood. The air was very dry there, and the oldest of them could have been put into position centuries before. Cairns of stone covered over the bodies. The ground was rock, impossible to dig. An iron gate closed the way into the burial ground, but it had been wrenched askew and hung half off its hinges. A few dwarf pines grew in the corners. Tufts of yellow grass rattled in the breeze.

'Typical human mountain folk,' said Stonbrak disapprovingly. 'Good land's scarce, I understand, but a duardin would have the decency to put the dead in proper tombs, not leave them under piles of stone like this.'

Maesa and Stonbrak approached with their weapons ready and stepped over the bent gate. The burial ground was too big to see all the way across. The land rose ahead of them, hiding part of the cemetery from them altogether. Bone chimes hanging from the trees rattled. Cowbells clonked. Fabric ribbons snapped and fluttered.

Stonbrak advanced ahead cautiously. His foot caught on a stone and kicked it skidding across the bedrock. Not far from the entrance, the cairns were broken into and their rocks scattered. Fragments of bones lay amid the stones.

'It has been defiled,' said Maesa.

'Now that's a crying shame,' said Stonbrak. He knelt down, and picked one up. 'All of them broken. This one's not that old.' He held it up for Maesa to see. 'Cracked open. The marrow gone. The recent dead picked clean!'

Shattercap stiffened and stood on Maesa's shoulder, holding onto one of the prince's antlers. He sniffed in the direction of the peak standing over the burial ground and strained his ears.

'Master… I hear…' he said.

'Yes, over yonder,' said Maesa. 'Up the slope.'

'What can you hear?' demanded Stonbrak. He put the bone back and got up. 'I can hear nothing over this wind. Is it coming?'

'The stout one's hearing needs sharpening as much as his wits,' said Shattercap.

Maesa patted the spite. 'Do not insult our companion. Weeping, Master Stonbrak. That is what we hear.'

Stonbrak tilted his head. 'Of course I could hear it. I just thought it the wind, that's all,' he said defensively.

They crept up the slope, keeping low. On bare rock, Stonbrak moved almost as quietly as Maesa. They reached the brink, keeping in the lee of a beehive cairn more handsomely built than the others. The weeping got louder.

Stonbrak leaned around the rocks, then pulled back in and put a finger to his lips.

'Over there. A human boy. I'd be wary here. There's a glow about him. He is not what he seems. He is almost certainly the beast we seek. We should attack together. I'll take the left, you go–'

Maesa strode past him, directly towards the boy.

'What are you doing?!' Stonbrak hissed after him. 'Where are you going? We should do this together!'

The boy was sat on a grave enclosed by masonry. The oldest graves were the finest, and though eroded by millennia of wind, their craftsmanship was obvious still. The boy was filthy, clad in rags, perhaps fourteen years of age, though both Stonbrak and Maesa found it hard to judge the years of men.

Maesa approached slowly. 'Who are you?' he asked softly. 'Why do you sit upon this grave and weep? There are plenty of places better for you than here.'

'Typical overwrought aelf puffery!' Stonbrak grumbled. He stood up from his hiding place.

The boy looked up suddenly, and gasped. 'An aelf, and a duardin?'

'What is your name, boy?' Maesa asked. Shattercap peered down, shaking in terror.

'Master…' he whimpered. 'Master, please.'

Maesa ignored him. 'What is your name?' he repeated.

'Filippo,' said the boy. 'My name is Filippo. I don't understand, why are you here?'

'We're looking for a creature terrorising these parts,' Stonbrak called from a safe distance. 'I think you know what we're talking about.'

The boy frowned. 'No, I do not. I come here for the peace, and the quiet. I come to forget.' He looked at his hands. The dirt covering his face was tracked by his tears. 'I was once so happy – we lived in the high pastures here, far from the village, friends to the high herders. But the last winter, it was so cold… So very cold. The snows came early, covering over the fields before the hay was in. My father vanished bringing the goats down from the mountain. Frost sabres took our horses. Mother tried to scare them away, but she was wounded, and died.' He shuddered. 'The smell of her wounds… My sister and I were left alone, with nothing to eat. I… I…'

'Uh-oh, here we go, Maesa,' said Stonbrak. 'His eyes! Look at his eyes!'

The boy's eyes became round black holes. His jaw swung loosely from his skull, opening wider with every word, and his voice dropped, becoming deeper, daemonic, tainted by the misery of the hungering dead.

'I was hungry, so hungry,' Filippo said. His fingers were lengthening, drooping like wax heated over a fire. 'She was weak, young. I needed to eat. I chased my sister into the snow, but she couldn't get far. I needed to eat. I was so hungry.'

Maesa stepped back. Filippo's mouth snapped and swung so low it brushed his knees. Grunts escaped the reeking maw his mouth had become. It was impossible to tell if they were meant to be words. His arms seemed to unravel like balls of dropped string, the growing hands slapping onto the ground, where they flopped about with a life of their own. His torso grew. Bones cracked as his ribs shifted under his chest, making his ragged tunic squirm, until with a series of painful snaps they expanded outward, forcing his shoulders wide.

'Grungni's underbeards! It's him all right. Strike now!' Stonbrak called.

'We must wait until its true form is revealed,' said Maesa.

Filippo shook with the pain of his transformation. His spine burst up between his shoulders. His tunic vanished into tattered shreds of glowing ectoplasm. His back arched. His head snapped back, inflating like a bladder filled with air. Sharp teeth ripped out through his gums. His arms continued to grow, until they were twelve feet long. His fingers were as big as swords. Horribly, his legs and lower torso remained those of a small boy. He howled at the sky.

'Hungry! So very, very hungry!'

'By all the gods of Azyr, Maesa, kill the bloody thing!' shouted Stonbrak.

The Mourngul's head snapped round whip-fast. Its arm shot out, knocking Maesa from his feet. The aelf crashed down onto a cairn, sending stones bouncing everywhere.

'I don't like to say I told you so, but I did,' muttered Stonbrak.

The Mourngul howled again, chilling the blood in Stonbrak and Maesa's veins. It reached down, crossed its hands across its waist, then ripped them across its stomach, tearing off its own pelvis and legs, and leaving them to evaporate into ghostly vapours. It lifted itself up on its immense arms and peered down at the prone aelf.

'Right then,' said Stonbrak decisively. 'I'm coming, prince.' He stepped out from behind the cairn and circled around the back of the Mourngul.

'Idenkor, stay back!' called Maesa. He flipped backward as the Mourngul's claw raked down and smashed the remains of the cairn to pieces. Maesa held his sword ready, but the Mourngul was so powerful that he had little chance of successfully parrying its blows. It hopped from hand to hand, its limbs so long it moved with a jerky speed that surprised them.

The duardin was coming up behind the Mourngul. The runes engraved into the axe shone with the trapped light of the forge.

Maesa leapt to the side, dodging another blow, keeping the Mourngul occupied.

'Barak Gorn! Khazuk! Khazuk!' shouted Stonbrak, taking his chance. He broke into a short sprint, and ran up a sturdy grave pile and leapt, bringing his axe down hard on the Mourngul's back. The blade bit deep, and Stonbrak hung from the shaft. The Mourngul let out a piteous howl and began slapping at its back with one hand, hopping about on the other in a circle as it tried to keep its balance.

Stonbrak whooped, swinging around from the Mourngul's back as it flailed away, attempting to dislodge him. 'Aha! Have at you, undead thing. You're keeping me from my breakfast tankard!'

The Mourngul hopped through the graves on one hand, flattening the wooden headboards and smashing cairns. Maesa ran after.

'This will end poorly,' said Shattercap.

'The Song of Thorns will finish it,' said Maesa.

'Be careful, wicked prince! So much magic is within it, one blow will not be enough!'

'Duly noted, small evil.'

The Mourngul swatted at Stonbrak first with one hand, then the other. Failing to knock the duardin free, it slapped both hands flat on the ground, and began to bounce from one to the other, spinning around and around until its hair whipped out around it and Stonbrak was clinging on for his life. Up and down the Mourngul went, neat as a carousel ride at a steam fair.

Suddenly, Stonbrak's axe popped free from the beast's back, and he sailed up and over, arms wheeling, coming down hard among the graves in a hail of displaced stone and splinters of ancient wood, where he lay insensible.

The Mourngul bounded after the merchant, but Maesa leapt into its path. The Song of Thorns passed over the thing's thumping hands, cutting into semi-corporeal flesh. It howled, and snatched its hand away from the pain, became overbalanced and crashed down, coming to rest not far from Stonbrak. It shrieked and pawed at its wound. Ectoplasmic magics leaked from it, dissipating on the air like blood diluting in water.

'Thou hast hurt it!' Shattercap crowed.

Maesa approached cautiously. Downed, the Mourngul was a collection of bones wrapped in sagging flesh, like a tent collapsed in a storm.

'So hungry, I am so hungry! Feed me! Feeeeeed meeeeee!'

It reached out its uninjured hand. Iron-hard claws punched into the rock, and it dragged itself along leaving a trail of glowing fluids to boil off on the ground. It clattered its teeth together, snapping its jaws like steel traps.

'Hungry.'

Maesa held his position, sword ready. Wisps of energy spiralled out from the wounded spectre into the hungering Song of Thorns.

'Look deep within yourself, Filippo!' Maesa shouted over the thing's moaning. 'You are cursed. Fight the magic that imprisons you!'

'Master. Master, it means to strike!' Shattercap warned.

Maesa jumped back as the Mourngul lunged at them. Somehow, it contrived to get its wounded arm underneath itself, and used it like a catapult to fling itself forward. It caught the prince a glancing blow with its shoulder. Maesa felt like he'd been hit by a falling tower. A delicate rib broke and ground under his close-fitting mail, but he managed to turn the impact into a spin, drew back his arm, elbow bent, and scythed the Song of Thorns deep into the creature's shoulder.

The Mourngul screamed. A flood of bright magic was sucked into the Song of Thorns, and it bounded away from the source of the pain.

Maesa let it go. He clutched at his side. His breath came raggedly. 'You were right, small evil. One blow will not finish it.'

'Two will hardly do, either. Hit it again! Hit it again!' shrieked Shattercap.

The Mourngul lolloped around in a wide circle, picking up speed, then switched direction abruptly and came bounding back at the prince. As it came at them, it snatched up a cairn, bones and all, and flung it overarm at the aelf with the force of a trebuchet. Stones bounced down all around him. Maesa was fully occupied ensuring none hit him, and was nearly snatched up as the Mourngul swiped at them on the way past, its nails snagging on his cloak, and spinning him around before it tore free.

'Master!'

The familiar weight of Shattercap vanished from his back. The spite was dragged into the air. He scampered down the cloth, but the Mourngul plucked and snatched at the spite, until it had him pinched between its filthy talons.

'Master, master, it has me! Its touch burns with cold!'

The Mourngul lifted Shattercap high, its mouth tipped back and gaping wide as a pit. Shattercap glanced down and squealed, kicking his legs without effect. The spectre had him fast.

'The mouth, the mouth!' he cried.

'I will devour you, chattering morsel,' the Mourngul howled, and dropped the wriggling spite into its gullet. Shattercap screamed as he fell. 'Hungry, so huuuuunnnnnnnnngry!'

'Shattercap!' Maesa shouted. He held up his sword. 'Ashellan! Unduneth! Callineth! Alarielle, Alarielle, Alarielle!'

The sky flooded with dark clouds. Lightning crackled down from the sky, spearing the Mourngul.

The Mourngul howled. Maesa was already running, the Song of Thorns held back two-handed, ready to thrust like a spear, and he plunged the wooden blade into the beast's hollow chest. The Mourngul staggered backward. Lightning poured from the sky over both of them in electric torrents. Ghostly light glowed within the creature as its essence was dragged into the blade. It fell onto its back, Maesa riding it down and pushing his sword in deeper.

'You are not alone in hungering,' he said through gritted teeth. 'The Song of Thorns is a soul leech. It will eat your essence. Submit to me, and I will end your suffering.'

The creature was diminished. The boy could be seen through the monster. 'Yes! Yes! Please, end the hunger, end the hunger!' he said, in his boy's voice. Then his head shook so fast it blurred, and the Mourngul's grotesque face was snapping again at the aelf, and it spoke deeply once more. 'No,' it said. 'No. Huuuuuungrrryyyyyy!'

The Mourngul pushed through the net of lightning, and swiped Maesa away. Maesa crashed onto his back, jarring his wounded rib. He lay winded as the monster plucked the Song of Thorns from its chest and threw it to one side, where it clattered away, lost among the stones.

The Mourngul's palm slapped onto Maesa, pinning him to the ground. It weighed very little, but the power of its grip was immense.

'I have you now. Hungry!' It bent down, the exposed cartilage in its nose twitching as it sniffed at him. 'Sweet, sweet aelf flesh.'

Drool as cold as frozen graves slipped from the Mourngul's mouth and ran down Maesa's face. Its guts hung from its torso, flapping anchorless in the breeze, dripping digestive juices onto the stones. The aelf arched his back, but he might as well have tried to dislodge a mountain. Grey tombstone teeth descended.

The Mourngul paused. Its ragged stomach made a loud gurgling. It moaned.

One ragged tail of intestine squirmed. A soft hiss of gas escaped the end, and with a wet wriggling, Shattercap fell from the gut and landed on the ground, shocked, but very much alive. He let out a sneeze.

'Ick! Ick! Ick! Shattercap all covered in… Shattercap doesn't want to think about what Shattercap is covered in. Horrid, horrid! Most horrid thing…'

The Mourngul belched. Its long jaw clicked. It looked from the spite to the aelf.

'Hungry.'

'Shattercap!' Maesa gasped from under its crushing claw. 'It has me!'

Shattercap blinked rancid juices from his eyes, and stared at the prince. He jumped up and wrapped his hand in the thing's dangling guts, and yanked, eliciting an agonised howl from the beast. It went back, like a horse dragged by the reins, and Maesa was suddenly free.

'Master, master, I have it!'

The Mourngul bent its head down on its unnaturally long neck, and peered at the spite.

'Morsel! Morsel! Cease your jabbering, and feed me.'

'Uh-oh,' said Shattercap. He released the guts and fled. 'It wants to eat me again! Master! Help me! Cut it down with thy magic blade!'

Maesa ran unevenly in the direction the Song of Thorns had flown.

'Run, Shattercap,' he whispered. 'Run.'

The spite leapt over a grave marker, the Mourngul's hand chasing him, shattering the wood to splinters. Shattercap glanced over his shoulder. Stonbrak was unconscious in a pile of rocks, and he saw the prince was unarmed.

'Your sword! Where is your sword?' he squealed.

Shattercap ran ahead of his pursuer. The Mourngul's furious passage smashed graves and cairns to nothing. By now, much of the burial ground had been laid to waste by the spectre's rampage. Shattercap ran like an ape, long arms working as much as his feet to propel him. He was fast and nimble, but the Mourngul's reach was long, and it raked at him with its dagger nails. Shattercap ran screaming before it. Maesa limped from grave to grave, searching without luck for his lost weapon.

'Hungry! Hungry!' the Mourngul howled. 'Huunnnngrryyy!'

The Mourngul caught Shattercap with one of its long fingers, tripping him. Shattercap flipped over, went into a dizzying roll down a hill, and fetched up with his backside bent over his head.

He had fallen out of the Mourngul's sight. He was safe, for the moment.

The spite scampered away, keeping to the shadows of skulls and broken rocks. The Mourngul swung its head back and forth, sniffing at the air, then moaned in pain as an ironwood arrow smacked into its shoulder. It wheeled around, and loped after Maesa.

Shattercap caught his breath. His tiny heart hammered in his chest. He crept away from the beast, terrified by its howls as Maesa filled it with arrows.

He would have run then, all his desire to be good abandoned, had not the gods taken a hand. His little foot kicked a pebble aside. That hit a bigger rock, which fell and hit something made of wood, whose voice, when it was struck, Shattercap knew.

'Master's sword!' He scampered for it, and stared down at the dusty weapon. Its edge glowed with deadly power. He hesitated, wary of it, fearing that if he touched it, it would suck him dry and leave his body a husk.

He was out of cover again and could see his master. Maesa was leaping over the Mourngul's arms, loosing arrows. The Mourngul bristled with shafts, but they seemed to have no effect upon it. Only magic would end the beast.

The Song of Thorns.

'Master!' Shattercap shouted. 'The sword, the sword! I see it! I fetch it for you, good prince. I bring it to you!' He bent down. The sword was lodged between stones. He pushed his scrawny arm down.

Maesa saw him the instant he reached out for the hilt.

'Do not touch the Song of Thorns!' the aelf cried.

Tiny claws crackled at their proximity to the magic sword. 'I nearly have it!' he squeaked. The rock grazed his chest. His breath was trapped.

Maesa was running for him. He was angry, far angrier than Shattercap had ever seen. 'Do not touch the Song of Thorns!'

Shattercap kept his resolve. The Mourngul was coming. The thump of its hands shook the ground. The grave-stink of the magic animating it choked him. He did not look up, but thrust his arm in deeper. 'I must, the thing will kill you...'

His small hand grasped the hilt. Shattercap was small, but imbued with the wiry strength of forest spirits, and he dragged the Song of Thorns free.

'I have it! I have it!' He stood tall and lifted up the hilt, the blade scraping on the broken stones. 'I have it!'

Then the blade's edge brushed him. Shattercap's triumph turned to horror. The world flashed away, and he found himself in a prison made of fibrous wood, full of wailing dead.

From far away, he heard Maesa cry.

'Give it to me! Give me my blade!'

He felt a hand about his neck. Another snatched the sword from Shattercap, and the vision fled.

Everything happened so quickly then. The Mourngul was bearing down on them. Maesa spun around to face it. Shattercap, still gripped by the neck, swung out as Maesa lunged with lightning speed as the Mourngul reared over them and its mouth came snapping down.

'Taste my blade, wretched ghoul,' Maesa spat.

He rammed the Song of Thorns into the Mourngul's mouth. The hungering throat took the whole length of the weapon, then Maesa's arm, before it came to a scraping stop against bone, and the point slid out of the spectre's back. A peal of thunder cracked overhead. The Mourngul screamed. The magic that sustained it was drunk away by the Song of Thorns. Its body shrivelled, and vibrated around the weapon, deflating into nothing, until its boneless arms were wriggling around like eels, and only its head remained full size. The arrows studding its skin fell away. As the spectre was consumed, its screams became higher, and weaker, until they were the moans of a boy.

Filippo's ghost fell from the end of the sword, and lay on the ground.

'I am so hungry,' he said.

'It is nearly done,' said Maesa wearily.

Shattercap was choking. Black spots prickled his sight. He smelled the deep forests and the silent pools of glades, calling him back.

'Master, please, you squeeze too tight!' His tiny claws raked Maesa's hand. 'Master, please!'

The aelf looked at him as if he did not recognise the spite. 'Shattercap?'

With the last of his breath, Shattercap gasped, 'You're strangling me!'

With a look of profound dismay, Maesa dropped his companion, and stared at his hand in disgust.

'Good prince,' Shattercap wheedled, and pressed his forehead to the ground. 'Shattercap sorry. Shattercap sorry for touching nice sword...'

Maesa dropped to his knee and reached out a hand to calm the spite. Shattercap shrank away.

'Shattercap, I did not mean...'

Shattercap shivered, curled into a ball of complete submission.

Filippo's ghost wept, drawing Maesa's attention back. 'Our task here is not complete,' he said.

Maesa pushed himself back to his feet. Shattercap had never seen him so spent. His hand was pressed to his side. The precious blade of Alarielle dragged on the ground.

Filippo looked up at him. 'What happened to me? Who are you? Where is my sister?'

'You are cursed,' said Maesa. 'We fought. I pierced your heart. The Song of Thorns bled away the death magic around your soul.'

Filippo was confused, but his face cleared, and he gasped. 'No, no, that thing. I do not wish to become that thing... I am free?'

'No. And you can never be while Nagash rules the kingdoms of death. It sorrows me to say, but you doomed yourself by your actions in life. The Lord of the Undead has judged you for your crime. To be that thing is your punishment. You are his forever. Soon the transformation will come upon you again. Death magic will accrue to your soul, and you will hunger anew. Nagash has a twisted sense of justice.'

'What am I to do?' sobbed the boy. 'I cannot spend an eternity as a monster. My sister. I murdered her. But I was so hungry...'

Shattercap's tiny heart fell. 'Poor, poor boy.'

The dark clouds were blowing away. Weak sunshine touched the Song of Thorns. 'Nothing can save you,' said the prince. 'Nothing, except a final blow from my sword.'

Filippo's ghost got to his knees and bowed his head.

'Then do it,' he said. 'Do it for my sister. I cannot... I cannot live with the taste any more. Her screams. The blood. The taste! Please, finish me.'

'Forgive me,' said Maesa.

The Song of Thorns fell. The soul of the boy parted like mist around the gleaming edge. Filippo cried out as the blade severed his final link to the Mortal Realms, a shriek that rose as the sword drank in the last shreds of his being.

The cry hung on the wind, then died. The bells and bone

chimes in the trees clattered. The flags snapped. Grit hissed over the ground.

Maesa sheathed his weapon, and stared off over the bones and rocks of the wrecked burial ground. Shattercap crept to his master's feet. The aelf had become as lifeless as a statue. Hesitantly, he reached out and tugged at Maesa's tunic, jumping back when Maesa glared down at him.

'Wicked prince, dost thou hate me?' Shattercap said quietly.

The prince frowned. 'What?'

'Thou hurt me,' said Shattercap. He fiddled with his fingers. 'I was trying to be good. I was trying to help thee.'

The furious look on Maesa's face passed as quickly as black clouds race from the sun. 'I am… sorry, Shattercap.' He smiled, and Shattercap's soul filled with joy. 'Come to me.' Maesa reached out his arm. 'Let us remain friends.'

'Oh, master!' Shattercap squeaked. He jumped up onto Maesa's arm and ran up onto his shoulder.

'My prince,' said Shattercap quietly into Maesa's ear. 'When I touched the sword, I felt them. So many, so many trapped inside. All the ones we have faced, all the ones thou hast killed, they are all in the sword…'

Some of the aelf's weariness returned. 'Do not speak of it, small evil.'

'But the sword…' Shattercap continued. 'So many voices within! So much pain. They… they cannot get out. Thou can set them free! Thou should release them! This would be good, yes? I am learning to be good. You can be good too. Are you going to free them from the blade?'

Maesa said nothing.

'Good prince, wouldst thou let them free?'

Maesa sighed. 'We must attend to our companion.'

Shattercap was wise enough not to ask again about the sword, but Maesa's unwillingness to discuss it left him frightened. Surely a blade like that could not be good, and if it were not good, could the one who bore it be bad? These thoughts troubled him as Maesa picked his way stiffly through the graveyard to where Stonbrak lay.

Maesa got down by his side, took out his canteen and poured a little water onto Stonbrak's face. 'Come now, master duardin, it is time to awaken,' he said.

Stonbrak groaned.

'He lives,' said Maesa. 'Let us see to his wounds.'

'I'm all right! I'm all right. Just a glancing blow,' Stonbrak said. 'Let me be a moment.'

'Allow us to help you up, Idenkor,' said Maesa. Gently, he helped Stonbrak sit.

'Oof,' said Stonbrak. 'Look at this, his claws went right through my mail! Duardin mail!'

'Are you hurt?'

Stonbrak scowled. 'I said duardin mail! The creature's claws broke the links, but not a scratch on me.' He held up the tattered sleeve of his armour and the jerkin beneath. 'This journey is costing me a fortune in repairs.' He squinted up at Maesa. 'The beast?'

'It is gone,' said the aelf.

'Good. Now we can have breakfast.'

Maesa offered his hand, but Stonbrak pushed it away and got up himself.

'I'm fine!'

'Thou dost not look fine,' said Shattercap. 'There is ugliness on thee, as every day.'

'Well I may be ugly, but I am unhurt.' He bent over to catch his breath. 'As you said, prince, a difficult foe. Stronger than I expected. These creations of the death god are sometimes hardier

234

than you might expect.' Stonbrak still had his axe in his hand, which seemed to surprise him. He put it back into his belt loop.

'Indeed,' said Maesa. 'The servants of death are more active than I have seen before, and my life has been long. Thringsson's warning was not an idle one.'

'What does it mean?' asked Shattercap.

'I am not sure, small evil. But I fear the storm that follows on the tail of this wind.'

'That's all well and good,' Stonbrak huffed. 'But first things first. Seeing as we've vanquished their hungry revenant, I believe the villagers owe us drinks and bacon.'

'Greedy,' said Shattercap.

'Practical, twigling. We can't all live off raindrops and sunshine.'

'And lovely plump babies,' said Shattercap wistfully.

'Shattercap…' Maesa warned.

The spite cringed. 'Sorry, master! I'll be good.'

They went back down the mountain, and Shattercap tried not to think about the Song of Thorns.

PART FIVE

THE ROAD
TO HYSH

CHAPTER SEVENTEEN

THE PROBLEM WITH BHARI ZHONDR

The campfire spat with dripping fat. The gar-hare was cooking slowly in the wet weather. Maesa and Stonbrak sat together away from the smoke, sharing a log and precious little else, both staring into the fire but seeing different things. Reflections in Stonbrak's eyes turned the leaping flames into miniature foundries, Maesa's into fields of angry stars. Rain beaded their cloaks with pearls of water, adding steam to the clouds of smoke. Summer days lingered long in that part of Ghur, and silver light clung to the cloudy night. It lacked colour, and the air was heavy. Beyond the light of the fire, the world was a woeful place, damp and grey, matching the travellers' mood.

'I asked you a civil question,' said Stonbrak. 'There's no need to be so rude about it.'

'You rebuke me for my manners, and yet you show none yourself, master duardin,' said Maesa coldly.

'It was a simple question!' Stonbrak protested.

'One I told you not to ask. It is most private to me, and I do not wish to share an answer.'

'Says the aelf who'll tell all and sundry about his dead wife, whether they're interested or not!'

'You go too far, Idenkor!' said Maesa with a sudden flash of passion. He swept his cloak aside, and rested his hand on the hilt of his sword.

Stonbrak peered at it sidelong. 'Well, well!' he said. 'So you'll not talk about that blade but you'll happily threaten a friend with it. Typical aelf.'

Maesa released his grip and held his hand open.

'I… I am sorry,' he said remorsefully.

'You should be,' said Stonbrak grumpily.

Maesa paused. 'You called me friend.'

Stonbrak leaned forward and puffed out his cheeks, and poked with deliberate care at the fire. 'I did. You are. So there you have it.' He adjusted the gar-hare. 'It's nearly done, thank Grimnir.' He huddled into his cloak. 'Miserable weather.'

'Yes,' said Maesa.

Stonbrak's emora mount came up behind him and butted him in the back. It made a questioning chirr and clacked its beak.

'Ow,' he growled, but reached back and scratched between its feathers nonetheless. The bird made a pleased gobbling in the back of its throat. 'Not now, Bhari.'

'Bhari,' said Maesa. 'Why did you give it that name?'

Stonbrak scratched his beard. 'Because I didn't like Bhari Zhondr when I was a beardling, and I don't like this bird either,' said Stonbrak. The way he stroked between Bhari's eyes suggested this was not entirely true. 'Fine pair of drumsticks on it though. If we ever get hungry, we can eat you, yes we can. Who's a good bird?'

The emora gave him a hard stare.

'That is mean, bearded one,' Shattercap said. He was hiding beneath the log, and nothing was visible of him save the pinprick glows of his eyes.

'It was a joke,' said Stonbrak.

'Bad beardy!'

The bird chirred.

'Why did you not like this Bhari?' asked Maesa.

'Bhari Zhondr was a boastful fool,' Stonbrak said. 'He was cruel too, in the way of young ones.' Stonbrak's face coloured. 'He was cruel to me.'

'How?' said Maesa.

'He was always on me, Bhari Zhondr,' said Stonbrak. His voice had become deep and rumbling, in a way that anyone who knew duardin well would recognise as a sign of shame. 'Mocking my craftsmanship, spoiling my work when he thought it better than his own. His grandfather was head of the jewelsmith's guild.' He shook his head. 'Anything he didn't get through his family, he got with his fists. But I was proud. I wasn't scared of him, and he hated me for my defiance, and so he plotted to humiliate me.'

Stonbrak stared deep into the coals of the fire, and kept his gaze there. Bhari the bird laid its head on the log next to Stonbrak. Its fat body dropped heavily to the ground behind him. Stonbrak continued to pet it as he spoke.

'There was a *kvinn*, a duardin-maid who I loved more than the brightest gem,' he said quietly. 'Always from afar. We duardin love rarely, but when we do, we love deeply, something you say you know a lot about!' he added sharply, with a look at Maesa. 'I was young to be so smitten, but smitten I was. I told my friend Bjorki about it, damn fool I was. Without my knowledge, Bhari Zhondr tormented my secret out of him. He saw how he could get at me, and he hatched a most horrible plan.' He huffed, and adjusted the gar-hare again. 'Over the next few weeks, I received a series of rune sticks purporting to be from this maiden. They spoke kindly to me, but urged me not to respond, for fear her father would find out. I doubted them at first, but they were so sincere, so gentle, I fell under their spell. I could not verify the truth of it, not without discovery, and every time I saw her, I dropped my eyes, but smiled, sure of the bond between us.

'Waiting for the rune sticks became a weekly torment, with a sweet joy at their arrival. My smithing suffered. The oldbeards we were apprenticed to had words with my father, and I was given a birching more than once. I did not care. All I cared about was those rune sticks.

'Then, one day, a rune stick came, and I remember the words it said to this day.' He coloured deeply, and cleared his throat. 'It said, "My dearest Idenkor, I would have a token of your affection, to keep by me, so that you can be close to me, though you are far."

'Immediately, my mind set to racing – I would give her the most precious thing any beardling can, but first I resolved to craft a box to put it in. I worked harder then than I ever had or ever have since, making a box of filigreed silver so fine and artful my masters ceased their grumbles about my lack of application. I even received a compliment from my father. Can you believe it! Another rune stick came, suggesting a meeting, at dead of night in the Iron Master's Hall. My heart leapt! The box was ready. I prepared myself to place my treasure within.' Stonbrak fell silent, and poked at the fire roughly.

'What was the gift, master beardy?' said Shattercap.

'My beard!' Stonbrak snapped. 'I cut a tress from my beard. It wasn't very long, and it was very straggly, as the beards of young duardin are, but a beard is a duardin's pride, and I wanted her to have something personal. I took a knife, and cut a piece, and laid it with shaking hands in the box. Then I went to the forge and worked up a good sweat so I'd smell good and proper.'

'Poo!' said Shattercap from his hiding place. The sound of a flapping hand accompanied his exclamation.

'Proper duardin smell of sweat, and smoke, and metal!' Stonbrak said between his legs to Shattercap. 'Bah, I probably smelled like a beardling, all coppery and of yak milk.'

Maesa raised an eyebrow.

'Never mind,' said Stonbrak. 'Anyway, I'll bet you can guess who was waiting for me when I got to the Iron Master's Hall.'

'Bhari Zhondr?' said Shattercap.

'Aye, Bhari Zhondr. He came out first to laugh at me, then all his cronies. They took the gift. I was humiliated. Word got back to the maiden and her father, and the humiliation got worse. Cutting your own beard off for a woman is an extreme act for my people, in case you're wondering – it's the sort of thing poets do.' He spat the word. 'I was a laughing stock. I had to leave my apprenticeship, which cost my old dad. He wasn't best pleased. First thing I know, I'm apprenticed to the merchant guild, at a hefty wage cut I might add, and shipped out to Chamon on a nine-year trading circuit while my brother back home gets better and better at the jeweller's arts.' He stopped, saddened. 'But you know his story. It took years for the hullaballoo to die down. I was ashamed. Forty-six, what kind of an age is that to have your heart broken?' He shook his head. 'Lucky for me, my new master was a wise and kind old soul, who talked me out of anything stupid, and made me see things weren't so bad as all that. I've known duardin snap under less pressure.' He sniffed deeply. 'But not Idenkor Stonbrak. I applied myself very diligently to my new role, and gathered much wealth. I mean, partly thanks to Jurven's skill, but they could see I was good at what I did. That shut everyone up. So, that's why Bhari Zhondr.' He patted his mount. 'I get to ride him around all day, tell him what to do, and if he annoys me enough, I can eat him.'

'What happened to the maid?' Maesa asked.

'Well,' said Stonbrak. He pulled the gar-hare off the fire. 'She only married Bhari bloody Zhondr, didn't she?'

Shattercap tittered, then gasped. 'So sorry,' he said, and sounded like he meant it.

Stonbrak handed Maesa a portion of the meat. Maesa gave him some back, and passed half of what he retained under the log. Shattercap ate it noisily. Maesa tasted his gently.

'This is well prepared, Idenkor.'

'Thank you,' said Stonbrak.

'That was a personal tale you relayed.'

'Yes, it was,' said Stonbrak. 'A second one at that.' He started to speak, then stopped, then started again. He looked at Maesa with eyes that welled. 'But though I've told people about Jurven before, I have never told anyone about Bhari. Not ever. I prefer to think it didn't happen.'

Maesa nodded. 'I know your race better than you think, Idenkor,' he said. 'You are proud, and sincere of heart. Telling me that story is as sure a sign of friendship as you could ever offer me.'

Stonbrak hunched over his meal and shrugged. 'That's all right.'

Maesa put his hand into one of his bags resting against the back of the log and pulled out a bottle of wine. He passed it to Stonbrak, then pulled out another. Carefully, he laid his meat aside and pulled the cork.

'In return for this great honour you have shown me, I will relent.' Maesa drank from the bottle as daintily as if he sipped from the finest crystal glass. 'I have decided I will tell you how I gained the Song of Thorns, after all.'

CHAPTER EIGHTEEN

GREEN WITCH

They were getting wetter when Maesa began to speak, but with the fire burning well to their fore, they were warm enough, and their cloaks kept out the worst of the damp. They finished their small meal, and drank together as Maesa told his story.

'There was a time before I met with Shattercap,' said Maesa, 'or with Aelphis, the king of the stags, when I wandered alone without purpose. I went to many lands, and had many adventures, as the foolish would call them, these brushes with death and disaster. I came one time to a great swamp in Aqshy, a vast land of lakes and low islands full of trees draped in moss. While there, for the first and only time in my life, I became lost...'

There was a hut on the island, there was no doubting it. It was well camouflaged, the profile an extension of the island's natural contours, the roof mossy as the rest of the ground. Three trees growing as one from the top further hid it, their interlaced roots providing support to the walls. Maesa might not have seen it at all, were it not early, the hours before dawn, and a single candle shone between the roots, lighting up a solitary window.

Maesa watched the window for half an hour before deciding to move on the cottage. The swamp objected to his presence, and the normally sure-footed aelf tripped and blundered his way to the island. Roots seemed to snag him purposefully. Branches reached down to hit him across the face. A shallow pool opened up and swallowed him to his chest. His body was covered in insect bites, his skin bruised. The swamp had been meting out this treatment to him ever since he had stepped into it, and he was wearied to his bones. He would have left, if only he could find the way.

Even the island, which seemed level and free of hazard, tripped him as he walked its perimeter. The hut's door was small, and virtually invisible behind a bushy fern. He rapped on it tiredly.

No voice answered him, but the door opened, dragging against the packed earth of the cottage floor.

There was no one inside; nevertheless, the cottage welcomed him. The sense of hostility he had endured outside was absent. A small iron stove put out a welcome heat, and Maesa went to it, keen to dry his sodden clothes. He put down his filthy pack and checked Ellamar's bones. Her remains were tight and dry in their wrappings. With relief, he put them away again. There was a three-legged stool hanging from a peg on the wall, which he took down to sit on.

The cottage was tiny, more of a burrow than a house. Polished roots made up the majority of the walls, with the spaces between filled with wattle panels covered in clay. There was a small sleeping platform at one end of the cottage, high off the floor in a hollow directly under one of the trees, with a curtain to screen it off. Cupboards built into the walls lined all the opposite end. Dried herbs hung from the ceiling. With their fragrance and the roots around him, he felt embraced by the swamp rather than rejected by it.

Before he knew what he was doing, he had stretched out his legs, leant into the softness of the wall and fallen into a deep sleep.

A soft dabbing at his face woke the prince. He came to with a start, nearly falling from the stool.

There was an old woman tending his bites with a rag soaked in astringent oils.

'Easy there, kin of Teclis, kin of Tyrion,' she said. 'You've been a-sleeping in my house.'

Maesa stood. He towered over the woman, and his head brushed the ceiling of the cottage.

'I rarely sleep,' he said. 'You enchanted me.'

'No, no,' she said. 'You are very tired, that is all. You've come a long way to get here. I've been waiting a while for you to show, but you're here now, so that's all right, ain't it?'

'Who are you?'

'Goodwife Melisin,' she said, and executed an ironic curtsey. 'Pleased to be making your acquaintance, your highness.'

Maesa looked down at her. She was a human, as far as he could tell, and very ancient for her kind, so old all loveliness that her race could possess had long ago withered. Her nose and chin were as pronounced as a grot's, her skin wrinkled and back humped so high it nearly came level with the top of her head. Her eyes had a sharp intelligence, however.

'Places like this can be traps,' said Maesa. He hesitated. 'Yet I see no evil in you.'

'Well isn't that nice to know,' she cackled. 'It is true. I'm a nice one.' She nodded out of the room's single window. 'My swamp don't like you much,' she said. 'Sorry for that. I'll have a word before you're on your way, see if I can't make it a bit easier for you. Thing is, it's been a bit on the hostile side these last couple of centuries. Don't take well to strangers. You'll see why soon enough.'

'What are you talking about? I am a–'

'Yes, yes, an exiled nomad, an aelf of the Wanderer Clans. Prince Maesa, last of his house, banished by his own people for fancying the wrong kind of lady, la-di-da.'

'How do you–'

'Never mind that,' she interrupted again. 'First things first, let's see to these bruises and these bites. You'll be no use to us at all if you're not fighting fit, so sit down, and be quiet awhile, there's a dear.'

Maesa sat back on the stool and did as he was told. The woman dabbed on more of the oil. His skin tingled, and the itching subsided. Then she hobbled off to one of her cupboards and opened it, revealing a mass of stoppered bottles. She pulled one out and came back to the prince.

'Whortlewood, for the bruising,' she said, then proceeded to smear a greasy unguent onto his injuries.

'I don't need your aid, madam,' he said.

'Yes you do,' she said. 'Too proud by half you aelves are. You're hardy, but you can be hurt. Still, as I reckon it you lot of the greenways are the least pompous of the bunch, and the best of the wild aelves.' She grinned at him. 'That's a compliment, by the way.'

'Thank you,' he said. His arm was losing its stiffness. He flexed it. 'You know your herbcraft.'

'I do,' she said. 'Now drink this.' She poured a thick liquid into a wooden cup. 'I know what you lot are like when you're love-lorn, don't look after yourselves properly.'

He sniffed the cup.

'Just drink it. It ain't going to kill you, it's good for you. Now, I've got something here that you need to listen to while you get that down you.'

He drank the liquid, and a delightful, warm sense of relaxation suffused him.

She went to another cupboard and took out a misshapen log about the size of Maesa's smallest bag. She got down on creaking knees and fussed around it, propping it up with small, colourful rocks and carved bits of branch, and Maesa saw it was a section of tree. Contorted, still covered in bark, perhaps rotten. Not much use for timber or for burning. Melisin poked it. It rocked, but did not fall over. She then fetched several small bottles, and spent some time dripping oils and tinctures onto various parts.

'Right,' she said. 'That'll do it.' Melisin cleared her throat. 'Oi, Findelfil. Wake up. He's finally here. Findelfil's been getting a bit distant of late,' she explained to Maesa. 'It's a good job you've come now. I don't think he'd have lasted much longer.' She turned her attention back to the lump of wood. The bottom and sides where it had been cut away from the tree had been sealed with resin. 'Findelfil! The prince has come, wake up!'

A pale blue light flickered in the hollow at the top. Melisin sat back on her heels, all her joints popping at once, and gave a gummy smile. 'Aha! That's my lad. Here he comes.'

The glow brightened, and coalesced into dots and shimmers that danced around one another, emitting a tinkling like the bells on a horse's harness heard from far away. These solidified, becoming the outline of a head, shoulders and a ghostly arm, which further sharpened until they took on the seeming of solidity, and the partial figure had grown around the wood. It had the features of Maesa's people – the sharp bones, the beauty, the ears tapering to a point – but an arboreal soul looked back from its shining eyes. This was no aelf. At best, it was the memory of one, expressed by the imaginations of the trees, a mark of remembrance for an alliance long broken.

Findelfil was a Tree-Revenant, a creature of the Sylvaneth, and a horribly mutilated one at that. Maesa had met such beings in the past. They were the foot-soldiers of the glades, part living wood and part spirit, kin to the spites and the dryads. Most often, they had legs, torsos and a left arm of living wood, the upper part of their bodies, their heads and their right arms expressed by the magic of Ghyran as a tangible spirit form. Findelfil was missing most of his woody parts. Now Maesa understood why the timber was sealed with resins.

'Champion of Alarielle, I greet you,' said Findelfil. Words like the breeze through leaves soughed from his mouth. 'As life made me so, I am Findelfil, warrior of the forest.'

'I greet you in return, noble spirit, with great respect. As life made me, I am Maesa, of the Wanderer Clans. But forgive me, I am no champion of Alarielle. You flatter me. The compact between she and my people is over, though it shames me to say so.'

'What you know, oh prince, is not so important as what is true, and what is true is what you are,' said Findelfil. 'The trees and the boughs have whispered of your coming for decades.'

'Ain't that the truth,' muttered the goodwife. 'I've been waiting a long old while this time.'

'I never gave up hope,' said Findelfil. 'Now you are here, and you will aid me.'

Maesa made a face. 'What if I do not wish to?'

'You will, for that is what is meant to be,' said the revenant. 'I am the last of the glade-kin of my household, who were slain by the evil that dwells in the heart of this swamp. I ask that you return me home, and overthrow the evil, and plant my soulpod so that I might grow again and call the spirits of my people back.'

'A small task for me, then,' said Maesa. 'To fight and kill something that destroyed a whole band of your kind, noble spirit. I will surely die.'

'You will not, for that is not what is intended to happen,' said Findelfil sombrely.

'Fate has a way of tricking us,' said Maesa. 'What is this foe?'

'A fearsome plague daemon,' said Findelfil. 'It has made its home amid the ruins of my glade-kin's dwellings.'

'For a single daemon to do what you say it did, it must be powerful,' said Maesa. 'If that is the case, I shall have no chance against it.'

'You will prevail. We were killed furtively, weakened by disease. We were half dead when it came against us openly. You will not be, and you shall have help.'

'In what form?' said Maesa.

'Our greatest treasure, that we held in trust for Alarielle's champion. It is yours, prince, you need only take it and wield it.'

'A weapon then?' asked Maesa.

'A sword like no other,' the revenant said. 'Use it, and keep it. Know the favour of Alarielle. She is the Goddess of Life. Surely her patronage would be useful to you, when you seek to over-come death?'

Maesa did not ask how the revenant knew of his quest. There was magic at work there. He thought a moment on the offer.

'I shall accept,' said Maesa.

'As was foretold,' said Findelfil.

'On one condition,' said Maesa.

'Name it,' said Findelfil.

'That your mistress aid me in my quest, and return my love to me if she can.'

The revenant smiled. 'She always helps you, oh prince. You are her favoured hero. The weapon is the key to your success.'

'I know nothing of that.'

'It is true nevertheless. The weapon has always been yours.'

Findelfil's spirit form flickered, and withdrew back into the remains of his wooden body.

'Oh, right then,' Melisin said, as if she had not been paying attention. She got up off her knees with a groan. 'He's no more to say. That's that then, laddie, all going to plan. I'll give you the necessaries to get through the centre of the swamp without dying. Potions you'll have, and medicinal things, some Aqua Ghyranis. 'Tis a black place now, full of death.' She raised a finger gnarled with rheumatism. 'But first, I'll make us something to eat.'

CHAPTER NINETEEN

PLAGUE BEAST

Having extracted binding oaths from Goodwife Melisin that no harm would come to Ellamar's remains, Maesa left the bulk of his belongings in the cottage. He donned his mail and his horned helm, and took his weapons, and a satchel of Melisin's potions, but nothing else. He tied a rope to the life-wood remains of Findelfil, slung him over his back and set out into the swamp.

Melisin's home vanished quickly. After only a few dozen yards, Maesa could not tell where the witch's house was. There were a number of low islands sporting clumps of trees, and any one of them could have been the location of her cottage.

'She will mind the bones of your beloved well,' said Findelfil from Maesa's back. When he manifested to speak to Maesa, the weight increased greatly. 'Pay attention to our task. You must go towards the very centre of the swamp.'

'It may take some time,' said Maesa. 'The trees here objected to me before.'

'They will not now,' said Findelfil. 'They protect what is left of the goodness of this place. Now they know you not to be a foe, they will not hinder you, they have been told to let you pass.'

Findelfil fell silent, and his stump became easier to bear.

What the revenant said was true. Maesa found the swamp altogether more forgiving. No roots trapped his feet, and no brambles reached out to claw at him. The insects let him be. Paths appeared where there had been none, and though only animal trails, they sped his passage.

Yet it remained a grim place. The trees were squat and heavy-boughed, with slimy black bark. Their leaves were close set, and combined with the mist hanging over the water, kept the light in the swamp muted. Occasional Hyshbeams infiltrated the canopy to spear the ponds, and lit up the water with an amber shine, showing fish swimming round in lazy circles. Maesa grew to like the swamp. It was an honest place, and though unpleasant, it offered the deep peace of wild countries.

The calm did not last. The airs took on a sickly smell. What was the healthy scent of wood rotting down gained an edge of putridity. Shortly thereafter, Maesa began to encounter single dead trees, then stands of dead trees, and pools of thick black water with oily rainbows upon their surfaces, over which buzzed large, aggressive flies. The higher ground became stinking ooze crawling with vermin. Though there were now no leaves to block the light, the landscape was covered by an unnatural gloom.

Findelfil returned to Maesa. 'We are close,' he said. 'The corrupt heart of the swamp. I will guide you to it, and show you the blade. The rest is up to you.'

A mournful, slobbering howl cried out of the rotted dark.

'Your daemon has our scent,' said Maesa.

'Then be quick!' said Findelfil.

Maesa loosened his sword in his scabbard and strung his bow. He took a fistful of arrows from his quiver and held them by the bow stave, and ran. Nothing there smelled wholesome. A feculent reek rose from the soil. The pools bubbled mephitic gas. Maesa could not keep the smell out. It made his head spin. He attempted to breathe through his mouth, but that was worse, so he ran gasping, Findelfil heavy on his back.

'So much harm has been done here,' Findelfil said despondently. 'Keep on ahead, prince of the Wanderers.'

Something heavy heaved itself through the muck. A sorrowful gibbering spoken in a dozen fragmentary languages came from an uncertain direction. There was the splash of feet paddling through the water, and a breeze sourer still raced over the poisoned swamp.

Maesa slipped. The lump of wood housing the revenant's soul dragged at his back, and the rope dug into his shoulders. Every step added to Findelfil's weight.

'Quickly!' said Findelfil.

'You are growing heavier,' said Maesa.

'It is this place,' said Findelfil. 'The magic that sustains me is harder to maintain here. It is the curse of the Unclean Ones. I feel it in my sap. Go on, or we shall both perish.'

Maesa dug deep into his reserves of strength, and pushed himself forward.

'There!' exclaimed Findelfil.

They came to an open area of mud where the trees had rotted down to soft, black spikes, all save one giant, away over the pools. Collapsed in by decay, but so vast its remnants were still as high as a tower of stone, was a castle made from a tree.

'Alas,' said Findelfil, 'the Tower-in-Bloom, dead now. Our goal is there.'

Maesa struggled through the filth, the weight of Findelfil growing all the while. The cries of the beast-daemon echoed over the swamp, but came no nearer. Good that was, for Maesa's progress was reduced to a pained staggering, the blood to his arms cut to a trickle by the rope dragging at his shoulders, so that his fingers went numb around his bow.

The stump of the Tower-in-Bloom grew bigger. Findelfil got heavier, and Maesa became slower. His feet slapped hard into the mud. He was covered in filth, and the stink near overcame him.

Fifty yards ahead was a wall of braided trees around the tower, all dead and disintegrating. From a gate whose arch had rotted through, stairs led up to the tower, promising safety. Maesa found the remains of a causeway sunken in the mud leading to the gate, yet Findelfil grew heavier, and heavier, until the prince was leaning forward like a man dragging at a timber wagon.

The mud plopped and bubbled. Across a wide swathe of the ground, little horns rose up from the morass, then little faces, in which were set little eyes glittering with mischief and little teeth sharp as knives. Fat bodies next, and spindly arms, then webbed feet with pointed toes peeking out from fat bellies. Nurglings, daemon imps of the Plague God.

With supreme effort Maesa brought up and drew his bow, sending a badly aimed arrow into the imps, yet there were so many, he could not miss, and the arrow popped a round stomach, which gushed pus and maggots into the morass. The imps thought their friend's demise funny, and tittered a high-pitched, maddening laugh. Arms held over their heads, bellies swaying, they waddled towards the prince, the look in their eyes and their grinning teeth leaving no doubt to their intention.

'If they catch me, they will strip the flesh from my bones,' said Maesa. He shot again. Two more died, but there were scores more, if not hundreds.

'Save your arrows,' urged Findelfil. 'Run!'

'I can barely walk,' said Maesa. He bent low under Findelfil's weight. The stairs beckoned, thirty yards, then twenty remained, but the bounding, capering tide of Nurglings advancing on the causeway was closer.

Maesa fell forward, finally pressed down by the weight of the revenant. The Nurglings bounced towards him, singing songs that lodged themselves in his mind and repeated themselves with infuriating persistence.

He surged to his feet just as the first Nurgling reached out its claw for his ankle. Maesa kicked it as he stood, and it flipped over and over, back into the horde of its fellows.

'Do not drop me,' warned the revenant, 'or this land is lost.'

Maesa staggered on. He drew his sword, and swung it leadenly about his feet. The blade swiped through the imps as easily as if they were rotten fruit. But these were merely the vanguard of the force, and their real strength was not far behind. As they drew in on him, they rose up, standing on each other's shoulders, in a defecating, urinating, giggling, singing mass as tall as a man. Maesa walked backwards as it advanced on him. He cut more of them down, but the mass remained; he might as well have swatted snowflakes in a blizzard. As he was within arm's reach of the dead tower's curtain wall, the living wave crested and broke over him, burying aelf and revenant in an avalanche of soft, filthy bodies.

They bit at him, and though his mail proved beyond their ability to penetrate, this covered only his torso and upper arms, and his legs and hands they sank their teeth into freely. Maesa cried out, no longer fighting, pushing through the heaps of their fat, damp forms to find the way.

His hand touched the wood of the tower. The instant it did, a set of fangs bit into his palm. The pain was so sharp he almost did not notice that the weight of Findelfil had returned to normal.

His burden lessened, Maesa sat up. He flung out his arm, throwing off the biting Nurglings, freeing his sword so he could cut at them with his blade. The press of them diminished, and he shoved himself up, and kicked out around himself, booting the giggling things away. A space around him cleared; he fell back against the wall, protecting his rear, and groped his way to the entrance. There, he made his way backwards up the steps, his sword held out, and many a glance cast behind himself in case of ambush from within the tower.

The Nurglings did not follow, but crowded the entrance, giggling and waving at him, like a crowd come to see a ship off from the docks.

His limbs shook. Fever sweat sprang up on his skin. He fell through the gate and lay slumped upon the ground.

'The bite of the Nurglings is laced with disease, but a little of the spirit of the glade remains,' said Findelfil. 'Here in this tower, Alarielle's love for life clings on. That is why you live.'

Maesa gaped. Ropes of saliva ran from his mouth, and he shook.

'Open your bag, take out the potions the goodwife gave you, or you will die.'

Maesa was unable to speak, but nodded. Unsteadily he slipped the ropes binding Findelfil to his back off his shoulders, and pulled open his satchel. His fingers were weak, and shook so much he could barely undo the toggle. His skin turned yellow, and withered before his eyes. He pulled out one of the bottles Melisin had given him. It blurred as his vision failed.

'I cannot see,' he gasped. His throat was closed by swelling glands. His voice was an ugly rasp.

'Drink!' urged Findelfil. 'Quickly! Before your strength deserts you completely.'

Maesa pulled the cork with teeth that wobbled in his gums. His body was afire with fever. His bones ached. Thick tears crawled down his cheeks. They smelled rank.

With moments left to him, he poured the liquid into his mouth. Immediately, he felt better. Where it touched his tongue, it returned to its normal size. His nose cleared, and the tears stopped. When the liquid hit his throat, the swelling subsided, then stilled his churning stomach. A sense of great wellbeing radiated from his gut out into his limbs, and on to his extremities, leaving him gasping with relief.

'Enough!' warned Findelfil. 'Too much will kill you as surely as the diseases of the Plague Lord.'

Maesa took the bottle away from his mouth. 'It is Aqua Ghyranis,' he said. He looked at his hand. The bites had become scars that faded before his eyes. 'Wondrous life water.'

'Alarielle's purest gift, augmented by a few herbs of Melisin's choosing,' Findelfil said. 'Few of the wells remain now, so many have been poisoned. You are fortunate. It is a great gift.'

Maesa put the cork back in carefully, and replaced the bottle in the bag. All his ailments were gone. Indeed, he felt better than he had before, rejuvenated, his body tingling with the call of spring. He took a moment to rearrange his gear, and gripped his sword.

'Where to now?' He looked up the stairs. They curved round and went out of sight, into the darkness of the tower's interior.

'Go up, and to the centre. There you will find the promised blade.'

The tree's wood was black and grey. The steps were spongy underfoot, and hollowed out in places, their timber eaten down to damp sawdust and sludge. Luminous fungi provided enough light for Maesa to see, but only just, and he went carefully, lest another foe ambush him. Yet Findelfil had spoken truly: some vestige of Alarielle's grace must have kept the tree free of the enemy, for he met no foe. He climbed around pits in the wood, stabbing two of his ironwood arrows into the soft walls to hold himself up. There were places where the outer skin of the tower was eaten right through, and Maesa looked out over the swamps. He watched a large shape disturb the mist. The wake it left swirled violently.

'It is coming!' said Findelfil. 'We must be quick!'

Maesa heeded him, and moved faster up the tower. He came out from the stair into what had been a great hall, now open to the elements. Huge, fluid buttresses twined around and braced one another, but their spreading tops were blunted by decay, supporting nothing but the sick, drizzling sky. Filthy matter choked the spaces between, and piled up against the walls in drifts were the mulched remains of the tree's upper reaches. Colourful lightning flickered in the sky, though no thunder accompanied it, and the weather grew oppressively close.

'Go to the centre of the tree,' said Findelfil.

Maesa proceeded, crossing the threshold from sapwood to heartwood, and though both were coloured by exposure and sickness, the heartwood was harder, and less decomposed. Designs emerged through the dross on the floor, the looping whorls the tree folk favoured. As he neared the centre of the hall, carvings became firmer of edge, and light glimmered still in the deepest, growing in strength until, at the very centre, all the design was hard-edged and shone with soft green magic, and the wood yet lived. There was a tree stump of polished wood, unmarred by time or Nurgle's fancies, and from the top of it grew a rose bearing a single, immense pink flower, with huge thorns on the stem. The shortest of these was as long as Maesa's hand, the very largest four feet in length. Golden light emanated from the space above the rose, illuminating it softly.

'There. The blade,' said Findelfil.

'I see no sword,' said Maesa.

'Take me from your back,' said the revenant. 'Our journey is almost over. I will show you what we have come for.'

Maesa did as he was asked. Findelfil's spirit portion manifested, and he pointed with an elegant arm.

'There. The longest thorn. Break it from the rose. It is yours by right. Take it.'

Maesa set Findelfil on the ground. He reached to push the lesser thorns aside, for every one looked razor sharp, but the rose pre-empted him, and its twisted stems unwound, and the thorns moved themselves, leaving Maesa a clear route through to the longest. At the junction between thorn and stem, there was an indentation in the wood akin to a hilt. He put his hand around this, and gasped in surprise, for a sense of great power flowed into him, accompanied by a gnawing hunger. It seemed familiar somehow, as if he and it renewed a forgotten association.

'Take it!' said Findelfil.

Maesa gripped and pulled. The thorn came away, leaving a pale scar on the stem. He brought the thorn out of the bush and looked at it wonderingly.

'A living blade,' he said.

'The Song of Thorns, Alarielle's gift to you, back in your hand where it belongs,' said Findelfil. 'Now place me on the stump. Protect me while I heal this place.'

The rose shrivelled from pink to pale brown. Petals dropped, and the stems of the bush lost their green and became grey, and broke into dust, showering the stump with a wholesome decay, so unlike that gripping the rest of the tower tree.

The tree groaned. Wet wood split. They heard branches fall into the meres outside. A moan hooted from the swamp.

'Now!' said Findelfil. 'It comes.'

Maesa placed Findelfil upon the stump. Twigs thrust out from the polished surface, and bark began to grow across the bare wood. Findelfil's remnant was gripped tightly by the twigs, and they pushed into wood and spirit flesh. He groaned, and put his head back. A thickening branch pierced his throat and grew from his mouth, sprouting leaves above his face.

Under Maesa's feet, the patterns in the floor pulsed. The light crept out, filling black channels with life magic, infiltrating the walls and the pillars. Wet dried. Blackness shrank away to reveal living wood of a deep red.

As Findelfil's spirit pushed outward into the dead tower, Maesa turned to face their enemy.

A heavy impact shook the tower tree, followed by a scrabbling and a scraping of a large body hauled up the stairs. Maesa left his metal sword driven into the floor, found a deep cleft in the wall, and slipped out of sight. He listened as the thing sighed and burped its way up the tree into the hall. It emitted outraged squeals when it caught sight of Findelfil and the spread of magic returning life to the wood, and it charged the stump. When it thundered by Maesa's hiding place, finally he saw it.

Maybe once the creature had been some form of lesser godbeast, or the offspring of something divine, for it was huge and carried a hint of lost nobility. In shape it was a scuttling creature – a centipede or similar inflated to huge size, every portion of its segmented body as large as an ogor's shield, with a pair of legs attached to each. For feet it had claws long as swords.

The head was wholly corrupted. An insectile face hung slackly below a throbbing tumour, and from this sprouted three humanoid upper torsos, all gangrenous of flesh, bearing black swords in their rotting hands, their heads each with single eyes and single horns. Daemonic parasites had taken the body for their own, perverting it to their master's ends. Long fibres spread from the daemonic flesh, and had burrowed through the creature's carapace into the soft parts beneath. Lesions covered it, and the lumps of lesser growths, while puffy fungi hung fruiting bodies from its joints. It smelled of death, and of unwholesome places.

The thing stopped. The mouths of the triple daemons snapped open and closed soundlessly, but the mandibles of the true mouth gaped, and it was from this that the bubbling moan came, accompanied by a stinking froth that hissed on the floor.

The possessed godbeast swerved forward, towards Findelfil. Maesa slipped out behind it, and strung his bow.

'Daemon! Daemon! Here is fresher prey,' he called.

The beast stopped, twisted round on itself, rearing up the fore-quarters so the triple parasites swayed. Legs spread in a threat display raked dead wood down from the walls.

Maesa's first arrow pierced the leftmost daemon's eye. Yellow slime burst forth, and it yammered silently, while the possessed godbeast's mouth squealed and dribbled. The daemon dropped its sword to claw at the arrow. To some, perhaps, it would have seemed amazing that it did not die, but Maesa knew the scions of Nurgle could survive impossible injury. It was at least blind, and its meld-brothers were dismayed enough that the creature forgot the rapid spread of life, and dived down at its attacker.

The daemons rooted in the beast rode the head down as if they were mortal knights at the charge. It battered into the wall, smashing away great lumps of rotten wood and gouging a furrow, opening up the crack where Maesa had sheltered. Black swords slashed at Maesa, who dodged, but in missing him, their blades cut into the pattern on the floor, and where they did, the new magic faded, and the rot returned.

Maesa leapt, landed lightly on the wall, and pushed off, flipping over as a run of legs sliced down and into the tree, tearing off a large section of dead wood. Green, wholesome light poured out from healthy tissue revealed beneath the rotten surface, and the beast reared back, and the daemons covered their eyes.

Maesa loosed off four more arrows in quick succession. One took a daemon parasite in the shoulder. Two thumped into the throbbing tumour joining them to the beast. The fourth hit the creature's carapace, and skidded off. He ran ahead of the thing, drawing it away from Findelfil, who was engulfed now by a mass of rising shoots and the brilliant, green play of life magic. When Maesa shot again, the daemons were ready, and their mount-host rose up to take the arrows for them, before they plunged after him.

The wall of the tower was close. Maesa was running out of space.

Still running, he slipped his bow back into its case, and drew the Song of Thorns from his belt. It was far lighter than any metal weapon, but he did not doubt the keenness of its blade. Wood as sharp as the finest ground steel glinted at him, imbued with a magic all its own.

The creature dived down at him. Maesa ran obliquely towards it, bounding along the wall and leaping over its raking claws. He slashed down with the sword, trusting its enchanted edge to deal with the beast's chitinous armour. He was not disappointed: the sword cut through a leg joint, severing the limb, and continued into a second. The beast moaned. The daemons twisted and hissed. They came at him again, and Maesa aimed to parry their black blades. Such weapons were sprouted directly in the Garden of Nurgle, and the slightest nick would condemn him to a painful death. And yet they did not touch him. The Song of Thorns flashed and sang a humming, vibrant song, deflecting both swords and flinging them back forcefully, before cutting across and decapitating one of the daemons.

The remaining two, blind and sighted, howled silently. A terrible, pained shriek escaped the beast, and a flood of foul light was sucked from the daemon's corpse into the sword. With it came a rush of awful power, filling Maesa with unnatural might.

Every blow that came at him he deflected, and countered with another that took limbs from the beast. The remaining daemons would not risk themselves now, and made their host do the work. He lured the creature through the hall, making it twine and bend around the columns. Where it struck, it shivered away their rotten outer layers, revealing green wood racing with light that pained the daemons, and made them reckless. Maesa led the beast on a swift pursuit, until it became tangled around the columns, and Maesa judged the time and position right.

He passed under the creature, dodging its stamping legs, and out behind. There, he ran up a stairway that ended in mid-air but was even now regrowing, and leapt upon the back of the creature. The daemons commanding it strained to see behind themselves, and tried to bend the creature round to bite. But it was stuck fast, and although the length of it heaved up and down and thrashed from side to side, Maesa was soon upon the infected head. The Song of Thorns slashed out, cutting away the head of the central daemon. The last, the one he had blinded with his arrow, he ran through with the spine. As they died, a flood of potent magic passed into him, and Maesa directed it downward, instinctively using the Song of Thorns as if it had been his sword since birth. Magic roared from the sword, obliterating the canker atop the beast's head. Rotten flesh exploded in every direction, throwing Maesa clear with the blast. The parasited creature flicked back its ruined foreparts, a final cry vomiting from its broken mouth, then with a heavy impact fell down dead and still to the floor.

Maesa picked himself up. He attempted to brush the stinking fluids from his clothes, but he was so encrusted it did no good. And yet the Song of Thorns was clean, and glowed with a pure power.

Findelfil was lost in a riot of climbing vines braiding him and the trunk into a solid mass. All around him life returned. The pillars flexed and moved with new growth. Fresh boughs extended towards each other from their tops, their leaves and twigs interlacing where they touched. Beyond this new ceiling the sky was clearing, the green-tinged clouds racing away.

'Well, that's you showing your worth again.'

Maesa turned to find Goodwife Melisin stood behind him, and

though she wore the same form as before, he knew then that she was no human female.

He dropped to his knee, and held up the Song of Thorns.

'Alarielle,' he said, for he had guessed it could only be she.

Goodwife Melisin cackled. 'That obvious, is it? Then look at me anew, and see you are correct.'

Maesa raised his head. Goodwife Melisin melted away before him, and a giantess stepped through her shed disguise and stood before the prince.

'Rise to your feet, Prince Maesa of the Wanderer Clans,' said Alarielle. Her voice was commanding music, stern, though not overpowering, and the sound of it filled him with life.

He did so, still holding out the sword to her.

'I thank you for the loan of this sword,' he said. 'I am pleased to be of service.' There was little else he could say. He could not deny her, or complain at his use; she was a goddess, and he, though noble and powerful in his own small way, was only a mortal.

'Sheathe it. The sword is always yours, your service is always mine. I am glad of it. Once more you earn it, once more you keep it.' She surveyed the tower tree, now unfurling huge boughs that climbed upward, making new walls and bringing the stump back up to its ancient height. 'There are laws for gods as there are for mortals, and we cannot be everywhere at once. This outpost of the glades is many worlds away from Ghyran, but precious all the same. An agent such as you is valuable, and beloved. You are among my most capable champions, Maesa.'

'If it can atone for the wrongs done you by my people,' he said, 'then I am honoured.'

'Your people betrayed me, it is true, but your debt was long ago repaid.' Her eyes were blank opals, her beautiful face as imperious as it was lovely. 'I pity you. Fate has little mercy for mortals involved in the affairs of gods.'

'I was told you might help me.'

'I shall,' she said. She faded out of view. 'When the time comes, I swear.'

Alarielle vanished, leaving him under a brilliant sky, where sunlight streamed into the renewed tower tree before the ceiling closed over his head, reborn.

Maesa finished his story, and sat back.

'I went then through a greening swamp. The goodwife's cottage was gone, and my pack was in a tree hollow where it had stood. I retrieved the bones of my love, and departed none the wiser, but richer by the Song of Thorns.'

'Why, I wonder?' said Stonbrak. 'Why did she give it to you? And what did she mean about it always being yours?'

'Who can tell?' said Maesa.

'Cryptic,' said Stonbrak. He had managed to light his pipe despite the rain, and now puffed on it thoughtfully. 'The gods were always thus. Even those of the duardin are inclined to obliquity.'

'It is so,' said Maesa.

'So you've served her all this time?'

'For a long time.'

'How long?'

Maesa shrugged. 'The years blend into one. I have performed tasks for her, she has favoured me. This sword is one gift, Aelphis was another. From time to time my questing takes me places I do not intend to go, and I find foes to overcome.'

'Like the Mourngul?'

'Perhaps, though that could also have been happenstance. Serving Alarielle has made me inclined to help those who need it, in case she is working quietly. The gods do not always show themselves overtly.'

'Isn't that the truth!' said Stonbrak. 'Many's the time I've wished for Grungni to intervene in a negotiation, and show the other party the error of their ways. But I have to do it all alone.' He peered over his pipe bowl thoughtfully. 'Do you have any of that life water left? It's valuable stuff, if you'd be willing to part with it.'

Maesa shook his head. 'I refused to use it as exchange, and I hoarded it for decades, but the last of it I used in Shyish, seeking out the realmstone of my Ellamar. That part of my quest was a success, thanks to Alarielle. Now, it is almost over.' Maesa dropped a log onto the fire, where the rain sizzled off it in steaming plumes. 'We should rest. We have a long journey ahead of us before we say farewell to Ghur.'

CHAPTER TWENTY

THE DEEP OF NIGHT

Shattercap huddled safe and warm under the log. It had been a long time since he had felt so comfortable. The dry earth cradled him, moist wood roofed him in. Nothing could get to him in there, not without facing his razor talons and needle teeth. It was poor lodgings compared to the delightful crannies he had once called home, surrounded by his own kind and the slow, lazy thoughts of trees. He missed the fungal smells of the forest floor, and the memories the trees kept beneath the leaves. But that was before Svarkelbud, and the blackening of his heart, and Shattercap's exile with the prince.

He would have been sad, but the grain of sand kept him happy. It had been weeks since he'd been able to take it out and look at it, but there, under the log, it was safe enough.

Though a single grain of sand, in his hand it seemed as big as a gem would to a man, and it was as precious too. A perfect cube, the six sides shone with shifting colours: purple, blue, red and gold, then back again, in looped play that repeated with subtle variations, so that it was nearly the same but always different, and evolved through limitless patterns of hue and intensity. It was hypnotic to look at, warm against his skin, and comforting to the heart. He knew he should not have it, he knew he should not have taken it, but it was too late to undo what he had done, for he feared the prince's reaction if he gave it back now. Besides, such feelings he felt when he held it! If he shut his eyes tight, and thought past his own memories, he could remember another time that he had not lived but, through the sand, could nevertheless remember. Times of happiness in a small cottage deep in the forest. A love intensified by a lack of longed-for children, and the sorrowful knowledge that life is finite. Shattercap gripped the grain tightly and felt these things that made him cry and happy at the same time. He was a spite. A creature of magic born of the trees. His emotions were not those of men or aelves or duardin, but through the sand he felt the pain of Ellamar, and her joy, and that changed him.

A sound outside disturbed him. His tiny fist closed over the cube, and stuffed it into a pouch on the inside of his loincloth. Through slitted eyes he peered outside, and saw Stonbrak come awake. Frightened of discovery, he scrambled back far under the log, curled up, and pretended to be asleep.

Stonbrak did not know what roused him from his slumber, but he woke with a question that was sharp and insistent in his mind, like a pick worrying loose shales. He rolled over, and tried to go back to sleep, but the thought would not leave him, and as it troubled him, the ground seemed to become less and less comfortable; too soft with grass and earth, not nearly rocky enough to support him solidly.

He sat up. His blanket fell away. The rain had stopped, and shreds of cloud drifted over the heavens. Constellations shone where distant starlight caught the scales of the great godbeasts.

Outlying portions of Ghur floating high beyond the realm glowed moon-bright, catching the light of Hysh hours before it would rise over the great continents. The fire was a mound of cherry coals that gave out little light. Maesa was a shadow past the log. Nearby, Aelphis snuffled into the ground, tearing up mouthfuls of fragrant herbs. Bhari Zhondr dozed, his legs drawn under him, his head tucked under one stumpy wing.

Stonbrak got up and walked to where the prince sat motionless. Stonbrak had his boots off, and dew wetted his broad feet.

'Maesa,' Stonbrak said. He spoke quietly, not wishing to advertise their presence. That part of Ghur was peaceful, but many dangerous beasts roamed the night.

The aelf did not reply. He sat cross-legged, his palms upward on his knees, his back straight as a spear.

'Maesa,' Stonbrak repeated. He came closer, and peered under the aelf's hood. In his shadowed face, his eyes were pale opals, no colour or pupil visible, but rolled back so only the whites showed. Stonbrak waved his hand in front of the aelf. There was no response. Maesa breathed slowly, his exhalations and inhalations as measured as the waves of the sea.

Stonbrak straightened up. He looked about, and harrumphed quietly. He put more wood on the fire, then got back under his blanket. For a while he stared into the flames, the question refusing to leave him. Then he had another thought: there was someone else he could ask. He got out from under his blanket again, and went over to the log.

'Hsst! Shattercap!' he hissed.

There was no answer.

'I know you're in there, little twigling. I've got something I need to speak to you about.'

'Go away,' Shattercap said from under the log. He sounded frightened. 'Shattercap is sleeping.'

'Hey, hey!' Stonbrak said. 'It's not about you, it's about Maesa.'

Shattercap's head poked out from under the log. 'What dost thou want?' he said suspiciously.

'Something's bothering me, twigling.' Stonbrak looked at Maesa, but the aelf remained motionless. 'At the Inn of the Brazen Claw, the aelf stated that he did not possess the Song of Thorns when he first encountered you, and yet this evening when he spoke of the green witch and Alarielle, he asserted that he won the sword before he fought Svarkelbud. Which is it?'

Shattercap frowned. 'Shattercap doesn't understand.'

'Did he have the sword when he met you or not?'

The spite yawned. 'Maybe. Sometimes he has it, and sometimes he doesn't.'

'What's that supposed to mean?'

'What dost thou think, beardy? It means sometimes he has it and sometimes he doesn't!'

'That makes no sense.'

'Yes it does,' said Shattercap. He slid back under his log. 'Now go away. I am sleepy.'

'Shattercap!' Stonbrak said loudly. He kicked the log. Nothing he said or did encouraged the spite back out of his hole, so he went back to his rest.

Stonbrak fell asleep intending to put the discrepancy to Maesa first thing in the morning. But his dreams were full of soft green forest light, and an enchanting song, and by the time the realm of Hysh shone round the rim of Ulgu onto Ghur, he had quite forgotten, and did not think of it again until after the end of their time together.

PART SIX

THE REDE
OF ATURATHI

CHAPTER TWENTY-ONE

SETTLER'S GAIN

Runes on the arch flared at the rhythmic taps of the Lumineth gatekeepers' staffs, the barrier cracked open, and the light of Hysh flooded through into Ghur unfiltered. Stonbrak threw up his hand to his goggles and gave an involuntary cry. He was not alone.

'Lords of the forgotten holds, that pains me,' said the duardin. His skin wrinkled around his eyes as he screwed them tight, but try as he might, he could not look into the brightness.

'You will become accustomed,' said Maesa, who stared unaffected into the glorious light. The liquid metal of the great gate finished folding back from a vista of unparalleled beauty. Cerulean skies. Slender spires of exquisite construction, the air between crowded with people borne on crackling clouds of magic, or by wondrous machines.

Silver bells on the tops of the gatekeepers' staffs tinkled.

'The way is clear! You may enter! Xintil welcomes you! Bathe in the light of Hysh and be enlightened!' They chanted this as a refrain, ringing their bells all the while.

The crowd upon the steps moved forward. Guarding the portal

alongside the Lumineth were a number of Stormcasts. The Tempest Lords had their keep in the city, but they could have been of any host, for the glare of the Realm of Light behind them made them into silhouettes blacker than the darkest shadow, hiding their colours. A summer breeze blew down the stairs. Shattercap leaned out from Maesa's shoulder, expression wondering.

'So pretty! So much light. So warm, so lovely! I smell magic, master, much, much magic!'

'Aye, and I can't see a bloody thing,' grumbled Stonbrak. He stubbed his toe upon the steps. Maesa caught his friend's shoulder, and steadied him. 'This better be worth it.'

'Mayhap it will, but do not mention the eye here.' They shuffled up a couple more steps. Checks were being undertaken at the top of the stairs, documents scried, auras read.

'I don't see why...'

'Because we do not know the situation regarding the aelementor,' said Maesa.

'You won't be able to hide what you carry from them,' said Stonbrak, squinting painfully at the mages and aelf-kind questioning the travellers crossing the gate.

'We will have to tell the truth. The Lumineth carry many magical artefacts on them, and much realmstone. What we bear is not that remarkable, at first glance.' Maesa spoke softly out of the corner of his mouth, and his words were lost in the hubbub of the crowd. Even that was dangerous. Aelven ears were sharp. 'However, it will pay to be discreet.'

'As long as it does pay,' said Stonbrak.

They reached the head of the line of travellers. There was a small platform before the shimmer-curtain of the gate. On the far side, those admitted to Hysh blinked and stumbled in the radiance of the realm as they headed down more stairs into Settler's Gain. An aelf in clothes so white they were unbearable to look upon sat at a desk to one side. Tempest Lords towered over the Wanderer and the duardin.

'One of our kin from the nomad clans of forest, leaf and glade,' said the functionary. His tone was pleasant enough, but there were notes of pity, and of scorn not quite hidden beneath. 'State your name and your business in Yllurai Xhen, most glorious of the cities of Sigmar.'

Before they could answer, an aelf mage spied them, and made a beeline right for them. Without word of warning, he appraised them, passing glowing wands over their bodies and gear.

'They have magic upon them, of death and of light. And there is this.' He pointed his wand at Shattercap distastefully. The spite cowered.

'He's an aelf,' said Stonbrak. 'You're all magic.'

'Not all magic, nor all aelves, are equal,' said the mage. 'While spites are known troublemakers, domesticated or not,' he added. He was haughtier than the functionary, and did not hide his contempt for their rustic cousin so well.

'Shattercap is my faithful companion. I assure you he will behave himself,' said Maesa.

Shattercap nodded enthusiastically. 'Yes, yes! I am good. No harm here. Only goodness!'

'As for myself, I am Maesa, a prince of the nomad clans, born to a high and ancient house,' said Maesa. 'I have upon my person some grave-sand of Shyish, a little aetherquartz.' He gave the mage a level stare. 'And the bones of my beloved.'

'To what purpose?' the functionary said, taking quick notes in the fluid Lumineth script.

'My own purpose. I have business with Ireath Talvari of the Lyceum Radiance.'

'Do you have a letter of invitation to visit with him?' asked the functionary.

'I do not. I come only with hope to petition him for magical assistance. My motives are pure, but they are my own.' He paused. 'A matter of the heart.'

'Matters of the heart,' said the mage disdainfully. 'Wild aelf sentimentality.'

The functionary gave the mage a hard look. 'What about your duardin friend?'

'He can answer for himself,' said Stonbrak, stepping forward. 'I am Idenkor Stonbrak, a merchant of the coastal hold Barak Gorn near Melket in Ulgu, come to see if there is a market here for the artefacts my people fashion.'

'Do you have examples of your wares?' asked the functionary.

'You doubt my word?'

The pen scratched over the document, both feather and parchment as dazzling as the functionary's robes.

'Do you have examples?' repeated the functionary.

'No, alas. All sold on my travels. I merely scout the market on my way home.'

'And why do you travel together?'

'Happenstance,' said Stonbrak, 'and for safety's sake. We met in Shyish, fought side by side there, and decided to proceed together. There are fell spirits abroad, and we have faced many perils on our journey.'

This seemed to satisfy the aelf. 'No mounts, goods, or other dependents?'

'We are as you see us,' said Maesa truthfully. Aelphis had gone back into the secret ways of the Wanderers; Bhari the emora sold on, to Stonbrak's mixed feelings.

'Then you may pass,' said the functionary. 'Welcome to the Ten Paradises.'

They passed through the shimmering barrier of the gate, and so by one step moved from Ghur into Hysh.

* * *

Stonbrak waited for Maesa in a hostelry at the side of a vast plaza. Diligent human servants served drinks in disposable yet exquisite clay beakers. A single aelf watched them closely, so closely that Stonbrak wondered if their cheerful demeanours were the product of genuine happiness or facsimiles born from fear.

Stonbrak had bought a pair of smoked-glass spectacles to replace his goggles; the slit design protected his eyes in most circumstances, but in Hysh they simply weren't up to the job. The new glasses reduced the glare to acceptable levels, and came complete with little side panels to cut out the light in his peripheral vision. Apparently, they were in great demand, and many non-Hyshians wore them. They were so light and well made he forgot he was wearing them, and though they were fashioned by aelves, he privately concluded they were good work. The wine he sipped he felt differently about. It was in every way perfect: lightly fizzy, sweet and sour notes perfectly balanced, dancing on his tongue in a manner that evoked long, joyful summer days, with a complexity of flavours in the aftertaste that were sublime.

Of course, he didn't like it; it wasn't ale. He had limits.

He drank it anyway.

The plaza was a huge plain of sunlight-baked stone surrounded by beautiful buildings with roofs of the most scintillating blue. Towers of every size pierced the endless noon, their tops capped with onion domes and slender turrets. Everything was on a monumental scale, so big that the groups of people gathered across the square looked like intimate family groups rather than the crowds they were. Multitudes clustered around artworks, fountains, and the plaza markets, where coloured awnings provided shade from the relentless light. Naturally, the colours went with the buildings perfectly. The shades' colours were too well judged to be personal choice. Settler's Gain looked like any other city, full of bustle, freedom, a million minds making a million choices that somehow came together to grant a composite character to the whole, but if you looked closer, there was little unplanned to Settler's Gain, and it lacked vitality because of it. There was a guiding hand at work in everything. This was a city where nothing was left to chance.

'Try too hard, these aelves,' Stonbrak said to himself.

'Huh?' said Shattercap dopily. Shattercap had attracted sharp looks, but only a few. There were plenty of other strange and magical creatures abroad in the city, and most people seemed to find his presence unexceptional, so he brazenly sat cross-legged out in the open, on the table where it wasn't shaded, basking in the light, his eyes tightly shut.

'This place,' Stonbrak muttered. 'It's too perfect. Looks alive, feels... sort of stale.'

Shattercap giggled.

'Are you all right? You're quiet, twigling, not said much,' said Stonbrak. 'You've not asked when Maesa will be back, or whined or mewled once. Are you ill?' He peered at the spite. Shattercap was swaying, a blissful expression plastered over his face. Despite his earlier suspicions about the brightness of Hysh, he was enjoying it.

'Lovely light. Lovely lovely lovely light,' said the spite. 'Lovely lovely.'

As Stonbrak watched, the spite shuddered, and a ripple passed through the leaves on his back and elbows.

'Are you... sprouting?' asked Stonbrak.

Shattercap sighed.

'Oh, by Grungni's beard, you are sprouting and... and you're drunk!'

Shattercap giggled. Stonbrak pressed his hands into the table and sat up straighter.

'Great,' he said. 'That's all I need. A Hysh-drunk plant daemon.' He finished the wine. Like the dark glasses, it had been ruinously expensive. 'Hey, you,' he called at a young human. 'Get me another of this watery aelf drink, would you? And make it cold. It's perishing hot here.'

The girl bowed, and moved off quickly while studiously giving no impression of haste.

Huge as it was, the plaza was only one of many in Settler's Gain. They'd chosen that particular one because it was right by the campus of the Lyceum Radiance. An impressive collection of fluted towers and fussy bastions, the Lyceum Radiance was close to the city limits, and in the plaza you could smell the spicy sand of the Xintil Desert wafting over the walls. In that district, the bones of the earth pushed through the ground. Crags, mesas and low hills had been integrated into the sacred geometry of Settler's Gain so well that they appeared more built than natural. A case in point was the dome of rock the lyceum was built around, each artificial addition so cleverly placed that rock and turret seemed to have sprung up from the earth together.

And yet – and yet – the hill was not completely tamed. The lower parts were heavily carved, but to Stonbrak, its smooth, high reaches looked like nothing so much as the back of a skull. It was too blunt an eminence, too heavy, too brooding, to submit entirely to the art of the aelves. As he gazed on it, he remembered the story of Pludu Quasque, and his brief description of Aturathi's character. Looking at the rock that once housed the spirit, Stonbrak imagined something uncompromising.

The towers' walls were blank for half their height. A hundred feet above the ground, they swelled out into tumbling gardens, carefully tended in the desert heat, and above that glittered with a profusion of windows. There appeared to be no way into any of them at street level. People were coming and going, but they were rising up by magical means to the gates in the gardens, their ascents marked by cracks of thunder, or the screeches of summoned beasts. There was no access from the ground.

It was nearly two hours before Maesa returned, or so Stonbrak guessed. It seemed to remain noon. There was no sun in the sky to mark the passage of time.

'I take it from the look on your face that they are not going to let you in to see this Ireath Talvari,' said Stonbrak as Maesa approached.

'They are not,' said Maesa. He took a seat, and gestured for wine. 'They say Talvari will not see anyone, and that the lyceum's precincts are as sacred as a temple, so even if he would, I cannot go inside as I am not a student, nor a stone or light mage.'

'You could mention Quasque,' said Stonbrak. 'That'd get you an audience. Or you could just tell them that you have the eye.'

Maesa looked to him sharply. 'Please, Idenkor, be quiet. There are attentive ears all around.'

'Well, you could,' said Stonbrak. He drained his cup, and when the server returned with wine for Maesa, asked that it should be refilled. He was feeling delightfully light-headed.

Maesa waited until the server had gone before he continued in a low voice. 'I cannot risk them taking the eye from me. I must return it to be sure of a boon from this aelementor. I must think awhile. I will not reveal what we have until I am sure of the consequences.'

'You're an aelf. They're aelves. Just talk to them. Sort it out.'

'So we will converse as friends, because we are all aelves?'

'That's how it works, isn't it?'

'Then you would as easily deal with a duardin of this city as you would of your own hold?'

'Hang on a minute, I'm not saying–'

'Or a Fyreslayer, or a Kharadron Overlord determined to cheat you with the laws of his Code?' said Maesa. 'The kindreds of aelves are not so close. The aelves here look upon me and my kind as wild and uncivilised, lacking true appreciation for their kind of order. They do not trust us. They mock us for our simple ways, and call us dirty. We aelves are not one indivisible mass, but many kindreds, and many individuals in each kindred.'

'Dirty?'

'Yes.'

'So what do you think of them?'

'They are arrogant, and patronising.'

Stonbrak smiled. 'Ha! Now you know how the rest of us feel when we're talking to aelves.' He slugged down his wine and stood.

'Where are you going?'

'You need to get in there.'

'I do.'

'Well then, can you do that?' said Stonbrak. He pointed at a group of young human mages floating up the sides of the lyceum on beams of directed light.

'I cannot.'

'Then, my aelven friend, let's go another way.'

'I am intrigued to discover what you mean,' said Maesa.

'Aren't you just?' said Stonbrak, who was almost as drunk as Shattercap. 'Come on.'

Stonbrak led Maesa around the rock dome, the Aturath Knoll, as the locals had called it. The Lyceum Radiance ringed it completely, but towards the desert side of the dome, where it sloped down to earth more gently and appeared less imposing, the nature of the buildings changed, becoming a warren of tenements and service structures where humans hurried about. It was a beautiful warren, and proportioned so finely you could almost forget the hive of activity it housed, but it was a warren nonetheless. No Lumineth who breathed the rarefied airs of magic dwelled there.

'That should do,' said Stonbrak, jabbing a finger at a service gate. A road built onto the knoll wound between the stacked buildings.

Where the road ended, there was a cleft in the stone that led to a place where the knoll became sheer. 'We climb that, it'll take us up to that crack – that'll make it easy enough to go up onto the dome.' He squinted. 'With a bit of hard climbing, maybe. But when you're up there. Pfft!' Stonbrak mimed shooting a bow. 'You do your woodland hero thing, get a rope on an arrow across to the tower and sneak in.'

'It is true that I may pass unseen.' Maesa looked up at the sky. It was growing not dark exactly, but less light. 'Hysh comes to the end of its dominance. It is Ulgu's turn to wax.'

'Does it ever get dark here?' asked Stonbrak incredulously. 'The folk of Ulgu maintain it does not, that even when our realm is at its zenith, and enjoys its gloomy noon, it is still bright here.'

'A twilight comes as the realm's magic wanes. It is never truly night,' said Maesa. 'But it will be dark enough, soon enough.'

'Wouldn't it be better to go now, while it is too light to look up?' said Stonbrak. 'We'd not be seen.'

'There is too much aerial traffic, too many wise birds and cunning minds riding the winds,' said Maesa. 'My abilities would be useless. Best to wait until the Lumineth take their pleasures, and the humans cease their labours.' He looked to Stonbrak. 'I am afraid you cannot come with me.'

Stonbrak looked like he was about to make a fuss, but then he nodded reluctantly. 'I knew it would come to this.'

'Thank you for your understanding, my friend. I have this for you.' Maesa took a pouch from his belt. 'In here is all the wealth I yet possess. Gemstones from many realms. It is not enough to recompense you for your company, but I would that you have it.'

'What's this for?' asked Stonbrak.

'You expected a reward for returning the eye. It is likely there will be none. If I am successful in replacing it, I do not know what will happen, or even if my Lumineth kin will be pleased that it has been done. If I find myself needing riches, I can always find more. If I am not successful, I will not be coming back, and I will not need these gemstones at all. I am sorry I lied to you.'

'Lied?' spluttered Stonbrak. 'You never said one word of a lie, you damned aelf.'

Maesa was perplexed. 'I let you believe we would be rewarded.'

'You think I couldn't see that myself? Why, the arrogance of aelves. I...' He bit off his words. When he spoke again, his voice was tight. 'Ach, I knew that.'

'You did?' said Maesa, surprised.

'Of course I did!' said Stonbrak. 'Just because I'm a duardin doesn't mean I'm obsessed with treasure. I mean, all right, I do like treasure, I'll admit it, treasure is good, but there's more to life, and more to duardin, than hoarding wealth, like honour, kindness and friendship.'

'Then I am humbled.'

'You're being patronising again, aelf.'

'Then I am also sorry.' Maesa gripped the duardin's shoulder. 'Listen to this, and know I mean it sincerely, no matter what you may think of my manner. I am glad you are my friend, Idenkor Stonbrak. My burden has been lifted while I have been in your company. I have been alone for too long. You helped me see beyond my obsession for a while.'

'You're all right.' Stonbrak patted the aelf's hand awkwardly. 'There are too few bonds between our peoples.'

'The realms are poorer for it,' agreed Maesa. 'I will treasure mine with you always.' He let Stonbrak go.

'You'd better take this,' said Stonbrak. He pushed aside his beard, and unclipped his coil of rope from the baldric he wore across his chest. 'You'll need it. I can get some more.'

'Thank you,' said Maesa, slinging the rope over his shoulder. 'Farewell.'

He crossed the street.

Now the light was fading, it was going fast. It was a strange sort of evening by the standards of other realms. With no Hysh to sink beyond realm's edge, and no Ulgu to eclipse it, there were no lengthening shadows, no fine sunset, but an odd dimming that started in the sky instead of the ground, and crept downwards as the lands of the realm further lost their luminescence. It was not very dark, but Maesa seemed to slip into it, become one with the failing day, so even when Stonbrak looked at him directly he was oddly hard to see.

'Hey, Maesa!' Stonbrak called gently.

'Yes?' Maesa stopped.

'Be careful. And come visit me with Ellamar in Barak Gorn, when you are reunited.'

'I shall.'

'Bye-bye beardy!' Shattercap whispered, and waved from Maesa's shoulder. Then the aelf passed through the gate in the wall around the human compound, and moved over to the darker side of the street.

Stonbrak watched Maesa becoming a shape that melted into the shadows of the Lyceum Radiance. When he blinked, it was like his friends had not been there at all.

'Aye, bye-bye, twigling,' Stonbrak said softly.

CHAPTER TWENTY-TWO

THE EYE OF THE AELEMENTOR

Only once did Maesa risk discovery, when a door cut into the rock of the knoll opened and a human bustled out, a pile of unfinished parchment balanced in his arms, forcing Maesa to flatten himself against the rock. The man went by only inches from him, close enough for Maesa's skills to be useless, but luckily the man was too busy keeping his burden balanced to notice the aelf. After that, Maesa hurried himself on up the paved road towards the cleft.

The dome of the Aturath Knoll lined one side of the street, the lyceum buildings the other, both radiating the heat of the day back out as the sky turned a pale, silvery blue. Reliefs were carved into the stone, a ribbon history of the lyceum crowded with the figures of Lumineth and grateful human supplicants. The images flowed over natural features, accentuating both carving and stone. In niches were tiny, hyper-accurate statues of a bull-masked aelementor Maesa assumed to be Aturathi. Magical lamps in others flickered a rainbow of colours. Even stones that looked to have rolled from the knoll's sides had not, but were carefully placed to draw the eye to pieces of art, and the least pebble of them was carved with interlocking runes. Plants grew in cracks, not one a weed, all these deliberately placed too. When the soft Hyshian twilight deepened, their flowers lit up like lanterns, sending inviting signals to insects that glowed themselves in complementary colours, and whose seeming wildness was belied by the small hives and bug-houses just visible beneath the eaves of the buildings.

The road ended abruptly in a row of potted trees. The work on the pots was fine, but they were cruder than those of aelven make, and Maesa thought them crafted by humans under Lumineth tuition, then placed tastefully out of the way where they would not diminish the beauty of the city.

He did not look around to see if he was observed, for if he had been seen, it would be too late anyway, but headed directly up the cleft. He moved with aelven lightness, bounding from one hold to another, so that he did not so much climb as leap up the rock, until, at the top of the cleft, it became so steep even Maesa had to employ his hands.

'Sit steady, Shattercap,' he said, and began to climb in earnest.

The dome's rock was a smooth stone, with small grains. It did not lend itself to the formation of handholds, and would have defeated most human climbers, yet Maesa inched his way up the cliff. Time passed as he pulled himself towards his goal. Cool wind blew in from the desert. Hot thermals rose from the city, stirring Maesa's cloak and tugging awkwardly at him. Bells tolled in the city towers. Hysh's night, such as it was, was short, and Maesa spent most of it clinging to the rock.

Eventually, his limbs on fire with the effort and fingertips bloodied by the stone, Maesa reached that part of the dome where the rock curved more gently, and he went more quickly, eventually being able to walk. He came to a stop atop the dome, and looked out over the city of Settler's Gain.

The great towers of the Lyceum Radiance seemed much smaller from above, with only one or two of those that floated in the air coming close to the top of the dome. Welcoming yellow light glowed in several of the windows, but many were dark, the occupants no doubt taking advantage of the brief twilight to sleep.

The city was lit up as other realms were in the hour before Hysh rises, bathed in mellow orange. In forgotten corners touched lightly by the lanterns, a gloaming developed, but no place grew any darker, and the sky never lost its blue. The crystal asylums that floated over the buildings like angular moons, their facets glinting with reflected lamps, were the most prominent feature of the sky. There were few stars.

Quickly, he strung his bow, fitted an arrow, pulled to full draw and loosed into the rock at his feet. The ironwood penetrated a few finger depths, enough so that when he tested the arrow, it did not budge. Maesa took Stonbrak's coil of rope from his shoulder, made one end fast to the arrow in the stone, then tied the other to the head of a second. He nocked this to his bow, sighted down on a dark window, made adjustments for the weight of the rope, and shot again.

The rope uncoiled with a hiss. The arrow, slowed by the rope's weight, arced gracefully at its target and disappeared within the room.

Maesa took up the slack, wrapped it round the arrow in the rock until it was taut, and gave a few hard tugs. The rope held. He slung his bow, took hold of the rope, and followed it until the curve of the rock took it up over his head.

'You mean to climb, master?' said Shattercap, nervously eyeing the drop.

'I do not,' said Maesa. He took off his sword belt, unhitched the scabbarded Song of Thorns and pushed it through the strap holding his bow case quiver to his back. Having done so, he folded the belt over twice, flipped it over the line, gripped it in both hands, and hung his weight from it.

'Oh, master!' said Shattercap. 'Oh no, on no, master, how do we know the rope will hold?'

'When we arrive, we will know it was safe. If we don't, it was not,' said Maesa. He jumped forward, swinging his feet ahead of him, and slid down the line.

Rope whined under the leather. Friction warmed the belt, threatening to burn it through, but before it gave, Maesa flew through the window, let go, and landed. He tossed the smoking leather aside, and waited, ready to fight.

There was nobody there. He relaxed and took in their sur-roundings. They appeared to be in someone's laboratory, for alembics glinted on benches, and books packed shelves built into the curving walls. Maesa's arrow had buried itself deep into one of these, piercing the book, the wood, and the wall behind. Traces of alchemical agents made the room smell strange, but they could not hide the scent of humanity linger-ing on everything.

Maesa took out his bow, and fired another arrow back the way he had come. It cut the rope, and stuck into the rock. Maesa quickly wound in the line.

He coiled the rope and stowed it, then retrieved the arrow from the bookcase. He looked back outside. From the higher towers, the arrows he had left in the top of the dome would be obvious to anyone who looked that way.

'Once more we find the clock against us,' he said.

Luckily, the door was unlocked.

The alchemist's laboratory occupied nearly the whole of the tower pinnacle. Outside, Maesa and Shattercap found themselves upon a small landing. Maesa descended the stairs with no more noise than a breath of air, and stole into the main body of the lyceum.

The halls were shadowed. Blue crystal lamplight made it feel cold. Maesa went slowly at first, pausing at every corner, and listening for people moving about the high halls, but there were few, and spurred by lack of time, he abandoned caution and hurried, following the scent of damp stone and sand back towards the rock. Where the buildings met the knoll, there were large chambers carved into the bedrock. The first two were impressive, but did not hold what they sought, and Maesa moved on.

At the end of a long corridor bored through the knoll, a set of bronze gates stood ajar. A cool draught carried out the sound of falling water and the smell of moisture.

'Living things!' said Shattercap.

'The aelementor is in there,' said Maesa, certain of it, and slipped through the gates.

Quasque's description had done little to capture the majesty of Aturathi's chamber. It was startlingly lit by hundreds of lamps hanging on golden chains. The ceilings were inset with mosaics so realistic that they seemed alive, their tesserae microscopically fine. The images depicted the aelementor in conference with the aelves, giving them counsel and aiding them in their wars.

At the back of the chamber, the living rock was exposed, and had been left unadorned. A deep fissure let flow a spring of clear water, whose edges were fringed with mosses and ferns. This passed through a hole in the floor, the complicated tile design around it beaded by spray.

It was by the spring that the aelementor sat in a throne of brilliant marble. His bull mask stared ahead, his great war axe laid lightly across his knees. Maesa approached on soft feet. Shattercap cooed and leaned forward.

'Great magic here, so much power!' he said.

Aturathi's body appeared to be rock, and though of a different kind to the throne, there was no join to see. His armour was of stone and metal, with long blue tassels and many crystals set into it. It looked like it had been donned by the aelementor, but at the same time, it also seemed carved. Aturathi was lifelike enough to appear a being enchanted, enough like a statue to seem only a masterwork of art. His shoulders carried an exact replica of the knoll, and as Maesa approached, his breath caught, for he could see clearly in its forward face two tiny arrows, and from one of them dangled a severed thread.

'His eye,' said Maesa. He pointed up to the bull mask. One eye was crystal, shining with trapped power, the other was an empty socket where a twin jewel should sit.

The jewel in Maesa's pouch.

'We must put back the jewel, and reawaken him,' said Maesa, as much to himself as to Shattercap. 'Once he is roused, I shall ask for his favour.'

Maesa went to the dormant spirit's feet, and clambered up onto his mighty knee. He stepped over the shaft of Aturathi's axe, and stood face to face with the soul of the mountain. There was no hint of life in the stone mask, but a sense of immanence hung around the being nevertheless, more potent and vital than the greatest mortal, as if Aturathi could at any moment step down from his throne and call the very earth to war.

Maesa's hand closed around the eye. It was warm, ready to return home. He lifted it out, and its light shone through his hand, silhouetting his bones.

'Soon, my love,' he whispered, and reached up to place the eye back into its socket.

A voice called across the hall, breaking the silence.

'Woodland prince, I bid you stop.'

Maesa pushed forward, hoping to foil the ambush by replacing the eye.

His hand would not move.

Magic prickled Shattercap's skin. Gravity pulsed in slow, tangible waves that rippled through his flesh, turning him and the prince about.

The gates stood open, dramatically framing, no doubt intentionally, an Alarith Stonemage. His body glowed with a soft nimbus of power, a gem at the tip of his staff radiated intimidating magic.

'Drop the jewel, and I shall release you,' said the Stonemage pompously. 'This is a temple as much as it is a school. You profane the resting place of a great being. Surrender Aturathi's eye, and you shall go free with the lightest of punishments for your offence.' The mage floated within the fane as he spoke, silent lightning leaping over the temple floor from his staff.

Aelf faced aelf. Shattercap whimpered, looking from one to the other. Their faces, like their souls, were wrought of the same stuff, but the twain could not be more different. The Lumineth was cool, aloof, supremely confident, all characteristics Maesa shared, but when seen in comparison to the Lumineth, the Wanderer seemed feral and fickle, as if his poise would desert him and he would fling himself into frenzied abandon at the least provocation.

Maesa smiled cruelly. The Stonemage drew himself up, becoming haughtier.

'You have little to smile about, woodland kin. Drop the jewel.'

'Do I not?' said Maesa. 'You think me too uncivilised to see what your intention is here?'

The Stonemage's nostrils arched, and he tilted his head. He moved his staff, and the pressure gripping Maesa increased. Maesa continued to speak with panting breath.

'You are Ireath Talvari, I guess. You knew I would attempt

to bring the eye home. Have you been observing your student, Quasque, all this time, I wonder? He respected you. You did nothing to help him.'

'What I see and expect is no concern of yours, child of the forest. Relinquish the eye, and there will be no harm.'

'Not so quickly. This trespass, it is a great insult?' said Maesa.

'Of the worst kind.'

'Then where are the guards, and why are you alone?' said Maesa. 'I think you cleared these halls tonight because you knew I was coming, and you wished none to see you take the eye from me and replace it yourself, so claiming Aturathi's boon for his restoration.'

Shattercap's eye was drawn by the prince's fingers moving slightly on the stone.

'That is no concern of yours,' said Talvari. 'I am archmage here. I deal with intruders as I see fit.'

'You Lumineth are known for your rivalries, your need to appear better than your friends and comrades,' said Maesa. 'We laugh about our cousins, in our hovels in the forest. We mock your pomposity and your striving to achieve, to build in stone where woody bower is adequate. I never thought to be a victim of this arrogance myself.'

'You go too far, woodlander. Ireath Talvari is fair, but you have had your chance. It pains me to spill aelven blood, but if you will not relent, so be it.'

Talvari lifted his staff. The pressure increased on Maesa and Shattercap. The spite squealed, and jumped from the prince's shoulder. He fell badly, lying stunned outside the magical field on his back.

'Perhaps... another hand... will see the... task done...' gasped Maesa, and dropped the jewel.

The eye fell weirdly through the magic gripping Maesa, pulled in towards the aelven prince in a gentle curve. Shattercap watched it with wide eyes. It was beautiful, so beautiful.

'Shatt…er… cap, take it!' Maesa was contorting, his limbs bent at unnatural angles by Talvari's crushing spell. The gem fell.

Shattercap leapt.

'Stop!' shouted Talvari.

Shattercap caught the eye in the air, wrapping his arms and legs around it, and carrying it down to an undignified landing that saw him rolling and bouncing across the sleeping aelementor's lap.

The Stonemage's attention switched to Shattercap, his grip loosening on Maesa enough that the prince was able to whisper a spell of his own. Green light flared along the network of his veins, life magic filling him with strength. Behind him, the ferns of Aturathi's spring danced, and with a cry, Maesa burst free of Talvari's hold, leapt from the statue, rolled across the floor and came up with his bow in his hands, arrow nocked.

'Put the gem in the socket, Shattercap,' Maesa cried. 'If you truly are good, now is the time to prove it.'

The spite scrambled. A beam of cold blue light shot from the crystal atop Talvari's staff, chasing Shattercap up the front of the aelementor's armour. Shattercap shrieked in terror, the heavy gem dragging at his arms. The long face of the mountain spirit seemed so far away, and the beam of crackling, killing light was close on his heels.

Maesa let fly. His arrow hit the crystal set at the top of Talvari's staff, breaking it into shards that melted into nothing before they could hit the floor. An explosion of freed magic blasted Talvari back, spinning him around so hard his robes flew out, and he slammed into the wall.

Shattercap hung one-handed from Aturathi's breastplate, clawed feet scratching on the marble and bronze of his armour.

'Quickly!' shouted Maesa.

'I cannot, wicked prince, help me!'

Maesa turned to climb again upon the slumbering spirit, but

Talvari rose up from the ground, hands encased in balls of lightning, and flew with a savage cry at Maesa. His clothes were in disarray, his hair out of place, and a trickle of blood ran from his perfect nose.

Talvari lifted a clawed hand, and the floor ripped up, casting a hail of sharp stones and broken tiles at the woodland prince. Maesa passed his hand through the air, drawing a rune of Ghyran. Flowing stalks of light budded, placing a shield between him and the Stonemage's wrath, but Maesa's magic was by far the weaker, and the debris crashed into the shield and through it, hammering Maesa back and sending him sliding across the floor to the edge of the spring.

Maesa raised his bloodied face. 'Shattercap, now!'

'I try, my master, I try!' Shattercap could find no purchase on the slippery stone. Tiny muscles burning, he heaved the gem up onto the spirit's war mask, and pushed it with trembling fingers towards the socket. The gem clinked and skidded on the mask. Whimpering with the effort, the spite pulled himself up as far as he could, and the eye kissed the edges of the empty socket, but it would not go in.

'I can't! I can't!'

Talvari floated back up into the air. He spat blood from thin lips. 'You should have listened to me,' the Stonemage snarled. He snatched his fist up and back, and hands of stone rippled out of the floor, catching Maesa's legs, melding into each other, and pinning the prince in place.

'Hopeless,' Talvari said. 'You are no mage.' He turned his attention to Shattercap, and twitched a finger.

The jewel rose spinning from the spite's grasp, hovering now directly before the socket.

'I will replace this, and claim what is rightfully mine. Then I shall let Lord Aturathi decide what to do with you for profaning his temple.' He sneered. 'He is not known for his merciful judgements.'

Shattercap squeaked, reaching for the gem, fingers brushing its edge. He strained. Talvari shouted, and the gem wobbled away from him. An ironwood arrow hissed through the air, clipping one point of the spinning jewel. It was knocked free of Talvari's influence, into the socket. It was not enough. The jewel was not seated, and teetered.

Shrieking defiantly, Shattercap gave his all, swinging his legs up enough that he could push, his tiny hand arresting the gem's fall before it could begin. With a gentle click, it went home.

'No!' yelled Talvari. 'This is my lyceum, my temple, my right to wake the aelementor!'

Brilliant light burst through the room, followed by a shock-wave. Shattercap was thrown clear, the mage buffeted and swung about. Maesa swayed in the stony trap, exerting all his strength to prevent himself falling and breaking his legs. A second burst of light erupted from the second eye. Aturathi trembled, the aether-quartz in his helm-mask glowing bright as twin suns. A lambency flowed from the realmstone, passing into his limbs, igniting other crystals set into his armour. His long, furred limbs shimmered, turning from rock to flesh, the hairs on them stirring as they took on the colours of life once more. The ground rumbled. The lamps jangled on their chains. Cracks appeared in the high ceilings, ruining the works of art. And yet, this spoiling of the temple heralded rebirth. With a deep sigh, Aturathi took in a breath, and his chest expanded under his armour. His hands moved on the shaft of his axe. His hooves shifted, and the delineation between demigod and throne became clear, then absolute.

'I live,' said Aturathi. With a noise like the rumbling of the earth, he stood, and surveyed his temple with glowing eyes.

Talvari flew forward to attack Maesa, but Aturathi held up a hand, and the aelven mage was arrested.

'Enough. Cease your warring,' he said, in a voice deep as time.

He turned to look upon Maesa, his eyes flashed, and the stone gripping the prince's legs parted, becoming hands again that released their grasp and withdrew into the floor, leaving ripples behind on the tiles. 'No blood will be spilled on my account.'

'Great Alarithi spirit!' Talvari said. 'This interloper came here with no permission.'

'I know all. I see all. He came to restore me. You sought to steal his prize, and take my blessing. Is this what I can expect from the Lumineth of these days? You gabble lies as easily as your forebears at the time of the Spirefall. Did you not jeopardise my return for the sake of your own power? Did you sit back and do nothing while a portion of my soul languished in the dungeons of the ratkin, leaving all toil to a mere human boy? I know the minds of all beings who stand upon my sacred ground, so you will be silent, Ireath Talvari.' Aturathi's great bull head turned, the stone flesh of his neck grinding like millstones. 'Where is the one who awoke me?'

Maesa came forward, Shattercap in his arms.

'He is here,' said Maesa, presenting the spite. 'By rights whatever boon you might grant belongs to him.'

'Wise you are, and noble. I know the desires that torture you, and yet you make no claim to my gift, and rightly so, unlike Ireath Talvari.' Aturathi turned his attention on Shattercap. 'Woodland spite, aelemental as I am – hail, little kin, and well met. You brought me back from deathly sleep. Because of that, I and this mountain will live again. For this service, I shall grant your heart's desire. What is it to be?'

Shattercap looked up at his master.

'You know what I wish, great Aturathi,' Shattercap said. 'I wish to be good.'

'That I cannot grant. Goodness can only come from within,' said the aelementor.

'I know.' Shattercap gripped Maesa's finger in his tiny hand. 'So I say, aid my master, the good prince. Please. Help him find his way back to his Ellamar. That is what a good person would do.'

Aturathi nodded. 'So be it,' he said. 'I know of your quest, prince.' The room, the knoll, the very air, began to vibrate. Talvari looked on impotently, angry, but wisely keeping his silence. 'I can show you what you need to do. Do you wish this?'

'More than anything!' said Maesa.

'Then open your mind to my mind, and see how your quest can be completed.' Aturathi's eyes flashed, and Maesa collapsed insensible. When he recovered, his eyes glistened with tears.

'I know what must be done, and how,' he said wonderingly. 'After all this time, we can be together.'

'I give you this warning,' said Aturathi. 'If you proceed, you risk much. It is not too late to turn back.' His neck ground as he looked upon Shattercap. 'Already, you have done much good, showing this one the way to righteousness. Let that be enough for you. That is my rede.'

Maesa slowly got to his feet.

'Great Aturathi, I thank you for your counsel, but I will not be dissuaded. I cannot be.'

'So be it,' said Aturathi.

'Great one,' said Maesa. 'This place you have put into my mind, how do I go there?'

'I will open the way,' said Aturathi. 'My last favour to you. A realmgate to your place of destiny.'

The aelementor swung his axe to the vertical, and pounded its haft to the floor. From the point of striking, cracks opened in the tiles, running outward on crazed paths. Upon hitting the wall they raced upward, into the rock whence came the spring, gathering behind the waterfall into a fissure. Blue light shone in a curtain that divided in two, opening on a different vista, where rain pounded slippery stone, and the wind hunted the clouds across the sky.

Cold, wet air blasted Maesa, lifting his hair into damp strings that whipped about his face. On the far side of the realmgate, lightning flashed. Shattercap scampered into Maesa's arms, eyes wide.

At that moment, Talvari, still gripped in Aturathi's invisible prison, chose to break his silence. 'Do not pursue your quest, Wanderer,' he said. 'Listen to the aelementor. It will end in sorrow.'

Maesa locked eyes with the fuming Stonemage.

'You have lost, Lumineth. Leave me be.'

'Look into my spirit. See I speak as one bested. What reason do I have to lie? Aelf to aelf, I tell you, you are in peril.'

Maesa frowned. He saw no deception, and he turned to Aturathi.

'Oh, great spirit, tell me, will I be successful?' A pleading edge cut his words, and they bled emotion.

'The price is steep, and the outcome uncertain,' said Aturathi. 'I can give you no sure answer to this question. You meddle in the magics of many realms. It is beyond my ability to see. I am mighty, but you are enmeshed in the affairs of gods.'

'That is no answer, spirit! Please, I beg you, tell me true. Will I hold my Ellamar in my arms again?'

Aturathi stood over him, tall and silent as a mountain. All in the chamber waited for his response, and it was long in the coming.

'Yes,' said the aelementor eventually. 'You shall hold her.'

Maesa let out a deep sigh of joy. Aturathi gave Shattercap a look that made him squeal. Maesa bowed deeply, collected his weapons, set his face into the storm and strode through the gap. As he left, Aturathi released Talvari, and moved towards him. The mage's face hardened as he prepared to face the aelementor's judgement. Maesa and Shattercap saw no more, for the rock grew back over the fissure, and vanished with a clap of thunder, leaving them far from Settler's Gain, and Hysh.

PART SEVEN
THE UNDYING
MAGISTRATE

CHAPTER TWENTY-THREE

THE RITUAL

Maesa emerged upon the lip of a bowl of stone set into an island floating in a tempestuous sky. Gusts of wind threatened to toss him over the edge into the clouds. He surveyed the heavens around them. Beside the rock, there was nothing solid to be seen, no other isles, no winged beasts. It was gloomy, the light spread into an unforgiving grey that dazzled yet failed to illuminate.

'Where are we?' said Shattercap.

'I do not know,' said Maesa. 'This is a metalith, but of which realm I cannot say. Some place caught between, perhaps.'

'Like Shadespire?' asked Shattercap.

'Maybe. There are more such places, though not known to many.'

A display of purple lightning cracked across the sky, filling the interiors of the clouds with frightening lilac shapes.

Shattercap whimpered. 'I do not like it, wicked prince.'

'It is not a place to be liked, little spite, but it does have power,' said Maesa. 'We are here for my purpose, and when it is fulfilled, we shall depart, we three. I will not tarry here longer than is necessary, I swear.'

'How shall we depart?' asked the spite, glancing behind them at the endless skies. 'There is nowhere to go.'

To that, Maesa had no answer.

Rain lashed, wind shoved, the very weather now worked against Maesa at the conclusion of his quest. He seemed not to notice, but moved as if in a dream, his aelven soul buoyed up by joy, his body trembling, descending steps hewn into the rough rock of the bowl. The centre had been planed flat, and was carved with geomantic sigils by long-dead hands, so that when the pair reached the centre of the island and looked up, they felt they were in an arena of sorts. The steps were the sole entrance, as Shattercap had said, there was no obvious way out. Once the stairs reached the lip of the bowl, they simply stopped, going nowhere.

'We must begin,' said Maesa. In the bowl the wind's might was curtailed; only the strongest blasts intruded, bringing with them a spattering of rain. Maesa's voice overcame them, and echoed strongly from the walls. 'Down you go.'

Maesa placed Shattercap upon the rock. The spite blanched and shivered. 'So cold, no life!' he hissed. No plants grew in the metalith's exposed cracks, not even the smallest patch of lichen. 'Oh, do let us leave! It claws at me. It burns my feet! Sucks at my spirit! It is like the Sands of Grief, all over again.'

'We will not be long,' said Maesa.

'Please, master! This is not a good place, thou art...'

'Silence!' said Maesa, harshly now, forgetting Shattercap's bravery in his desire to be with Ellamar. His violet eyes burned. 'I must do this,' he said. Seeing Shattercap shrink from his anger, Maesa calmed, the fierceness smoothed from his face. 'You must understand. I have waited centuries for this moment. I must have

her back. I must…' His hands clenched. 'I have to. Do you understand? I will perish without her. It is…' His voice broke.

Shattercap approached carefully, his hand out, hesitating before
he touched the prince's arm. 'Master, master, thou art good. Thou
art kind. Shattercap is sorry. Please forgive.'

Maesa drew in a breath that seemed to fight him; he was drowning in sorrow as only an aelf can, but he nodded, and gulped at
the air. 'Yes, yes, you are good, Shattercap.'

'Truly?'

'Truly.' Maesa unslung the pack from his back, taking out the
hourglass full of Ellamar's soul-sand, then the leather-wrapped
bundle of her bones. It was so small, the size of a babe in arms,
and he cradled it with the utmost care of a new father, and put
it upon the rock.

'I must lay her out. I must make her ready to receive flesh,' he
said. 'Dear Shattercap, good Shattercap, go to the brink and keep
watch, I have no idea what dangers may patrol these skies.'

'Hunting eagles?' Shattercap quailed.

'Perhaps. Be careful. We must have some lookout.' Maesa looked
at him pleadingly. 'Please.'

The spite bit his lip. 'Very well. I will be careful, thou must too.'
And he bounded away up the edge of the bowl, braving the full
force of the wind and whatever horrors rode it.

Maesa's mind was full of detail of the spell he must perform.
Without Aturathi's help, he would have had no chance of success, and yet as he prepared, he could not help but find his actions
familiar, as if he had dreamed them some time, long ago.

The feeling unnerved him, so he shook it off. At the centre of
the arena, the patterns came together tightly, the lines shrinking
and passing over and under each other in complex knotwork.
Within small ovals trapped by the patterns were sigils that made

little sense to him, esoteric pictograms that bore no resemblance to the flowing runes of the aelven kindreds, man's writings, or the angular cut marks of the duardin. They appeared crude and menacing compared to the artistry of the pattern surrounding them, but he ignored this in his desperation. He could not turn back now.

He brushed the patterns free of grit, untied the thongs binding up Ellamar's swaddling, and unrolled the leather. It took some time to free her bones from their silk wrappings.

Upon the central area, he laid out the skeleton of Ellamar lovingly. Her bones were old and brown and polished in places from much handling, so ancient, so brittle, and yet he had borne them without damage for longer than he could remember. He placed them out as if she were lying on her back, although the nature of the bones meant she appeared as an exploded diagram of a person, the ribs like bows laid flat, the skull resting on its base rather than gazing up at him adoringly.

He remembered the eyes that had inhabited that skull, the soft, beautiful flesh that had covered it.

He looked to the rim of the bowl. Shattercap scampered around the rocks on all fours, stopping to sniff at the air. The spite was brave. Maesa would make sure he was rewarded for his friendship. Already brimming with heady emotion, the prince felt a rolling wave of affection for the creature.

The life-sands came next. He opened the top of the hourglass purchased from Throck and Grimmson months before. He hesitated before upending it as he must, for he suffered a terrible fear they would blow away and that would be that.

'Trust in the spirits of the earth,' he said to himself. 'Aturathi would not lie.'

With a silent prayer to Alarielle, he tipped over the glass.

The sands came out sparkling with the promise of life that was and may yet be. With a careful hand he poured them in a circle around the bones. They did not blow away in the gusting wind as he feared, but floated down unaffected, each grain shining with an inner lucency. When settled in a perimeter around the bones, they projected a shifting curtain of soul-light that, while beautiful, made the bones seem older and more worn than before, casting each rough patch, each pit, into harsh relief.

Again he looked to Shattercap. The spite was watching him this time, and Maesa nodded at him.

Within the glowing circle, the light spread. The grooves of the carved pattern were lighting up, and spilling out, as if slow waters reclaimed channels dried by drought.

'As her soul must return, so souls must be expended,' Maesa said.

Reverently, he drew the Song of Thorns, and held it flat in his palms. For a long time he regarded it.

'Forgive me, you have been an admirable weapon,' he said, though his contrition was small. There could only ever have been one end to the blade from the moment he first lifted it; he had known that from the beginning. The Song of Thorns made him a sort of necromancer, and it shamed him.

But shame could not stop him. He flipped the hilt into his palm, held the point to the sky, and called out.

'Souls I give for one soul. By the grace of Alarielle, I ask mercy from the Lord of Death, Nagash, and by ancient compact call back Ellamar, the much-loved, from his grip.'

So saying, he let his arm fall, reversing the blade and driving it point down directly into the heart of the central pattern, in the middle of Ellamar's skeleton.

Thunder cracked. Lightning raced across the churning skies.

Silence. Maesa took a step back, then another. The light from the soul-sands streamed into the Song of Thorns, and went out. The sky darkened, as if in eclipse, and at the brink of the bowl Shattercap peered upwards nervously.

'Ellamar? Ellamar?' Maesa said. Thunder answered. Rain fell in fat drops, individual at first, then coming in drenching crowds. 'Ellamar!' he said again, fearing the sword had betrayed him.

He fell to his knees, and screamed in dismay. The rain was washing the sand out into the pattern. He scrabbled at the grains, but they were grey and lifeless, having lost their colourful hue, and he could not gather them, and those he could stuck to his fingers like corpse ash.

'Shattercap!' he howled. 'Shattercap, help me! Something is wrong, oh, something is wrong!'

The spite bounded down from his lookout, skidded as he ran upon the wet stone. Maesa's eyes locked with his, and then the world exploded.

A bolt of lightning struck at the Song of Thorns, then another, and another, each sending out a burst of hot, scalding air. The final strike became rooted to the hilt, and energy poured from the churning sky in a torrent.

The spite raced to the aelf's side. 'Master, look!' said Shattercap.

A moan rose from the sword, a phantom's wail at odds with the weapon's own fierce, arboreal spirit, for it was not the sword that spoke. A glowing mist detached itself from the blade, and floated free, coalescing into a human form wailing with death's agonies. A face formed, hands, and feet, and the moaning also defined itself into words.

'Free, free, free,' it said.

'Why, 'tis the boy from the graveyard, the hungerfiend!' said Shattercap.

'Yes. Filippo,' said Maesa. 'It is happening. Shattercap, it is happening!'

The boy's soul turned its ghostly face upward, the moaning ceased; it smiled and flew away.

Another mist emerged from the smoking sword, then another.

A huntsman, a beast, the souls of ratkin, orruks, men and others. The first released, the others came in a trickle, then flooded into the space around the sword and the column of dancing lightning. Those that had been corrupted in life were free of their curses, and rose purified from their captivity, streaking away into the wild heavens about the metalith, their wretched cries becoming shouts of liberation.

More quickly they came, until all the bowl was full of racing ghosts, and the light of their souls glanced from the rain. They passed over and through the travellers on their way to their rest, sending shudders through the spirits of both.

'So many thou hast slain, my prince. So much death,' said Shattercap.

'They are only those that perished while I held the Song of Thorns,' said Maesa. 'There were many more before. My hands will forever be steeped in blood, but that matters not one whit if it brings my Ellamar back to me.'

The fanatical way he spoke frightened Shattercap. Only terror of the spirits whirling around them kept the spite at Maesa's side. On and on they came, until the flood abated, and the last spirit struggled free and passed over their heads.

The lightning snapped off, leaving the Song of Thorns smoking. Thunder rolled drumbeats far away. Shattercap made to move forward, but Maesa restrained him.

'It is not yet done. Wait, and watch.'

The Song of Thorns shone with captured lightning. There was a pulse, a wash of warm air, and the pattern all across the bowl filled with light. The sands ignited, each becoming a star, rising up to make constellations that drifted over the bones. These star points descended upon Ellamar's remains, joining together, until they formed a shell of light around her.

Shattercap gasped. 'Is that... her?' he asked.

Maesa nodded. His beloved was re-forming before their eyes. The shell was a perfect sculpture, capturing her likeness from the days of beauty. 'Her soul returns to us,' he said.

Another boom of thunder. The metalith shook. Water bounced from the surface as if from a struck drumskin. Ellamar's bones clacked upon the rock, leapt up, joining one to another, holding themselves within her likeness as they would have been when alive. Ribs spread arches. Vertebrae lined up, an osseous serpent; the pelvis hoisted itself over leg bones rolling into realignment. Finger bones jostled for their true position. Shoulder blades rasped into place. Last was the skull, rolling back, and dragging across the stone, so the occipital bone mated with the spine. The jaw clicked once, twice, fitting itself to the phantom face hovering around it. Then it relaxed on itself, losing the stiffness of death, as if Ellamar's body were solid around it and not made of light, but flesh, supporting it and supported by it. The brownness of the bones faded, becoming white, becoming pink. Roughness smoothed.

From the feet came a rolling transformation. Connective tissues kindled from the burning soul light. Ligaments linked bones, uniting the scaffolding of the body. Cartilage filled the gaps. Muscles followed, raising ridged landscapes across the bone. Tendons stood white against bloodless red. Filigrees of veins branched and spread. Nerves, alive with the jolting energies of life, squirmed into place. In the hollows of the torso, organs grew like fruit, the great lengths of her guts writhed, then settled, packed tight and ready to live.

Her eyes budded, inflated, bloomed like flowers, filling raw sockets. Beaded fat rolled into position. By the time the last sheaths of muscle fibre had covered over the round of her skull, skin was already carpeting her limbs. Nails grew like swift ice on toe and finger.

The Song of Thorns throbbed throughout this process of reanimation, sending pulses of life magic from its woody blade into the body, which, having grown around it, was now pinned in place. As the skin reached the pelvis, a burst of magic from the sword restarted her heart, and Ellamar drew her first breath into virgin lungs. She arched her back, lidless eyes rolling in her face in panic, her hands reaching for the sword.

She screamed with the pain of rebirth. Maesa looked away, unable to bear it. Shattercap watched on, horrified yet curious.

The screaming subsided, became a soft sighing, almost a sound of pleasure. Her head lolled to one side. Breasts grew over her chest. Skin covered over her face, her head. Hair sprouted. Her eyes, now lidded, closed, and perfect lips parted slightly. From gory horror she turned to sleeping maiden, and seemed at peace.

Thunder pealed once more, spent of fury, creeping away to shudder other quarters. The rain hastened after it, and a break in the clouds permitted Hysh's shine to caress the stone a moment.

'Master, look, look!' said Shattercap. He tugged at Maesa's hand. 'See! She is sleeping!'

'It is over?' Maesa asked.

'Yes! She is back. She is beautiful, so beautiful!'

Maesa turned hesitantly to look. Upon seeing Ellamar lying whole upon the rock, caught in a single beam of sunlight, he cried out, and wept.

'Ellamar! My Ellamar!'

He ran to her side. The Song of Thorns remained in place, the blade sunk through her stomach above the navel. But there was no mark or blood. It seemed instead a woody umbilicus, a bringer rather than taker of life. It was grey now, and marked with dark spots: dead. As Maesa approached, it collapsed into dust, leaving Ellamar with a white, oval scar.

She opened her eyes.

'Maesa? Maesa, what has happened?' she asked drowsily. 'I had the most terrible dream that I grew old and died, and you were full of grief.'

The autumn prince went to her side, twirling off his cloak onto her nakedness, for the fresh pink of her body was beginning to pimple with the cold.

'It is true, my love. You did die, but I have brought you back from death.'

'Truthfully?' She frowned.

'Truthfully. Look around you.' He took her hands in his. She sat.

'This is not our home.'

'No. That is long gone.'

'Hello, pretty,' said Shattercap.

Ellamar frowned. 'What is that?' she said. 'It's so hard to remember anything. The mirrors?' she said. Her confusion cleared. 'Your pet from the city of the mirrors!'

Shattercap's expression rumpled. 'Shattercap not a pet!' he said.

She laughed, and Maesa laughed with her through his weeping.

'Come,' he said, helping her to her feet. 'We have done grave insult to Nagash, and although the magic was properly done, he will regard our success as his failure, and treat us accordingly. We must depart this place.'

'Where are we?'

Maesa gave a smile far more awkward than the kind usually seen on aelves. 'In truth I do not know. However, no place is truly an island, even if it looks to be one. There may be some way to access the pathways of my people. Or perhaps some other portal. Rest, my love. Recover your strength. Shattercap and I will search this place properly.'

He made to embrace her, but suddenly she cried out, and pulled away. She clutched at the scar the Song of Thorns had left. When she brought up her hand, it was bright with blood.

'Something is wrong,' she said, staring in horror at the red on her fingers.

'My love!' Maesa said in dismay.

A terrible screech cut the air.

'Master!' Shattercap wailed. He pointed to the sky. Dark shapes came through the clouds, fluttering in the wind, cruel glaives held before them, as much iron accusations as they were weapons.

'The Hounds of Nagash!' Maesa said.

Ellamar moaned, and clutched at Maesa's arm. 'There is something... missing. I am not whole.'

Maesa cast about for a means of escape, but saw none. The Glaivewraiths descended, more than a score of them. They ringed the bowl, and circled it in silent parade, glaives up, before stopping, and lowering their weapons at the three in the centre.

'What now, master?'

Ellamar cried out and she fell to her hands and knees. The wraiths screamed. Maesa reached for the Song of Thorns, and found his belt empty. His bow was away from him, and as he went for it, a wraith rose up through the rock and blocked his path, then shook its canine skull, stopping Maesa short.

Ellamar moaned. Shattercap whimpered.

'Maesa!' Ellamar screamed. She looked up at him, her eyes wide with fear. Her body was disintegrating, coloured motes of it flowing off her, exposing the layers of her body so soon after they had been laid down. Her scream turned to a rising shriek, and she collapsed, leaving nought but the grave-sands of Shyish to curl in the breeze.

'Ellamar!' Maesa was frozen in place. 'Ellamar!' He clenched his fists, rage and sorrow shaking his body. He looked from one undead monster to the next, confounded. They did not move, but floated in position, weapons levelled, watching him.

'Why do you not attack?' he shouted. 'What are you waiting for? Take me for your damned master!'

In answer, the sky split.

CHAPTER TWENTY-FOUR

THE MAGISTRATE

In the thin air facing the metalith steps, some dozen feet above, there came a dazzling flash. When it faded, an arched realmgate was open there. Stacks of human skulls made the columns, a gargant's skull the keystone. The eyes of them all shone red, and through the gate spilled the purple sorceries of Shyish.

At the lip of this gate appeared a plate of bone, fashioned from the skeleton of some monstrous beast. Another folded up out of nowhere beside it, carved flanges locking into place, then another panel. Each one clicked like cast knucklebones as they connected, creating a set of bone stairs that led from the portal to the metalith. They knocked and clattered, until with a final, hollow clack, they touched the rock.

Out of the rift and down the steps an osseous nightmare stalked. Huge legs, humanoid in form, bent heavily at the knee, edged their way out. Attached to their tops was no body, but a platform of fluted ribs and carved scapulae. As it tilted and the feet tentatively negotiated the steps, it revealed itself as a palanquin, with a raised rim made of jawbones, though all magically sculpted and fitted, and a throne, white and startling, rising up in the middle. In the throne sat a giant man, a golem of bone, an Ossiarch who looked like a suit of hideous armour. It sheltered no flesh, but souls bound and blended into gestalt, whose stolen light shone through gaps in the bone plates. It was an artificial being, crafted by sorcery, and every inch malevolent.

The palanquin scuttled down the stairs. There were legs at all four corners, half aware, from the way their toes tapped out a route to follow. The wraiths parted for the palanquin. It crept fussily onto the metalith and came to a halt before the travellers.

The being turned its cruel, unmoving face to look upon Maesa. It wore robes of purple, and a tall crown evoking Nagash's own: a frame of bone with purple silk stretched over it. Its hands gripped at the arms of the throne. The legs bearing the palanquin shifted skittishly.

'Prince Maesa,' the Ossiarch said. It had a hollow voice, gruff, a daemon bound to a cave tempting innocents in. 'Again we meet, and again you fail.'

Maesa looked helplessly from the Ossiarch to the soul-sands of his dead wife.

'Save her!' Maesa said impulsively.

'It cannot be done. You will soon know why.' The Ossiarch shifted in its throne. The palanquin took a step sideways, then back.

'Who are you?' Maesa said.

Although the face of the Ossiarch did not move, could not move, it grunted with vile amusement.

'Who indeed? I am a magistrate of Nagash. My given task is to judge those who offend the Lord of the Undead, and by all the gods, aelf, your offences are grave. You and I have met many times before. Do you not recall?' The magistrate laughed.

Maesa stared up at the monster on the throne. 'You mock me. What transpires here?'

'What, what, what – ah, I do so enjoy these conversations of ours. Your suffering is as piquant to my senses as it is just.' The construct leaned forward, a sudden and unnatural movement. The mute legs of the palanquin shifted about. 'Centuries ago, you attempted to cheat the Lord of Death. You stole the soul of your dead wife from her appointed place in the kingdoms of the unliving.'

'Impossible,' said Maesa. 'I retrieved it only months ago.'

'This time,' said the magistrate. 'See.'

Six arms unfolded from the deck of the palanquin, opening like the petals of a bone flower. They spread wide, and between them was projected a shimmering field of magic. Upon it, an image formed. It showed Maesa, and Ellamar, running from a horde of screeching, half-vampiric things.

'This was the first time, the closest you ever came to success. You failed.' The magistrate sat up straight. 'If it were not for the intervention of Alarielle, who opposes Nagash in all things, you would have suffered the fate of spiritual annihilation. A fate you richly deserved.' An image of Alarielle appeared alongside Maesa's fruitless flight from the ghouls. Before her, huge and menacing, floated the head of Nagash made gargantuan. 'She invoked ancient treaties between the realms of Life and Death. An accord was struck, and a crueller fate decreed.'

'What?' said Maesa, his voice tiny.

'You are cursed, prince!' said the magistrate with a flourish of his sculpted hands. 'Cursed to repeat the same quest over and over again. Each time you fail, or die in the process of failure, you are reborn by Alarielle's will and returned to the beginning to repeat it all again.' Other images shivered into being. Some showed Maesa and Ellamar together, the majority a myriad of deaths. 'That way, thief of souls, you must experience the grief, the loneliness, the horror of losing your beloved over and over and over again. And each time, you are given enough hope to dare to dream she might be returned to you. That inflicts its own wounds on your soul, until at the last you and I meet, again. I have the unique and privileged pleasure of telling you what path of doom you tread once more, before your memories are stolen, and your punishment recommenced.'

The magistrate moved its head a little. The witch-lights of its eyes left shining trails.

'Before Nagash returned to claim his rightful dominion over the dead, death offered idleness to departed souls. After he came, he gave them purpose, for he is a just and wise ruler. You shall have neither rest nor purpose, for you are deserving of neither. For you, there will be only suffering, for ever and all time. Nothing but an endless road of grief and disappointment, of terrible, unrelenting *life*.'

'No,' breathed Maesa. 'No! I will not accept this! Ellamar died, I wandered, I found how to bring her back...'

'Is that so?' said the magistrate. 'Then tell me, how much do you remember? How sharp is your memory?'

'I remember. I left our cottage, I roamed the realms, I came back to myself... I... I...' Maesa could not say more. His memory was a shifting thing, treacherous as a fog bank over rocks.

'You aelves have an acuity of mind. Yet you do not. You cannot remember clearly, can you? If you stopped to think, and order your recollections, you would find them full of holes, and events out of sequence, contradictory and duplicated.'

'How can you know this?' said Maesa.

'You know what I say is true, Prince Maesa. You have suffered since before Sigmar returned, you will suffer an eternity more, and you will never, ever know the companionship of your lover again.'

'No!' screamed Maesa. Hands clawed, he leapt at the palanquin, but a twitch of the Ossiarch's hand sent out a lash of energy that lifted Maesa off his feet and sent him crashing to the ground.

'You cannot oppose me, mortal. I am an unliving embodiment of the will of the God of Death!'

The images blinked out. The palanquin advanced. Maesa got onto his knees, his strength spent. Shattercap shook with terror.

'The kingdom of death is far greater than that of life, for what lives does so briefly, and what is dead is dead forever,' said the Ossiarch. 'The kingdom of life is ever in flux, while that of death can only grow. My lord Nagash lends us our souls for a brief time, before calling them back to his protection. He is generous, but his bounty has its limits. You were presumptuous to think you could take what is his.' The magistrate leaned back in its throne. The palanquin shifted. 'Now, prepare to forget and to suffer anew.' The dark, sinister lights of Shyishan magic played around the magistrate's hands. 'But first, the final dagger thrust to your heart,' said the magistrate. Its voice took on a mocking tone again. 'You were close this time, so very close. You would have broken your curse, had you not been thwarted by one who is so very dear to you.'

'Who?' said Maesa, but he was already looking at Shattercap.

The spite stood trembling. He reached into his loincloth, and brought out the precious grain he had stolen, holding it out to Maesa between pinched forefinger and thumb.

'I am sorry, so sorry. I did not know! It was so beautiful, so pretty, I wanted it, a piece, a little piece, of the love thou knewest.' He dropped his head. 'Nobody loves Shattercap.'

'Shattercap... Shattercap...' Maesa's features were slack with horror. It quickly turned to rage. 'How could you? How could you do such a thing to me? You have ruined everything, you treacherous, evil, wicked little brute!'

Maesa raged and ran at the spite. The magistrate did nothing to stop him, but laughed. The spite was terrified, shying away from the wraiths lining the stone walls. Nimble as he was, he could not outpace a wrathful aelf. Maesa snatched him up by the ankle, ignored the raking of Shattercap's claws, and grabbed him about the neck.

'You are wicked. You are deceitful. I hate you, I hate you!'

'Prince, please, please!' Shattercap's voice choked away. His eyes bulged.

'Yes, yes, kill it. Break its neck and send its worthless spirit back into the soil,' said the magistrate. 'Were it not for your treacherous companion, I would have no hold over you. In death, you reap what you sow in life, and you have planted a bad seed with this one. Add murder to your list of crimes with impunity, there is no greater punishment than that which you face already.'

Maesa's hand squeezed. Shattercap's struggles weakened, his arms fell limp. His breath was a hiss. Maesa's wild, violet eyes rounded. His anger fled him. He released his friend just in time. Shattercap fell to the ground, retching and coughing.

'So sorry,' he croaked. 'So sorry.'

Disappointment, not rage, dominated the aelf when he spoke. 'I should have known. I should never have trusted you. It is in your nature to be wicked.'

Shattercap broke into a blubbery, snotty weeping. 'So sorry, so sorry!'

Maesa faced his judge, and drew himself up.

'I have learned my lesson, would that I could remember it and apply its learning. Give me my punishment.'

'Bold you are,' said the magistrate. 'Years of the most awful kind of pain an aelf can endure await you.'

'I go to it hopefully,' said Maesa. 'I go to it knowing I have survived it, and knowing that one day I will succeed and I will hold my Ellamar again. It has been foretold.'

'Count on nothing, prince,' said the Ossiarch. 'The world is changing. Nagash rises. If you return here again, it will be after journeying a glorious Necrotopia. This will be the last time you perform this task, and then I shall see you destroyed, as you should have been at the very beginning.'

A half-man of moulded bone unfolded from the palanquin deck. In his hands he held an hourglass made of two crystal skulls welded together. The Ossiarch moved its arms in ritual fashion. The grave-sands of Ellamar's soul spread over the arena rose up, gathered together, and flew unerringly into the glass. The half-man snapped closed the top, imprisoning the soul within.

'Ellamar will be returned to where she belongs. Now you,' said the magistrate. The break in the clouds closed. Gloom descended. Around Maesa's feet purple light played, illuminating his face from below, and making it ghastly.

'Shattercap!' he said quickly. 'I am sorry. Try to be go...'

A column of magic consumed him. It vanished, and the autumn prince was gone.

Shattercap felt very small and very alone. His tiny chest heaved with sobs.

'Master!' he said.

The magistrate's throne crabbed around, until the Ossiarch was looking at Shattercap. 'And finally, you.'

Its eyes flared with building power, but the expected blow did not come. A softening of atmosphere enveloped Shattercap, and the clear, pure, kind voice of a woman spoke, the most beautiful voice he had ever heard.

'This being is none of your concern. He is a spirit under my protection, of my domain. You cannot touch him, and you shall not.'

Shattercap dared not open his eyes, but leant into the comforting presence. Green light shone through his eyes. The smell of shoots and growing things overwhelmed the dry scent of the undead, and singing birds drowned out the hissing of the Glaivewraiths.

'Enjoy this little victory,' the magistrate said. 'Soon your time will be done, and the kingdom of death unending will raise its banners over all things. Green will fade to bone, and the glorious, unchanging permanence of death shall hold sway. Perhaps in the end Maesa will be spared, his mighty soul harvested, and given immortality within an Ossiarch shell, where he will be troubled no more by the emotions you inflict upon him. Oblivion could be his, and his pain over, were it not for your intervention.'

The magistrate's horrible voice grew distant. Shattercap felt himself move without moving. He was still crying, still frightened, but he could no longer feel the presence of the undead. The soft, protective presence became a warm body. A huge hand cupped him. Soft fabrics moved against his skin. He nestled into them, and was no longer afraid.

'Open your eyes, Shattercap, spirit of the woods.'

Shattercap did as he was told, and looked up into the radiant face of the goddess Alarielle.

CHAPTER TWENTY-FIVE

THE GRIEVING PRINCE

'Look, Shattercap. I have brought you home,' the goddess said. She wore the form of a giantess, mostly human in aspect. A pair of wing-like branches with long foliage for feathers sprouted from her back, and her left arm ended in a Branchwraith's claw. She was terrifying, evidently divine, and had an edge of boundless fury to her, like the sea, or a mountain pass on the verge of avalanche, but her face was beautiful, and her pupilless eyes shone with a healing power that Shattercap basked in.

Shattercap should have been afraid of Alarielle, but the comfort of her presence was so great. She was, in some respects, kin of his, and being at her side was as natural as breathing to him. He did as she bade, and surveyed their new location, gaping in delight at what he saw. From his perch nestling in Alarielle's hand, he looked out through a deep green forest riotous with life. Animals and birds cried from the trees. The undergrowth rattled with the passage of small beasts. Insects chirred from blades of grass or flew by, wings whirring. Ungulates called to one another through the undergrowth.

'Most worthy goddess, have you brought me home to Ghyran?' he asked.

'Indeed I have,' she said.

Shattercap gave a small gasp of joy. His tiny claws gripped her thumb, and he stood up. 'And is this my forest?'

'Alas, no,' she said. 'Though it is very like it, enough that you will be happy here.'

'Did it burn? Did Lord Fangmaw bring down the trees and kill all the good things?'

'No,' she said. 'Fangmaw's hordes were scattered. Upon the foundations of the city Maesa visited, there is a new settlement founded by Sigmar. Axes flash, and trees must die so that men might live. But though your forest is diminished, it lives still, and into the wastes created by Fangmaw, new growth spreads. There are glades guarded by the dryads sprouted from the soulpods Maesa retrieved. It is always the way, Shattercap. Life ebbs and flows. The magistrate was wrong to say death will reign triumphant. Very wrong. Without life, death is nothing.'

'Then where is this place? It is...' He smiled nervously. 'It is beautiful.' Little tears gathered at the corners of his eyes. He smiled as other spites flitted past, tiny humanoid forms held aloft on butterfly wings. 'I can stay here?'

Alarielle smiled down at him with a mother's love. 'There are spites aplenty in these trees, little one. Good and bad. You will be welcome among them, as a prince yourself.'

Shattercap clapped his hands and capered around the goddess' palm. 'Hooray! Hooray! No more horridness, no more cold, no more awful, deadly places!'

Alarielle laughed at his antics, but then Shattercap faltered, frowned, and stopped.

'But what of the wicked prince?' Shattercap looked down, ashamed. 'I called him that, but he was good really, so kind to me, and what I did...' He looked up at her again.

'Yes. The prince. Come, if you would see him a last time, it is not far.'

Shattercap nodded. 'I want to see him. I want to say sorry, but he will be angry.'

Alarielle's smile was sad. 'He will not see you, and if he did, he would not know you.'

Alarielle strode through the forest, the trees bowing their crowns before her and drawing back to clear a path. Flowers sprang up from the forest floor so that she and Shattercap proceeded always on a shining, fragrant carpet of many colours. With deep musical creaks the trees got up behind them, and shuffled back into position, shading the ground again, but wherever Alarielle trod was glorious daylight, and crowds of jubilant spites accompanied her.

They came to a clearing, where a small crag broke the forest canopy. The overgrown ruins of a house nestled into the rock by a spring of pure water, just a hump on the ground, little more than a pile of mossy stones. It was a beautiful place, but Shattercap was oppressed by its atmosphere. Sorrow smothered everything, and there the noises of birds and animals were absent.

Alarielle walked around the ruins. Past the crag, a vista opened. Bare rock tumbled into a valley, and the waters of the spring hopped down a series of pools to join a river, flat and silver, winding its way through the woods.

At the brink of this slope knelt Prince Maesa, his head bowed, still as a statue. A neat cairn of stones had been raised at the top of the slope.

'The prince!'

'Hush now,' said Alarielle. 'I hide us from him, but make no loud noise.'

Shattercap peered over the thumb of Alarielle's cupped hand, as if it were a parapet, and Maesa an enemy who might dare the castle to slay him.

'What will become of him?'

'What the magistrate said was true. He has forgotten everything, so has the spirit of Ellamar. The first time he underwent this process, the house on the far side of this crag was whole – now it is centuries fallen, the gardens he and Ellamar enjoyed are filled with mighty oaks. He sees none of this. For him, Ellamar's death occurred only yesterday, and his heart is broken in twain.'

Maesa was singing very quietly, the funeral laments of the forest aelves.

'Why do you make him suffer so?' Shattercap asked. 'Why not let him die? The magistrate said this is your fault.'

Alarielle sighed. 'This is a cruel world, Shattercap. The forces of Order must have their champions to oppose the forces of Death and Chaos. No hero has a happy story. Tragedy is the obverse of their coin. On one side, glory, the other, misery. I would release him, but I need him. He is one of my finest champions. Where he goes, good follows. He is a reminder of the bond that once was, between the aelves and myself.'

'But, but, he has no magic sword! He has no friends!'

'Not so, little one. His story is circular. The Song of Thorns is timeless, it will grow again, and he will bear it again. Aelphis too will return to his side. I will see to it. That is Maesa's nature, to wither and die and be reborn, as a plant will through the seasons. His curse is simply not to know, to not enjoy spring, summer, or the crisp, cold days of winter, but to remain forever gripped by autumn, the most melancholy of seasons. He is the autumn prince, my champion, my hero.'

'So, he will wander, and lose himself, then he will come back here, and take her bones, and wander more, all to bring her back to life, but never to succeed?'

'Sometimes he dies here of grief. Other times, like the last, he comes close to succeeding. Success is the only chance of release for both of them. You may blame me, but the only reason Nagash agreed to my request is because he is cruel. He enjoys seeing Maesa suffer, for he knows it pains me, and I am his rival. Cruelty is his great vice, and his great weakness. By being cruel, he gives me a champion, and the possibility of release for Maesa. You see, where there is life, there is hope, and through his love, Maesa lives, and so he may one day succeed.' She smiled down at the spite. 'That is enough. That is his fate, not yours. You may go now, and live with my blessing among my woods and glades, and by doing so, spread your goodness to others of your kind.'

'Good?' said Shattercap. 'But I must learn to be good. Good prince taught me goodness. And he failed! Failed! I spoiled everything.'

'He did not fail. You are good, Shattercap. Your theft of the sand was your last selfish act. Remember in the temple of Aturathi, at the Lyceum Radiance, you gave up the opportunity to have whatever you wanted so Maesa could be whole? By the sacrifice you made, and the remorse you feel now, you are reborn, remade. You have nothing more to learn.'

Shattercap spread his fingers over his chest, and felt it all over. 'I don't feel any different,' he said.

Alarielle laughed. 'Come now, I will take you to your new friends.' She began to turn.

'Wait!' said Shattercap, scuttling around her hand to keep Maesa in sight. 'The prince hurts, in here.' Shattercap tapped his heart.

'He does. That is his punishment.'

'He doesn't always,' said Shattercap. 'He didn't when I was with

327

him, not so much. Do you think he will win? Big horn-head said he would!'

Alarielle seemed happy to hear that news. 'If so great an aelementor prophesied it, then it is assured that he will. With good friends, and some luck, he may one day succeed. Until then, he must wander, in grief at first, and then with hope, for that hope then to be dashed and horror to be realised, before he must relive it all again.'

Shattercap set his jaw. 'I cannot leave him.'

'It is not your curse.'

The spite became firmer. 'I will not leave him.'

Alarielle's expression saddened. 'You are sure? With you at his side, he stands a greater chance of victory, but to go with him, you must forget too.'

'I am sure,' said Shattercap. Then, 'Would I still be good?'

'Of course! You are altered to the core, but the core is all that will remain. Everything else, your times together, your adventures before, everything, that will all be erased.'

The spite nodded, already decided.

'If Shattercap will still be good, that is enough,' he said to himself. He looked down at his dirty feet, and he cleared his throat, and when he looked up into the infinite deeps of the goddess' eyes, he was somehow changed, swollen with the magic of the green places, and his tongue and little mind loaned their wisdom, and he spoke clearly, from the soul of the forest itself.

'What is memory but a fleeting thing, a reflection on the water. A picture from the past that holds no shape, but teases us with inconstancy, always tempting, unobtainable. Why have that, when my friend is suffering? Friendship now, no memory of then, that is the better choice. Abandon sentiment bled by time for moments vibrant, a forever spring for me, no loneliness, no blank past, but a future to be lived, grief shared, at the side of this autumn prince!' He nodded again. 'Yes, yes, I would have that.'

He looked up the overgrown garden at the weeping aelf.

'And this time, I shall be there from the start.'

Alarielle bent down and kissed the top of his pointed head. 'So be it, little one. Go with my blessing.'

Maesa knew nothing but profound sorrow. His soul was drowning in it, his mind foundering upon black reefs of misery. Warnings spoken by the elders of his people came back to him, that he would know nothing but pain. In that moment, he saw those words were true.

Yet he felt no regret.

Inside the stone cairn the body of his love lay, life fled, but nothing could take the memories of their time together. There was grim comfort in that.

A soft footfall nearby roused him. There upon the path through his garden, he saw a woodland spite. The creature grinned, holding up his long-fingered hands to wave. He was altogether ugly.

'Who are you, spite, to intrude upon my grief?' Maesa said sharply. 'Begone to your forest and let me be.'

'Weep not,' the spite said. 'Love is dead, but friendship comes, in me.'

'A friend? Did Alarielle send you?' Maesa asked. 'She is the mistress of spites.'

The spite wrinkled his nose, like he was trying to remember. 'She did not send me, I sent myself.'

'But you know her?'

'Yes!' said the spite. 'She is... She was... There?'

'Alarielle?' Maesa scrambled up, and peered into the trees, but he could see nothing. 'Will she help me?'

'I think she already has. I remember bones. You need the bones.' The spite put his head into his hands. 'You need... I can't remember what you need.'

'If you have come to torment me, I will not bear it!' Maesa's hand flew to his sword hilt, surprising him. He thought all emotion but sorrow gone.

'No torment, good prince. I come to comfort you through thick times and thin, I swear.'

Maesa's hand gripped the leather binding of his sword hilt, and then relaxed, and let it drop to his side. He wiped tears from his beautiful face. 'Comfort I would welcome.' He knelt down before the spite. 'Tell me, if you are to be my companion, what is your name, what is your nature?'

The spite grinned from ear to ear – those things he did know, and he pronounced with a little bow.

'Shattercap am I,' he said. 'And as life made me, I am good.'

Saddened still, a little hope glinted deep in the aelf's violet eyes.

'As life made me, I am Maesa,' replied the prince. 'And perhaps we shall be friends.'

ABOUT THE AUTHOR

Guy Haley is the author of the Siege of Terra novel *The Lost and the Damned*, as well as the Horus Heresy novels *Titandeath*, *Wolfsbane* and *Pharos*, and the Primarchs novels *Konrad Curze: The Night Haunter*, *Corax: Lord of Shadows* and *Perturabo: The Hammer of Olympia*. He has also written many Warhammer 40,000 novels, including the Dawn of Fire books *Avenging Son* and *Throne of Light*, as well as *Belisarius Cawl: The Great Work*, the Dark Imperium trilogy, *The Devastation of Baal*, *Dante*, *Darkness in the Blood* and *Astorath: Angel of Mercy*. For Age of Sigmar he has penned the Drekki Flynt novel *The Arkanaut's Oath*, as well as other stories included in *War Storm*, *Ghal Maraz* and *Call of Archaon*. He lives in Yorkshire with his wife and son.

YOUR NEXT READ

GODSBANE
by Dale Lucas

As rumours of a fearsome weapon from the past begin to surface, numerous factions within Hysh clash for the right to wield the Godsbane. Can Lumineth loreseeker Thelena Evenfall navigate a tumultuous landscape of battles and betrayals to defend the citizens of Settler's Gain?

YOUR
NEXT READ

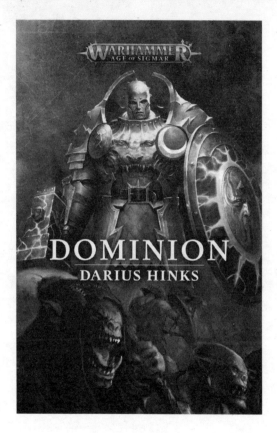

DOMINION
by Darius Hinks

Witness the destructive forces that are on the rise in the Realm of Beasts first-hand, and see the indomitable defences of Excelsis tested like never before.

YOUR
NEXT READ

SOULSLAYER
by Darius Hinks

Gotrek marches to war alongside his newfound kin, the Fyreslayers.
Yet the Slayer's soul burns brightly enough to spark the interest
of the Idoneth Deepkin...